Roxy Blues

Other works by Pierce Kelley

Father, I Must Go, (iUniverse, 2011);

Thousand Yard Stare (iUniverse, 2010);

Kennedy Homes: An American Tragedy (iUniverse, 2009);

A Foreseeable Risk (iUniverse, 2009);

Asleep at the Wheel (iUniverse, 2009);

A Tinker's Damn! (iUniverse, 2008);

Bocas del Toro (iUniverse, 2007);

A Plenary Indulgence (iUniverse, 2007);

Pieces to the Puzzle (iUniverse, 2007);

Introducing Children to the Game of Tennis (iUniverse, 2007);

A Very Fine Line (iUniverse, 2006);

Fistfight at the L and M Saloon (iUniverse, 2006;

Civil Litigation: A Case Study (Pearson Publications, 2001;

The Parent's Guide to Coaching Tennis (F &W Publications, 1995);

A Parent's Guide to Coaching Tennis (Betterway Publications, 1991).

Roxy BLUES

A Novel

PIERCE KELLEY

iUniverse, Inc.
Bloomington

Roxy Blues
A Novel

iUniverse books may be ordered through booksellers or by contacting:

iUniverse
1663 Liberty Drive
Bloomington, IN 47403
www.iuniverse.com
1-800-Authors (1-800-288-4677)

ISBN: 978-1-4620-9307-6 (sc)
ISBN: 978-1-4620-9306-9 (hc)
ISBN: 978-1-4620-9308-3 (e)

Printed in the United States of America

iUniverse rev. date: 12/30/2011

"To Danny, Susie, Keith, Sam, Shari, Mark, Nicole, Walter and all those afflicted with addictions, whether as a result of the misuse of drugs or alcohol, or due to excessive gambling, eating, debting, or any of the other causes of what becomes a compulsive disease, that they gather the strength to find the cure, so that they can stop the insane behavior that is ruining, or has ruined, their lives."

"The tears happen. Endure, grieve and move on.
The only person who is with us our entire life is ourselves."

Irish Proverb

Acknowledgements

·⁙·

I thank those who have supported and encouraged me on this and other projects. I wish to specifically thank Sue Pundt, Paul Christian Sullivan, Dennis Geagan, Doug Easton, Scott Harrison and Tug Miller, who have read drafts and offered their insights into this and other works. I thank Matt Sky for the cover design and for his editorial comments and suggestions. I thank Sue Pundt for the picture of me on the back cover, taken in Glacier National Park.

The pills depicted on the front cover are not the Roxy Contin tablets referred to in this book, but they are similar to the actual pills. The street name for those pills is Roxy Blues, because they are bluish in color. RoxyContin comes in other shapes and sizes, but they all contain OxyCodone. The RoxyContin pills are fast-acting, whereas the OxyContin products are time-released.

I felt this was a story that needed to be told after hearing story after unbelievable story of incredibly poor decisions made by people addicted to the drug. They gave me insight into the world of those who, despite the threat of jail or prison, the loss of jobs, income, children, health and other pleasures of life, continue to use this extremely powerful addictive drug which can ruin lives.

There is a large segment of our population that has little awareness of this particular problem. Drugs have been a problem in our country for decades, but when I mentioned the term "Roxy Blues" to people, most had never heard of it. On the other hand, when others heard the term, they immediately shared a horror story or two.

I acknowledge and thank those who shared their stories of being addicted to RoxyContin, OxyContin and derivatives of OxyCodone. They were, and some remain, truly powerless to combat their illness. I could not have written this book without having people who truly know and understand the power of addiction explain it to me. If I have been successful in telling this tale, I have been able to describe those addictive forces and explain the problem to those who have little or no knowledge of the subject in a way that makes the problem comprehensible. I hope that I have been able to do so.

Pierce Kelley

Prologue

⸻

Jeremy awoke to the sound of a car door slamming. Then he heard another door slam. He bolted upright, sprang out of bed, and ran to the door. He turned on the outside light and opened the door. When he walked outside he saw two cars in the driveway and saw a stranger walking towards him, with Sally ten feet behind.

Jeremy's smile turned to a frown.

"Who are you?" he demanded.

Slim stopped in his tracks, realizing what was about to happen. As Sally was rushing to get in between the two men, Slim responded,

"My name's Slim," and then, though he knew full well who it was, he asked, "Who are you?"

"What are you doin' here, Jeremy?" Sally demanded. "When did you get out?"

Her tone of voice was not welcoming, warm or even close to friendly.

"Who's he, Sally?"

"He's a friend." She turned to Slim and said, "You'd better go."

Before Slim had time to leave, Jeremy persisted,

"No, who the fuck is he, Sally? What's going on here!"

"That's none of your business, Jeremy! You haven't been around for five months and now all of a sudden you show up and think everything is going to be just like it was? It isn't!"

Sally got in between the two men and said to Slim, "Go! Now!"

Slim stood his ground at first, but then walked backwards, very slowly, toward his car, keeping his eyes on Jeremy as he did so. Jeremy walked towards him, keeping the same distance between the two men. Sally stayed in between them, facing Jeremy, keeping her arms up, pushing against Jeremy's chest, to stop his advance. He threw her hands to the side several times and kept walking.

"So who is he, Sally! You found yourself a boyfriend, did you?"

"He's just a friend, let him go. I'll explain later," she responded, in a softer tone of voice, trying to lower the tensions that were escalating.

"Oh yeah? I doubt that! Hey, you! Come back here!"

Slim reached his car, opened the passenger side door, reached underneath the seat and pulled out a Smith & Wesson 45. Then he sneered,

"I ain't goin' anywhere, Mister, and you'd better watch your mouth!"

Jeremy saw the gun and stopped.

"This is my house! Get your fucking ass off my property! Now!"

"What you gonna do, little man? Call the police?"

Jeremy's mind was racing. All he'd wanted to do was make love to his wife and see his baby. He wasn't ready for this.

"You put that gun down and I'll kick your fucking ass, that's what I'll do!"

"Oh yeah? You and who else you scrawny, little mother-fucker!"

Sally stayed in between the two men, but Jeremy kept moving forward, pushing her out of the way, but she managed to stay in the middle. The men were less than six feet from each other. Jeremy stopped. The two men stared menacingly at each other.

"Okay! That's it! You get out of here, Slim! And you go back into the house, Jeremy! Now!" Sally shrieked. She put her hands on Jeremy again, pushing hard on his chest. He pushed her away, again, but this time she fell down. Jeremy stopped when he was a foot away from the gun which was pointed in his face and said,

"I ain't afraid of you! Go ahead, pull the fucking trigger! You fucking coward! Steal a man's wife while he's in jail!"

Slim pulled back the hammer until it clicked and said,

"Make one fucking move towards me and I'll blow your head off, mother fucker!"

The two men stood their ground, neither moving an inch, glaring at each other, less than a foot apart. As they did, they heard,

"Yes, this is Sally Thibodeaux. I need a deputy out here now! Somebody's about to get killed!"

Though both men heard what she had said, neither moved and neither looked away. Slim thought to himself that he'd better get out of there before the law arrived. He had some things in the car he'd rather they not find.

Jeremy thought to himself that he didn't want the law coming to his house for any reason. He didn't want to do anything that would put him back behind bars. Despite that, neither made the first move, until Slim slowly released the hammer, and said,

"Don't do anything stupid, little man. The law's gonna be here any minute."

He took a few steps sideways, angling to get around the car and into the driver's seat, while keeping the gun pointed at Jeremy's head, not saying another word.

Jeremy looked him straight in the eye and said,

"Get your fucking ass out of here and don't come back!"

Slim opened the door with his other hand, while keeping the gun pointed at Jeremy, got in, started the engine, and peeled out of the driveway, leaving Jeremy standing where he was and Sally still sitting on the ground with her cell phone in hand, giving directions.

"Tell them not to come, Sally. I don't want the law here." Jeremy said sternly.

"It's too late for that, Jeremy. They're on their way. Yes, I'll stay on the line. Yes, I'm safe now, I think. Yes, that's right, about a mile behind the Dollar Store."

Jeremy was angry, and hurt. His heart was pounding. He didn't know what to say or do, but he knew that he'd better get out of there before the police arrived.

"Where's my truck?" he demanded.

"I sold it." Sally replied, defiantly.

"You sold it?" he said, accusingly.

"That's right! I needed the money, Jeremy! We didn't have any!"

Jeremy didn't know what to do. He didn't want to be there when the police got there. He was afraid of what he might say or do.

"Give me the keys to your car!"

"No!"

"Give me the keys to your car, Sally! My name's on it, too!"

"No! Then what will I do for a car?"

"Sally, give me the damn keys! I'll go over to my mother's house and leave you alone. We can figure all of this out tomorrow!"

They heard the siren of the approaching police car.

"Too late now, Jeremy! You're going back to jail!"

Chapter One

·❙❙·

"Holy shit! Did you see that?"

"Yeah. He's a big mother-fucker! Get your ass in the boat!"

"Here! Take this bag!"

"Drop the bag, Jeremy, and get in the fuckin' boat! Now!"

"No! Take it! I'll be alright."

"Jeremy!"

Jeremy turned and saw a dorsal fin headed his way. Realizing the trouble he was in, he squirmed, twisted his torso, did a scissors kick with his legs to thrust the hundred pound bag of clams onto the back of the boat, and followed the bag onto the flat transom at the stern of the boat.

Ben pulled the bag into the boat with one arm and helped Jeremy into the boat with the other. Jeremy came wriggling into the boat, breathing heavily as he did.

"Damn! I did something to my back right then. It hurts like a son-of-a-bitch!"

"Jeremy! Look at this shit! That shark is circling back to get your ass! He's wondering where you went. Look at him!"

Jeremy crawled up to his knees, then onto the wooden bench on the side of the boat and looked out in the water to see a dorsal fin in the water, heading towards the boat less than twenty feet away.

"It's a Bull! He's gotta be ten feet long, if not more. He's huge!"

"Damn! I've never seen one that big around here before. Have you?"

"No."

"I didn't see him until he butted me with his snout!"

The two men were screaming back and forth at each other as the shark headed straight for their boat. They were in a thirty-footer with a ten foot beam, so they weren't worried about the shark sinking them or doing any damage to the boat, and they saw sharks most every day, but this one was different. It swam directly beneath them as the men watched, less than four feet from what would have been certain death or serious bodily injury if Jeremy had still been in the water with it.

"He must weigh a good four hundred pounds or so, don't you think?"

"I have no idea. It's a lot bigger than me, that's for sure."

"It's three times your size, Jeremy. You'd be an appetizer for him."

"That ain't funny, Ben. He could've taken a chunk out of me already. I'm lucky he just butted me."

"No, that's what they do. They head-butt before they attack."

"Look at the size of those pectoral fins! They're like flippers they're so big."

"That's gotta be the biggest shark around here since that fourteen foot Tiger shark cruised through here a couple of years ago. You remember that?"

"I heard about him, but I never saw him."

"Me neither, but Bulls are more dangerous than the Tiger and even the Great White."

"No way!"

"Yeah they are. I saw it on a National Geographic thing last year. I swear. They're the sharks that are most likely to attack a human, and they like being in shallow water, close to the coastline."

"Like here."

"Yeah. Like right here."

"Where'd he go?"

"He's over there," Ben said, pointing to the other side of the boat. "See the water moving? He's so fucking big he leaves a wake when he goes. He's gone. You're safe."

Ben turned his attention back to Jeremy and asked, "So how are you, man? You okay?"

"No, I'm not okay. I hurt myself trying to get myself back in the boat and get away from that damn shark."

"Where's it hurt?"

"My low back. Damn that hurts!"

"We've got some more bags to get up, Jeremy."

"I'm not going back in that water today, Ben. You're going to have to do it."

"You afraid of that shark?"

"Damn straight I am, but that's not why I'm not going back in. I really fucked up my back. I'm not shittin' you, man."

"Well I don't particularly want to get in the water either, not after the way he butted you like he did, but your uncle won't be happy if we come in light, and that shark is on his way somewhere else, lookin' for somethin' else to eat other than us. I'll do it."

"My uncle will understand if we come in light. I hope this isn't something too serious."

"Jeremy, you lie down or do whatever you have to do to get comfortable. I'll get the rest of the bags. It's just gonna take a little while longer than usual, that's all," Ben said as he jumped in the water.

Jeremy laid down on the floor of the boat and tried to get comfortable. He couldn't find a position that didn't cause him pain. He put some life preservers under him but that didn't help much. He lay there watching as Ben hoisted the bags into the back of the boat by himself and then, since there wasn't much room to put them, he had to climb into the boat and move bags so that he could get the rest of the bags on board.

"Ricky told us to bring in fifty bags today. How many you got so far? Jeremy asked.

"I count forty three."

"Shit, man! I gotta get somethin' for this pain! That's enough. He's not going to mind if we come in seven bags light. I'm hurt, man!"

"This won't take me but another fifteen minutes or so. You can hang in there that long, can't you?"

"Ben, this is killin' me!"

"I'll go as fast as I can, Jeremy. Hang in there, man."

While Ben was doing the work of two men by himself, Jeremy was doing his best to get out of his wet suit and into some dry clothes, but he was having trouble doing it by himself.

"Ben, you gotta help me, man. I can't get myself out of this damn wet suit!

"Shit, man! You must be hurt."

Ben pulled the wetsuit off of Jeremy and then went back to getting the clams on the boat. Twenty minutes later, after Ben got the last bag on board, he started the engine and said, "We're outa here." Ben pushed down on the throttle and the engine responded with a roar, but it was a windy day and the water was choppy.

"Slow down! Don't go so fast, Ben. It hurts more when the boat bounces like that."

"You are hurt, aren't you, man?"

"Ben, I don't remember ever hurtin' this bad before in my life!"

Half an hour later, after Ben had tied up to the dock behind the Southern Clam Farmers building, Jeremy slowly made his way out of the boat, bent over like an old man, holding his back. His uncle, Ricky Thibodeaux, watched him as he walked towards him.

"What happened to you? Ricky asked.

"This huge Bull shark came up and bumped me as I was lifting a bag up and I did something to my low back while I was trying to get out of its way and get back in the boat."

"A Bull came after you?"

"Yeah, it did, and it was really big, Uncle Ricky. The biggest shark I've ever seen."

"Did you see it, Ben?"

"I did. It must've been ten feet long and four hundred pounds, at least, maybe more. It was the biggest damn shark I've ever seen."

"So where's it hurt?"

Jeremy put his hand in the small of his back, in his lumbar area, and said,

"Right here."

"Go home, take some Advil, get some rest, and see how it feels in the morning. Let's hope it's nothin' too serious. Maybe you strained a muscle or somethin' like that."

"I don't think I can drive myself home, Uncle Ricky. It hurts bad."

"Alright. I'll have Harley give you a ride. Call me at the house later and let me know how you're doin'."

Ricky Thibodeaux turned and yelled,

"Harley! I need for you to drive Jeremy home. Use the van so he can lie down."

Harley immediately jumped to his feet and ran to get the van as Jeremy and Ricky walked slowly off the dock towards the two story metal building that housed the entire clamming operation. The building was over a hundred feet long and fifty feet wide. They opened the back door and entered a room where three men were washing, sorting and bagging clams. They had the radio turned up full blast. Ricky yelled loud enough to be heard over the music, barely,

"Turn that damn radio down! I can't hear myself think in here. Hey, Adrian! Go help Ben get those clams off the boat!

Adrian immediately stopped what he was doing and did what he was told to do. Jeremy had trouble getting into the back of the van, but he was able to put his butt on the floor and pull his legs in behind him. He laid down, flat on his back and said,

"God that hurt! Drive slow, Harley. I don't want to be thrown around back here."

"Hold onto somethin', man! I gotta get back. We've got two boatloads of clams waiting for us to clean and bag up, and that don't include yours."

"I can't reach a damn thing, Harley! Just go slow. It won't kill ya to go slow for a change."

Ten minutes later Jeremy hobbled into his house. He went straight for the medicine cabinet and then the couch. After a few minutes he got up and went into the bedroom to lie down. The couch wasn't comfortable enough for him. When he found a position that caused him the least amount of pain, he reached for the phone by the side of the bed and called Sally. After hearing what happened, she said.

"I'll take an early lunch and be there as soon as I can. You want me to bring you anything?"

"Maybe stop and get some more Advil from the Dollar Store."

"How about some of that Icy Hot? Maybe that will help."

"We can give it a try."

"A hot bath might do you some good, too. I'll be there in an hour or so, unless you want me to come home now?"

"No, I'm okay where I am for now. I just hope the pills help it go away."

When Sally got home, the first thing she did, after putting her baby on the bed with Jeremy, was to start drawing a hot bath for him.

Samantha, who wasn't a year old yet, had learned how to walk, and when she tired of crawling all over Jeremy she slid off the bed and stumbled into the bathroom to see what her mother was doing. Sally picked her up and walked back into the bedroom.

"So how bad is it? Do you think you should go to the doctor? she asked.

"If it doesn't get any better, and soon, I'm not going to be able to go to work tomorrow, that's for sure."

"Just sit in that hot water for a while and see if that doesn't help. Be careful getting in. It's really hot."

Jeremy hobbled from his bed to the bathroom, put his right foot in the tub and immediately pulled it out. "Damn! You're not kidding that's hot! Why d'you make it that hot?"

"Because I'm thinking that you probably have a strained muscle and this is supposed to loosen up the muscles. It'd be better if we had a whirlpool, but we don't."

"I thought you were supposed to use ice to prevent swelling. Are you sure this is gonna help?"

"You might be right about that, but it depends on if it's a muscle strain or sprain, I think, but I'm not sure. You want to call a doctor first?"

"Who are we gonna call? We don't know any doctors."

"I'll ask my Dad. He'll know. Want me to call him?"

"No, don't bother. I'll just get in this thing and see what happens."

Jeremy put both feet in the water and slowly eased into the tub.

"It does feel good. I hope it helps."

"Just stay in there until the water cools off. Then we'll put on the Icy Hot after you dry off. I know people use that for muscle pain, but that might be after the swelling's gone down. I don't know. I've got to get back to work. Want some lunch before I go?"

"No. I don't feel much like eating right now. Thanks anyway."

Jeremy stayed in the hot water while Sally and Samantha ate their lunch. When they were done, Sally gave Jeremy a kiss and said,

"Call me if you need anything. See you later."

Ten minutes later, Jeremy got up, dried himself off and put the Icy Hot on his low back. Then he laid down in the bed and fell asleep. When he woke up two hours later, his back was throbbing. He called Sally.

"It's not any better. I think I'd better go see a doctor. Who should I call?"

"I don't know. I'll ask my Dad and call you back."

After she spoke to her father, she called Jeremy and said,

"He said to call Dr. Malpartido. That's who Ian saw when he slipped on the dock that time and fell down the stairs."

"How am I going to pay for this?"

"He said you should be covered by Workmen's Comp. You need to have your uncle call in the claim."

Jeremy called his uncle and told him that he was thinking that he needed to see a doctor.

"I'd rather not file a claim unless I have to, Jeremy."

"Do you want me just to go see him and see what he says before we actually file the claim?"

"No, if you're really hurt, and it sounds as if you are, that's what it's there for."

"I'm hurt, Uncle Ricky. I can hardly walk. The Advil didn't do me any good and neither did the hot bath. I'd like for a doctor to tell me what's wrong with me."

"Okay then. You call to make an appointment and I'll take care of things with Worker's Compensation. Let's hope you're gonna be alright, Jeremy."

"Amen to that. Thanks, Uncle Ricky."

Jeremy was able to get an appointment to see the doctor later that afternoon. He called Sally and told her that she would have to take him to Dr. Malpartido's office in Chiefland when she came home and that he had to be there by 4:30.

Once she got home, Sally drove as Jeremy put the passenger seat as far back as he could, with pillows under him.

After filling out all the forms, they sat in the waiting room for half an hour before being called in to see the doctor. They sat for another ten minutes in one of the rooms inside the office. When the doctor walked in, he had a file in his hand and was reading it.

"So you hurt yourself at work this morning and you have severe pain in your low back. Is that it?"

"Yeah, that's about the size of it, Doctor."

"No prior back problems before today?"

"Nope. Never."

"Stand up."

Jeremy stood up.

"Can you touch your toes?"

"No way."

"Bend forward as far as you can and tell me when you feel any pain or discomfort."

Jeremy bent forward, not even coming close to reaching his knees, and said,

"That's as far as I can go before it starts to hurt."

"Extend your arms to your side."

Jeremy did as he was told.

"Turn to the side as far as you can."

"Which way?"

"Both ways. Do your left first."

Jeremy turned to his right no more than a foot and said,

"That hurts. I can't go much further than that."

"And the other way?"

Jeremy turned to his left and went about the same distance, maybe a little further.

"I can't do much better on that side either."

"Take off your shirt and lie down on the table for me, please. Face up."

Jeremy did as he was asked to do.

"Lift this leg for me as far as you can."

Jeremy raised his left leg up to about a 45 degree angle.

"Now the other leg."

Jeremy was only able to raise his right leg up six inches or so before he let out a groan and said,

"That's the best I can do on that side."

"Do you have any shooting pains in either of your legs?"

"Yeah. I've been feeling some tingling in that right leg, like it's gonna give out on me and I'm going to fall down every now and then."

"Turn over and let me have a look at your back."

Jeremy did as he was asked. The doctor palpated his back and touched some spots that caused Jeremy to yelp in pain.

"Okay, you can sit up now."

The doctor sat down at his desk and began writing on his chart.

"I'm afraid you may have herniated a disc in your low back, but I'll need an MRI to confirm that. I'm going to want to wait a week or so, let the swelling go down, and see what happens before I order one. For now, I'm going to give you some medications for the pain. You should experience some relief fairly soon. It's a fast-acting medication."

The doctor handed Jeremy a prescription.

"When do you think I might be able to go back to work?"

"When your body tells you that you can. For now, you'll need to take things very easy and not do anything to hurt yourself more."

"Right now, all I can do is lie in bed and even that hurts."

"The medication I have prescribed for you will help with the pain. It won't help the underlying problem any. I want to see you back here in a week. If you're not any better, then I'll send you for an MRI."

"Anything I should be doing between now and then?"

"You should not do anything that will cause you pain. Don't bend, lift or twist. Your body will tell you what you can do and what you can't. I'll also give you a prescription for Robaxin. It's muscle relaxant and it should help some, too, but if you have a herniated disc, there isn't much you can do to make it better, but if the disc isn't herniated, and it's a severe sprain or strain, then the best you can do is give it time to heal and not aggravate the situation."

"So I won't be working for a while then, will I?"

"No, you won't."

The doctor was writing on a pad as he said,

"I'm going to let Workmen's Comp know that you are unable to work at this time and that you're going to be out of work for at least a week and maybe much longer. Let's see how you're doing in a week, Mr. Thibodeaux."

He stood, smiled and said, "Good luck to you, sir."

With that, the doctor left the room. On their way out, Jeremy and Sally stopped at the front desk and told the receptionist that it was a Worker's Compensation case. They were told that they weren't required to pay anything, not even a co-pay.

When they were in the car, Sally asked,

"So what did he prescribe for you?"

"I don't know. He didn't say. Here is the prescription. You tell me."

Sally took the prescription and said,

"I can't read his writing. One is for Robaxin, but I can't read the other. It starts with an O, or maybe that's an R"

They took the prescription to the CVS store in Chiefland and waited in the car while the prescription was filled. Fortunately for them, Samantha had slept through most of the visit to the doctor, but she was now waking up and getting fussy. Sally took her to the playground at the McDonald's next door to let her move around. Samantha liked the swing best.

Jeremy laid down on the back seat and tried to get comfortable, but there was no position he could get in which didn't cause him pain. He ended up lying in the grass under a tree next to the car.

An hour later, the medicine was ready. The label read RoxyContin. Jeremy took two of the large, bluish pills right away, and one of the Robaxins.

Sally read the information sheet that was inside the package the pills came in. "It says you should take only one of those RoxyContin pills at a time and that you should have some food with it."

"Okay, I'll have a hamburger and a coke at McD's."

Twenty minutes later, as they were pulling into their driveway, Jeremy began to experience some relief.

"Man, these pills work! I'm feeling better already," he said as he slowly and carefully got out of the car. "I'm not ready to do anything other than get back into bed, but I don't hurt near as much."

Jeremy took two more Advil and got back in bed.

"You want any dinner, Jeremy?"

"No thanks. I'm not hungry. That burger was enough. I'm sleepy."

"It says you might experience some dizziness, disorientation and some other side effects, and that it might make you sleepy, too, so that's what it's supposed to do."

"I slept two hours this afternoon. I might go back to sleep again. Say, Sally, would you mind sleeping in the other room tonight? If I wake up in the middle of the night I might want to watch a movie or something. I can't sleep that much. I know it."

"Sure, I don't mind. I'm going to feed Samantha now and get her ready for bed. You're feeling better, yes?"

"I'm not in as much pain. I'm much better than I was. That was awful. What are those pills again? OxyContin?"

"It says RoxyContin."

Ten minutes later, Jeremy was asleep.

Chapter Two

⊹

They were made for each other. Jeremy was the son of a fifth generation family from the Rosewood area, not far outside of town. Sally was the daughter of a family that had lived in Cedar Key since Cedar Key's glory days, which were shortly before the outbreak of the Civil War. They were born days apart at the Community Hospital in Gainesville and may have passed each other on the way in and out. When they were old enough, they started school together in the same pre-school classroom, and they would share a classroom for the next fourteen years until they graduated from the only school they would ever know.

Cedar Key, a town of 850 people, according to the 2010 census, has only one school, which houses classrooms for children ranging in ages from four to nineteen. Sally was always one of the girls chosen to be a princess for the Clamerica celebration, or to be on a float during the Fourth of July parade, or be the prom queen, or involved in whatever holiday pageant was going on, together with the other thirteen or fourteen girls in her class, who would participate as well, and most of the time she was the queen bee.

Jeremy was the star player on a basketball team that would rarely celebrate victories over their competitors who came from much larger schools. He also played baseball and ran track for the school. It was too small to field a football team.

Both were above average students, but college was never in either of their plans. The mud of the tidal waters surrounding the thousand islands which comprise the islands of Cedar Keys was in their blood. They were destined to be fishermen.

The Thibodeauxs and the Richards were among those who had been commercial fishermen for decades. However, in the early '90s, when Sally and Jeremy were still in diapers, both families leased areas of the Gulf, not far from shore, from the State of Florida, and planted clams. The "net ban," as it was called, banned fishing with large nets that scraped the bottom of the Gulf to capture the fish which were then sold to restaurants and seafood markets on Florida's Nature Coast. The problem was that the process killed many other creatures of the Gulf unintentionally.

The ban destroyed the fishing business in Cedar Key. Those resourceful enough to make the transition to farming clams became far wealthier than they could ever have imagined possible in a span of less than a decade. Cedar Key now provided over 60% of the clams for the entire state and it shipped clams all over the country as well.

Not long after the ban went into effect, the State of Florida issued its first commercial lease to one enterprising Cedar Key man, a transplant from New York, named Billy Leeming, who saw what the future held for aquaculture. He leased a five acre plot in the waters of the Gulf, less than a mile from the harbor of Cedar Key, and put millions of tiny clams in hundreds of burlap bags in water deep enough so that the bags would never be exposed to the forces of the sun and deprived of water. As the clams grew, he, and dozens of others like him, transferred the ever-growing clams into larger bags with fewer clams inside until the clams were large enough to be harvested and sold.

The Thibodeauxs and the Richards were Billy's friends and competitors. There was enough water for all of them and a demand for as many clams as the community could produce. The clams began at an infinitesimally small size, visible only under a microscope, and were allowed to grow until they reached a maximum size of 2 inches. Some, known as pasta clams, were harvested at 5/8ths of an inch. Others were sorted into sizes of 7/8ths, one inch, an inch and a half, and two inches.

There were setbacks and many natural disasters involved in the growth of the clamming industry, such as hurricanes which dropped millions of gallons of fresh water on the fragile clams, and killed them. Predators, such as redfish, black drum and other bottom feeders, found ways to break the bags and destroy the crop, which required the farmers to make improvements to the bags. And there were thieves. Who could tell one clam from another after a bag was stolen and the clams put in other bags?

Billy Leeming, the Thibodeauxs, the Richards, and many others, succeeded. The businesses were all family-run, no franchises or large corporations involved. The operations involved a lease, a clamming boat, a facility to clean and bag the clams, and a way to get the product to market. Jeremy and Sally had been in the business since they were old enough to walk and tell the difference between a pasta clam and a "cherrystone." The cherrystone is a clam in between the "little necks," which are about an inch in size, and the "top necks," which are usually harvested when they get to be at about two inches.

Jeremy and Sally would follow in the footsteps of their fathers, mothers, grandparents, great-grandparents and other ancestors and make a living from the fruits of the sea. They were in love with each other before they knew the meaning of the word. From the time Jeremy first pulled Sally's hair and she flattened him for it people knew that their destinies had been pre-ordained.

Sally was the first girl Jeremy ever kissed and Jeremy was the first boy for Sally as well. There were a few digressions through the adolescent years when April Cummings, Becky Crawford and Anna Whitman gave it their best shots at Jeremy, while Timmy Loyd, Tom Landis, Roy Taylor and Josh Stathem tried to convince Sally that they were more deserving of her love and affection.

Two weeks after graduation, a festive group of hundreds of friends and relatives witnessed the happy couple exchange vows of eternal love through good times and bad, sickness and health, for better or worse. Matt Hodges and the Clam-diggers provided the musical entertainment. The community park overflowed with people and good wishes. The match was made in heaven. Reverend Jim Wright presided over the event and sealed the deal.

With financial assistance from their parents, and a loan from the Cedar Key branch of Capital City Bank, they soon became the proud owners of a two acre plot of ground six miles out of town off of State Road 24 in Rosewood, though it had a Cedar Key mailing address, with a brand-new double-wide trailer, the one with real Cypress logs on the outside. They could walk to the Dollar Store from their home.

Rosewood had been the site of a racial disturbance at the turn of the twentieth century which had become the subject of a movie and the object of a lawsuit nearly a century after the event occurred, but it was of no consequence to Jeremy and Sally. No such problems existed anymore. Besides, they had heard a different version of what had actually happened. There wasn't much racial diversity in the community these days. They knew all their neighbors and all of their neighbors knew them and everybody got along just fine.

They both continued to work with their families by day. Sally worked for her father's clam business and Jeremy for his uncle's. They entered adult life with plans for prosperity and progeny. Ten months later their prayers were answered with the arrival of Samantha Grace, a seven pound, eleven ounce bundle of joy. Their cups were running over.

Jeremy's specialties in the clamming business were his physical strength and his ability to hold his breath under water for an incredibly long time. The best clam leases were in the waters closest to shore, but not too close. Divers who could stand in waters up to their shoulders on high tides and water at their knees when the tides were low were the fortunate few. Most had to dive to depths of eight to ten feet on a high tide or to six foot depths on low tides.

As soon as they accumulated enough money to do so, Jeremy and Sally bought themselves a two acre deep water lease and began their own business, on the side. They kept their jobs with their families and knew that it would take a few years before they could be on their own, but it was a start.

With Samantha constantly at her side, on her back or in her arms, Sally no longer went out on the water anywhere near as often as she used to, or as often as she wanted to, and she learned about the packaging, shipping and marketing side of the business. Jeremy was the diver and the handler of the clams. He sorted them, weighed them and bagged them.

Sally grew into a tall, thin body, with brown eyes and wavy brown hair which she wore at shoulder length and occasionally highlighted with blonde streaks. Despite years of orthodontic work in her early teenage years, she had a small gap between her two front teeth, of which she was self-conscious, and she often put her hand over her mouth when smiling or laughing to hide it.

Jeremy was the same height as Sally, or maybe an inch shorter, though he'd never admit it, but he was barrel-chested and had big, muscular arms and thick fingers. He kept his hair short on top, sometimes shaving it completely, with a pencil-thin mustache and a swatch of hair below his lower lip. On a dare from friends while in Tampa one night during his senior year, he had a tattoo of a shark, the mascot of Cedar Key's school, emblazoned on his left bicep. He, too, had light brown eyes and brown hair. They were the result of generations of breeding from the stock of the scrublands of Levy County. There weren't many blue eyed, blonde haired people in the mix, nor were there any red-heads with green eyes in the gene pool.

The hardest part of being a clammer, as far as it being physically challenging, was hoisting up a fully loaded clam bag weighing over a hundred pounds from a depth of ten feet, and then doing it over and over again for hours. Once the bags were loaded onto the boat, they had to be unloaded off the boat and carried a hundred feet or more to a room where they were placed in a machine which washed and sorted them. The clams were then placed in bags of different colors, depending upon the size of the clams, in quantities of a hundred. After being bagged, they were put in refrigerated coolers, awaiting either a local sale or a delivery by truck or van to local destinations or for shipment by air via FedEx or UPS.

Jeremy's job ended once the clams were in coolers. Others were responsible for the packaging and shipping side of the business. His uncle had two daughters and they worked in the office and handled most of the paperwork.

Sally's job began when the clams were in the coolers. She was happy to be working for her father since he not only didn't mind Samantha coming to work with her, he insisted upon it. Samantha had her own room in the shop, complete with a bed and enough toys and games for five children.

During Jeremy's sophomore year in high school, his father died in a tragic car accident. Prior to that, the business had been run by his father and his uncle. Once his father passed, his uncle took over the operation. Though Jeremy liked being in the water, he would occasionally be required to drive a delivery truck and work in the office doing paperwork, too. He was being trained by his uncle to take over the business when the time came for him to retire.

During the months of November through March, it isn't uncommon for air temperatures to drop down into the teens several times. During the winter of 2010 a record was set when temperatures were below freezing for thirteen days in a row. Even in full-bodied wet suits the waters of the Gulf are unwelcoming, especially in the dark hours before dawn when work sometimes begins.

In the hot months, beginning in April and ending in October, the waters can be a welcome relief from the heat when temperatures hover around the century mark, but the sun's rays are a fearsome enemy. It isn't uncommon to see men with distorted noses or ears who lost the battle with the elements after years of exposure to the sun.

But the sand-fleas, or "no see-ums," even more than the sun, are the scourge of the clammers. There is no relief from them except with a poisonous, Deet-based product being liberally and continuously applied, together with other lotions to block the sun. Most men don't spend the time to take the necessary precautions, viewing them as somehow less than manly.

People said that Jeremy had the hide of an alligator because he refused the Deet but, at Sally's insistence, he applied the sun block lotions. She didn't want him to end up with skin cancer, like so many of their ancestors had, when the only protection was a hat with a broad band, which was of no use whatsoever in the water.

Jeremy wasn't ten feet tall, but he felt like he was bullet-proof, and he was cocky. He knew that if he ever got in a fight, which he rarely did, there were all the Thibodeauxs and Richards cousins there to guard his back. All but newcomers to the area were related in one way or another to the Thibodeauxs and the Richards, either by blood or marriage or both.

They might fight with each other every now and then, and it was usually on a Saturday night down on Dock Street at one of the bars with live music where a family feud would erupt, but woe to the unwary visitor who happened to be on the opposite side of an altercation with Jeremy or his kin. The police knew the families all too well and gave them a wide berth. Many family members had been police officers over the years.

There weren't many men in Cedar Key's Police Department, and no women, and they mostly write speeding tickets and keep a look-out for drivers leaving the bars after having too much to drink. There was an uneasy truce between the police and the locals as a result of an incident in which one of the brood wound up on the wrong end of a Taser. A million dollar settlement calmed the waters but people like the Thibodeauxs, the Richards and the other families felt that anyone who hadn't lived there as long as they had were outsiders, and that included the entire current police force.

Scrub pines, cabbage palms, and cedars strong enough to survive the arid, dry, sandy, moisture-less, nutrient free soil, provided the natural environment for the hardy souls who called the area home. It was an hour drive to Gainesville, two hours to Tampa, three hours to Tallahassee, and half an hour to the smaller communities of Chiefland, Bronson and Crystal River. Nobody came to Cedar Key by accident. It wasn't on the way to or from anyplace. People were there because they wanted to be there. To Jeremy and Sally it was home, their home.

Chapter Three

————— ılı —————

Jeremy awoke the next morning to the sounds of Samantha babbling. Sally was busy getting ready for another day of work. Jeremy gingerly crawled out of bed and walked slowly into the kitchen where Samantha was sitting in her high chair, eating breakfast.

"So how do you feel?" Sally asked.

"I'm sore, but I feel better. When am I supposed to take some more pills?"

"It says no more than two pills a day, so you're supposed to take one tablet every twelve hours, I'd say."

"It's been more than twelve hours. I'll take some more of that Robaxin, too."

Sally handed him the pills and a glass of water. He swallowed the pills immediately.

"How did you sleep?"

"Like a rock. I didn't wake up once. How about you?"

"I slept okay. That bed in the other room isn't bad, but I like being in our bed with you better. I hope we don't have to do that for too long."

"I feel better than I did yesterday, but I'm not going to be able to do anything or go anywhere today. I'll give Uncle Ricky a call here in a few minutes and let him know what's going on."

"Can I leave Samantha with you, or no?"

"Not today, okay? I'm not sure that I can pick her up right now. Let's see how it goes. Maybe tomorrow."

"That's fine. I'll see you at about noon. If you need anything, just give me a call."

Once Sally and Samantha had driven off, Jeremy called his uncle.

"So can you sit in a chair or do anything?"

"Not now, Uncle Ricky. I've been up for less than half an hour and I'm ready to get back into bed again. I took one of those pills last night and it knocked me out."

"What is it you're taking?"

"RoxyCodone, or something like that."

"RoxyContin?"

"Yeah, that's it."

"You be careful with that stuff, Jeremy. You don't want to use it for any longer than is absolutely necessary, you hear?"

"Yeah, I hear you, Uncle Ricky."

"I'm serious, Jeremy. I've known people who've had a lot of trouble with that stuff."

"I'll be careful. I promise."

"I've never known you to be sick or injured a day in your life."

"I can't remember being sick too much, other than the flu a couple of times, and maybe the mumps, and I know I've never hurt myself before like this."

"But you need that stuff to help you with the pain, huh?"

"Oh yeah. It worked like magic last night. I was in some serious pain, but within twenty minutes of taking that stuff the pain just about went completely away and I was asleep within an hour. I slept through the night with no problem. Today I'm sore and stiff, but it doesn't hurt near as much as it did yesterday, but I took another pill as soon as I woke up."

"So what does the doctor think it is?"

"He thinks it might be a herniated disc."

"When's he going to know for sure?"

"If I'm not better by next week, he's going to send me for an MRI."

"Let's hope not it's not a herniated disc. If it is, they might have to operate on you."

"That's what he said."

"When you're better, I can put you to work in the office. You can do the paperwork until you're able to get back in the water. What did you do to hurt yourself that bad anyway? You've seen sharks before."

"I was in deep water so I was kickin' with my feet to get myself in the boat and pushin' with my arms to get the bag in the boat, and at the same time, I was lookin' to see where he was so that I could keep out of his way. I must have twisted too much because as I was getting in the boat I felt a really sharp pain in my low back. I knew it was something serious right away, because it was like nothin' I'd ever felt before, and that was it."

"Well, let's hope it's not as serious as they think it is and you don't need surgery. You take care of yourself, Jeremy, and, when you feel better, come back to work and do whatever you can, okay?"

"Thanks, Uncle Ricky, I will."

"Call me every couple of days and let me know how you're doing."

"I will."

Within half an hour after taking another of the blue pills, Jeremy fell asleep. He was awakened by the noise of the front door opening when Sally and Samantha returned for lunch.

"How do you feel?" Sally asked.

"Dopey. I slept all morning."

"How about your back?"

"I'm not feeling pain like I did yesterday, but I haven't done much since seeing Dr. Malpartido."

"I guess that's good."

"It's good I don't have pain, but my back is as stiff as a board. I can't move much."

"Want some lunch?"

"Not really, but I guess I should eat something."

Sally put Samantha in her little stroller and began fixing lunch for everyone. Samantha was able to walk, but she was at the stage where she was dangerous. She might walk into a table and hit her head, or walk into a chair and fall down, so she needed constant supervision. Jeremy wasn't able to help. He was lying down on the couch trying to find a comfortable position. In the stroller, Samantha could walk, or roll, all over the house without hurting herself.

After lunch, and after Sally and Samantha had gone back to work, Jeremy took some more Robaxin and tried playing his guitar. He had to put it down within a few minutes because it hurt him to sit and hold the guitar in the normal position. After less than twenty minutes he was back in bed watching a video.

When Sally got home, she put Samantha in the sand box Jeremy had built for her and went inside. Jeremy was barely able to walk outside, sit in a chair, and watch Samantha play. Though she pointed at the swing, indicating that she wanted him to put her in it, Jeremy wasn't able to oblige. He was afraid it would hurt too much just to pick her up, let alone push her.

Jeremy sat outside with Samantha until the no-see-ums got so bad they drove the two of them inside. He was sound asleep not long after dinner, after taking another blue pill. Sally slept in the other room again that night.

When it was time to go back to see the doctor, Jeremy still wasn't able to drive. He sat on the passenger side and put the seat all the way back, with pillows underneath him. After seeing him, and noting that the swelling was down but there was little improvement in motion or mobility, Dr. Malpartido ordered an MRI.

A week later, Sally took the whole day off and drove Jeremy to Gainesville for the examination, leaving Samantha with Jeremy's mother. After successfully negotiating the traffic, something they didn't see much of in Cedar Key, and finding the MRI facility in Gainesville, they were promptly taken into the room where the test was to be performed, after Jeremy filled out the necessary paperwork.

A young woman dressed in white nurse's garb told Jeremy to lie down on a table. He noticed that there were wheels on the table. Once he did as he was told, the attendant slid the table into the machine which completely covered his head and torso, all the way down to his knees. As she did so, Jeremy immediately demanded to be taken out of the cylinder into which his body barely fit.

"I didn't know what to expect, but I didn't expect that. My nose was about an inch from the top and my arms were pressed up against the side. I felt like a sardine in there."

"But you've got to do it, Jeremy. There's no other way for the doctor to find out what's wrong with you." Sally told him.

"You don't have machines that aren't bigger than that? he asked.

The attendant replied, "They do, they're called Open MRI machines, but they aren't as accurate and that's not what the doctor ordered."

"You're gonna have to tough it out, Jeremy." Sally offered.

Jeremy thought about it for a few seconds, took a deep breath, and said, "Okay, let's do it."

The attendant slid the table back inside the machine and started it up.

"This is going to take a little less than an hour, so make yourself as comfortable as you can and be patient. If you really can't stand it anymore, tell me and I'll pull you out, but if I pull you out before the test is complete, it will ruin the results and you'll have to do it all over again, at an additional charge."

"Who pays if that happens?"

"I don't know. It's never happened with one of my patients," the attendant replied.

"Tell me every fifteen minutes how long it's been, okay?"

"I will," the attendant said.

"I'll be right here, baby," Sally said as she put her hands on his ankles. "I'm with you."

"I wish I'd known what to expect. I'd have taken a pill to put me to sleep if I'd have known it was gonna be like this."

"You can do it, Jeremy. Be strong, sweetheart."

After a few minutes, when he realized he could still breathe and he adjusted to the situation better, he settled down. His heart rate became more regular, but he was still nervous.

"Is it fifteen minutes yet?"

"No, it's not quite ten minutes yet, Mr. Thibodeaux," the attendant responded.

"Damn! This is hard!"

Fifty minutes later, the attendant said,

"You made it, Mr. Thibodeaux. Congratulations," as she slid the board on which Jeremy was lying out from the machine.

"How did I do?"

"Oh, I can't tell you that. The doctor will have to read the results, or a radiologist. You can call your doctor and make an appointment to see him. I doubt he'll give you the results over the phone, but he might."

"But it's Friday. I'll have to wait until next week to find out?"

"I'm afraid so, Mr. Thibodeaux."

"We're going to see him on Monday anyway, Jeremy. We'll find out soon enough. There's nothing you can do about it anyway."

"Yeah, but I'd like to know now. I want this thing to go away already."

Once they were home, and though he was in much less pain, he was still unable to do much, other than slowly move about his home, basically going from the bedroom to the couch. Picking up Samantha, who weighed less than twenty pounds, was still more than he could handle.

On the few times when he tried to hold Samantha, Sally had to rush over to him and take Samantha out of his arms when a sudden pain came on and he felt as if he might drop her. The weekend went much like every day since the incident on the boat occurred. The Robaxin seemed to have little effect on the back problem, but the blue pills provided relief from the pain and put him to sleep.

On Monday, Jeremy was still unable to drive himself. He was in fear that he'd have a sudden pain that might cause him to have an accident. When those shooting pains came over him, he felt a weakness in his body that completely disabled him. He was hoping for good news, but expecting the worst.

As soon as Dr. Malpartido walked into the room where Jeremy and Sally were sitting waiting for him, he took the MRI film and put it up on a screen that allowed them to see the spine, the discs, spinal nerves and the spinal cord. The doctor used a ruler to explain the results.

"You have an injury at the L4-L5 level. This is your sacrum, and these are the discs in your lumbar spine. This is called L-1; this is L-2; here's L-3, this is L-4 and this is L-5. The L is for lumbar. Now, in each disc there is a gelatin like substance which acts like a spacer and keeps the bones apart and allows space for the nerves.

"Your spinal cord runs inside a sheath inside the spine from top to bottom. There are nerves that run off of the spinal cord, called spinal nerves. What has happened to you is that the gelatin substance, which is inside your disc between the L4 and the L5 bones, has escaped and it is impinging on one of your spinal nerves, as you can see.

"If the substance moves around but doesn't get outside of the sac, that's called a bulging disc. I've read where maybe as many as half the people in the United States have bulging discs and they don't even know it. But where, as here, the substance has escaped the disc and presses upon that nerve, it can cause excruciating, and disabling, pain. That's why you are in so much pain."

"So what can you do to make me better?"

"With a disc that is herniated, like yours is, and where the gelatin-like substance impinges upon a spinal nerve as yours does, generally there is only one way to correct the problem, and that is by surgery."

"Surgery…that's what I was afraid of. I'm not going to be able to go back to work for a long time, am I?"

"It's going to take several months, at the very least, and that's if you have a full recovery."

"Am I going to be in this much pain until the operation?"

"Probably not. You're going to figure out which positions cause you pain and which ones don't. You're going to figure out what activities hurt you and which ones don't. Do things that don't hurt you and don't get yourself in positions that cause you pain. It's that simple, but herniated discs don't cure themselves. Some people learn to live with the pain and discomfort and for whatever reasons they decide not to have the surgery. In your case, you're a young man and you use your body to earn income. You want to get better and go back to what you have done all your life, right?"

"That's right."

"So you have to have the surgery. Since you were hurt at work, your employer's Workmen's Compensation carrier will pay for the surgery, and I'd say you should have the surgery as soon as possible."

"What's that going to involve?"

"The surgeons will clean out the area and get the disc substance away from the spinal nerve. You'll feel immediate relief once the pressure is off the spinal nerve, but it will take a while for you to heal."

"So what do I have to do?"

"Nothing. I'll let Workmen's Comp know the results of the MRI and that I recommend surgery. They'll tell you where to go from here."

"Will you still be my doctor?"

"Yes, I'm your primary treating physician. When the surgeons finish their work, you'll come back to me and I'll be responsible for your post-surgical care. I'll be the one to decide when you can go back to work. Are those pills I prescribed working?"

"Yes. They take away the pain. The Robaxin pills you gave me, the Icy-Hot and all the other things I take don't seem to do any good at all."

"No, they won't do much good, not with the injury you have. As I said, the only thing that will help you is surgery, but the medical profession has made some great strides in that department lately. There is a procedure available now that is less invasive and can be done on an out-patient basis. There are still risks involved, but there are risks with any surgery. I have used a group out of Orlando before, with good success, and that is who I'm going to recommend for you."

"So when am I going to see you again?"

"I'll make an appointment to see you in two weeks. I don't know how long it will take before you'll be able to get in to see the surgeons. Worker's Compensation will decide that. I'll want to see you in two weeks. I'll give you a prescription for two more weeks of that pain reliever now."

The doctor stopped in the middle of writing the prescription and asked,

"Are you sure you need this? I thought I gave you enough to last you for a month the last time."

Jeremy lied and said, "I'm all out, Doctor. I just use one in the morning and one at night, just like you told me, but I don't have anymore. Can't you give me more than that, so I don't have to keep getting those prescriptions filled all the time?"

The doctor wrote out a prescription and handed it to Jeremy.

"I'll give you a two week supply, no more, and you be careful using these," he warned.

"I understand, but this stuff really works, just like you said it would. I know it won't cure my problem, but when I take it I can get to sleep and not be waking up in pain during the night. I don't know what I'd do without it."

"Mr. Thibodeaux, I'm sorry I don't have better news for you but, as you can see for yourself, the results from the MRI are very clear. The only way you are going to fix the problem is by getting the pressure off that spinal nerve. You have a herniated disc at your L4-L5 level."

At that, the doctor stood, extended his hand and said,

"Good luck, young man. I'll see you in two weeks."

Chapter Four

The next day, Jeremy went into to town to see his uncle and explain what Dr. Malpartido had told him.

"A herniated disc, huh? Well, you won't be going back in the water for a while, Jeremy. It looks like you're going to have to use that brain of yours instead of that strong back you've relied on all these years."

"I'm afraid so, Uncle Ricky."

"Can you come back and work in the office?"

"Not yet. I spend most of my time lying in bed or sleeping. I can't drive yet and I can barely stand. I still can't stand and hold Samantha for more than a few seconds at a time."

"Damn, Jeremy! You hurt yourself good, didn't you?"

"Yeah, the doctor showed me the results from the MRI and explained it all to me. There isn't any doubt about it. I need surgery."

"At least Workmen's Comp is going to pay the bills."

"And they're supposed to pay me about two-thirds of my salary while I'm off work. They're going to tell me when I can come back to work, Uncle Ricky. I can't come back until they say so."

"But I need you here now, Jeremy. Don't get me wrong, you're my kin and I'm behind you all the way. You'll always have a job here, but if you can work doing anything, I want you here. Understand?"

"Yeah, I understand, Uncle Ricky, and when I'm able to work I'll be back. Hopefully I'll be back in the water, swimming. I'd much rather do that than work in the office any day."

"I know you would, Jeremy. You're a worker. You do what the doctors tell you and get yourself better. If there's anything I can do for you and Sally, just ask."

"Thanks, Uncle Ricky. I will."

The two men embraced.

"Good luck, Jeremy. I hope it goes well for you."

The days passed slowly with few changes. Jeremy grew tired of watching videos and he started watching day-time television shows and CNN, and soon that bored him, too. After two weeks with no word from Workmen's Compensation, when he returned to see Dr. Malpartido, the doctor offered, "Maybe you need to hire yourself a lawyer. Many people in your situation do."

"I've never even spoken to a lawyer in my whole life, I don't think," Jeremy said. "There's one or two lawyers in Cedar Key, but I don't know them. They're not from around here."

"There's three now. That man who opened that new restaurant, the Old Fish House Café, is a lawyer, too," Sally interjected.

"But I've never said a word to any of them."

"Well, that's up to you, Mr. Thibodeaus, but tell me, what's your pain level? Do you still need the medication I have prescribed for you or can we discontinue that at this point?"

"I absolutely still need those pills, Doctor. As far as I'm concerned it's a miracle drug."

"Well, we've got to be careful with it. It can have some serious side effects. I'll write you another script for two more weeks. I don't need to see you until after the surgery, really, because there's nothing else I can do for you, but I'll follow with you until the surgery is approved and you meet with the surgeon. You should see one soon. I'd suggest you call Worker's Comp and talk to the adjuster assigned to your case."

"Or maybe just hire an attorney and let him do that," Sally offered.

"Or do as your wife has suggested. That's up to you," the doctor responded, as he stood up, readying himself to move onto his next patient. Jeremy stood, extended his hand and said,

"Thanks, Dr. Malpartido. You've helped me."

The two men shook hands, and the doctor responded,

"You're welcome, and good luck, Mr. Thibodeaux."

On the ride home, after they had the prescription filled again, Jeremy asked Sally,

"So do you know any attorneys who could help me?"

"You remember when Joey fell out of that tree and broke his arm while working for that tree farm in Chiefland?"

"Yeah."

"Well he ended up getting a woman lawyer out of Crystal River and she really helped him."

"Okay, so find out who it was and I'll call her."

Later that day, after making a few phone calls, Sally came home and gave Jeremy the name and number of the attorney.

"That's who Joey used. You gonna call her?"

"Yeah. I'll call her right now. I called that adjuster four times now and she never returns my calls. I'm tired of lying around the house like this, not able to do anything."

Jeremy made the phone call and, after he hung up, asked Sally,

"Can you take me this afternoon? She can see me at 4:30."

"Sure. Call and see if your Mom can watch Samantha. I'd rather not take her with us for this."

"She said I had to bring my last few pay stubs. Do you know where they are?"

"Of course," Sally said as she walked to the drawer where she kept all of their receipts and things they'd need to do their taxes.

Jeremy made the phone call and his mother was glad to be of assistance. She was always happy to have Samantha with her and rarely refused their requests. Samantha had her own room in her grandmother's house and was as happy there as she was at her own house.

They found the office, which was located on State Road 19 not far from the most well-known landmark in Crystal River, the Plantation Inn, without any problem. After filling out the necessary forms, they went in to meet with Virginia Hayfield, a short, thin woman in her mid-thirties with blonde hair and glasses. She stood as they entered her office and greeted them with a smile.

"I'm sorry to hear of your problems but I'll be happy to help. Dealing with Workmen's Comp can be difficult. They don't return phone calls, right?"

"That's right," Jeremy said. "And weeks go by without anything being done. I want this thing to be over with as soon as possible. If I've got to have surgery, then let's get it done and move on."

"I agree with you. Have you received your first check yet?"

"No, I haven't."

"Well sign these papers and I'll get to work for you right away. Look them over first but basically they just say that you have retained me to represent you and you authorize Worker's Comp to discuss your case with me."

"How much is this going to cost me?" Jeremy asked.

"Nothing now, and if all goes as I expect it will, I'll be paid by Worker's Comp so you won't owe me anything, but the contract says I am to receive 10% of whatever you get, including your average weekly wage checks. Did you bring the last several months of pay stubs as you were asked to do?"

"Yes. Here they are."

"Great. Unless you have any questions or reservations about doing this, just sign the papers and I'll get started first thing in the morning."

Jeremy looked at Sally and asked, "What do you think?"

She gave him a look as if to say that it was up to him.

"I don't have any questions. I'd say go ahead and sign it. That's why we're here, isn't it?"

Jeremy signed the documents and said,

"Is that it? Do you want to talk about what happened or anything else?"

"Not right now. One of the documents you signed authorizes me to get your medical records. From what you told me it happened on the job. Worker's Comp isn't contesting that part, so it seems pretty clear that you were hurt at work and that you have a serious, disabling injury which prevents you from working. You are entitled to benefits and they are slow giving you those benefits. It's pretty normal stuff for me. I'll get your work records and your medical records and do my best to get you in to see the surgeon to whom Worker's Comp is sending you as soon as possible. The main thing I will do for you, really, will be to keep the Worker's Compensation adjuster on her toes and make sure she does her job right. Sound good?"

"Yeah. I was expecting I'd have to pay you a lot of money."

"Nope. That's not how it works with Worker's Comp. The legislature made some changes a few years back so there's not as much money for lawyers to make any more, but I get paid some money just by making sure your medical issues are properly dealt with and to get you back to work as quickly as possible. Don't think that there won't be any disagreements along the way. They get paid by the Worker's Compensation Fund, which gets its money from employers who pay insurance premiums, so they can be slanted in favor of the employers at times, which is why you need a lawyer."

"I'm glad we came to see you. Thanks for being willing to help us."

"You're welcome. I'll give you a call once I have a chance to talk to the adjuster and we'll get this thing moving. I promise."

At that she stood and said,

"I was able to squeeze you in today on short notice but I have another client in the waiting room who I need to see. Again, thank you for calling upon me to be of service to you."

Jeremy and Sally stood, shook her hand and said, at the same time,

"No, thank you."

A few days later, Jeremy received his first check from the insurance company. It was for about 60% of his average weekly wage. The next day he received a phone call from Ms. Hayfield in which she told him that the referral to the Lumbar Spine Surgery Specialists in Orlando had been approved. Jeremy had an appointment to see a Dr. Livengood for a surgical consult in a week,

"Damn! That attorney is good!"

"Maybe this is going to work out okay after all," Sally said. "I'll be happy when we can sleep in the same bed again."

Jeremy and Sally hadn't had sex since the incident. Jeremy said, "I'll see if Mom can watch Samantha on Saturday night. We need some time together."

Sally looked over and smiled knowingly. They loved each other and this was the first obstacle their love had to overcome.

That Saturday night Sally bought some clam chowder from Tony's, which had been crowned the world champion clam chowder maker for the third time in a row, in New England no less, using Cedar Key clams. Her friend, Jeannie, gave her a quarter bushel of oysters, and she picked up some corn and some other things at the outdoor market on State Road 24. They had a romantic, candle-lit dinner, with music playing softly in the background.

After dinner, they made love, being extra-careful so as not to cause Jeremy any pain, which was hard to do, because he wasn't able to move much at all. Then they watched a movie they'd received in the mail from Net Flix, holding each other tenderly as they did, and they slept in the same bed for the first time since the incident, too, but not before Jeremy took two of the blue pills, just to make sure he would sleep pain-free through the night. One pill was no longer enough to do the job.

Chapter Five

---⫶⫶⫶---

The drive to Orlando took them almost two hours. When they arrived at the Lumbar Spine Surgical Specialists, they were immediately impressed by the four story structure with huge tinted glass covering the entire façade of the building. As they entered the building, they saw a sign that said "Cafeteria" and noticed the television sets, linen table cloths, cushioned chairs, plants and flowers that made it look more like an expensive restaurant than a cafeteria.

The receptionist told them that the doctor was running a little late and that it would be another twenty minutes before he would be able to see them. She said they were welcome to help themselves to the food and drink in the cafeteria, which was free to all patients and their companions. It was almost noon and they hadn't eaten any breakfast before they left, so they had hot sandwiches, made to their specifications by a chef who took their order, fresh vegetables, some fruit and drinks. It made them feel quite special.

As they were finishing, a young, female attendant, dressed in a starched-white frock, walked up and told them that the doctor was ready to see them. They followed her onto the elevators up to the fourth floor.

Dr. Livengood was an athletic-looking man with a dark sun tan, who appeared to be in his late forties, with streaks of grey running through an otherwise full head of black hair. He was dressed in green surgical garb. He stood as they entered and extended his hand, saying,

"I'm sorry to have kept you waiting. We had to squeeze a patient who had somewhat of an emergency situation onto my schedule today and it caused me to run a little late. I hope we haven't inconvenienced you too much. I noticed that you had to come a long way to see me."

"Oh it was no trouble at all. We had lunch while we were waiting. It was really very enjoyable. Thank you for that."

"It's the least we can do for our patients. We try to make this otherwise unpleasant situation as pleasant as is possible, and we hope that when you leave us you will tell others that your experience with LSSS was far beyond your expectations, and that you had a positive result which was better than what you had hoped for."

"I hope you can do that for me. I'm afraid I may never be able to swim in the water and do my job as a clammer again."

"We're going to do our very best to make sure that when you leave our care that you can say that you are as good, or better, than you ever were."

"Thank you, Doctor."

"Well, this is what is called a surgical consult. It has been authorized by your Worker's Compensation Insurance Carrier and the purpose of it is to allow us, the Lumbar Spine Surgical Specialists, to make sure that you are an appropriate candidate for surgery. We need to meet with you, talk to you, review your medical chart and make certain that we think we can help you.

"Unfortunately, there are times when we determine that a person, for one reason or another, is not a good candidate for our services. It's one thing to look at a file with the name Jeremy Thibodeaux on it, but quite another to actually meet with you, see what you look like, palpate your spine, do a screening, look at your MRI, see if there are any contra-indications to surgery…things like that. I'm going to ask you to meet with my assistant, Lilly Rose, and she is going to ask you a series of questions and administer a few tests. After you do that, I'll meet with you again and let you know what I think. How's that?"

"Whatever you say, Doctor."

"Good! I like a cooperative and compliant patient. That's a good start.

It won't take more than half an hour. You stay here and I'll be back to see you then."

The doctor left the room and another young woman sat down in a chair next to him and began asking questions of Jeremy. The woman also took his temperature and blood pressure, felt his pulse and measured his heart rate and did all of the other standard tests. Half an hour later, when she was finished, Dr. Livengood re-entered the room, holding a chart in his hands and said,

"I've reviewed your MRI and it looks as if you are an excellent candidate for this surgery and I'm pleased to inform you that the Lumber Spinal Surgery Specialists will accept you as a patient."

"That's great. I'm happy to hear it," Jeremy responded.

"Now, let me explain to you exactly what we're going to do. The surgery I will perform upon you is called "minimally invasive." That means that we will make the least possible intrusion into your body. This is laser-guided surgery and a very small incision will be made just above the L4-L5 area and a sheath will be inserted into the hole we make in your skin. Inside that sheath I'll put the laser, which I can control with instruments.

"I can direct the laser to exactly the area I want to be in, which will allow me to not only visualize the area, but also perform the surgery without having to actually put my hands on you. Now, this is still a very delicate matter because anytime a spinal nerve is involved you must be very careful, and I will be. I have performed this surgery a thousand times on patients just like you over the last ten years. This is truly a revolutionary improvement in the care and treatment the medical profession can provide to a person with a problem such as you have.

"You won't be left with a huge scar; we won't be fusing your spine; you won't be put under by general anesthetia; and you won't be required to stay in a hospital for several days, as is the case with the more typical surgery for a herniated disc. Instead, you will be awake throughout the entire procedure, which will last for less than an hour, you'll have a local anesthetic, for the incision, and you can leave here an hour after the surgery is over. Now, you will need to have someone with you to drive you home, and since your wife is here with you today, I assume she can be with you then and that won't be a problem. We like to keep you here for an hour or so after the surgery and see you the day after surgery as well, just to make sure that there are no complications."

"So we will need to be here for two nights?" Sally asked.

"That's correct, and that's the bare minimum. Sometimes we ask some of our older patients to be with us for three or, on rare occasions, four days."

"We have a one year old, so we'll have to figure out what to do with her for those two days, but I'm sure that won't be a problem."

The doctor stood and said,

"Well, it was nice to meet you but, as you can see, we are quite busy here, and I have several people waiting to see me. If you have any other questions, my assistant, Randi, will answer them for you. She will also schedule the surgery for you as well. She controls my schedule and she is a task-master," he said with a smile.

Jeremy and Sally stood, shook hands with the doctor, and he left the room.

Moments after he was out of sight, Randi came in, with a smile on her face, and, after introducing herself, sat down and said, "So when would you like to have this surgery performed?"

Jeremy asked, "How soon can we do this, Randi?"

"Well, first it must be approved by your Worker's Compensation adjuster, and I will contact her today. That's a formality, since they agreed to send you here, but the earliest the doctor could perform the surgery, if it was approved right away, would be a month from now."

"A month! I was hoping for next week," Jeremy exclaimed.

"He's really tired of being in pain and unable to do anything at all, like hold his baby," Sally offered.

"I understand," Randi responded, but Dr. Livengood is a very busy man. There are hundreds and hundreds of people wanting to get his help, but not everyone is accepted. Fortunately for you, you were, but you'll have to be patient. One thing at a time. Today you passed the qualifying examination, which is a good thing."

"I understand," Jeremy said, "but please schedule me for the first available date and time once Worker's Comp approves it, okay? I'm ready to go whatever day of the week or time of the day is good for him. You call and we'll be here."

"I understand," Randi responded, "and I will do that for you. For now, I'm going to schedule you for the second week in June, which is five weeks from now. That's a Tuesday, so you'll need to be here by Monday morning for a pre-surgical consult. The doctor will see you that afternoon, after we have all of the test results. How's that?"

"If that's the best you can do, that'll be fine, I guess."

"It's the best I can do, but if there are any cancellations, which are rare. I'll let you know. So," she said with a smile, "unless you have any questions, you're free to go. I'll be in touch once I get the okay from Worker's Comp."

Neither Jeremy or Sally had any other questions and they stood to go.

"You need to read over all of the instructions and the information sheet that is included in this packet," Randi said as she handed Jeremy a thick manila envelope, "and if you have any questions after reading it, just call me."

"Thank you," Jeremy and Sally said at the same time.

"Follow me and I'll show you out." Randi escorted them to the elevator and stood with them until they were safely in the elevator. They saw her smiling face as the doors to the elevator closed. It took them three hours to get back to Cedar Key because they caught the beginning of rush-hour traffic in the Orlando hub.

When they hadn't heard anything from Workmen's Compensation by the end of the next week, Jeremy called Virginia Hatfield. By the end of the next day, the surgery was approved. A day later, Randi called to let Jeremy know that the surgery was confirmed for the date she had given them, a few days short of four weeks away.

There was nothing Jeremy could do to improve his condition. Surgery was the only option. He found ways to adjust to his circumstances, but there was still very little that he could do. Sitting in a chair for more than ten minutes was painful and he could hardly stand being on his feet for more than five minutes at a time. His uncle wanted him to come back to work and to do whatever he could in the office. Jeremy asked his lawyer about it and she told him that it would be better if he didn't do that until after the surgery, after the doctor cleared him to return to part-time work.

She said that since the doctor had told him, and Worker's Comp, that he was totally unable to work then he should do exactly what the doctor told him to do. Uncle Ricky wasn't happy about it, but he understood. Besides, since Jeremy couldn't sit or stand for very long there wasn't much he could do. He spent most of his time moving from his bed to the couch and back.

He was about to run out of the RoxyContin pills, so Jeremy made an appointment to go back to see Dr. Malpartido. Again, as always, Sally had to drive. Jeremy had tried to drive himself to and from his house to Cedar Key but it caused him too much pain.

"I don't understand. You shouldn't be out of pills. There must be some mistake," the doctor said when Jeremy asked him to refill the prescription.

"I don't know what the problem is. I take the prescription to the pharmacy and they give me pills. I take two a day until they're gone. Maybe they aren't giving me the right number of pills."

"I doubt that, Mr. Thibodeaux, but it's possible."

The doctor stared at the chart, and then asked,

"Do you think that we can cut back on the pills, Mr. Thibodeaux? I really don't want to keep you on this medication for too long."

"No, I don't. If I don't take those pills every twelve hours, or if I'm late in taking them by just an hour or two, the pain comes back. I don't know what I'd do without them," Jeremy told him. He wasn't about to tell the doctor that he was now using two pills at a time and that he really wanted the doctor to prescribe more pills, not less.

"Please understand that once that surgery is completed, provided all goes as planned, I'm not going to prescribe this medication to you any longer. As I've told you, there are some potentially serious side-effects to this drug, including dependency upon it."

"Once I'm not in pain anymore, I'm not going to take this medicine ever again. It numbs me and puts me to sleep. I never took drugs at all before this. Even when many of my best friends started smoking marijuana or taking pills of some kind or another, I never did. I hate having to take this stuff, but I'm glad I have it. I remember the pain I was in when I first came to see you. I don't want to be in that kind of pain ever again."

"I don't doubt that you are in pain, Mr. Thibodeaux, and I'm sure these pills help with that."

"I need them, Doctor."

"Alright, Mr. Thibodeaux. I'll give you more pills, but this may be the last time. I hope the surgery is successful. When is it scheduled for?"

Jeremy told him. "Alright, I'll give you a prescription that will take you through the surgery and for one week past that date. I want to see you then and see how you're doing. Provided the surgery is successful, I'm going to discontinue that drug altogether as soon as possible, understand?"

"That's fine with me. Do you think I will be able to go right back to work after surgery?"

"No, no, no, no. There will be a period of rehabilitation. If this surgery works the way it is supposed to, however, it shouldn't be long. You're going to have to rehabilitate and strengthen the muscles in your legs, arms and back that you haven't been using since the incident. That's going to take a while. I'll send you to a physical therapist to help you with that. It might be six weeks or two months before you can go back to work, and even then we'll go slowly, allowing you to work part-time for a while and increasing your hours as we go, depending upon how you're doing."

"I need to get him out of the house, Dr. Malpartido. He's driving me crazy. Actually, I'm driving him all over the place, too, so it's a double shot of trouble for me. When do you think he'll be able to drive again?" Sally asked.

"He can drive whenever his body tells him he can. It's a matter of how much pain he can tolerate. I don't expect that he'll be doing any driving for at least a month after surgery, but I could be wrong. It could be sooner. It depends on how well the surgery goes. I don't want him driving after taking any medication."

Dr. Malpartido handed Jeremy the new prescription and they went to CVS to have it filled before heading home.

The weeks passed slowly until the day for the surgery finally arrived. Jeremy and Sally left Samantha with his mother and left as early as they could on Monday, after Sally had taken Samantha to her grandmother's house, in order to be in Orlando for the 9:30 for the pre-surgical appointment. They arrived in time to check into their motel room before going to LSSS. All went well that day, and they were in bed early, anxiously awaiting the surgery.

Sally had been allowed to participate in all the meetings and examinations on Monday, but on the day of surgery, she wasn't allowed in or near the room where the surgery was performed. She sat in the cafeteria and ate breakfast, watching television, for an hour while Jeremy underwent the surgery.

Although he was awake, he was in a dazed condition and, since he was lying on his stomach, in a prone position, he couldn't see anything that was going on. Even though he was told not to take any medications either the night before surgery or the day of surgery, he took two of the blue pills the night before, telling Sally that he was afraid he wouldn't be able to sleep.

Sally was in the post-operative room, waiting, when Jeremy was led into the room after the surgery was completed. Jeremy was nauseous and became sick to his stomach several times. The nurses told them that it wasn't uncommon for patients to throw up after surgery and not to worry about it. It was a natural reaction to the medications.

When Sally asked how it went, Jeremy could only say that he hadn't felt a thing. When she asked how his back was after the surgery, Jeremy wasn't able to tell. He wouldn't know until the anesthetic wore off.

Dr. Livengood came into the room as Sally and Jeremy were sitting there, and he told them that as far as he was concerned the surgery was a complete success.

"Everything went absolutely perfectly. I was able to visualize the area very clearly and I was able to do what needed to be done to remove the substance that was impinging on your spinal nerve root. I extracted the excess fluids with no difficulty and cleaned up the area. You should experience an immediate relief from the symptoms that brought you here and I expect that you will have a complete recovery."

"Do you think I'll be able to go back to work as a clammer? Diving in the water and bringing up clam bags like I did before the incident?"

"I see no reason why not, but I'm going to leave that up to your primary treating physician, who will undoubtedly put you on a rehabilitation program. I will want to see you in two weeks just to make sure that the small incision I made in your low back has healed well and that there are no complications."

"Do you expect me to have any pain once the anesthetic wears off?"

"It isn't unusual for patients to have some minor discomfort in the area of the incision, but it should go away in a day or two, if you have any. You shouldn't have the kind of pain you've been having since the incident, though. That was exactly the problem I was to correct. My nurse will want to see you tomorrow to make sure you don't have anything other than the normal type of pain we would expect you to have. Unless there is a problem, I won't see you tomorrow. If I don't, let me take this opportunity to say that it has been my pleasure to serve you and I thank you for being such a good patient."

Dr. Livengood stood to leave, but before he left, Jeremy asked,

"Doctor, do you think it would be possible to write me a prescription for the RoxyContin for a few days, maybe a week, just in case? I have been taking it since shortly after the incident and it has provided me with much-needed relief."

"I don't see why not. It's a common pain medication for a medical problem such as yours. I'll have my assistant bring you in the prescription before you leave."

Sally looked over at Jeremy with a puzzled look on her face. After the doctor had left the room she asked,

"Don't you still have some pills from Dr. Malpartido's prescription?"

"Yes, but that's about to expire and Dr. Malpartido said he wouldn't give me anymore, remember?"

"Do you think you're going to need them?"

"I don't want to take the chance. You don't know how bad the pain has been."

"Don't you think it's a good idea to wait and see if you have any pain? The surgery was supposed to take that away now that there is no pressure on the spinal nerves, right?"

"Sally! I'm the one who's been laid up for months now! I know what it feels like! You don't!"

"Okay, okay. I was just asking."

"If I don't need them, I won't use them, okay? I'd rather have them and not use them than be in pain and not have them."

"Alright. Whatever you say."

The nurse gave him a prescription for a month's supply of the RoxyContin. He stuffed it in his wallet, hiding it from Sally.

Later that day, the anesthetic wore off and Jeremy noticed a sensation that was more like a bee sting than anything else. Other than that he was pain free.

"I'm a little sore, but it's nothing, really, just a little sting from the incision, but I feel better than I have since I got hurt. Wow! That's amazing!"

"Remember what the doctor said. Take it easy. You're going to have to get your strength back, so don't do too much."

"I feel fine. I really do. I mean, I'm still a little groggy, a little nauseous, but I don't feel any pain!"

Jeremy gave Sally a big hug and said,

"I'm going to be my old self again!"

Sally smiled and said,

"I hope so. This has been hard on all of us."

"I can't believe it! Want to go out to dinner or something?"

"Jeremy! Take it easy. Let's just stay in the motel room and watch a movie. Don't rush things."

That night, Jeremy took two blue pills after dinner, telling Sally it was as a precaution. Later, they made love to each other. He was more active than usual, and Sally had to repeatedly tell him to be careful.

The next morning, the pain in his back at the incision site was gone and he felt no pain in his back. It was a new feeling for him and he was still a bit unsure of whether or not it would be a permanent thing. After seeing Dr. Livengood's assistant for less than ten minutes, they were on their way back to Cedar Key.

The first thing Jeremy did when they drove over number four bridge was to pick Samantha up from his mother's house. Jeremy immediately hugged her and lifted her over his head.

"Jeremy! You take it easy!" Sally scolded.

"I feel fine. I really do."

"Well you've got to see Dr. Malpartido next week and he's going to send you to physical therapy for a while, so you're not 100% there, Clamboy. Put her down!"

"I'm fine, Sally. I feel great. I really do," he responded.

"Do what the doctors tell you, Jeremy!" his mother chimed in.

"Okay, okay, okay, but I'd like to go to see Uncle Ricky right now if it's okay with you."

"Are you going to drive yourself?"

"No, not yet. I'll let you do the driving for just a little while longer."

"Thank you. I'll be happy to do that for you, but not for too long. I haven't been home in two days and I want to spend some time with Samantha, too."

They met with Ricky and he said that as soon as Jeremy was cleared to return to work he wanted him back.

They called attorney Hatfield and gave her the good news.

"Don't be in a hurry to get back to work. Follow your doctor's orders and make sure that Worker's Comp approves everything that you do," she told him.

Jeremy and Sally went back to sleeping in the same bed and made love, with fewer restrictions, like they hadn't done in many months. At Sally's request, Jeremy didn't take a pill before bed, but when he wasn't able to sleep, he waited until after she dozed off, and then he got up, took two pills, and went right to sleep.

The next day, by the time he got up Sally and Samantha were gone. He had some breakfast and marveled at how well he felt. He didn't take any pills with breakfast, as he had done for the last two months, but by noon he could feel his body craving the pills. He reasoned that he should listen to his body and it was telling him that he needed the pills. He didn't put up much resistance.

By mid-afternoon, he couldn't stay in the house any longer. He felt fine and could see no reason why he shouldn't get out and do something. The first thing he did was get in his truck and drive down to the Dollar Store to buy a few household things they needed. Then he decided to drive down State Road 24 from the Dollar Store to town and back, just to see how it felt. After two successful trips with no soreness or stiffness, he pronounced himself able to drive again.

"I'm okay to drive now. It didn't hurt a bit," he told Sally when she came home from work.

"Just take things easy, Jeremy! Don't rush things! Do what your lawyer and your doctors are telling you." Sally reminded him.

That night, Jeremy and Sally made love twice, something they hadn't done in almost two years, ever since Samantha was born. The pills made Jeremy feel more powerful, and they seemed to give him more energy, too. When he thought Sally was asleep, he snuck into the bathroom. As he was taking the pills, Sally walked in behind him and asked,

"I thought you were going to stop taking those."

"I think I'm just too amped up right now. That sex was great, but now I'm still so excited that I can't sleep." He lied and told her, "I'm just taking one pill per day, not two like I used to. I'll stop. Just not yet."

Sally shrugged her shoulders and said, "Whatever, but that doctor told you to be careful, Jeremy."

When Jeremy went to see Dr. Malpartido the next week, he prescribed twelve sessions of physical therapy.

"I want you to go three times a week for four weeks and then come see me when you're finished."

"Do you think I need it, Doctor? I feel great. I really do."

"Do you want to go out and hurt yourself again? You're like an athlete who hasn't played a game in several months. You don't go right back into the game without stretching and practicing, do you? Trust me and just do as I say. See you in a month."

"And what about a prescription for RoxyContin? I'm having trouble sleeping without taking a pill, and I still have an occasional pain."

"I was afraid of that. I think you've developed a chemical dependency on these pills. Here's what I will do for you. I will give you a prescription but it will be for a smaller dosage and I want you to take one pill once a day for the first week and then take a pill only once every other day for the second week. By the third week, reduce it to once every three days and I want you to be off of it altogether by the time I see you again, okay?"

"Whatever you say, Doctor."

Dr. Malpartido gave Jeremy a prescription, but when Jeremy had it filled, he noticed that the bottle was a little different. The cap had a greenish cover and the pills were a bluish-green. He read where the dosage was for 15 milligrams of OxyCodone, not 30 as with the blue pills.

"Damn! He thought to himself. "I'll just have to take four of these things, that's all."

When he told his uncle about the month of physical therapy, Ricky wasn't happy. He didn't understand why Jeremy couldn't come back to work right away, at least in the office.

"Goddamnit Jeremy! We've been short-handed for months now! When are those people going to let you come back to work?"

"I'd say in a month or so, Uncle Ricky."

"And what are they going to let you do once you come back?"

"I think I'm going to be able to go back to what I was doing, Uncle Ricky, but I've got to do what the doctors and my lawyer tells me to do. It's all about Workmen's Compensation and their rules."

"Okay, Jeremy. I understand, but I want you to give me the name and the telephone number of whoever it is I have to call and talk to about this. If you're alright, and you tell me you are, I want you working, you understand?"

"I understand."

His uncle calmed down a bit, put his arm around Jeremy and said,

"I'm glad to hear that you're going to be alright, Jeremy, and I hope you're back to normal real soon. Take care of yourself and do what the doctors tell you, but stay in touch and let me know how it's going. I've got a business to run, you know, and these are difficult times right now. I need you around here. Besides, if you play your cards right, this might become your business. You know that."

"I know, Uncle Ricky, and I appreciate all you've done for me. I do."

Jeremy started physical therapy the next Monday. For an hour, he received instructions on what exercises were best to strengthen the muscles in his abdomen and low back. Every session he spent fifteen or twenty minutes in a whirlpool. He received massage therapy in the area of his sacrum and L4-L5. He also spent time on a treadmill, walking, and doing exercises to strengthen his arms and legs.

Ever since the injury, and for what had become several months, Jeremy had been completely inactive and all of the muscles in his body had weakened, much more than he realized. He was surprised at how out of breath he was and how easily he tired out. He had taken his conditioning for granted, because he had been so active all his life. Despite the weakness and occasional soreness afterwards, the sessions were entirely pleasurable and he looked forward to them.

"But you told me that I'm supposed to do exactly what the doctors and my lawyer told me to do, and that's what I'm doing!" Jeremy protested when Sally asked him about going back to work. She could see nothing wrong with him.

"Then why are you still taking those blue pills? The doctor told you to stop."

"He gave me another prescription for a smaller dosage and tells me to take less and less."

"But that's not what you're doing. You're still taking the same as before."

"No, I'm not. I'm only taking one a day, not two as I used to."

"But you're still taking the blue pills. You didn't tell Dr. Malpartido that Dr. Livengood gave you a prescription, too, did you?"

"I didn't know how I was going to feel after the surgery. I wanted to make sure I had some pain pills if I needed them. He gave me green pills this time. They're not as strong. I'll start taking them once I'm out of the blue pills."

"I think you're getting hooked on them, Jeremy."

"I can stop if I want to. They help me go to sleep, that's all."

The return visit to Dr. Livengood was uneventful. Everything was fine. The staff took a picture of him with the doctor and said it would be put on the wall with his testimonial about how successful the surgery had been for him.

A month later, after he had completed the twelve sessions with a physical therapist, Jeremy went back to see Dr. Malpartido.

"So it seems as if you've done well with the physical therapy. Are you ready to go back to work?"

"I think so."

"I'm going to clear you for light-duty work. I'll place a 20 pound restriction on how much weight you can carry and a requirement that you do no work that requires repeated bending or stretching for the next six weeks. I'm going to want to see you in six weeks and we'll see how you're doing then. Okay? Any questions?"

"Can I have another prescription for the pain medicine, just in case I have a problem?"

Dr. Malpartido looked over the top of his glasses and said,

"We've talked about this. I've told you that I don't want to see you become dependent upon this medication and that it is an extremely powerful drug. I hope you took me seriously. Do you have any pills left?"

Though it wasn't true, Jeremy told him he didn't.

"Here's what I'll do for you. I'll give you one last prescription. You'll have enough pills for a month. The pills I'm prescribing are not as strong as the last pills I prescribed for you. I am trying to wean you off of the OxyCodone, but once you run out, that's it. No more. If you find that you have a craving for more, tell me, and I'll send you for some drug counseling. You may well have developed a dependency, which is a normal side-effect of using the drug, but it is a serious side-effect.

"I'm not going to see you for six weeks. When I see you again, you should be off the pills altogether. At that time I want you to tell me that you have stopped using this medication entirely, okay? If a problem with your back occurs, call me right away, okay?"

Jeremy assured the doctor that he didn't have a problem with the pills, but he had the prescription filled before heading home. This time they were white pills. The strength was 5 milligrams of OxyCodone, less than the green pills and much less than the Blues. He thought to himself,

"These things are hardly worth taking! I'll have to take a dozen of these to make up for two of the blue pills. I guess it's better than nothing."

He didn't tell Sally about it and kept the pills in his car.

Ricky was happy to have Jeremy back to work, even though it was only in the office. With the 20 pound lifting restriction, he could still carry the small bags with 100 clams in them that were sold to the public, which was another of Jeremy's activities. Everyone was glad to have him back, but that was no surprise since he was related to most of the people who worked there.

Sally was glad that he was back to work, too, and she didn't recognize any restrictions on his ability to do things around the house, other than an unwillingness to do various tasks. She was tired of taking out the garbage, vacuuming the floor and doing all of the housework with little or no help. "There is nothing wrong with you now, Jeremy! And you can help me more with Samantha, too."

"Okay, I will."

"And are you finished with Virginia Hatfield? When was the last time you spoke to her?"

"Not since after the surgery, just to tell her that it helped. I'll call her tomorrow."

When he called his lawyer, she said that she would keep her file open until the case was officially closed by Worker's Comp. In case another problem developed in the future, it was very important that the records show that he complied with all of the requirements."

"So do you think I'll need your assistance any further?"

"I don't think so. If a problem comes up, call me, but at this point, from what you've told me, I expect Dr. Malpartido to release you to go back to work full-time with no restrictions the next time he sees you, unless a problem develops."

"And you'll get your fee from Worker's Comp?"

"Yes, I will, or that's what I expect."

"Well thanks for your help. I'll call you if anything goes wrong."

"Jeremy, call me in a couple of months, just to tell me that everything is going well and you're not having any problems whatsoever, and then I'll close my books on this case, okay?"

"Alright, I will."

"And remember, if anything happens in the future to aggravate the situation, if it happens at work, you'll be covered."

"But what if it doesn't happen at work?"

"That's a different story. If it doesn't happen at work, it's not covered. You should keep that in mind, and call me if anything happens, no matter what it is or where it happens. I handle cases other than just Worker's Comp. I might be able to help you with other things, like car accidents, slips and falls…things like that."

"Well, I'll keep that in mind, and thanks again for all you did to help me."

"You're welcome."

"And I don't owe you anything?"

"Not at this point, but let me make sure that Workmen's Comp pays my bill in full before I make that final."

"That's fine. Just let me know. You were great."

"Thank you, and good luck."

Jeremy followed his doctor's orders and slowly and gradually returned to his normal work schedule. When he saw Dr. Malpartido six weeks later, he was cleared for a return to work with no restrictions.

"Do you still have any of the medications I prescribed for you?"

"Maybe a few, but I don't use them unless I absolutely have to," he said, even though it wasn't true. He was now taking even more than two a day, because he could add on a green or a white pill any time he wanted to.

"Only if I'm real sore after a particularly hard day's work."

"Jeremy, those aren't muscle relaxers. That medication is for pain. There is a difference. I don't want you taking them unless it's absolutely necessary, and then only if you are in pain, serious pain, not just minor discomfort."

"I won't, Doctor. I promise."

"Actually, I'd like for you to throw the rest away right now. You don't need them anymore. Will you do that for me?"

"I will," Jeremy replied, knowing full well he had no intention of doing so.

Chapter Six

⫻⫻⫻

Three weeks later, when Jeremy was down to his very last few days of pills, he became concerned and decided he'd better do something about it. He told himself that he had tried to do what the doctor had told him to do, but he just wasn't able to do it. He needed those pills.

Although he no longer went to the bars on Dock Street, except for an occasional beer after work with the boys, he knew everyone in town and everyone knew him. He knew where to find what he was looking for.

As soon as he walked in to Frog's Landing, he spied a familiar face. It was Brianne Greene, a girl he and Sally had gone to school with. He sat down next to her and exchanged greetings. After having a beer and talking about old times, he asked her about drugs.

"Roxy Blues? Yeah, I can get you as much as you need, Jeremy, but they aren't cheap. How much do you want?" Brianne asked.

"How much do people usually buy? A hundred? Two hundred?"

"People buy what they can afford, Jeremy. Those things are expensive. They can cost up to $15 per pill, depending on what you get. The Roxy Blues are the fastest-acting ones and they're the most expensive. Sometimes people buy them one at a time."

"Damn! So I've got $250. How much can I get for that?"

"Of the Blues? That would be about twenty pills. I can give you a little discount, since we're old friends and all. I'll try and get you twenty five pills for that amount of money. That's a good deal, Jeremy."

"But they only cost me about twenty bucks from CVS, and that's for thirty pills. Why are they are so expensive?"

"That's because they're so damn good, Jeremy, as you know."

"That's true, they are, but..."

"And they're illegal. When you buy them at CVS with a prescription that's an entirely different story from buying them on the street."

"Yeah, but a hundred times more expensive, or whatever it is?"

"That's the way it is, Jeremy. You want them, you're going to have to pay for them.

"You can't get me a little bit better deal, Brianne?

"I'm already giving you a great deal, Jeremy. I can't do any better than that."

"Where do you get them?"

"That I can't tell you, man. If I did, you could go straight to the source and cut me out of the deal altogether."

"I didn't mean that. I just meant how you get them. I mean, you don't get them from the drug store, or the manufacturer. I know that."

"Sometimes we do. People with prescriptions get them and need to sell them to make some money, but most of the time it comes from someplace else. Let's just say it comes from someplace over around Orlando. You don't know the people and you don't want to know the people. Trust me, Jeremy."

"That's good enough for me. I don't need to know. I just need to know you."

"That's right."

"So when do you want me to give you the money?"

"You give me the money and I'll give you ten pills right now. I'll get you the rest next week. How's that?"

"That's will hold me for a week. That's all I've got with me right now."

"You're doing more than one a night? Be careful, Jeremy. That's not as bad as some people I know. Some people are doing five a day. You're not shooting up or snorting anything, are you, Jeremy?"

"Naaah. I just swallow them."

"If you're smart, you'd get out now, Jeremy, if you can. This isn't something you can play with. You're only going to want more and more, trust me. Are you still in pain? Why won't your doctor give you any more pills?"

"I had surgery and he says I'm all better now."

"Are you?"

"I'm okay, I just use them to help me get some sleep and after a really hard day out in the Gulf, that's all."

"Yeah, right. Me, too," Brianne said, with a laugh. "Maybe you could get some with lesser strength, you know. Save the Blues for special occasions."

"Yeah, my doctor already tried that with me. Those whites are hardly worth taking and I have to take two of the greens to feel anything."

"I can hook you up with whatever you want, Jeremy. Just give me a week to fill the order. I don't usually carry any extra pills with me. The ones I'm giving you were for somebody else, but he didn't show up, but that's okay. I can get more if they do without any problem, it just won't be today."

"How much for the greens?"

"Usually $11 to $12 apiece, but I can sell them to you for 8 dollars apiece."

"And the whites?"

"Nobody buys the whites. You really want any of them? People end up taking lots of them at a time."

"How much are they?"

"Five dollars apiece."

"And that's the best price you can get me?"

"Yeah. We don't sell many of them. It's really a pain because I've got to get so many of them to make it worthwhile, and they can get bulky. We don't like that. We use them as teasers, or samples, that's about it."

Jeremy thought about it for a while and said,

"Say, Brianne, Next time, which will probably be next week, I'd like to have enough to hold me for a month at a time. I'd rather have them all be the Blues."

"That's about a thousand dollars of pills, Jeremy."

"I know," he responded. "I'll have the money. Don't worry about that."

"Whatever you say. I'm giving you the best deal I can, and $10 a pill is a great deal for the Blues, Jeremy. That'll be a hundred pills."

"Let's do it. I just had that surgery a few weeks back and I still need them."

"That surgery didn't work?"

"Yeah, it worked, but I still have the pain every now and then."

Brianne looked at him, knowing that he was as hooked as any of the others were who bought from her. She knew he might have been kidding himself, but he wasn't kidding her. She knew. She was as hooked as he was.

"I'm only here once a week or so. They have karaoke here on Tuesday nights and Doug and I come most every Tuesday for that. I'll see you next week, Jeremy."

"Great! See you then. Same time. Do you sing?"

"Yeah."

"Doug too?"

"No way."

"What time does that start up?"

"About 8:30 or 9:00."

"I'm in bed by then. What time do you get here?"

"I can meet you here at 6. We have dinner here, shoot some pool and shoot the shit with whoever is here before the music starts up. We usually leave for home around 11."

"Alright. I'll see you here on Tuesday at 6. Thanks, Brianne."

"No problems, Jeremy. Does Sally know about this?"

"No, and I'd rather she not."

"That works for me. That's why I asked. Take care of yourself, Jeremy."

When he met with Brianne the following Tuesday and received the additional pills, she asked,

"How are you keeping these from Sally?"

"I leave them in the car so she won't find them."

"That's a bad idea, Jeremy. You get stopped by a cop for anything, like a broken tail light or whatever, and they search your car and find them, you're busted, man."

"Cops won't search me. I know 'em all."

"Not the deputies, you don't. They got guys from all over working the roads, plus there's a few of the town's police that aren't all that friendly, either. It's not like when we were kids. We don't know them all anymore, or at least I don't. I'm tellin' you, don't leave 'em in the car and don't leave 'em in your pockets, either. You be careful, Jeremy, and hold on to those scripts the doctor gave you, if you have any."

"I gave 'em to the pharmacy. I don't have 'em anymore."

"Well, if you get any more, make a copy before you hand it in. It could save your ass."

Jeremy didn't say anything in response. He took a swig from his bottle of beer and asked,

"So what songs do you sing, Brianne?"

"I do Janis pretty well, after a few beers, that is. I like 'Me and Bobby McGee' and 'Take Another Little Piece of my Heart' the best."

"Maybe Sally and I will come some night just to listen."

"Hey, you can get up and sing. Lots of people do."

"But we can't sing."

"There's lots of people who get up and sing who have no idea how bad they sound. It's just about having some fun."

"We'll come and listen, at least the first time or two. I don't hardly sing at birthday parties."

"Come on down. It's every Tuesday."

"Maybe we will. Thanks, Brianne."

"Anytime. Tell Sally I said hello. She probably still hates me."

"What she doesn't know can't hurt me, Brianne. I'm going to leave that alone. You two never did get along, ever since about 5th grade."

They laughed. Jeremy paid his tab and headed out the door. When he got home, he put the pills inside a pocket of the only sports coat he owned, which was hidden deep in his closet. Sally would never have a reason to look there. Every night before bed, he'd take two pills, always making sure that Sally didn't see him do it. Every now and then he'd take three. He wanted more, but he couldn't afford them. He couldn't believe how much they cost.

"Maybe you should find yourself another doctor, Jeremy," Brianne told him. "There are people who come to Florida from all over the country getting these pills from doctors and pharmacies every day. Florida is the "pill capitol" of the country."

"But I don't know how to do that, Brianne."

"I'll see if I can't get you the name of a doctor who can help you out, Jeremy. That would be cutting into my business, of course, but bein' as we're old friends and all, I'll do it."

Brianne had been attracted to Jeremy all during their school years, but she'd never had a chance to get next to him because Sally was always there. If anything ever happened between the two of them, Brianne wouldn't have been disappointed.

One Saturday afternoon a few weeks later, Jeremy and Sally drove to Chiefland to do their weekly shopping trip at Kringle. They took Samantha with them. She liked the playground at McDonald's and, after shopping, the three would spend some time at McDonald's.

On this particular day, Jeremy was pushing the cart, with Samantha in the seat, as Sally was picking out some fresh vegetables. She would drop one package in after another as they strolled down the aisles. Jeremy had his hands full watching Samantha, who was now a year and a half old and had grown tired of just sitting in the cart. She now wanted to stand up in the cart, but she wasn't old enough to realize that she could fall and get hurt if she wasn't careful.

Next thing Jeremy knew, he heard Sally cry out. He turned and saw Sally lying on the ground. He grabbed Samantha, pulled her out of the cart and rushed over to Sally.

"What happened?"

"I fell on something. I don't know what."

"Are you alright?"

"I hurt my back."

"You want me to get somebody?"

"No, help me get up. I think I'll be okay."

"You sure?"

"Just help me up."

Jeremy helped her get to her feet.

"The back of your pants are wet. You must have slipped on some water or something."

"I didn't see anything."

Jeremy looked around, but didn't see anything either.

"You must have landed in a puddle and dried it up. I don't see anything now. How do you feel?"

She held her low back and said, "My back hurts."

"What do you want to do? You want to take Samantha out to the car and wait for me to finish up the rest of the shopping or do you want to call for some help now?"

"I'll wait for you in the car."

"You want me to walk you out to the car?"

"I'll be alright."

"I'll be out as fast as I can."

"Man, this hurts!" Sally said as she slowly limped out of the store. Jeremy watched her walk away and decided it would be best to follow her out to the car.

"You sure you don't want to see somebody about that? A paramedic? Report it to someone? Anything?"

"No. I just want to get home. I'll be alright."

Jeremy left the cart inside the store and, while carrying Samantha in his arms, walked out to the car with Sally. Once she was safely inside, lying down on the passenger's side with the seat back as far as it would go, he went back to finish up the shopping, keeping Samantha with him. When he got to the car, twenty minutes later, Sally was still lying down on the passenger seat, just as he had done months before. He put the groceries in the trunk and asked,

"Want to get anything at Walgreen's or CVS before we go home?"

"Do you have any of that stuff the doctor gave you left? The muscle relaxer stuff?"

"You mean the Robaxin?"

"Yeah, that stuff."

"Yeah. I stopped using it after a while and never did get a refill."

"And we've still got the Advil, right?"

"Yeah. I bought a new bottle at the Dollar Store last week."

"I'll be alright. Just get me home."

"No McDonald's today."

"No, don't even mention the word."

It was too late. Samantha started to cry as they drove past. She pointed her finger as if to say, don't forget to stop. They went through the drive-through and got her an ice cream sundae, which made her happy.

When they got home, Sally drew herself a hot bath and gingerly got in. Half an hour later, she had Jeremy massage her low back and liberally apply Icy-Hot. An hour later, she asked,

"Do you still have any of those blue pills? This is killing me."

"I think I have a few left. You stay here. I'll go check."

Jeremy returned a few minutes later with one of the Roxys and a glass of water.

"I hope this helps," she said.

Half an hour later, she was asleep.

The next morning, when she awoke, it was ten o'clock. Three hours later than she usually woke up.

"Man, those things work! I slept like a rock."

"How do you feel?"

"My low back is sore, but I'm not feeling anywhere near as much pain as I did yesterday. I feel a little spacey, though, like my mind isn't working right."

"Is there anything I can do for you? Anything you need?"

"Not now, but unless this gets a whole lot better I'm going to want to see Dr. Malpartido."

"Today is Sunday, so there's nothing we can do today, unless you want to go to the Emergency room."

"No, I can wait 'til tomorrow, but if that pain comes back, I'll take another one of your pills."

Later that afternoon, the pain returned. She took another pill and fell back asleep, but before getting back into bed, she called her father and told him she wouldn't be in to work the next day, which was a Monday.

When she woke up the following morning, and the pain hadn't gone away, she asked Jeremy,

"Would you mind calling and making an appointment with Dr. Malpartido for me? You're going to have to drive me there so I guess it will have to be in the late afternoon, unless you can take part of the day off."

Jeremy made the call and took the latest time available, which was for late in the afternoon, so that he could get as close to a full day of work in as possible. Jeremy took off from work a couple of hours early and drove her to Chiefland. They left Samantha with his mother.

"Am I going to need an MRI like Jeremy did?" she asked the doctor, after he completed his initial examination.

"Maybe, but I don't think so. I think you may just have a severe strain, which is more of a muscular thing. A sprain involves a ligament. Your husband had a herniated disc. Your symptoms are different from his."

"But my pain is right around my tail bone, just like his was, and it's a throbbing pain and it's constant. This is killing me."

"But it's not shooting down into your leg as his was. That's called radiating pain. Let's give it a week and see what happens. I'll give you a prescription for the pain. Take two Advils three times a day and stay off your feet as much as possible. Put a soft pillow under you when you sit down."

He handed her a prescription for Vicodin.

She looked at it and said,

"This isn't the stuff you gave Jeremy. Can't I have what you gave him?"

"I'd rather not give you that. It's very strong. I don't think you need it. Vicodin should work just fine."

"But I took that RoxyContin the last two days and it really helped. I'd like to stay with it."

Dr. Malpartido turned to Jeremy and said,

"I thought you said you would throw the rest of that medicine away?"

"I meant to, but I never got around to it."

The doctor sighed and said,

"Alright, but I'm only going to give you the 15 milligram dose, not the 30. This is powerful medicine."

"Whatever you say, Doctor, so long as it works."

"Take one pill in the morning and one at night until the pain starts to go away, and then only if you need it. Now, this didn't happen at work, so that's different from the way we handled your husband's case, too. How are you going to pay for this? Do you have health insurance?"

"I have it through my work. I've never made a claim before, other than for when Samantha was born, but that was covered. This is the first time I've ever hurt myself."

"Alright. Your insurance should pay for all this, but you'll have a co-pay and a deductible. Just give your card to the woman at the front and they'll figure it out. I'll see you back here next week."

Before they handed the prescription to the pharmacist, Jeremy made a copy at the photo center, where there was a photo copy machine.

"Why d'you to that?" Sally asked.

"Just for our records. Once we give them the form, we don't know what it said. My lawyer said it was a good idea."

"Really? I don't remember her saying that."

When Sally talked to her father about it, he confirmed that she had health insurance coverage through work.

"We can't afford it, Sally, because it's so damn expensive, but I got it for you and me, and a few others. Don't mention it to anybody else at work or everybody will want me to get it for them, too."

"Thanks, Dad."

"Maybe you ought to see a lawyer about that fall at Kringle. There shouldn't have been any water on the floor like there was," her father suggested.

"But I didn't report it or anything."

"You can do what you want, but I'd say talk to a lawyer about it. They won't take the case unless they think they can make some money off of it, and they won't charge you any money to look into it for you."

Sally called several lawyers over the next few days, but no one would even agree to meet with her. One said unless she was hurt badly it wasn't worth his while. Another said that he wouldn't ever even think about suing Kringle because people thought of it as "their" store and would never return a verdict in her favor. A third said that if surgery was necessary that she might consider taking the case. A fourth said that since she hadn't filed a report it would make the case too hard to prove. The only one that offered her any helpful advice told her to immediately go back to Kringle, file a report of the incident and then call back once she knew exactly what was wrong with her. The lawyer still wouldn't see her, but at least she spoke to her and said she might help.

That night, when Sally took the green pill, she could tell the difference. She wasn't able to fall asleep right away like she did when she took the blue pill, and it didn't affect her like the blue pill did.

"Just take another one of the greens," Jeremy told her. "Two 15s is the same as one 30."

"Okay."

That weekend, when they did their shopping, Sally went back to Kringle and filled out an incident report, like the lawyer told her to do. The following week, she went back to see Dr. Malpartido again.

"So how are you doing?"

"I'm still in pain, but I'm better."

"No shooting pains going into either of your legs?"

"No."

"Let's try a little massage therapy, maybe some electro-stimulation, and some whirlpool. I think you have a bad sprain, that's all. Not too serious. It's very painful, I'm sure, but it's not nearly as serious as what Jeremy went through."

"Thank God for that! Do you do those things here?"

"Yes. Wanda will help you with all of that. If you just wait here for a few minutes, she'll come get you."

"When will I see you again?"

"I'll get reports from my assistants. If I think I need to see you I will. You'll be coming here three times a week for the next several weeks."

"Three times a week! But I can't drive myself and Jeremy can't take that much time off or we won't have any money coming in."

"I'll get them to give you the latest appointment possible. I think you're going to be able to drive yourself before too long. That's the best I can do for you. Trust me, these sessions are going to help you."

"You're going to like the massage and the whirlpool," Jeremy added.

"I'll also give you another prescription for the pain, but I don't want you driving after taking these, understand?"

"I understand."

"Good. Stay here and Wanda will be in to see you shortly."

"Will I start today?"

"Yes."

"How long will it take?"

"About an hour, maybe a little more this first time."

The doctor stood and left the room.

"I'll go do some shopping while you do all of that," Jeremy offered. "I'll be back in an hour or so."

When Jeremy returned, Sally was waiting.

"So how was it?"

"I feel great. You were right. That massage and the whirlpool made me feel much better. That electric thing didn't do much for me. The heat on my back feels good, too."

"So it's better?"

"Yeah. Let's see how long it lasts."

Two hours later the pain returned. Sally took two of the greenish pills and went to sleep. Over the next few weeks Sally's condition continued to improve. She was able to drive herself by the next week. She started going back to work for a few hours a day during the third week. By the fourth week, though she was still a little stiff, she told Dr. Malpartido that she was going to have to stop coming.

"I know we only have to pay the $10 co-pay, but the deductible was $500 and with the gas, leaving work early and all the rest, I don't think we can't afford it anymore. I love having the massage and the whirlpool, and doing the exercises, but I'm driving myself now, and with me not working as many hours as I was before I got hurt, I'm thinking it's money we don't have to spend. You've told me it's nothing too serious and that it will continue to improve as long as I don't do something to hurt myself again. I think I'll be alright."

"Well, I'm here if you need me. If you just take it easy for a while longer and don't do anything to aggravate your condition, I think you'll be fine.."

"That's hard to do when you have a two year old child. Just picking her up causes me pain."

"Then don't pick her up."

"That's easy for you to say. Can I have one last prescription to help me get through these next few weeks, or however long you think it will last?"

The doctor looked at her and said,

"You know what I told your husband. You must be careful with these pills. I will give you one more prescription, but that's all. You should only use these pills if you need them to control the pain and only if you can't tolerate the pain or discomfort. But as I did with him, I'm going to prescribe a lesser dosage of the OxyCodone. Once this prescription runs out, that's it."

He shook her hand and said,

"Good luck. I am glad to have been able to help you."

Dr. Malpartido had given her a prescription for the white RoxyContin tablets, which had 5 milligrams of OxyCodone in them. Even though Sally knew the dangers of taking the pills, every night before she went to bed she'd find a reason why she needed to take one. She'd tell herself that it was important that she get a good night's sleep, or that she had over-done it at work or around the home that day and felt some discomfort, or because she was in a foul frame of mind and she wanted to change her mood. She took six of the white pills that night.

She didn't know that Jeremy was taking the RoxyContin, too, but he saw her take pills every night and didn't say anything to her about what he was doing.

Once Sally was feeling better, she and Jeremy resumed their love making. She experienced similar sensations just as Jeremy had after taking the RoxyContin. With both of them taking the pills, it made the whole experience seem better for both of them. After several weeks of taking the pills, as prescribed by Dr. Malpartido, and afterwards, she stopped making excuses or rationalizations. She admitted to herself that the reason she kept taking the pills was because she liked doing it. Jeremy had long since come to that conclusion, and he accepted it.

She had learned the differences between the white pills, the green pills and the blue ones, just as Jeremy had. When she ran out of the whites she asked Jeremy for one of his. He obliged, but after a week or so of that, she realized that he should have run out by then. She asked him,

"How is it you haven't run out of your pills? You didn't get that much from Dr. Livengood, did you? Dr. Malpartido told you to throw the rest away, but you still have pills for me. I don't see how you could have any left. What's going on, Jeremy?"

At first, Jeremy told her that he hadn't taken any in a while and he was about to run out, but she pressed him on it, thinking that there was no way that could be true. She told him that she was worried about what to do when he did run out, because she wanted to get more pills, even though Dr. Malpartido wouldn't prescribe them for her. Jeremy told her that he thought he might know where to get more. When he said that, she realized that he wasn't telling her the whole truth, and she asked,

"Okay, Jeremy. What is it you aren't telling me? Where are you going to get pills?"

Jeremy didn't want to tell her it was Brianne. The two women really didn't like each other and, although they didn't fight like they used to back in grade school, they avoided each other. Sally had always been the pretty one and Brianne hated her for it. Brianne had grown out of her scrawny, pimple-faced, awkward teen years, dyed her hair blonde and matured into a woman who attracted guys at the bars. Sally hadn't seen her since high school.

"I can't tell you, Sally. I promised I wouldn't. It's someone we both know and can trust, but it's better if you didn't know. Leave that up to me."

Although Sally was still the more beautiful of the two, she had settled into being a wife and mother and never saw much of her old school mates.

She didn't have eyes for anyone but Jeremy whereas Brianne was used to mingling with all kinds of guys at the bars. She wasn't married or living with anyone, but she was spending a lot of time with guys who either supplied her with drugs or used drugs with her. Brianne turned heads when she walked into a bar. Sally knew nothing about any of that and accepted Jeremy's explanation.

As long as he could supply them with pills, there was no problem, because it didn't matter all that much to her. What mattered was her being able to have the pills when she wanted them. To her way of thinking, lots of people took sleeping pills, over-the-counter medications, caffeine, alcohol and all kinds of things to help them get through the day. She and Jeremy were doing the same thing. To her, they didn't have a problem. The fact that it was illegal was more of an inconvenience than it was an impediment.

The pills helped them to enjoy the sex, which was more frequent and longer lasting than it had been in a while. The side effects of dry mouth, lightheadedness and an occasional headache were offset by the euphoria they experienced and the increased sexual appetite. It made them giddy and act silly. They laughed when one or the other had a lapse in memory due to the drug, thinking it was funny. They said stupid things but they both laughed at whatever was said. They were inside their home, not worried about interacting with other people, so they could do and say whatever they wanted to. And it helped put them to sleep and eliminated any of the aches and pains of the day. It had become an integral part of their daily lives. Then, one day, Jeremy told her that he was about to run out of pills.

"What do you mean you don't know where to get any more? How could you let that happen?"

"The person I buy from hasn't been around for the last three weeks. Nobody knows where she is. I'm going to have to find somebody else and I'm having a little trouble, that's all. I'm going to have to go up to the Lion's Lair tonight with one of the new guys at work."

"Does he know you're doing drugs?"

"No. I just told him I'd go drinking with him one of these nights and tonight is the night."

"Why don't you buy from someone around here? Someone you know and can trust?"

"I'd rather people around here don't know our business, Sally. That's all."

"Well you be careful, Jeremy."

When Jeremy came home that night, Sally met him at the door.

"So did you get any?"

"Yeah, thirty of the greens."

"The greens? Why not the Blues?"

"That's all I could afford. The Blues were too expensive."

"More expensive than before?"

"Yeah, much more expensive."

"What took you so long?"

"I had to shoot the shit with those guys for a while. They were checking me out and making sure I wasn't going to turn them in, I guess."

"So who were they?"

"Some guys from up around Branford. I'd never seen them before."

"Who's this new guy at work?"

"His name is Randy. He's an older guy. Been around the water all his life. He doesn't talk much but he knows what he's doin' on a boat. While I was out sick, Uncle Ricky needed a couple of helpers and he hired him. He's been there over six months now, ever since I got hurt."

"So how much did it cost you?"

"More than what we've been payin', I can tell you that."

"How much more?"

"About $5 a pill," Jeremy responded.

"This is going to cost us a lot more money. Can we afford this?"

"I think I'm due for a raise. I think he'll pay me more now. I haven't missed any time off work since I've been back, other than to take you to see the doctor."

"I'll ask my Dad for a little extra pay, too. I'll tell him that you're not making as much money now as you had been before you got hurt, which is true."

"That would be nice. Think he will give you one?"

"Let's hope so. We're going to need it. So these are 15 milligrams and we take two of these?"

"That's right. It's the same amount of OxyCodone as with the blue pills. Wait a few minutes before taking them. I've got to shower first. I went there straight from work. We'll take them at the same time."

While Jeremy was battling his back problems in the beginning, their sex life changed dramatically for the worse, but then it got much better as he got better, with the help of the pills. When Sally got hurt, their sex life ended until she got better, and now that they were both openly using pills, and finding out that they enjoyed making love to each other while both were under the spell of the pills. It opened new doors for them. They experimented more. The pills had changed things in ways they had never imagined.

They'd been together for years, made love to each other a thousand times, neither had ever made love to anyone else, and they had grown to take sex for granted to some extent. The pills altered their state of mind and dulled their senses to some extent, which had the effect of making the love-making sessions last longer. After each had reached orgasm, they were sound asleep within minutes. Although it was a big expense, given their limited income, they were able to keep their budget under control, though there was never anything left over for their savings account.

Jeremy and Sally were blissfully happy. Both were back to work, doing their jobs. Jeremy got the raise he was looking for. Sally's father gave her a raise, too. Both adored their beautiful daughter, who would be two years old in another few months, and both were still very much in love with the other.

Chapter Seven

⫘

Six months later, as Jeremy was at the post office in Cedar Key to buy some stamps, Brianne walked in.

"Hey, Brianne! How are you? I haven't seen you in a while. Where have you been?"

"Hi Jeremy. You don't want to know. I've been to hell and back."

"Sorry to hear it. You look good."

"Thanks. I've cleaned up my act."

"So what happened? Want to tell me about it or no?"

"Jeremy, before I tell you, let me ask you this…are you still doing those Roxy Blues?"

"Every now and again, whenever I get a pain in my back like I had before. You know how it is. Those things work."

"Yeah, they work, until they take over, and then they'll kill you. If you don't need them, don't use them, and even if you do need them, I'd still say find something else for the pain. It's not worth it."

"Why? What's so bad about them? I think they're great."

"Well, first off, they're illegal, unless you have a prescription."

"Yeah, well we had prescriptions."

"We? Sally has started using them too?"

"She fell at the Kringle a while back and they've helped her, too."

"That's the next thing, it's because they do work that you get to liking them and using them even when you don't have to."

"They help with pain, better than anything else I've ever tried, and a whole lot better than Aspirin, Advil, Motrin, Tylenol or anything else you can buy over the counter."

"That's true, that's why they're dangerous."

"And the sex is better."

"Yeah, for a while, until you need more to get that high you're looking for, and after a while there won't be any sex at all, trust me."

"And they help you get to sleep at night."

"They'll knock your socks off is what they'll do. They're powerful, Jeremy…really powerful stuff."

"So what happened to you? Why'd you stop using them?"

"I got arrested not too long after I sold that last bag of pills to you. For a while I thought it might have been you that turned me in, but then I found out who did and you had nothin' to do with it."

"I wouldn't have turned you in, Brianne. I gave you my word on that."

"Yeah, you did, but things happen when the law gets involved and people do things they thought they'd never do, especially if they're looking at going to prison. That's when all kinds of bad things start happening. You get real paranoid about who your friends are. You just get weird, that's all, and I was weird there for a while."

"So who turned you in?"

"I can't tell you that, and it's better if you don't know anyway. No good can come out of it. I'm trying to put all of that behind me now, Jeremy."

"So what happened?"

"I got probation, but not until I'd spent some time in jail since I couldn't bond out. I almost lost my kid because of it."

"You've got a kid?"

"Yeah, Destiny. She'll be three next June."

"That's about the age of our Samantha. I had no idea. Who's the father?"

"This guy from Crystal River. One of the men I was buying from. That's another thing that stuff will make you do…things you wouldn't do if you were thinking straight. I was having sex with all kinds of guys, as long as drugs were involved I was doing it. I was just all messed up on that stuff, having unprotected sex. I guess I'm lucky I just got pregnant and didn't get AIDS or some kind of venereal disease. He wasn't anybody I was in love with. He just caught me at the right time, or the wrong time, but when all this happened, it made me realize that I love my daughter more than anything else in the world and she's what made me straighten up. She's the best thing that's ever happened to me."

"Does he have much to do with her now?"

"No, and that's for the best. He doesn't even know it's his kid. Maybe it isn't the right thing for me to do, but he's still using and I really don't want that around her or me. I'm not telling him he's the father and he might not ever find out, unless the State gets involved and they go looking to find the father. I'm not going to ask him for child support or anything. If I did, he'd want to see her, have her half the time, share the holidays and all the rest. It's better this way, I think."

"And you almost lost her because of it?"

"Yeah. The State of Florida, Department of Children and Families, better known as DCF, got involved. I told them I didn't know who the father was and so they put her with my mother, but she really wasn't able to take care of her and if I hadn't got out when I did they were going to put her in foster care."

"Man! That's some serious shit, Brianne!"

"Yeah! And I'm still on probation. I will be for the next few years. I've got to go down every month and pee in a bottle to prove I'm not doing drugs. It's humiliating, and I have to pay money to do it."

"So you've cleaned up your act. That's good."

"Yeah, that's good."

"You still do karaoke on Tuesdays?"

"No, I try to stay out of the bars. They don't do me any good either. There's nothing in a bar that I'm looking for."

"Are you working?"

"I've got a job as a certified nurse's assistant at the Hospice in Chiefland. I'm thinking about going back to school to become a nurse."

"That'd be good."

"It costs money and it takes time, that's all, and between working a low-paying job and taking care of Destiny, I don't have much of either."

"So I guess that means I won't be able to get any pills from you anymore, will I?"

"No, you won't, and if you take my advice you won't buy from anybody."

"The last time we spoke, you were going to get me the name of a doctor who could help me with the pain, and maybe write some scripts for me. Did you ever get a name for me? Got anybody you could recommend?"

Brianne froze, looked Jeremy straight in the eye, and said,

"Have you been listening to me?"

When he looked away and didn't respond, she said,

"Have you heard a word I've said?"

"Yeah, I heard you. What do you mean? I just asked if you knew anybody I could talk to, that's all. I have pain every now and then."

At that, Brianne turned and said,

"Jeremy, I've got to go. I've got to pick up Destiny from my mother's house. Take care of yourself and think about what I told you."

Jeremy watched her walk away and thought to himself that she must have really been messed up to get into all that kind of trouble. She was selling, using, and hanging out with a rough group of people. Things he'd never do. Other than buying some pills every month he wasn't going to ever get involved like she had. When he went home that night, he didn't mention his meeting with Brianne to Sally. She still had no idea he'd been talking to her, let alone buying drugs from her.

Both Jeremy and Sally had long since healed up well and neither had any ongoing problems with their backs, other than an occasional flare-up when they over-did something, but those things went away in a few days, so neither had returned to see Dr. Malpartido in many months. Jeremy still kept the photocopy of the last prescription he had given Sally and he'd kept a few of the containers the pills had come in, "just in case," as he said, they ever needed them. If the police ever got involved, he could say they were leftovers from the prescriptions.

He went back up to the Lion's Lair in Chiefland every month and saw a guy he came to know only as "Rawhide," who sold him whatever he wanted. It was costing them more money, though. The price of the pills had gone up even more over the months. The greens were now $16 apiece and the Blues $30 apiece, but another problem had developed…Jeremy had started taking more than two a night.

After starting out only taking one blue pill, Jeremy started taking a green with a blue. He said he needed the extra pill to make him feel "right." He'd gotten used to the one blue pill and it just wasn't doing the same things for him anymore. A few months after that, he started taking two Blues a night. He was able to maintain the "high" by doing that. He began adding a white or a green to the two Blues and was now up to three Blues a night.

Occasionally, but not often, Rawhide would throw in a few samples of other pills. One time he gave Jeremy some pink tablets, which were 10 milligrams of OxyContin. The difference was the OxyContin was time-released whereas the RoxyContin was fast- acting. Another time he gave Jeremy a few grey tablets, which were 20 milligrams of OxyContin. They didn't do much for either Sally or him. They preferred the Blues.

In their minds, Jeremy and Sally rationalized that the drugs they were using had been prescribed by a doctor for them because of injuries they'd sustained and they were just using them on an as-needed basis. They just needed them every day, that's all.

Jeremy got in the habit of taking a blue, a white and a green with him to work and he'd have them in his pocket at all times. He'd never leave home without knowing he had some with him. He was starting to get the shakes every now and then and the only way to get rid of them was to take a pill. He'd take the white one first, and if that worked, he was fine. If he needed more, he'd take a green. There were days when he took all three. Since OxyCodone is a barbiturate, delirium tremens, or "DTs," were a common withdrawal side effect, which occasionally happened when it was time for Jeremy to take another pill.

No one knew what they were doing behind the closed doors of their house and they were keeping things behind closed doors. No one in either family suspected anything, or if they did, no one said anything.

But behind those closed doors, things were changing. The sex wasn't as good as it was when they first started using the pills, and Jeremy had started six months before Sally. Now that it was Sally who was more interested in having sex than Jeremy, there was a reversal of roles. There were times when he was unable to perform at all, but most of the time he just wasn't interested. That was normal, they thought. That's what happens to married people after they've been together for years. They were still in love with each other.

Several months later, Samantha celebrated her third birthday on a beautiful summer day in mid-August, with family and friends with a picnic at the park next to the cemetery. From all outward appearances, they were still the perfect Cedar Key family.

Chapter Eight

When their supply of pills got down to less than a two week quantity, Jeremy went up to Chiefland to get more. Whenever he walked in, Rawhide was there, shooting a game of pool with one of his buddies. Jeremy ordered two Buds, one for him and one for Rawhide, and put four quarters on the pool table so as to play the winner, who was usually Rawhide, just as he had done for many months. He then sat down at a table next to the pool table, and watched the game. He put his keys on top of the table.

While playing eight ball, or occasionally nine ball, they'd talk business. Jeremy would tell him how much money he had and how many pills he wanted. When the game was over, Rawhide would take a break, pick up the key to Jeremy's truck and leave Jeremy to play the next challenger.

Rawhide would put a container with the pills in it in the glove compartment of Jeremy's truck and remove an envelope with the cash inside. When Rawhide returned, he'd put Jeremy's keys back on the table where Jeremy had been sitting, they'd drink another beer, and Jeremy would leave after being there for an hour or so. That had been the pattern established from the dozen or more visits to the bar over the course of what was now more than a year.

On this particular night, when Jeremy walked into the bar, he found Rawhide playing pool, as usual. Jeremy put his quarters on the table but before he left to order two beers, as he always did, Rawhide said,

"Hey, Clam boy! Say hello to the Cowboy!"

Jeremy walked over, shook hands with a tall, thin man, in his mid-thirties, with a cowboy hat on and said,

"How's it goin', man?"

"Alright. How 'bout you?"

"Same."

As Rawhide was chalking his pool stick, he ambled alongside Jeremy and whispered, "The Cowboy here is going to be helping me out some with my business."

"Why's that, Rawhide?"

"I'm expanding the operation some. I've got people wanting me as far south as Orlando, as far west as Crystal River, as far east as St. Augustine, and as far north as Perry. I just can't be everyplace at once. You may not see me next time you come up here, but if you see the Cowboy here, you can do business with him. I'm going to show him how we do it tonight. That alright with you?"

"If you say so, Rawhide. I don't guess I have much choice in the matter, do I?"

"No, you don't. This has nothin' to do with you, but I figure you'd be okay with that so long as the supply chain is uninterrupted. Am I right?"

"That's right, Rawhide."

"Good! Then we have an understanding. Go buy me and the Cowboy a beer, will ya?"

"Sure thing, Rawhide. Bud okay with you, Cowboy?"

"That'll do."

Jeremy went and bought the beers and the three men clinked bottles to seal the deal. When their game ended, Rawhide and the Cowboy walked outside with the keys to Jeremy's truck and Jeremy played the next man up. When the two men returned, Cowboy put the keys back on Jeremy's table. Jeremy had another beer, played a game against the Cowboy, and left.

He wasn't happy about the change. He'd grown accustomed to doing business with Rawhide and felt safe. The fewer people who knew what was going on the better, he thought. It concerned him, but he didn't think too much about it.

He could understand how Rawhide couldn't be in Chiefland all the time. It was probably a good thing to have a back-up. What would he do if Rawhide wasn't there? He'd have to wait and see how things went the next month. He couldn't detect any difference whatsoever in the product, and didn't give it another thought. He didn't mention it to Sally. The less she knew the better.

A month later, when he entered the bar, he saw Cowboy playing pool but there was no sign of Rawhide. He put his quarters on the table, bought some beers, told the Cowboy what he wanted and the deal went down just the same. The only difference was the Cowboy always gave him a sample of what he was buying.

"I want you to see what you're getting. That's just the way I do business. Think of it as if you're gettin' somethin' for free."

After two beers and a few games of pool, he left for home. No problems. He liked the part about free samples.

That went on for the next several months. Jeremy never saw Rawhide again. It was all the Cowboy now. Nobody other than Sally, Rawhide, Brianne and the Cowboy had any idea that he and Sally were using an illegal substance. He wanted to keep it that way.

After four or five months of doing business with the Cowboy, after he gave the Cowboy the keys to his truck, the Cowboy said, in a low voice so that no one else could hear,

"Hey, Clam boy. I need to ask you to do me a favor."

"What's that, Cowboy?"

"I need for you to deliver a package to somebody in Cedar Key. Can you do that for me?"

"Who is it?"

"A guy named Carlos, says he works on a farm not too far outside of Cedar Key. Know the guy?"

"No."

"He's a Mexican…short, dark-skinned, skinny guy. About my age."

"Don't know him."

"He knows you."

"He does?"

"Maybe he said he knows who you are. I think that's what he said."

"I'd rather not, Cowboy. I don't want anybody in Cedar Key knowing what I'm doing."

"The guy doesn't have a car and can't get here and it's a long way for me to get all the way to where he is. He can get a ride to Cedar Key. With the price of gas goin' up the way it is I lose my profit just drivin' over there and back. I'll take $50 off your bill if you do."

"Fifty dollars, huh? I'm really not wanting to do this, Cowboy."

"Did you hear what I said? The Cowboy sneered. "Do you know how much trouble you're gonna cause me if I have do to do this?"

Jeremy thought about it for a few seconds and asked, "If I do this for you, how would I get in touch with him?"

"You know that place on the left as you're comin' into town where you can wash clothes?"

"Yeah, I know the place. It's called the Wash 'n Go, or something like that."

"You be there at 5:00 tomorrow and he'll be there. Just tell him the Cowboy sent you."

"So you already had this deal set up before even talking to me?"

"Yeah. I'm supposed to meet him there. If you don't do this for me I'll have to do it. He's expecting me, but I can call him and tell him it'll be you, if you agree that is."

"How will I get you the money?"

"I'll take care of that. You just give him the package. Will you do that for me?"

Jeremy thought about it some more. He really didn't want to do it, but he couldn't find a reason to say no, and he said, "I'd rather not do this, man."

The Cowboy's face turned into a frown. He turned to look Jeremy directly in the face. His tone of voice changed as he said,

"You gonna make me spend two hours of my time and drive a hundred miles when it wouldn't take you two minutes to do this? What the hell's wrong with you, man? I'd do it for you, that's for damn sure."

The Cowboy wasn't happy with Jeremy's reluctance to do him this favor. Jeremy could see out of the corner of his eyes that some of the other men in the bar were looking over at the two of them, probably wondering if a fight was about to break out or something. He felt threatened. He decided to give in to Cowboy's demands.

"So I don't have to do anything other than hand this guy the package, right?"

"Right, and you don't need to see what's inside either. I don't want you opening it up. He's getting the same stuff you're getting, nothing different."

"And I don't have to get any money, just hand him the package, that's it?"

"That's right. So you'll do it?"

Jeremy hesitated, but before he had time to respond, the Cowboy continued,

"That's an easy $50 if you ask me. You're gonna be there anyway. It's not out of your way at all. I don't see why you aren't jumpin' on that deal."

"Alright, but I really don't want to do this. I'll do it for you this one time, but that's it. Don't ask me again, okay?"

"Thanks, Clam boy. I knew I could count on you. I'll leave the package for Carlos in a brown bag next to your stuff." The Cowboy slapped Jeremy on the shoulder as he started to walk out of the bar.

The next day at 5:00 when he walked in to the Wash 'n Go no one else was in the building except for a short Mexican guy. Jeremy asked,

"Hey man. Have you seen a guy in here wearing a cowboy hat? He calls himself the Cowboy."

In broken English, the man responded.

"No, man. He's not here, but he told me you'd be coming in his place. Do you have something for me from him?

"Yeah. I've got a package from the Cowboy for you."

Jeremy handed the man the package and left. He was in and out of the place in less than a minute. On his way out, he bought a coke from the machine, in case anyone was to ask why he stopped there.

Two weeks later, as Jeremy was working in the back of the shop sorting clams, his uncle walked into the room and said,

"Jeremy, there are two Levy County Deputies out here to see you."

"Really? Why?"

"They didn't say, but you need to stop what you're doing and come with me right now."

"Okay."

"You have no idea why they're here, Jeremy?"

"No, I don't."

"Well, let's hope it's nothing serious."

The two men walked side by side, without speaking, down the hall and to the front of the building. Jeremy saw two unsmiling deputies standing next to their squad car. He didn't recognize either one. As he approached, the taller of the two said,

"Are you Jeremy Thibodeaux?"

"I am."

"We have a warrant for your arrest. You'll need to come with us."

"What for, Officer?"

"You'll be taken before a Judge within the next twenty four hours and he'll explain the charges to you."

"Did I fail to pay a ticket or something? What did I do?"

"Please put your hands behind your back."

"You're going to handcuff me?"

"Yes sir. It's standard procedure. Any time we put a person who has been arrested into a squad car we have to do this, sir."

Jeremy did as he was told to do. The other Officer opened the rear door on the driver's side of the vehicle and, after the first Officer had placed the handcuffs on Jeremy, guided Jeremy into the car. Ricky, who stood by watching a few feet away, asked what the bond was and one of the Officers said,

"He has no bond at this time, sir. The Judge will set bond in the morning."

"No bond! Jeremy, what did you do, son? Even murderers get a bond, don't they?"

"Nothin', Uncle Ricky. I have no idea what this is all about."

"Call me when you find out something."

"I will, and call Sally and tell her what happened to me, okay?"

"I will."

Once the two Officers were back in their vehicle, they drove off, leaving Ricky and all of the other employees standing together, watching them as they did so.

Jeremy asked,

"You guys can't tell me what this is all about?"

"Sir, you have a right to remain silent. Anything you say can be used against you in a court of law. You have a right to speak to an attorney. If you cannot afford a lawyer, one will be appointed to represent you. Do you understand these rights as I have just read them to you?"

"Yeah, I understand what you said," Jeremy responded.

"If you choose to speak to us about any matter, you may do so, but you will be waiving your right to remain silent. Would you like to waive your rights and discuss anything with us?"

"No, I don't want to talk to you, but you can't tell me what I'm charged with?"

"You are charged with a felony involving a drug-related offense."

Jeremy knew what it was about all along, since that was the only thing it could have been. He feigned innocence to make it look good in front of his uncle and the men he worked with. He figured it had to be that Mexican, or maybe it was the Cowboy, or Rawhide. He was sure it wasn't Brianne, but she was a possibility, too. Those were the only people who could possibly have turned him in. He was going to keep his mouth shut until he could talk to a lawyer.

Jeremy sat quietly looking out the window as they drove eastward on State Road 24 towards Bronson and the Levy County Jail. Whenever a car came along in the opposite direction, or if he saw people along the side of the road, he ducked his head, not wanting anyone to see him. As he sat there, he remembered that he had some pills in the front pocket of his jeans. He couldn't reach his pocket because his hands were cuffed behind him. He asked,

"Say, would you guys loosen up these handcuffs for me? They're on too tight and I think they're cutting off circulation. They might even be cutting into my skin. I might even be bleeding. Can you put them on so I can have my hands in front of me?"

"We'll be at the jail in a few minutes. I'll take them off of you once we're inside the jail."

Chapter Nine

⫻

The police cruiser pulled up to the jail compound in Bronson. A buzzer sounded as the large sliding doors on wheels mechanically opened. The vehicle pulled inside the compound and the sliding gate shut behind them once they were inside. Jeremy was helped from the vehicle, escorted into the building and taken to the central booking room, where the handcuffs were removed.

He was then taken through all of the various steps in the booking process. He was finger-printed, searched and all of his belongings, including the silver cross which hung around his neck and his wedding rings, were placed in a manila folder with his name on it. A guard made a list of every item as he inserted it into the folder.

As the guard was putting Jeremy's wallet in the envelope, he took out all the money, every piece of identification and all the little hand-written reminder notes and receipts stuffed in there, one by one. He left the two pills, a green one and a blue one, in his pants, hoping they would go undetected.

He was then required to take off all of his clothes and put on an orange prison uniform. The clothes, too, were put in the bag.

When the Officer checked the pants, to make sure nothing else of any value was inside, the guard let out a yell,

"Well, well, well…what do we have here?"

He pulled out the blue pill first.

"It looks like this might be one of those RoxyContin tablets we've been seeing so often lately."

Jeremy felt his body tense as he realized that he had been caught. The jailer then found the green pill.

"I'm going to have these examined and if they are what I think they are, you're going to have another charge or two lodged against you, Mr. Thibodeaux."

Jeremy hung his head, not saying a word.

He was then photographed. The orange jump suit had an inmate number across the front of it. A wrist band was placed on him by one of the guards.

"Don't take this off or lose this. You're going to need it," the guard cautioned.

Jeremy was handed a stack of materials about half an inch thick.

"These are the rules and regulations. Read them, and fill out this sheet naming who can visit you."

"Now?"

"Right now, and you can only list up to eight people."

Jeremy thought for a few seconds and then wrote down Sally, Samantha, his mother, Sally's father, and his Uncle Ricky. He couldn't think of anyone else.

"Can I add people to this list later?"

"No. Once your visitation list is turned in you won't be able to change that until you've been here for six months."

"Damn! Let me think…"

The only other person he could think of was Sally's mother, who lived in Crystal River, and Ricky's wife, so he put them down, just in case.

"When can they come see me?"

"All that is in the booklet I just gave you," the guard said sternly. "Read it when you get to your cell."

"What about my money?"

Jeremy had a little over twenty dollars in his wallet and some change in his pockets.

"That money will be put in an account in your name and you can use it at the canteen. That is explained in the booklet as well."

The guard handed Jeremy two towels, an extra jail uniform, two sheets, a pillow case, a container for holding things, like a toothbrush, soap, shampoo and toiletries, and some flip-flop kind of shoes.

After all the paperwork was completed, Jeremy asked if he could make a phone call.

"Who do you want to call?"

"My wife."

"That can wait."

"But I thought I was allowed a phone call?"

"That's if you wanted to call your lawyer. The rules about telephone calls are in the handbook, too."

Jeremy was then led down a long hallway to a pentagon shaped central guard station. He could see that four other hallways led out from there. The guard stopped in the middle, handed the paperwork to one of three uniformed men standing inside the glass enclosed office, and told Jeremy to follow him.

Half way down the hall the guard told Jeremy to pick up a mattress and a pillow from an open cell. Jeremy did as directed and followed the guard to a large cell at the end of the hall where over a dozen men sat on beds. He could see that several of the men were playing cards. Some were reading magazines. Some were sleeping. Few of the men seemed to notice that a new inmate had arrived.

"You men better not be gambling in there! If you are I'll take those cards away." He turned to Jeremy and said, "Take that bunk over there," pointing to one in the middle of the rows of beds. It looked like there might have been twenty beds in all.

Jeremy did as he was told. The sound of the metal doors slamming behind him resonated throughout his body. The first thing to hit him was the odor. It smelled like stale urine. The next thing to hit him was the dark, dingy room. Everything was painted grey and the lights weren't very bright. The next thing he observed was that there was nothing on the walls…no pictures, no photographs, no nothing, except for some informational signs and a clock.

He noticed three computers along the wall with chairs in front of them and a phone on the wall. He put what few things he was carrying underneath the bed and started to put the sheets on the mattress. Nobody seemed to notice.

Since he had been arrested in the afternoon, by the time he was fully processed it was well past 4:00. Before he was finished getting his bed made, he heard a guard announce "Chow time!" All of the men stood up and formed a line. Jeremy followed along. It was time for dinner.

Jeremy wasn't hungry and didn't eat any of the meatloaf, potatoes and carrots, but he ate the piece of chocolate cake that came with it. One of the other inmates, who saw that he wasn't eating his food, asked for his dinner and Jeremy started to give it to him.

A guard saw Jeremy about to give his tray to the other inmate and he called Jeremy over before he did.

"Thibodeaux! Come here! And bring your tray!"

Jeremy walked over to the door to the cell and said,

"Yes sir."

The guard told him, in a stern, unfriendly voice, "You're new here, but you need to read that booklet. Inmates are not allowed to exchange food with one another."

"I had no idea. I didn't know that."

The guard then lowered his voice and said, "And you'd better be careful about who you choose as your friends."

"I will. I don't know anybody in here. I don't have any friends."

"Well that guy you were about to give your dinner to is in here for a sex offense on a minor. He's not real well liked, if you know what I mean. Read that part about sexual assaults. You're one of the smaller guys in here, and one of the youngest, too. You be careful. That's all."

The guard turned and walked away.

After all the trays were returned and dinner was officially over, Jeremy went back to his bunk. As he sat there, he noticed that men were lined up against a wall to make phone calls.

There was only the one telephone on the wall. Jeremy got in line. He noticed that each man had to enter codes to be able to use the phone. He heard some making collect calls. Nobody had any money on them.

While he was standing in line Jeremy read the handbook about telephone calls. It said that phones were turned on at 8 in the morning and turned off at 10 at night. Service was provided by a "pay as you go" company and every inmate had to have a number to access the system. His booking identification number, which was on his wrist, was his PIN number. Even though Cedar Key was a local number from Bronson, it was still a call that had to be paid for. He could only make a collect call since he hadn't had time to get hooked into the system.

When it was his turn, he fumbled through and managed to make a collect call to his home. When Sally answered, she was frantic.

"Uncle Ricky told me all about it! So what are you charged with?"

"Drugs."

"How'd that happen? Who turned you in?"

"I can't talk about it now, Sally. Guys are listening and I've got no privacy here."

"So when can I come see you?"

"I'm supposed to be in court in the morning but I overheard one of the other guys saying we just go to a room here in the jail and don't get brought to court, so I don't think you'll be able to see me tomorrow."

"So when can I see you?"

"They gave me this handbook and it's got all the rules and regulations in here."

Jeremy turned pages until he came to the section on visitation.

"It says visiting hours are on Tuesday, Wednesday and Thursday from 1:00 until 4:00, and on Saturday and Sunday from 8:00 a.m. until 11:00 a.m., and then again from 1:00 until 4:00."

"That's it?"

"That's what it says."

"No night time visits?"

"I don't see where it says anything about night time visits."

"Can I bring Samantha?"

"I see here where it says no one under the age of 16 is allowed to visit. I don't know if that includes children of an inmate or what, but that's what it says. I'll have to ask about that."

"Damn, Jeremy! What are we going to do?"

"I don't know Sally. I've never been in trouble before. I don't know what's going to happen."

"And Uncle Ricky says you don't have a bond set or something crazy like that. Is that true?"

"That's what the deputy said, but the Judge is supposed to set bond tomorrow is what I've been told."

"We don't have much money for a bondsman, but I'll do the best I can to get you out of there. You know we don't have any money for a lawyer, Jeremy. I guess you'll have to get a Public Defender."

"Yeah. I'm afraid so."

"What can I bring you?"

"I haven't finished reading this thing but from what I can tell you can't bring me anything, not even money. The only way to do that is to deposit it into my account on line, or you could order it over the phone some kind of way, or you could go to the Sheriff's office. There's supposed to be a machine there you can make a deposit into my account by using it. I don't know how it's done. You'll have to figure it out."

"Not even underwear or socks or anything?"

"That's what it says. Anything I need I have to buy from the Canteen, including tennis shoes."

"Tennis shoes?"

"Yeah. That's what it says. That's the only kind of shoes you can wear for exercising. Otherwise I wear these flip-flops they gave me."

"Well, hopefully you're not going to be in there too long. Maybe the Judge will set your bond low enough so that we can get you out."

"Let's hope so. Say, Sally, I can't talk too long. There's a five minute limit and there are a bunch of guys waiting to use the phone. When are you going to come see me?"

"Tomorrow's Thursday, so I'd better go tomorrow or I won't see you until Saturday. I'll come right from work."

"Sally, if you're not here by 3:00 it says they won't let you in."

"I'll have to get off early. I'll see you tomorrow."

"Yeah…and Sally," Jeremy said haltingly, with his eyes welling up with tears, "I love you."

"I love you, too, Jeremy. We'll get through this."

Jeremy went back to his bunk, but it wasn't even 6:00 and he wasn't the least bit tired. He laid down and started to read the rest of the handbook.

There was a whole page on sexual assaults in the jail. He'd never been anywhere except for a locker room in school, or on a boat at work, where he was with nothing but other guys. He felt out of place. The more he read the more scared he became. He'd always been a strong kid, one who could take care of himself, and he wasn't afraid of a fight, but there were some really huge guys in there with him and nobody seemed very friendly.

Some of the other men easily weighed twice as much as he did, and some were a foot taller, too. There were a few guys younger than him, but it seemed as if most of the guys were at least five or ten years older than him and a few guys were as old as his uncle. He tried not to make eye contact with anyone and didn't strike up a conversation with anybody.

He read the rules on Housing, which said:

YOU SHALL make your bed promptly by 5:30 a.m. and the bed shall remain made for the rest of the day;

YOU SHALL be fully dressed by 5:45 a.m. each day and remain dressed all day from lights on until 2000 hours at which time you may dress down into your shirt and shorts. Lights out is at 2200 hours;

YOU SHALL sweep and mop daily;

YOU SHALL clean your showers, sinks and toilets daily;

YOU SHALL NOT hang pictures on the wall; keep them in your box;

YOU SHALL NOT use bed coverings, mattresses or pillows for other than sleeping purposes and they must remain on your assigned bunk;

YOU SHALL NOT lie on the bed while wearing shoes;

YOU SHALL NOT mark on the walls, tables or chairs;

YOU SHALL NOT cover any lights, bars or vents with paper or any other material;

YOU SHALL NOT allow paper or other debris to accumulate in your cell/dormitory;

YOU SHALL NOT change your assigned bunk or cell;

YOU SHALL be in bed, quiet, no talking, at the posted "lights out" time.

He read a long list of other things he couldn't do, such as fighting, indecent exposure, destroying property and other such things, but it also included refusing to work, refusing to obey an order, faking an illness, smoking and gambling, too.

"Damn! Guys can't smoke," he thought to himself. "I'm glad I don't smoke."

It also included profanity.

"Right! Guys in here ain't gonna cuss," he laughed out loud when he read that part.

He saw where the only clothes he was permitted to have were three plain white T-shirts, three plain white pairs of socks; three plain white undershorts and one plain white sweatshirt.

Besides sleeping, eating and working, the only things he could do were exercise for three hours per week and participate in classes. The only inmate programs were religious services, anger management classes, Alcoholics Anonymous meetings and courses on "Life Skills," which included topics such as Health and Nutrition, Parenting Skills and Workplace Readiness. There was also a library

By 7:00, he had read the rules twice and was bored.

He thought to himself, "No TV! Not even a radio! I hope I'm not going to be in here too long. I need to get out of here. This place will drive me crazy."

Jeremy thought about calling Sally again, but then he thought that there was really nothing else to say. He had to wait to see what happened in the morning when he went before the Judge.

By 10:00, Jeremy was ready to jump out of his skin. He was tired of lying in bed but not so tired that he was ready to go to sleep. He lay in bed listening to every sound that was made and every conversation he could hear, most of which he didn't want to hear.

Once the lights went out, there was no talking. Two guys in the corner were whispering back and forth and a guard came to the cell door and ran his night stick across it, saying,

"Quiet in there! No talking!"

It had been well over a year since Jeremy had gone to bed without taking one flavor of RoxyContin or another. He hadn't thought what that would be like. He didn't know what to expect. He was wishing he had a few of the Roxy Blues. He'd take three, if he could. He tossed and turned over and over again, with no success. He had no idea what time it was as there were no clocks in the cells, but it seemed as if the moment he finally fell asleep lights were on and people were yelling at him.

"On your feet and stand by your bed!"

Every inmate stood, as ordered.

"Collins!"

"Here."

"Weinstein!"

"Here."

"Harrison!"

"Here."

"Mulroney!"

"Here."

Jeremy listened as the names were called. They weren't in alphabetical order so he had to listen carefully. The last name called was his.

"Thibodeaux!"

And he responded "Here."

After all the names were called, and there were twenty of them, a guard yelled,

"All present and accounted for, Sergeant."

As one deputy was calling out the names, another deputy was walking through the dormitory, stopping every now and then to comment if something was out of place or otherwise amiss. After the "Count," as it was called, was completed, or cleared, the jailer said, "Make your beds, now!"

All of the men immediately began to do as instructed. As they were doing so, Jeremy heard the rattle of the food carts.

"Chow time!"

The men lined up. Food was served on trays to each man, who sat on his bed to eat it. This time Jeremy was hungry, since he hadn't eaten in almost eighteen hours, but he felt nauseous, too. He drank the juice and ate the toast, but left the eggs, coffee and grits on his plate. He couldn't eat. His hands began shaking uncontrollably. He put them under his legs so that nobody could notice.

He was as nervous as could be, more so than when he was getting ready for the surgery or when that bull shark was circling him while he was diving for clams. He'd much rather face either of those two dangers than go in front of a Judge as he would later that morning. He was also feeling a powerful need to take a pill.

Chapter Ten

At 8:00, a guard came to the cell door and yelled, "Thibodeaux!"

"Yes sir."

"Follow me!"

Jeremy followed the guard down the hall into a room on the other side of the booking area where he had been the previous day. As he entered the room he saw six other men seated in chairs facing a large television. The screen was blank. Several yards in front of the television was a podium. Once he sat down, the guard said,

"Listen up! When your name is called you are to walk to the podium and listen carefully to what Judge Salter has to say. Answer any questions asked of you. Do not speak until you are spoken to. If you have any questions, the Judge will give you an opportunity to ask them. You will be able to see the Judge and hear what he has to say and he will be able to see you and hear what you have to say. When your hearing is concluded you are to remain in this room until all hearings are concluded. No one leaves this room except in the company of a guard. Understood?"

Everyone muttered "Yes sir," or words to that effect.

"The Judge will appear on the screen at exactly 8:30. Remain quiet until he does."

The men sat silently and watched as the clock ticked for fifteen minutes. At exactly 8:30, the screen became illuminated and the face of an older man in a black robe, with black glasses and a balding head of gray hair filled the screen.

"Good morning. My name is Judge Marcus Salter and I will be conducting what is called a "First Appearance" hearing for most of you. The purpose of this hearing is to inform you of the charges against you and to set the amount of bail. I will also want to know if you have the financial ability to hire your own lawyer or if I will need to appoint a lawyer to represent you. Do not tell me anything about the charges against you because, if you do, anything you say can and undoubtedly will be used against you at the time of trial. This hearing is being videotaped and recorded. Now, the first case to be heard this morning is that of Jorge Gonzalez. Mr. Gonzalez, if you would, please step up to the podium."

A young Hispanic man seated two seats away from Jeremy stood and walked up to the podium.

"Are you Jorge Gonzalez?"

"Si, your Honor. I am," the man said in broken English."

"Are you able to understand me or would you prefer to have an interpreter?"

"I am able to understand."

"If you don't understand something I say, we have an interpreter in the courtroom here with me who can help. Just let me know if you need any help, okay?"

"Yes, I will."

"Mr. Gonzalez, you are charged with driving without having a valid driver's license. I see that you were convicted of the same offense three months ago. I am setting your bond at $1,000.00. Do you have the ability to hire a lawyer?"

"No, you Honor, I don't. With your permission, I will plead guilty. I am guilty."

"What says the State?"

"The State would want Mr. Gonzalez sentenced to a minimum of thirty days in jail with a fine of at least $1000.00, your Honor. We would also like Mr. Gonzalez to know that if he does it again the jail time will more than double as will the fine. This is a second offense. He served ten days in jail the first time and was fined $500. I don't know why he can't get a license, but until he does, he can't drive."

"Mr. Gonzalez, if you want to plead guilty right now and admit that you were driving without a valid driver's license I will sentence you to thirty days in jail and fine you $1000, which can be paid within ninety days, or sixty days after you get out of jail. Do you want to do that?"

"Yes. I do."

"Alright, you have a seat. I'll come back to you after I finish with the others here. The next case is Jeremy Thibodeaux."

Jeremy felt as if he'd been shot with a pistol when he heard his name called. He jumped out of his seat and walked to the podium.

"Are you Jeremy Thibodeaux?

"Yes sir. I am."

"Mr. Thibodeaux, you are charged with the unlawful possession of a controlled substance, which is a third degree felony punishable by up to five years in prison and a fine of up to $5,000. You are also charged with the unlawful sale or delivery of a controlled substance. That is also second degree felony, meaning that you could be sentenced to up to fifteen years in the State Penitentiary and fined up to $10,000 for that charge. Do you have the ability to retain your own lawyer?"

"No, your Honor, I don't."

"It says here you live in Cedar Key. How long have you lived there?"

"All my life."

"And you are married and have a child?"

"That's right."

"And you work for the Thibodeaux Clam Company. Is that your business?"

"No, that's my Uncle's."

"How much do you earn?"

"On an average week over the past year or so I earned $400, or $10 per hour for a 40 hour week. Sometimes we work a little more, sometimes less, depending upon the weather. I got a raise a while back and now I'm getting paid $14 an hour."

"Do you own your own home?"

"We're paying on it."

"How long have you owned it?"

"We got it right after we got married a few years ago."

"Do you own a car?"

"Yes sir. I have a 1999 Ford Ranger."

"Is it paid for?"

"Yes sir, it is."

"Do you have any money in the bank?"

"Maybe a couple of hundred dollars. I get paid every Friday but it all seems to be gone by the next Friday."

"Does your wife work?"

"Yes sir. She works in the office of a different clamming company."

The Judge hesitated and then said,

"Well, Mr. Thibodeaux, I think you probably make too much money for the Public Defender, but unless you get out of jail and are able to work you won't have any money with which to pay for an attorney, will you? What are the chances of you posting a bond to get yourself out of jail, sir?"

"That depends on how much it is."

"What says the State?"

Jeremy couldn't see who was speaking, but he heard a voice say,

"These are serious charges Mr. Thibodeaux is facing, your Honor. The State would ask that the bond to be set at $50,000 on each charge. The arrest of Mr. Thibodeaux is part of an ongoing sting operation in which other arrests are to be made. The State doesn't want to see Mr. Thibodeaux get out of jail and possibly do something to jeopardize the investigation. If he can't get out, his lawyer can file a motion to reduce the bond for him. We think a bond of $50,000 on each charge is appropriate, your Honor."

"Can you make that, Mr. Thibodeaux?"

"No way, your Honor. I need for it to be a whole lot lower than that."

"Mr. Thibodeaux, based on what the State has just told me, I'm not inclined to set your bond much lower than what the State has requested, so I'm going to set the bond at $50,000 on the Sales and Delivery charge and $25,000 on the possession charge. I'll go ahead and appoint the Public Defender's Office to represent you at this time."

At that, the Judge started to say, "The next case is…" and Jeremy interrupted,

"But Judge, I…"

"Don't tell me anything about your case. I suggest you talk to the lawyer assigned to represent you and let that person talk for you. The next case is that of Robert Dowling."

Jeremy hung his head and walked slowly back to his chair. He hardly heard a word of what was said to any of the other inmates. All he knew was that he wasn't getting out of jail that day and it might be a long time before he'd see his wife and his daughter again. He was feeling nauseous and felt beads of sweat forming on his temples.

It was 9:00 before he was put back in his cell. He was allowed to remain there until the other inmates returned for lunch. His mind raced through the various options he had. Maybe one of his relatives, like Uncle Ricky, or his mother, maybe, could put up the $7,500 cash and some land as security for the $75,000 so that he could make bail. His land was worth maybe a hundred thousand dollars, with the trailer on it, but he owed ninety something on it.

His mind was running through all the options he could think of as he sat and ate his lunch of ham and cheese on white bread, with potato chips and a cup of gator-aid. There was no way he and Sally could make that bond by themselves. Maybe her parents would help. They were divorced and each owned a house. Maybe his lawyer could file for a bond reduction. Maybe he could turn State's evidence against someone, but he didn't know who that could be. The only people he was involved with were Rawhide, the Cowboy and the Mexican. Brianne had been caught and done her time. Maybe Sally would have some ideas.

When the minute hand of the clock finally ticked to the twelve, with the little hand on the one, Jeremy waited anxiously for his name to be called. Every time a guard approached his cell, Jeremy leapt to his feet and walked to the door, certain that the guard was coming to tell him he had a visitor. He called the home number every fifteen minutes, but no one was there to answer. He couldn't call Sally's cell phone, because she couldn't accept collect calls on it.

By 3:00, he slumped down on his bed, knowing that she wouldn't be allowed in to see him if she arrived, since that was another of the rules he had read. He felt nauseous, again, and though he didn't get sick to his stomach, he felt like he might. He was sure he had a fever and thought he might be getting sick. He was sure it was because of him being in jail. He never got sick, ever. He was as healthy as a horse.

At 3:30, Sally finally answered the phone.

"Where have you been!" he screamed. "I thought you were coming to see me!"

"I did. They wouldn't let me in."

"Why not?"

"I came straight from work and I had shorts and a tank top on."

Jeremy let out a huge sigh.

"Shit! That's my fault. I should have told you. They don't let anybody in if they're wearing shorts above the knees or if their shirts don't have sleeves on 'em. That was my bad. I'm sorry."

"So what happened today?"

"The Judge set my bond at $75,000 and appointed the Public Defender's Office to represent me."

"Why is it set so high?"

"Because the State said my case was part of an ongoing investigation and if I was released I could mess up the whole operation. Something like that."

"Part of an ongoing investigation? What's that all about?"

"I can't talk about it over the phone, Sally. I'll have to tell you when I see you."

"But I won't be able to get in to see you until Saturday now."

"I know. Damn! I was so lookin' forward to seeing you. I miss you and Samantha so much!"

"I know, baby. I miss you, too. I can't believe this is happening."

"Also, you need to know that even if you went home and put on pants and a shirt if you didn't get here by 3:00 they wouldn't have let you in."

"So what time can I get in to see you on Saturday?"

"Visiting hours begin at 8:00 and they end at 11:00, but you can only see me for half an hour."

"Half an hour! Can I come back at 1:00?"

"No. Only one visit per day per person."

"Oh, man! This is going to be really hard!"

"You're tellin' me, and I can't see Samantha until I've been here for six months, and even then I won't be able to hold her or give her a hug."

"Are you going to be able to hold me or kiss me when I see you?"

"No, baby. We won't even be in the same room."

The two were silent for a few seconds.

"I went to the Sheriff's Office and put some money in your Inmate Account."

"You did? Thanks. How much?"

"I put a hundred dollars in there for you."

"Thanks. I'm gonna buy some shirts, underwear and some socks."

"That sounds exciting."

"That's about all I can get, that and a sweatshirt, but I won't need that for a while."

"How did the hearing go anyway? Did the Judge say how long you might be in there?"

"The Judge said I could be sent to prison for up to twenty years on the two charges."

"Twenty years! For both of them or total?"

"Fifteen for one and five for the other, plus I could get fined up to $10,000 on one and $5,000 on the other."

"Damn, Jeremy. This is a whole lot more serious than I thought. Johnny Jones got probation last year when he got arrested for drugs. He's still smokin' dope all the time from what I hear, and you remember Brianne? She got into some trouble a while back and she was in jail for a while but now she's workin' at some place up in Chiefland. I saw her the other day as I was drivin' by, on my way to the Kringle. She looked like she's a nurse or somethin'."

Jeremy didn't say anything about him having anything to do with Brianne, and said,

"I should find out more about what's likely to happen to me once I talk to my Public Defender, but for now I can't talk to anybody about any of this. I just listen when other guys talk and they don't have much good to say about the PDs. They call them Public Pretenders. I just hope somebody comes to see me soon. I feel like I'm about to throw up half the time. I feel weak. I've got a headache and I'm sure I've got a fever, I hurt, and I couldn't sleep hardly at all last night. When I finally did fall asleep they woke me up at 5:00 this morning…plus I'm scared in here, Sally. There are some mean lookin' dudes in here. I try not to look at anybody, and there's nothin' to do…no TV, no radio, no nothin'."

"No TV?"

"No."

"You just sit there on your bed?"

"That's about it."

"We gotta get you outa there, Jeremy."

"You're tellin' me. Say, Sally, I gotta go. There's about ten guys waiting to use this phone. I'll see you on Saturday."

"I'll be there early."

"Remember, you gotta be here by 10:00 or they won't let you in."

"I'll be there at 8:00. You be strong, Jeremy. Is there anything I can bring you?"

"No. They'll take anything you bring me away from you and throw it away, I think."

"Okay, I'll just bring me. I love you, baby."

"I love you, too, Sally. See you Saturday."

Jeremy went back to his bed to lie down, feeling worse than he'd ever felt before in his life, even when he got hurt. That was a physical pain. He could deal with that. This was a pain that he felt in every part of his body, his muscles, his stomach, but most of all in his head. He kept trying to figure a way out of the mess he was in, but had no idea how he could do it.

The trustees brought dinner at exactly 4:45. Jeremy couldn't eat. He drank the gator-aid, but didn't touch the hamburger or French fries. After putting his tray away, he went back down and fell asleep for a few minutes, despite the fact the other inmates were laughing and talking all around him. When he awoke, he saw that it was only 5:30. He had nothing to do except lie there until lights went out at 10:00.

Half an hour later, the cell door opened and a trustee came in pushing a cart full of books. Most of the men stood and walked toward the cart.

"Form a line!" a guard yelled.

The men lined up against the wall and one at a time they looked over the books and magazines. The several copies of Sports Illustrated went first, with Field and Stream and anything having anything to do with hunting or fishing going next. By the time it was Jeremy's turn, there was little to choose from. He picked out a book written by Louis L'Amour because it was about cowboys and Indians. He also picked out a detective kind of book, thinking maybe he'd learn some things about law.

He started reading the detective story first. It was about a murder and a detective who was hired to prove that the main character didn't do it. Jeremy hadn't read many books other than those he was required to read in school, and never any mystery books. He kept turning pages and before he knew it, a guard was yelling,

"Lights Out!"

Many of the men snored and made noises in their sleep. It seemed as if everyone else was asleep as he lay there, feeling tired, weak, sick to his stomach, and very much alone. As he lay there, the shakes came back, but this time it was his whole body, not just his hands. He had a headache and began to sweat. He also felt his body craving the blue pills, and it was a stronger desire than hunger or thirst or for anything he'd ever felt the need for before.

Chapter Eleven

-----------------------·⫶⫶·-----------------------

Sometime in the middle of the night, Jeremy fell asleep from sheer exhaustion. He was awakened by the clanging of bells and loud noises. Since he wasn't going to court, he would have to do chores just like the rest of the prisoners. First, though, he had to await the head count and then make his bed. After all the prisoners were accounted for, and beds were made, the breakfast cart rolled in, pushed by trustees, some of whom acted like they were the guards, or on staff at the jail. It was good to be a trustee. Those were inmates who had earned the right to get out of their cells, walk around the jail, talk to the guards, and act like they were better than the other prisoners.

Though he still felt sick, and nauseous, he knew he had to eat something, so he ate the toast, eggs and bacon and drank the orange liquid that was supposed to be orange juice. He couldn't eat the rock-hard grits. Once the trays were back on the cart and the cart was out of the cell, it was time to go to work.

For the next four hours it was,

"Thibodeaux! Grab that mop and mop that floor! Or Thibodeaux! Get that brush and clean those toilets! Or Thibodeaux! Take that trash and put it in that garbage can!"

There were several hundred prisoners, men and women, housed at the Levy County Detention Center, as it is formally known. Jeremy was in one of the dozen or more large cell blocks, called "pods." It didn't seem possible to keep all of the prisoners busy doing work details, but everywhere he looked, the inmates were working, under the watchful eyes of the guards, some of whom were easier to hear than others.

None of the guards called anybody anything other than "Inmate!" or by their last name. Even when an inmate talked to another inmate they called each other by their last names. Jeremy didn't talk to anybody for the first few days, though there were a few of the other inmates who were about his age, who seemed to be as unsure of themselves as he was, who he caught looking over at him every now and then. He wasn't sure if they were coming on to him or if they were just trying to make friends.

At 11:00, work came to an abrupt stop and men were allowed to shower before lunch was served at exactly 11:30. Jeremy ate the turkey and cheese sandwich and the bag of chips, though he still wasn't feeling well and he was sure he had a fever and thought he might have the flu. He considered telling the guards that he needed to see a doctor, but he decided he'd better not do that just yet, especially since he saw that part in the rules about feigning an illness. Besides, he knew that part of the problem had to do with him being unable to take the pills he had become accustomed to taking on a daily basis and he didn't think it was a good idea for the jailers to be aware of that.

After lunch, since it was a Friday and no visitors were allowed, from 1:00 to 4:00 the men and women were allowed to go out to separate exercise yards. Not everybody went, but Jeremy followed the others. He hadn't bought any tennis shoes yet, so he couldn't play basketball with the others, but it was good just to get outside in the fresh air.

He'd been a man who spent most of his life on the water and not under a roof, inside walls. He hated being in school because it prevented him from being outside. It was early May and the weather was perfect, not too hot and not too cold. He sat on a bench and watched the other guys play.

He also caught himself looking over at the women on a separate court. He missed Sally. He'd been with her every day of his life, just about, and not being able to lie next to her at night and make love to her was about the hardest part of being away from her, even though they hadn't been making love to each other on a regular basis in a while. He thought about Samantha and what she would be doing at various times of the day. He had to fight back tears when he did.

As he sat on a bench, taking in everything that was going on around him, he saw a door to one of the buildings open up. When it did, men walked over and got in line. He figured that had to be the Canteen, so he went, too. He saw a kiosk machine inside.

When it was his turn, he ordered the shirts, socks, underwear and size eight tennis shoes.

An inmate behind him said,

"You getting' the whole nine yards, huh, Thibodeaux?"

"Yeah, I guess so."

"There's nothin' else you can buy here except for clothes, candy and stuff. Just remember that if you buy any of that candy, you gotta finish it before you go back to the cell.

Jeremy turned and saw it was the sexual predator guy he had offered his food to. He said,

"Thanks, man." And walked away, not wanting to engage him in any conversation. He went back to where he had been sitting, but the guy followed him and sat down next to him. Jeremy immediately said,

"Hey, no offense, man, but I'd like to be by myself if you don't mind," Jeremy told the man.

The man responded,

"Listen, I know that guard told you I'm a sex offender and that you'd better stay away from me. They tell everybody that, but all I did was have sex with a sixteen year old girl who looked like she was twenty five, and now I'm lookin' at goin' to prison and having somebody put a sign in my yard sayin' I'm a sexual predator for the rest of my life. That coulda happened to any of us."

"But how old are you? Thirty?"

"I'm twenty eight, and I met her in a bar. I didn't know."

"Yeah, well that may be true, but if it's all the same to you, I'd like to be alone."

"Suit yourself," the man said, and he got up and walked away.

One of the other inmates, one about the same age as Jeremy, came and sat down next to him.

"That guy tell you it was a sixteen year old who looked like a twenty year old?"

"Yeah."

"That's what he tells everybody. One of the guards told me that wasn't true, that it was really one of his cousins. Nobody wants to have anything to do with him. He got beat up pretty good a few weeks ago because of it."

"What happened?"

"It was out here, like now, and some guys kind of formed a circle around him and before the guards could do anything about it, some guy beat the shit out of him."

"What happened to the guy who did it?"

"Nobody would tell who did it, not even that guy, so nothin' happened. I don't think the guards cared too much about it. They were probably glad it happened. What's your name, man?"

"Jeremy. How about you?"

"Sam. What you in for?"

"Drugs. How about you?"

"Same thing."

"How long you in for?"

"I go to court in a couple of weeks. If what my Public Pretender tells me is true, I'll be out and on probation."

"This your first time?"

"Yeah. You?"

"Yeah."

" Since we're under the age of twenty five, they go easy on us the first time I'm told."

"Not me. I got a $75,000 bond on me. They're talkin' about twenty years in prison."

"That's not going to happen, unless you're a dealer, and if you are you're in deep shit! They've got mandatory minimum sentences for dealers, depending upon how much shit you got caught with."

"Naah. I'm no dealer, just use enough for me and my wife, but they got me charged with delivery, too."

"That's bad. They only got me for possession."

"Pot?"

"Yeah. You?"

"Roxys."

"That's more serious. You need to talk to your PD and he'll tell you what's gonna happen. They're deal-makers. They'll tell you that you're getting a great deal. The hard part is getting them to come see you."

"Where you from, Sam?"

"Morristown. You?"

"Cedar Key."

"You a clammer?"

"Yeah. You a farmer?"

"Horses, mostly, but yeah, we make hay and do things around the farms. I got a business where we go around to all the farms and gather up the horse manure. We sell it as fertilizer. We also bring in fresh loads of sawdust for the stalls. It's a good business. There's lots of horse farms around Williston and down towards Ocala."

"Yeah, I know. I drive by them every now and then, but not too often. I mostly stick to the water. What cell you in?"

"They call 'em pods. Mine faces east, for all the good it does. We can't hardly ever see the sun. You?"

"I don't know. It's the one on the right as you walk towards the guard station."

"You full up?"

"We've got about twenty some guys in there, and that includes two extra cots."

"Eighteen in mine. That'll change, though. Guys come and go every day."

A bell rang.

"Time to go in. Nice meetin' you, Jeremy. Take it easy, and good luck."

"You, too, Sam."

Five minutes later Jeremy was back in his bed reading about a man named Sackett. The book was set in the early 1800s, at the time when the West was still wild and all lands west of the Mississippi were called "Indian Country." He liked reading about the Indians and what it was like for the Americans heading west.

Inside the book was a page that listed all of the other books written by L'Amour. When he finished this one, he'd see if he couldn't get some of the others. Reading was the only thing that he could do to pass the time. There were no computers in the cells and men weren't even allowed to do much of anything except read and play cards, and even then it couldn't be for money. Reading was the only thing he could do and it made the time go by faster, much faster.

Half an hour later, the dinner meal arrived. It was fried chicken with potato salad and beans, one of his favorite meals. He ate the whole thing. His muscles ached and he still felt like he might get sick, but he thought he'd feel better if he ate more.

When dinner was over, he was back in bed reading until it was lights out. Right before the order came to turn off all lights and go to sleep, the guards came in and did another head count and inspection. Supposedly a few inmates over the years had somehow obtained drugs in the jail and the guards were determined that wouldn't happen again, though many said it was a guard who sold the drugs to the inmates. Regardless, ten minutes later, Jeremy was in his bed, trying to go to sleep.

He still felt weak, nauseous, and he was sure he had a temperature over a hundred, and he couldn't sleep. While everyone else was sleeping, he lay in his bed, trembling, sweating, and worrying about what was to become of him.

When sleep finally overtook him, for the third night in a row, it was interrupted way too soon by the clanging of bells, bright lights and men yelling at him.

This was Saturday morning, though, a day when most everybody had visitors. After another head count, the making of the beds, and breakfast, the men then sat on their beds, waiting to see if they had any visitors.

Shortly after 8:00, a guard called his name. The guard pointed him to a little cubicle inside the pod. Jeremy sat down and saw Sally's face on the screen. She was dressed up like she was going to a picnic, with a bright, multi-colored shirt and her best blue jeans.

When he saw her, he broke into a big smile,

"You look great!"

"I thought I'd do what I could to cheer you up some."

"Well, you did. Can you see me okay?"

"Yeah, though it's not the same as having you sitting across from me or being able to hold your hand. How's it goin' in there for you?"

"Not much to do, so I've started reading a couple of books."

"Reading books? You haven't done that since Ms. White's History class, when she made you do it."

"I know. There's just nothin' to do except stare at walls. I'm actually enjoying the books I got."

He told her all about them and said,

"If I'm going to be in here for a while, I'm going to take whatever classes they've got, so I don't have to sit in my bed any more than I have to."

"What kind of classes?"

"There's a Parenting Class, a Life Skills class about nutrition and stuff, plus there's religious services. There's even an Alcoholics Anonymous meeting in here."

"Reverend Wright will be glad to know that you're going to attend services every now and then."

"He might even be one of the ministers who comes here. I don't know who it is, but I'm goin'."

"So did you buy clothes and all with the money I put in there for you?"

"I did, but I won't get them until next week. The guys play basketball on Monday and Friday afternoons, when there's no visitation, but I couldn't play because I didn't have sneakers."

"You meetin' some people, are you?"

"Just one guy about my age, but he's in a different cell. He's in here for drugs, too, and he says he's getting' out in a couple of weeks."

"So maybe you'll get out before too long."

"I hope so, but I'm charged with Sales and Delivery, and that's the biggest problem."

"Have you seen a lawyer yet?"

"No."

"So what's this all about Jeremy? Can you tell me now?"

Jeremy looked around and said, not over this computer thing, Sally. I don't trust them. Anybody in here would do whatever they could to get out of here, even if it means ratting out another guy, I'm sure. I'd rather not say too much."

"No, you'd better not say anything.

"Did I ever tell you about the guys I met up in Chiefland?"

"A little. Not much that I can recall."

"Well, anyway, one night, this one guy asked me to do him a favor and I think that's what it's all about. I never sold anything to anybody, but I don't want to say any more than that."

"Okay."

"And it was a set up. I never got any money or did anything like that, but I'm charged with sale and delivery of a controlled substance. I'm innocent of that, Sally."

"So what can you do about it?"

"I've got to talk to a lawyer and see what he tells me."

"Maybe they'll put you on probation like all those other guys in Cedar Key."

"That kid said my Public Defender would tell me what's going to happen to me. He says they make deals all the time. That's what they do. Say, did you talk to your parents or Uncle Ricky about maybe putting up the bond to get me out of here?"

"Uncle Ricky said that if you did what they say you did then you can just stay right where you are 'til you get that stuff out of your system."

"And your folks?"

"Ever since they divorced, my mother doesn't seem to have much money, and my father isn't working near as hard as he used to. I think he figures if he makes too much money she'll get it. Neither one of them has $7,500 to spare, Jeremy. I asked."

"I know better than to ask my mother. She doesn't have anything other than what she gets from Social Security for her disability, so I guess I'm here until we go to court."

"Didn't you say that the Judge might lower your bond once you got an attorney?"

"That's what he said."

"You want me to call the Public Defender's Office and find out what's going on?"

"Yeah. That's a good idea. At least you can find out who my attorney is, maybe."

"I'll do it first thing Monday."

"How's Samantha?"

"She's askin' where her Daddy is all the time."

"Yeah, I'll bet she misses me."

"Of course she does. We both do, especially at night."

"Yeah, we haven't been away from each other for years. I didn't think too much about it while we were together, but now that I'm not with you, I miss you all that much more."

"We're all sayin' prayers for you."

"I hope they work. Well, it's about time for you to leave. You gonna come see me tomorrow?"

"Of course I am, but it may not be until the afternoon. We're gonna go to church with my Dad, spend some time with him. It will be good for him to go, too. Ever since the divorce he doesn't get out much."

Jeremy put his hand up to the computer screen and Sally did the same.

"I love you."

"I love you, too, babe. We'll get through this."

The two were near tears. Jeremy sat and watched the screen as Sally stood and walked out of the room, closing the door behind her. All he could see was the empty chair and the empty visiting room. He sat there until a guard commanded,

"Other inmates are waiting, Thibodeaux. Your time's up."

Saturday night was no different than any other night. No movie or special event, though the library cart came through again. Jeremy wrote down that he wanted some more of the Louis L'Amour books. He took another two detective books, just in case.

He'd never had insomnia before, but he couldn't sleep, no matter how tired he was. He was worried about everything. In the beginning, he thought that the fever, nauseasness, dizziness and the rest might have been due to him being in jail, but the longer he was in jail, the more he realized it had more to do with him not being able to have any of the RoxyContin. He'd been taking the pills for well over a year, and was up to three a day sometimes, just before he got arrested. Again, sheer exhaustion caused him to doze off some time in the early hours of the morning.

Sunday morning began no differently from any other morning. First came the head count, then make the beds, then breakfast, then clean up, but there was no work detail on Sundays. Visitation began at 8:00, and most of the men, but not all, went to religious services, which were non-denominational, but because so many of the men, and women, attended church services they had to break them up into groups.

The men and women always went to church services separately, just as they did with everything else. Allowing the two sexes to get together was a sure way to cause trouble, so it just wasn't allowed. They did, occasionally, see each other, but it was always at a good distance.

Jeremy went with the 10:30 group, which finished just in time for them to get to lunch. If they'd been late, they'd have missed lunch altogether. That was the rule. Rules were never broken in jail, not without consequences. Sally came that afternoon and they talked about everything except the criminal charges.

That Monday, Jeremy went out for the recreation session, but Sam wasn't there. He watched the guys play basketball. They had teams and there was always a team on the side waiting. Sometimes there were enough guys to have two teams waiting to play, then those two teams would play after the first game was over, and then the winners would play. If there was enough time, the two losing teams would play each other. Jeremy was sure he'd be on one of the scrub teams, but he was looking forward to playing.

On Tuesday, when Sally came to visit, she got there just in time. Another ten minutes and they wouldn't have let her in.

"They only let me stay for half an hour anyway, so why won't they let me in after 3:00?"

"Sally, this place is all about rules. They make 'em and we can't break 'em. That's the rules. So did you find out who my lawyer is?"

"They couldn't tell me. They said the lawyer gets appointed at the arraignment. They said someone would be over to see you sometime this week."

"If I had money my lawyer woulda been here ten minutes after I got arrested."

"Yeah, but you don't, so you gotta be patient."

"That's easy for you to say. If it weren't for these books I'd go crazy."

"That's good you're reading books. Those classes might help, too. When do you start?"

"As soon as they'll let me."

They talked about the cars, the bills, the house and little things, and then Jeremy asked,

"How's things with Samantha?"

"She misses her Daddy, and so do I."

When Sally said that, Jeremy felt himself tearing up. He wiped away the tears and said, "Well, time's about up, I guess. It's been half an hour already."

"It seems like I just got here," Sally said.

"Yeah. I spend most of the day waiting 'til you get here and then the rest of the day thinking about you after you've gone. I love you, baby."

"I love you, too, Jeremy. We'll get through this."

When Sally was gone, Jeremy went back to his bunk and read, hoping that he'd be allowed into classes soon. After he'd been in jail for ten days, he was allowed into the Parenting Class, since he had a child who was three years old. A few days after that he was allowed into the Health and Nutrition class, since there were several empty seats in that one, but he wasn't able to get into the AA program. That program was packed and many of the men in the program were required to be there by court order. They had to get slips signed to prove that they had attended the classes.

As people came and went other people were allowed in. He'd have to wait until a seat opened up for that. Same thing for the Anger Management Class. A lot of guys were ordered to attend those classes, too, and they got first preference for seats when one opened up.

When he saw Sally on the following Thursday, and he still hadn't seen anyone from the Public Defender's Office, he asked Sally to call again.

"You can't do that yourself?"

"All I can do is send a note over to them and I've done that every day. I can't do anything until I get to see my lawyer. This waiting, not knowing what's going to happen, is killing me."

"I'll do what I can, baby. Hang in there."

Chapter Twelve

_____ ⊪ _____

The next day, just as he was about to go out for recreation period, the guard called his name.

"Now they come," he thought to himself.

Sure enough, it was someone from the PDs office, not an attorney, but an investigator.

"My name is Duncan Blake and I'm here to get some basic information from you. A lawyer will be over to see you after he or she sees my report and reviews the materials we get from the State. So anything you say to me is protected by the attorney/client privilege. First I'm going to ask you to tell me all about your history…school, jobs, where you've lived, wives, kids, all that stuff."

After Jeremy answered all his questions, the man said,

"Okay, now, tell me about what happened."

Jeremy told him about Rawhide, Cowboy and the Mexican, but the man knew about them and had heard the story before he was finished telling it.

"So you're representing other people who bought from these guys?" Jeremy asked.

"I'm not, but our office is, and yes, there are dozens of cases just like yours in our office, and they're still making arrests."

"So that's why my bond is so high, right? They don't want me to go out and tell anyone that those guys are cops."

"Well, Rawhide isn't a cop. He got caught and he decided to help himself by turning State's evidence and telling the police about everyone in the five county area who's using pills."

"Damn! I'm sure there are a lot of people who'd like to find his ass."

"You're right about that, but he's in protective custody someplace, and he's not involved in any of the sales. Like in your case, Rawhide didn't sell you any of the drugs you're charged with possessing, and Rawhide didn't give you the drugs you allegedly delivered to the Mexican. Cowboy did that, and Cowboy is a cop."

"And the Mexican?"

"He's a cop, too."

"So what about me? Can I get probation out of this? I've never been in trouble before."

"The problem you have is that they've got you charged with sale and delivery, too. They take that a lot more serious than simple possession. If it was just the simple possession count, I'd say you'd be out and on probation in no time, but because of that other charge, that's going to take a while longer."

"I'm not looking at twenty years in prison, am I?"

"No, no, no. They might try to put you behind bars for a few years if you're convicted of that Sales and Delivery charge, but no, you're not looking at any serious time."

"A few years is serious to me. I can't stand not bein' able to see my wife and daughter."

"You say he gave you $50 to deliver that package to the Mexican?"

"Yeah, that's right."

"I'm not a lawyer, but that could be a problem for you."

"He didn't really pay me to do it, he just took $50 off of what I paid him for the pills, and I didn't get a dime from the Mexican. All I did was hand it to him."

"RoxyContin, right?"

"Yeah. That's what the Cowboy told me. Actually, what he said was that the guy was getting the same thing I got, so I assume it was RoxyContin. I don't know."

"What kind?"

"What kind did I get you mean?"

"Yeah."

"I got the greens and the Blues."

"And they found some pills on you when you were being booked, right? Not at the scene where you were arrested, right?"

"Yeah. They came and arrested me at my work, and I had a couple of pills in my pants pocket. They found the pills as I was being booked."

"Doesn't sound like we have much of an argument about that, do we?"

"I guess not."

"That's not good, but they never went to your house and searched or anything?"

"No, they didn't."

"I guess they didn't think they needed to after they got you on the sales charge. Anyway, so you were taking the Roxy Blues…how are you doing in here?"

"It's boring as hell. Nothing to do except read for the most part."

"I mean how are you doing physically?"

"I feel terrible. I'm nauseous most of the time, can't sleep. I sit around and worry about everything. I've got a headache all the time. I'm sure I've got a fever. I feel like shit. Bein' in here isn't good for me."

"It isn't about being in here that's the problem. You're having withdrawal symptoms from not using those pills."

"You think?"

"I know it. You're not the first client we've had with this. The problem is a little like a Catch-22 because if we send you for treatment it's like admitting you've been using for a while, but since they know you've bought pills several times, and probably more, depending upon what Rawhide told them, they already know that you're a user. Do you have the shakes?"

Jeremy lowered his head and said, "Yeah."

"Pretty bad?"

"Sometimes. It's worst when I'm in bed and the lights are out."

"That's what I'm told. You'll get over it."

"When?"

"It takes a while, depending on how long you've been using. Maybe a month or two, maybe longer."

Jeremy was quiet for a minute, thinking about what the man had told him, and then he asked,

"Can they charge me for all those times I bought from that Rawhide guy?"

"Yes, if they have the evidence."

"Then why didn't they?"

"Because they probably don't have the evidence. When you bought from Cowboy, it was all set up in advance. They probably had the pills tested before they sold to you. That's what they call a "controlled buy."

"The Cowboy always gave me some samples of what I'd bought. Rawhide never did. With the Cowboy, he'd usually give me one of whatever I was buying."

"And he kept some, did he?"

"I don't know if he did or not. He might have. I didn't think too much of it at the time. I figured he used them, too. So that's what he was doing? Keeping some as evidence?"

"That's right. So maybe you'll get charged and maybe not. Do you want me to see about getting you some help or are you going to be able to get through this on your own?"

"Is there anything you can get to help me with these shakes?"

"Hell no! That would be illegal. They'd bust me for doing something like that. I'd lose my job, too. No way, Mr. Thibodeaux. You're on your own, unless things get so bad you need to see a doctor, and then maybe I can arrange a visit for you."

"I meant something legal to help me, not drugs…you thought I meant illegal drugs?"

"No. I'm talking about anything. It's against the rules for me to give you anything…not even an aspirin. The way the doctors do it is like with heroin or morphine addicts. They lower the dosage until it's down to nothing. That takes a while. How long were you using?"

Jeremy looked at him, still not sure if he could trust him or not, and said, "Not too long."

"Then maybe you can make it on your own."

"I'll give it a try. So when will I see a lawyer?"

"Someone will be over to see you within a week or so. You've got a right to a Preliminary Hearing after you've been here for twenty one days and they haven't filed an Information against you, so if that happens, and nothing has been filed as of today, somebody will definitely be here to see you before then."

"What's an Information?"

"It's a piece of paper, that's what it is, but it's a formal document that the State Attorney, or one of his assistants, files with the court. It's called a "charging" document because it charges you with a crime."

"When will this thing go to court?"

"You mean trial?"

"Yeah, I guess."

"The State is supposed to bring you to trial within six months of your arrest. Sometimes it's longer, sometimes shorter. It depends."

"And a bond reduction?"

"I'll see what I can do. Say, I'm sorry but I can't spend any more time talking to you right now. I've got a dozen more guys to see and it's getting late. I got all I need. That's all for now. On your way out, would you tell the guard to send in the next client? Thanks."

Jeremy went back to his cell, still hoping to have a chance to go outside for recreation, but it was too late.

"But it's not even 2:00!"

"Those are the rules, Thibodeaux. Back to your cell."

He told Sally all that he could about his meeting with the investigator the following day. He told her he wasn't going anywhere for at least another week, and probably longer.

The following Monday, a package was waiting for him at the kiosk. It was all the clothes he had ordered from the Canteen. The first thing he did was try on the shoes. He was ready to play some ball. Since teams had been chosen before he got his shoes, he'd have to wait until Friday to play.

Once Jeremy started attending the classes and playing basketball, he started meeting people. Although he hadn't played basketball in almost five years, he was still in better shape than most of guys out there, and although he couldn't jump as high as most, he could run faster and longer than most anyone else.

Since they played full court, usually, that meant a lot of running back and forth, up and down the court. He was huffing and puffing the first few times, but after that he was as good or better than most anyone else out there. Once the guys saw that he could play ball, they accepted him into the group, and soon the guards were telling him,

"No talking in the halls, Thibodeaux! You keep it up and you'll lose privileges!"

On the nineteenth day after his arrest, or two days before his Preliminary Hearing, a guard called him out of his cell, right after lunch. It was a Monday.

"Oh, shit! I hope this isn't going to take too long. I'll miss basketball," he thought to himself.

He walked into a visitation room up at the front of the jail, near the booking area, and there was an attractive young woman with a medium build, and short, light brown hair, sitting down at the desk, looking at a file. She looked up once he was seated.

"Good afternoon, Mr. Thibodeaux. My name is Sarah Panther. I've been assigned to handle the hearing which is to take place on Wednesday."

"You're a lawyer?"

"Yes."

"Okay. Well, nice to meet you. Thanks for coming to see me."

"Now listen, the only reason for the hearing on Wednesday is to make sure that there is a reasonable basis to believe that you committed the crimes with which you are charged. Since you bought pills from an undercover cop and delivered pills to an undercover cop, there isn't much doubt about it. The hearing is really a waste of time, especially on the possession charge for those pills they found in your pants pocket while you were being booked."

"So why go through with it? Do we have to?"

"I'd like to hear what the Cowboy says happened when he talked you into delivering those pills to the Mexican."

"Your investigator told you all about that, right? I didn't want to do that and never would have done it, except for the fact that he…"

"He told you he'd take fifty dollars off the price of the pills you bought, right?"

"Yeah, that had something to do with it, but he said all I had to do was hand the package to this guy. The whole thing took less than a minute. The Mexican didn't give me a penny. He like forced me to do it. I didn't do it for the fifty dollars."

"That's one of the big questions in this case. It could be the difference between you being home and in prison."

"So do you think you can get me off on this or am I dead in the water?"

"You have a chance. There's a defense called entrapment, and it's possible that it might work in this case. It's your only chance, I think."

"What do you need to know from me?"

"You ever sell drugs to anyone before?"

"No."

"Ever been arrested before? I know you don't have any convictions, but no prior arrests either, right? In this state or any other state?"

"No."

"You didn't bring up this business of making a delivery, he did, right?"

"That's right."

"We have a chance, that's the most I'll say, but we're not going to win on Wednesday. All we're going to do is ask some questions of the Officer. We'll raise the issue at a later date."

"Any chance of getting my bond reduced?"

"Not likely, not with this Judge, but maybe down to $50,000. Could you make that?"

"Probably not. My wife and I definitely couldn't, but maybe we could get some help from family if they all pitched in. It's possible."

"Okay, we'll deal with that later. First, let's see what happens at the Preliminary Hearing. I'll see you in court on Wednesday."

"Will I be brought to court or just appear by way of a screen like the last time?"

"You'll be taken to court."

"Can my wife be there?"

"Yes, she can."

"Is that it?"

"That's it for now."

Jeremy stood, looked at the clock and saw that he still had fifteen minutes to be in his cell and ready for recreation period.

"Thank you, Miss Panther. Is that an Indian name?"

"You're welcome, and yes it is. My father is a full-blooded Osage."

"Nice to meet you."

Jeremy turned and hurried to get to his cell on time so that he could make it out to the basketball games.

Chapter Thirteen

On Wednesday morning, after breakfast, Jeremy was allowed to shower before being taken to a holding cell at the front of the jail, awaiting transport to the courthouse. He sat with seven other men who were to be in court that day, too. He recognized most of the men and exchanged greetings with them.

Some were being sentenced to prison and would soon be in the hands of the Department of Corrections. Others were scheduled for trial that day. Another had a hearing on whether or not he violated the terms of his probation when he was caught drinking beer in his home by a Probation Officer who paid him a surprise visit. The ones who would be in front of a jury had street clothes on. Jurors weren't supposed to know that they were in jail. The others, including Jeremy, were in jail garb. All were as nervous and apprehensive as he was.

Once the van arrived to take them, their feet were shackled and they were handcuffed. They were then led as a group to the van. At the courthouse they were led into a cell at the rear of the courthouse where they sat with the restraints still on them.

Jeremy sat and watched as the other six men were taken to court. Two of the men were back before a guard came to get him. When it was his turn, he was ushered down a long hallway and into a courtroom.

When he walked in, the first person he saw was his Public Defender, sitting at a table. Just past that, he saw Sally sitting in the first row. She was dressed up like she was going to church. Two men and a woman sat at the table next to the table where his lawyer was sitting. He recognized one of the men as "Cowboy," though he had a coat and tie on and didn't look much like the man he'd seen in the bar all those times. In the jury box, he saw an Hispanic looking man who he thought must have been the Mexican from the Wash 'n Go. To his right was the Judge, a different one from the time before, and some women sitting at desks in front of the Judge.

His lawyer motioned for him to sit next to her and he did. Once he was seated, the Judge began,

"Are we ready to proceed?"

Jeremy noticed that the sign plate in front of the Judge said, Frederick Frick. It was a different Judge from the only other time he'd been in court, which was for the First Appearance hearing.

"Yes, your Honor," Ms. Panther responded.

"Alright then. We're here on the case of the State of Florida versus Jeremy Thibodeaux, case number 38-2011-CF-000471, to conduct a Preliminary Hearing. Mr. Thibodeaux is represented by attorney Panther of the Public Defender's Office. The State is represented by Thomas Whistler. Is the State ready to proceed?"

A short, wiry young man, in a black suit and a red tie, with dark black glasses and black hair, stood and said,

"We are, your Honor."

"Call your first witness, Mr. Whistler."

"The State calls Officer Rodney Fowler."

The man Jeremy knew as "Cowboy" stood and walked to the witness stand. After being sworn, he sat down and looked over at the prosecutor.

"Please state your name."

"Rodney Fowler."

"How are you employed?"

"I'm a detective with the Levy County Sheriff's Office."

"How long have you been so employed?"

"I've been a deputy for ten years. I've been a detective for the last four."

"Directing your attention to March 14 of this year, did you have occasion to meet with an individual by the name of Jeremy Thibodeaux on that date?"

"I did."

"And was that the first time you met him?"

"No. I first met the Defendant several months prior to that. At first, I only knew him as Jeremy. Through investigation, I determined that his real name was Jeremy Thibodeaux."

"Do you see the person you know as Jeremy Thibodeaux in the courtroom today?"

"Yes, that's him right there, the Defendant," the deputy said, pointing at Jeremy.

"And how is it that you first came to meet Mr. Thibodeaux?"

"He was introduced to me by a confidential informant as a person who was a user of a controlled substance and as one who wanted to purchase pills from the informant."

"Objection, your Honor. That's hearsay."

"Over-ruled, Ms. Panther, but your objection is noted."

"Where did that meeting take place, the first meeting that is?"

"In a bar in Chiefland called the Lions Lair."

"And what was discussed at that first meeting?"

"I was actually a bystander in that meeting. The purpose of the meeting was to introduce me to Mr. Thibodeaux and people like him who were buying product from my confidential informant so that I could do whatever was necessary to arrest those individuals who were committing drug-related offenses here in Levy County."

"And what occurred on that first night you met Mr. Thibodeaux?"

"My confidential informant sold Mr. Thibodeaux a large amount of pills for $2000, as I recall."

"And what were those pills?"

"Objection. This man is not qualified to testify as to the contents in the pills."

"Judge, these aren't the pills that the Defendant is being charged with possessing and selling. This is background information." the prosecutor interjected.

"Over-ruled. You may answer, Deputy Fowler." the Judge said.

"RoxyContins, which is a category II controlled substance."

"And how is it that you personally know that the pills were RoxyContins?"

"Again, I was an observer, and those drugs weren't tested. I just know that's what the Defendant thought he was buying and that's what the informant was selling."

"And did that sale take place in your presence?"

"Well, the way it went down was the Defendant, Mr. Thibodeaux, who drives a 1999 Ford Ranger pick-up truck, gave the key to the truck to my confidential informant while we were playing pool. He just put the key on the table while no one was watching and we picked it up. Then, after the game was over, the confidential informant and I walked out to Mr. Thibodeaux's car, where an envelope with the $2000 in it was in the glove compartment. We took the money and left a package with the pills. We then returned to the bar, gave Mr. Thibodeaux the key to his truck back, and he left half an hour later, after drinking a beer or two with us."

"When was the next time you met Mr. Thibodeaux?"

"The next month, I was in the bar, which is a place where drugs are bought and sold frequently…"

"Objection, your Honor."

"Over-ruled. Ms. Panther, the Court understands the basis for your objection, which is well-founded, but I believe the testimony is relevant for this proceeding. You will have the opportunity to cross-examine and clear that up. There's no jury here to be prejudiced. You may continue, Deputy Fowler."

"As I was saying, I was in the bar, playing pool, when Mr. Thibodeaux walked in."

"Was your confidential informant present at that time as well?"

"No. That was the point of the first meeting, so that suspected criminals would deal directly with me."

"And did Mr. Thibodeaux deal directly with you?"

"Yes, he did, except I added a little twist to the deal."

"What did you do differently, Deputy?"

"I gave Mr. Thibodeaux a free sample of everything I sold him. I told him that it was because I wanted him to be sure that he saw what it was he was getting, but the real reason was that I wanted to keep some as evidence. I took one of each type of pill out of the package he bought and attached that to my report. My informant told me that Mr. Thibodeaux usually only bought the blue pills but, after a while, he started buying green pills, too. When I dealt with him, he bought large quantities of the blue and the green pills. In fact, one time I sold him about a hundred white pills, too."

And how much did Mr. Thibodeaux buy of each of these illegal substances on March 14 of this year, Deputy?"

"If I can refer to my report," the Deputy said as he opened the file he was holding in his hands and flipped a few pages.

"He bought about a hundred pills that night. Sixty of the Blues and forty of the greens."

"The Blues are the highest content of OxyCodone, aren't they?"

"Yes. They have 30 milligrams of OxyCodone in them. The technical name for them is RoxyContin, but on the street they're called "Roxy Blues.""

"And the greens?"

"They contain 15 milligrams of OxyCodone."

"When did you next see Mr. Thibodeaux?"

"About a month later, he came back in the bar again."

"Did he call to arrange a meeting or just show up?"

"He'd just show up. That's how it worked. I tried to make sure that I'd be there every Monday and he knew that. When he needed pills, he'd come find me."

"Did the same events transpire as the previous two times?"

"Yes. Exactly the same, except that might have been the night he bought those white pills. If it's important, I can check to see."

"That won't be necessary. And when did you see him after that?"

"It was a month after that."

"And are we now at the point in time where the drugs that are the basis for these charges were bought and sold?"

"No. This went on for a few more months."

"Every time, same thing?"

"Yes."

"And so we're now at March 14, 2011. What was bought and sold that night?"

"RoxyContins."

"And did a sale take place that night, Deputy?"

"Yes, it did, on March 14 of this year, a sale took place."

"Did that take place in your presence?"

"Yes. I sold the Defendant the drugs."

"In the same manner as you described with the previous several meetings?"

"Yes."

"And how much did Mr. Thibodeaux buy that night?"

"He bought a hundred and fifty pills that night. Over the several months I was supplying him with drugs he began to buy more and more pills. At first, it was like fifty or sixty, and then it became a hundred pills was a month, and it increased to a hundred and fifty pills there at the end."

"How were the pills broken up that night?"

"A hundred and twenty of the Blues and thirty of the greens."

"But he's not charged with any crime relating to any prior sales, is he, Deputy?"

"No."

"And why not?"

"We were in the middle of a drug investigation and we weren't quite ready to spring the trap. I was still meeting new people and finding more buyers. I didn't want to 'blow my cover,' so to speak."

"So what is the basis for the charge that the Defendant sold or delivered drugs that night, Deputy?"

"On this particular occasion, as the deal was going down, I asked Mr. Thibodeaux if he would deliver a package to someone in Cedar Key for me at the Wash 'n Go there on State Road 24 as you get into town."

"And what did Mr. Thibodeaux say?"

"At first, he hesitated, and then he agreed to do it when I told him I'd take $50 off his bill if he'd do that for me."

"Did you threaten him or tell him that if he didn't deliver the package something bad would happen?"

"No."

"Did he have to think about it for a while or did he willingly agree to deliver the package for you?"

"I didn't have to talk him into it. Once I told him I'd give him the $50 off he pretty much agreed to do it right away. I mean, the whole conversation didn't last two minutes."

"And did he know what was in the package?"

"Of course he knew."

"Objection. This Officer can't testify as to what Mr. Thibodeaux knew or didn't know."

"Did you tell him what was in the package, Deputy?" the Judge asked.

"I didn't specifically tell him exactly what drugs were in the package, or how much was in there, but I did tell him that it was the same thing he was getting."

"Why did you take $50 off the purchase price of the other drugs?" the Judge continued.

"I offered to give him the money because he hesitated a little. He knew what it was. He knew it was illegal. He was glad to save $50 bucks."

"Thank you, sir. You may continue, Mr. Whistler."

"So you told him, specifically, there are RoxyContin drugs in the package?" the prosecutor asked.

"Objection, your Honor."

"Over-ruled. Next question, Mr. Whistler."

"I didn't say it's OxyContin, or OxyCodone, or Roxy Blues. No, I didn't do that. I told him it was the same as he was getting, which was RoxyContin."

"And did all of the acts you have described occur within Levy County and the State of Florida?"

"Yes, they did."

"I have no more questions of this witness, your Honor."

"Cross-examination, Ms. Panther?"

"Yes, your Honor. Thank you."

Ms. Panther walked up to the podium and began,

"What is the name of the man you have referred to as your confidential informant?"

"His street name is Rawhide. That is the name Mr. Thibodeaux called him."

"And what is his real name?"

"I'd rather not reveal that at this time."

The prosecutor stood up and said,

"Your Honor, the State of Florida does not believe that the name of the confidential informant needs to be revealed. Furthermore, that informant is involved in a number of criminal investigations, some of which are ongoing. The CI was not present at any of the crimes with which this Defendant is charged. The law in the State of Florida, and the United States, is as found in the case of Roviaro versus the United States of America, 77 Supreme Court Reporter at page 623, the government isn't required to reveal that information."

"I don't believe that the name of the informant is critical to the issue to be decided today, Ms. Panther, which is whether or not there is a reasonable basis to believe that this Defendant committed the crimes with which he is charged. We can address that issue at a later time, should you care to do so. Next question."

"When did you first hear the name of Jeremy Thibodeaux?"

"When Rawhide, the confidential informant, told me about him."

'Prior to the date on which you first met Mr. Thibodeaux, after being introduced to him by Rawhide, had you ever heard his name in connection with any other criminal investigation?"

"No."

"Subsequent to meeting Mr. Thibodeaux, and after doing an investigation into his background, did you learn of any other criminal activities in which Mr. Thibodeaux may have been involved, other than the use of RoxyContin, or an OxyCodone derivative?"

"No."

"And have you heard from any source whatsoever, whether it is a confidential informant whose name you won't reveal or another law enforcement officer, that Mr. Thibodeaux was involved with the sale or distribution of a controlled substance prior to this March 14 event?"

"No."

"And he doesn't have a reputation for being a drug dealer, does he?"

"Not to my knowledge. He may have in some circles. I don't know, but I'm not aware of that."

"So why did you decide to ask Mr. Thibodeaux to deliver the pills to Deputy Gonzalez at the Wash 'n Go in Cedar Key?"

"I had made arrangements to have a few other criminals make deliveries to Deputy Gonzalez that day, so it was really something that I thought of at the last minute. I mean, I had the package there for another person, but that person didn't show up, so I decided to see if Mr. Thibodeaux would do it."

"So it wasn't the same drugs as what Mr. Thibodeaux allegedly bought from you that day, was it?"

"Yes, it was. It was the exact same drugs, just not the same quantities. The person who didn't show up was to have bought a whole lot more, that's all."

"He refused to do it at first, didn't he?"

"He didn't refuse, but he hesitated. I think that's more accurate."

"He didn't want to do it, did he?"

"I wouldn't say that. I mean, I guess it's fair to say he wasn't too sure about delivering some drugs to someone he didn't know. It is illegal. He knew that."

"So why did he do it, Deputy?"

"He agreed to do it when I said I'd take $50 off of his bill."

"You didn't threaten him or make it sound like you'd be angry if he didn't do what you were asking him to do?"

"I didn't threaten him."

"He's a kid, right? Twenty two? How old are you, Deputy?"

"I'm thirty five."

"And he's what, 5'8" tall?"

"About that, I guess."

"And how tall are you?"

"I'm 6'3"."

"And you don't think you intimidated him into doing this for you?"

"No, I don't. He agreed to do it, plain and simple."

"And you didn't say anything about how inconvenient it would be for you to drive over there, and how easy it would be for him to just drop it off for you….nothing like that, right?"

"I might have said something like that, but he could have said no. He didn't."

"Now you've charged him with sale and delivery of a controlled substance, correct?"

"Actually, I filed a report and, based upon the report an arrest warrant was issued. So you could say that I had him arrested for sale and delivery of a controlled substance, but the State Attorney's Office formally files the charges, not me, plus he's charged with possession, too, and I had nothing to do with that."

"Okay, Deputy. That's true, but you had him arrested for sale and delivery of a controlled substance, correct? He was arrested because of your activities and your report, right?"

"Yes, that's right."

"But he didn't actually sell the pills, did he? You created that situation, didn't you?

"I set the trap. I think that's a fair statement, and I caught him."

You set up the crime, didn't you?"

"I gave Mr. Thibodeaux an opportunity to commit a crime and he took it. He didn't have to. He knew it was wrong. He broke the law."

"He delivered the controlled substance, right? You set up the supposed 'sale,' not him, right? He didn't have any idea who Deputy Gonzalez was, did he?"

The prosecutor rose from his chair and said, "You've asked several questions there, Counselor. Which one do you want him to answer?"

"Please re-phrase the question, Ms. Panther." Judge Frick said.

"Deputy Gonzalez had no idea who Jeremy Thibodeaux was, did he? To your knowledge, that is."

"Not to my knowledge. You can ask him. He's sitting outside the courtroom right now."

"I intend to, but I asked you that question."

"Not to my knowledge, no ma'am."

"And Mr. Thibodeaux didn't know Deputy Gonzalez, did he?"

"Not to my knowledge."

"And Mr. Thibodeaux never talked to the Deputy to arrange a price or how much was to be bought or where the deal was to go down, or any of that, did he?"

"No ma'am. I took care of all of that."

"And Mr. Thibodeaux didn't receive any money from Deputy Gonzalez, did he?"

"No ma'am."

"So what Mr. Thibodeaux did was 'hand' a package to an undercover officer, at your bidding, correct?"

"That is still a 'sale,' Counselor. Mr. Thibodeaux committed the crime of selling a controlled substance when he delivered that package to Deputy Gonzalez, in my opinion. That's why I charged him with that crime."

"But it was your idea, not his, to deliver an illegal substance to an undercover police officer, wasn't it?"

"I provided him with an opportunity to commit a crime, as I previously testified. He took it."

"A crime of "sale and delivery" of a controlled substance by Mr. Thibodeaux to Deputy Gonzalez would never have been committed on the 14th day of March, 2011, if you didn't ASK the Defendant to deliver a package to Cedar Key for you, would it?"

The prosecutor stood up again and said,

"Your Honor, at this point I am going to object. We are going far afield from what is at issue here today. Ms. Panther is trying to suggest that Mr. Thibodeaux was entrapped into committing this crime, but the point is a crime was committed that day. Whether or not the defense of entrapment exists, which appears fairly obvious it does not, is an entirely different issue."

"I agree with you, Mr. Whistler. Entrapment is a defense and that is not an issue I will rule upon today, but I am going to allow Ms. Panther a little more latitude here this morning. Not too much more, Ms. Panther, because Mr. Whistler' point is well-made. You may answer the question, Deputy."

"If I didn't ask Mr. Thibodeaux to make a delivery he wouldn't have made a delivery that day? The answer is pretty obvious. Of course not."

"So Mr. Thibodeaux wasn't PRE-disposed to commit the crime, was he?"

"I can't answer that question. It didn't take too much time for him to agree to do it. I'd say he was pre-disposed to commit the crime. He was ready and willing, in my opinion."

"So you don't see any problem with you, a law enforcement officer with ten years of experience, going out and inducing an unwary citizen into committing a crime which he was otherwise not inclined to commit?"

"Objection!"

"I will sustain that objection. You are getting into your argument there, Ms. Panther. Next question."

"So how much was the drug transaction involving Deputy Gonzalez going to be for?"

"Well, we really didn't set a price. I mean, it was, after all, just a trap that we set up."

"A trap for an unwary individual, wasn't it."

"Objection!"

"Sustained. Be careful, Ms. Panther. You're treading on thin ice now. Next question."

"And you don't see anything wrong with a law enforcement officer paying a citizen money to commit a crime?"

"Alright! That's enough," Judge Frick interjected. "I'm not going to allow any more questions along that line, Ms. Panther. Do you have any questions concerning the issue of whether or not there are reasonable grounds to believe that Mr. Thibodeaux committed the crimes for which he has been arrested? I allowed you much latitude because I thought you were trying to make a point with regard to the Sales and Delivery charge, which you did, but I've heard enough of that. Is there anything else you'd like to ask?"

"No, your Honor. I don't have any other questions. Thank you for allowing me the latitude you did."

"Any re-direct?"

"No, your Honor."

"Before you call your next witness, I have a question of the Officer."

The Judge turned to the Deputy and asked, "Officer, you are familiar with the portion of the statute that makes it a crime to purchase controlled substances, are you not?"

"I am, your Honor."

"So why, if I might ask, haven't you charged Mr. Thibodeaux with a crime on the occasions when he bought those pills from you as you testified?"

The Deputy squirmed in his chair and said, "Due to lack of evidence, your Honor."

"But didn't I hear you testify that you kept a sample from every drug transaction with Mr. Thibodeaux?"

"That's correct, your Honor, I did."

"So what happened to the evidence?"

The Officer cleared his throat and said, "The evidence has been misplaced and can't be located, sir."

The Judge turned back to the two attorneys and said, "Next witness."

"The State calls Deputy Gonzalez."

The deputy testified that he did not know Mr. Thibodeax and that he had never heard of him before. He also admitted on cross-examination that the delivery took no more than a few minutes and no words were exchanged other than "The Cowboy sent me," or something like that.

The State then called the guard who found the pill in Jeremy's pants pocket. After that they called a chemist to testify.

"Please state your name."

"Thomas Crow Cherner."

"And how are you employed?"

"I am an employee of the State of Florida and my job is to conduct experiments upon various substances, as in this case, to determine what the substance is."

"And what qualification do you have which would allow you to do so?"

"I have a degree in chemistry from the University of Florida and I have been employed by the State of Florida for over twenty years, doing this type of work."

"And have you been declared an expert witness in various courts throughout the State of Florida?"

"Thousands of times."

"We would stipulate that he is an expert, your Honor." Ms. Panther said.

The chemist went on to testify that the substances found in the package delivered to Deputy Gonzalez were OxyCodone derivatives, as were the pills taken from Jeremy at the time he was booked into jail. On cross-examination, Ms. Panther asked the witness to explain what RoxyContin is and the differences between the various colored pills.

"OxyContin is the brand name for a time-release formula of OxyCodone. OxyContin is available in blue tablets, that are 5 milligrams; white tablets, that are 10 milligram; gray tablets, which are 15 milligram; pink tablets, which are 20 milligrams; brown tablets, which are 30 milligram tablets; yellow tablets, which are 40 milligrams; red tablets, which are 60 milligrams; and greenish-blue tablets, which are 80 milligrams. Actually, there is a 160 milligram tablet, too, and that is available in other countries, but no longer in the U.S. It was considered too dangerous."

"So what is RoxyContin?"

"The difference between the two is that RoxyContin is a fast-acting pill that has an immediate effect, not like the OxyContin, which is a time-released tablet that operates over the course of a few hours."

"So what is the product we are involved with in this case?"

"RoxyContin."

"And how many of those products are there?"

"There are three RoxyContin pills available, and those are in white tablets, which have 5 milligrams of OxyCodone in them; green tablets, which have 15 milligrams of OxyCodone; and the blue tablets, which have 30 milligrams of OxyCodone in them."

"Have you heard the term Roxy Blues?"

"I have. I have also heard the term 'hillbilly heroin.' They both refer to RoxyContin and its derivates. A Roxy Blue is the blue tablet that has 30 milligrams of OxyCodone in it and it has an immediate effect."

"And it has a very serious potential for chemical dependence by those who use it. Isn't that right?"

"That is correct."

"If you would, please tell the court what the potential side-effects are for a person who uses a RoxyContin product?"

"Your Honor, I object. This has nothing to do with what is at issue today."

"I agree with you, Mr. Whistler, but I'd like to hear the answer to that question. I see so many of these cases. You may answer, sir."

"The clinically reported side effects include euphoria, memory loss, constipation, fatigue, dizziness, nausea, lightheadedness, headache, dry mouth, anxiety, pruritus, diaphoresis, dimness of vision, loss of appetite, nervousness, abdominal pain, diarrhea, ischuria, dyspnea and hiccups."

"And what are the withdrawal related side effects?"

"Your Honor…"

"Last question, Ms. Panther. You may answer."

"Anxiety, nausea, insomnia, muscle pain, muscle weakness, fevers and other flu like symptoms."

"No further questions, your Honor."

"Any further witnesses, Mr. Whistler?"

"No, your Honor."

"Do you wish to call any witnesses, Ms. Panther?"

"No, your Honor."

"Do either of you care to make an argument?"

"The State would say only that the evidence is more than adequate to bind the Defendant over for further prosecution."

"And Ms. Panther, do you wish to make an argument? If so, I don't want to hear any argument about entrapment at this time."

"No, your Honor. I have no argument on the possession charge and I'll reserve argument on that entrapment issue for a later day. I would suggest to the Court that the evidence on the issue of the Sales and Delivery charge is really such that it should only be a simple possession charge. All he did was take a sealed package, which supposedly had pills in it, and hand it to Deputy Gonzalez. That's not a sale."

"But it was a delivery, wasn't it, Ms. Panther? You don't need to answer that. I find that there is an adequate basis to believe that Mr. Thibodeaux has committed the crimes for which he has been arrested and that his continued confinement is justified. Anything further, Counsel?"

"Not from the State, your Honor."

"The defense would ask the Court to consider the issue of the amount of the bond."

"File the appropriate motion, Ms. Panther. I will not do so this morning. This case lasted longer than I expected it to. I have other cases to be heard before noon and I have to move on. Call the next case, please, Madame Clerk."

Jeremy and Ms. Panther stood as the clerk called out the next case.

"I'll be over to see you in a few days," Ms. Panther said.

"Can I talk to my wife for a minute?"

"No, not here. Sorry."

A guard came and began to escort Jeremy, who still had the leg irons on his feet and the handcuffs on his wrists, out of the courtroom. He looked over at Sally and asked, in a loud whisper, "Are you coming to see me today? " He saw her shaking her head up and down as he was led out of the courtroom.

Chapter Fourteen

ⵌⵌⵌⵌⵌⵌⵌⵌⵌⵌⵌⵌⵌⵌⵌⵌⵌ ᵢⵌᵢ ⵌⵌⵌⵌⵌⵌⵌⵌⵌⵌⵌⵌⵌⵌⵌⵌⵌ

Since it was a Wednesday, Sally was able to visit and she was there at exactly 1:00, the first visitor of the day.

"So that's what happened! Damn, Jeremy! You got set up!"

"Yeah. And that explains why I feel so sick all the time. It's been three weeks and I'm not right yet. I didn't know any of that stuff that chemist was talking about."

"You're getting better though. I can tell."

"Yeah? I don't feel any better."

"You look better, baby."

"You've got to be kidding. You're just saying that to try to cheer me up."

"You're right! Is it working?"

"No, but Sally," Jeremy whispered, you're not still doin' that shit, are you? After what's happened to me?"

"I still have pains every now and again and I have a few of those pills left."

"After what you just heard you ought to throw them away."

"Listen to you! You were the one that got me started on those things!"

"I know, but things are different now."

"I'll stop when I run out. So what happens next?"

"I don't know. My lawyer said she'd be over to see me in a few days."

They spent most of their time talking about Samantha and how she was doing, and about work, the weather, clamming and all of the normal, everyday things Jeremy wanted to find out about, since he couldn't be there. When their visit was up, Sally said,

"Say Jeremy. I took off the whole day today, so I'm going to have to work extra tomorrow. I won't be able to see you until Saturday. Take good care of yourself. See you then. Love you."

"I love you, too, babe."

Jeremy had settled into a rhythm at the jail. He knew what he would be doing at every hour of the day, whether he wanted to or not. He had started with the AA program and was nearing completion of the Parenting class. He had adjusted to life in jail and grew to dislike any changes to that rhythm, like when men came and went and new people had to be broken in to the system.

He wasn't having any problems in the jail. He kept to himself and minded his own business. He saw a lot of arguments and fights, though, and the guards were constantly coming into the cell at all hours of the day and night to break up the fights or other disturbances. A lot of times men would jaw at each other but nothing ever came of it, but that was enough to get the guards in. If something wasn't going on in his cell it would be in another of the cells on his wing of the jail, but he minded his own business and was never involved in any of the fights.

On Monday of the following week, while he was cleaning toilets, Ms. Panther came to visit.

"Glad to see you. I was busy on the bathroom detail. You saved me from that."

"Glad to be of assistance. This won't take long, but I wanted to let you know that I will file a motion to reduce your bond and I will file a motion at the appropriate time to try to get that Sales and Delivery charge thrown out."

"You can't do anything about the possession charge, can you?"

"Not that I can think of. They pretty much have you on that one I'm afraid. You had pills in your pocket. What am I going to do with that? That's called simple possession of a controlled substance."

"No illegal arrest issue? No search and seizure argument? No nothing?"

"Not that I can think of."

"So what am I looking at?"

"If it was just the possession charge, I'd have you out of here in no time. You'd be put on probation for a few years and required to go to drug treatment, but you'd probably already be on the street. The Sales and Delivery charge is the problem. They like to see a man do a little time in prison for those cases. There's a minimum mandatory three years in prison for the amount of pills you delivered."

"Three years? But I had no idea how much was in that package."

"That's true, and we can argue that, too, but I'm just saying you're not looking at fifteen years, which is the maximum on that charge, or anything close to that. How old are you?"

"Twenty two."

"Since you are so young you'd be in a youthful offender prison, and those aren't near as bad as the others."

"But I don't want to go to prison at all."

"I know that, and I think we have a good chance with this Judge on the entrapment issue. He's a hard man, but I think the fact that this drug is so addictive makes a difference to him, like they took advantage of your weakness to make this case. I could be wrong, but I think we've got a good shot at it."

"So when will that happen?"

"It'll probably be a month or two before we get it heard. I'm having the hearing transcribed now, and that takes some time, and there are some other things that will take place first, but I'll get it set for hearing as quickly as I can."

"A month or two? That's the best you can do? "

"Maybe a little sooner. We'll see. I'm awfully busy and I've got some trials coming up between now and then. I'll do the best I can, but I can't do anything until that transcript is typed up. The expense has to be approved, and there's a whole procedure involved with that in our office which takes time, and then it takes time for the Court Reporter to do the work. There's not much I can do to shorten it, I'm afraid."

"Thanks, Ms. Panther. I think you did a great job for me last week."

"At least that Officer told the truth, didn't he?"

"Pretty much. It was about like he said."

"That's not always the case, so you were lucky with that. Alright, I have ten other people to see here this morning. Sorry, but I've got to send you back."

"To toilet detail?"

"Sorry, Mr. Thibodeaux."

They stood, shook hands, and he turned and walked out to where a guard was ready to escort him back. He was lucky, the guard put him back in his cell.

Meanwhile, on the home front, Sally became concerned as her supply of pills began to dwindle. When she had less than a dozen, she made a call to Dr. Malpartido's office and scheduled an appointment. When she met with him, she told the doctor,

"My low back has been killing me lately. I can't sit at my desk for more than an hour or two and I can hardly hold my child in my arms anymore. She's getting too heavy for me."

"Well she is almost three years old, isn't she? She must weigh about forty pounds by now, doesn't she?"

"About that, but my back hurts when I lift much of anything. I could do things before I was hurt that I can't do now."

"Get on the table and let's see what's going on."

The doctor had Sally do straight leg raises, and he lifted one leg and then the other. She made noises as if it caused her pain as he did so.

"That hurts when I do that?"

"Yes, it does."

"Tell me when you feel pain. I don't want to hurt you. I'm just trying to figure out what exercises and movements cause you pain."

He went through a series of movements, palpated her low back, and, after ten minutes said,

"Alright, that's enough."

"What do you think, Doctor?"

"I'm not sure, Sally. Did you do anything to hurt yourself recently?"

"You mean other than when I picked up Samantha or carried a package that was too heavy for me, like I told you?"

"But no trauma or a car accident or anything like that?"

"No."

You may have done something to cause a slight sprain/strain, or maybe it's a little residual from the incident at Kringle, but it's nothing too significant."

"Well, I'm glad to hear it, but I'm still in pain."

"Here's a sheet with some exercises for your low back that I want you to start doing on a daily basis, okay?"

"Okay," Sally said, as she looked over the sheet. "I can do these. No problem."

"And do you have a place where you can get into a whirlpool every now and then?"

"Yeah. A friend of mine is the manager at the Old Fenimore Condominiums. They have a whirlpool next to their pool. She'll let me get in whenever I want."

"And do you have any more of those pills I prescribed for you the last time?"

"No, I ran out of them a while ago," she replied.

He looked at her curiously, wondering to himself if there was anything else going on. He suspected that, perhaps, some chemical dependency had developed with her, too. He knew about what had happened to Jeremy.

"How's Jeremy doing these days?"

"He's waiting for trial. He was set-up by some undercover police Officers and they tricked him into doing something he never would have done."

"That RoxyContin is a very dangerous drug, Sally. I don't want to see you develop any problems with it."

"It helped me, Doctor, like nothing else I've ever experienced before."

He thought about what he should do for a few seconds and then said,

"Alright. Here's what I'll do. I'm going to prescribe some RoxyContin for your pain, but it will be in a smaller dose than before. I'll want to see you back here in two weeks to see how you're doing. If you stop having any pain, and you stop taking the pills, call me and we'll cancel the appointment. Otherwise, I'll see you in two weeks, okay? I'm only going to give you a two-week supply."

"Whatever you say, Doctor."

"And Sally, please, unless the pain is really something you can't tolerate, don't take the pills. They are dangerous and can be habit-forming."

"I understand, Doctor. I'll do as you say."

Sally had the prescription filled and was disappointed to see that she was given the white pills that were, as she knew full well, not even half as strong as the greens. She also didn't like the fact that she'd only been given a fourteen day supply.

After nearly a month of visiting at least four to five times a week, Sally stopped going to see Jeremy as regularly. It slowed down to three days a week, usually Tuesdays, Thursdays and Saturdays. They were running out of things to talk about other than Samantha and the bills.

"It's hard for me to pay the bills, Jeremy, on only one income. My parents are helpin' out but they've got their own problems. They don't have much to spare."

"There's nothin' I can do to help while I'm in here, baby."

"When are you getting' out anyway?"

"If I can get out, it could be within the next month or two, if we can win a motion that she's going to file to try to get the charges dismissed. If not, I might be goin' to prison for a couple of years. That's what my lawyer told me."

"Nothing has changed since the hearing then?"

"No."

"This is hard on me, Jeremy. I miss you so much."

"Me, too, Sally."

Sally was tired of sitting at home with Samantha and watching television and movies. She started going to church on a regular basis, including Wednesday services, just so she could see people. At work, there weren't but a few people there in the office, and she didn't really have too many friends. Her whole life was Jeremy and Samantha, and now Jeremy wasn't around anymore.

After two months of Jeremy being in jail, she started going to Coconuts on Tuesday nights for the karaoke, just to get out of the house and see some people. She sang in the church choir and wasn't afraid to get up and sing a song or two. She told herself it was the best thing to do to have a little fun while Jeremy was in jail.

She'd go with some of her girlfriends from high school who were still around town. Most of them were waitressing at the Island Place, the Island Room, the Big Deck, Tony's Seafood Restaurant, Kona Joe's Island Café, Cook's Café, Seabreeze, the Pickled Pepper, or in the restaurants in Chiefland. Some of them were still in school at Central Florida Community College, which had a satellite campus in Chiefland. A couple of the women were attending Santa Fe Community College in Gainesville.

People from Cedar Key usually stayed in Cedar Key. There aren't that many of them, 850 as of the 2010 census, but they've been in the area for generations, like the Thibodeauxs and the Richards families. They said that once you got the "mud" in your feet, it got under your skin and you couldn't leave. And it was true…on a low tide, a person could very easily get stuck in the mud of Cedar Key and have trouble getting out.

Guys who didn't know her would hit on her. She liked flirting with them. It was nothing serious, but it wasn't anything she told Jeremy about. What he didn't know wouldn't hurt her.

Sally still had some pills left behind by Jeremy after he got arrested, plus she had the prescription for pills from Dr. Malpartido, but she had started to use a white or a green during the day, and one of the blue pills at night. She was taking more pills but her supply was dwindling. Before too long she'd be completely out of pills and she knew Dr. Malpartido would eventually stop giving her a prescription. She knew that she'd have to find a way to get more pills before too long.

When she went back to see Dr. Malpartido, she told him that she was still having the occasional pain and needed more pills. He gave her another prescription, but when he did, he told her,

"I'm giving you one last prescription, Sally. It should be enough to help you deal with the pain and discomfort you are experiencing. Again, if the pain isn't so bad that you can't stand it, don't take these pills. If you stop taking the pills, do it. If I see you again and you still want pills, I'm going to send you to a counselor. I don't want to see you end up where Jeremy is. I'm serious about this, Sally."

"I understand, Doctor. Thank you."

"Are you doing all the exercises I told you to do?"

"Every day."

"And those aren't helping any?"

"They help. I'm getting better. It just takes time, I guess."

"Keep doing your exercises."

"Okay."

"And the whirlpool?"

"I am doing that most every day, weather permitting. Samantha enjoys it when we go there. We swim, too."

"I could send you to a massage therapist, if you want, but that costs money and you'll have to pay the deductible and the co-pay. Do you want me to do that?"

"Not now. It's hard on me being a single parent. Besides, I can't afford the gas and the co-pay on one income right now."

"Okay, Sally. I'll see you in two weeks, though I hope you get better before then and don't need to see me. If you're feeling well, just call and cancel."

Sally had the prescription filled right away and saw that the doctor had given her another prescription for white pills. She wasn't surprised, and was glad to have them. They gave her a little bit of a kick to the Blues at night and there were days when she needed them to help her make it through the day.

Sally had learned the difference between the three pills and the effect which each had. Her body wanted the Blues most of all, but she saved them for special nights. Just like what had happened to Jeremy, she gradually started to crave more of the pills, just as he had done in order to get the "high" that she needed.

She'd been using them for several months now but wasn't concerned about the changes that were occurring in her life. She didn't mind the occasional dizziness, constipation or nervousness and didn't associate it with the use of pills, or didn't mind it enough to change her habits. She hadn't had to find pills on her own yet, but that was about to change. She would soon run out of her stash and Dr. Malpartido wasn't going to give her any more.

The next Tuesday night, when one of the guys from out of town who had been hitting on her for a couple of weeks came up to talk to her, she asked him if he knew anywhere that she could get some pills for the pain she had in her low back. The guy smiled, knowingly, showing a front tooth with gold, and said,

"Yeah. I think I know where I might find somethin' to help you out, but you'll have to come by my house to get it. I don't like to do business in public. I don't like carrying things in cars…too easy for the wrong people to find things."

"Great. When can I get some?"

'How soon you needing to get something?"

"Within the next few weeks."

"That can be arranged. Here, I'll give you my telephone number. Give me a call and I'll give you directions. How's that?"

The man wrote down his telephone number on a napkin from the bar and handed it to her.

"What's your name anyway?" Sally asked.

"Just call me Slim."

"Okay, Slim. I'm Sally. I'll be calling."

Sally stood and started to leave.

"Where you goin'? You don't have to run off now, do you? It's not past your bed-time, is it?"

"I've got a daughter to pick up. Gotta go."

"Okay, Sweetheart. I'll be lookin' forward to hearin' from you."

Slim wasn't in the bar on either of the following two Tuesdays, and Sally was about tapped out, so on the following day, she found the napkin with his phone number on it and made a call to Slim. He gave her directions to his house and they made plans to meet.

"You live all the way over in Williston? That's an hour away!"

"If you want what I got, that's where you gotta come, girl."

"I don't get off work until 4:00 today."

"I've gotta be someplace by 6:30 so if you're here by 5:30, no later, then I'll fix you up. Otherwise, we'll just have to do it on another day, that's all."

"I'll be there today."

Sally told her mother-in-law that she had to run to Chiefland to see Dr. Malpartido and dropped Samantha off with her. She made it to Williston by 5:30 and purchased a week's supply of the Blues. That was all she could afford. Slim offered her something to drink, but she declined.

"See you at Coconuts on Tuesday night?" she asked.

"Yeah, I think I'll be there."

The following Tuesday, Sally went to karaoke night at Coconuts, and Slim was there. She sized him up and told herself that he wasn't a bad looking guy, and that gold tooth was kind of cool looking, though she wasn't interested in him. She was in love with Jeremy. He wore blue jeans, a t-shirt and a baseball cap, just like most everybody else in the bar, and he had a mustache and goatee, but most everybody else had some kind of facial hair, too. He didn't have any tattoos, or at least none that she could see, and he talked nicely to her. He wasn't rude or vulgar. They played a few games of pool together and she was home by 8:00. What was the harm in that?

By the third month after Jeremy's arrest, Sally found her eyes wandering and her mind started playing tricks with her. There had never been anyone else besides Jeremy in her life, but now Jeremy wasn't in her life. He was in jail. She tried her best to keep those impure thoughts of sexual pleasures from coming into her head, but she couldn't help it. She'd have dreams about it. She didn't want to have those dreams, and there were men other than Jeremy in her dreams. She didn't want that, but she was a young woman and those kind of thoughts were only natural, she told herself. Everybody must have those same thoughts and those needs. It was normal, she told herself. She hadn't done anything wrong, yet, but seeds of discontent had been sewn.

Her father, who saw her every day at work and knew that she was going downtown after work every so often, because the men who worked for him told him all about it, became a little concerned after several weeks of late Tuesday nights and her being late to work on Wednesday mornings. One day he asked her,

"What's going on down there that you're so interested in?"

"Just singing with some friends and getting out of the house once a week, that's all, Dad," she told him.

One week, none of her friends could make it, but Sally went on her own. She felt safe there. She knew the owners and the barmaids. Nothing bad was going to happen.

A week later, when she ran out of pills, she called Slim and bought more. This time she bought a two week supply, which was more than she could afford, but it had become a necessary expense. She couldn't go a day without them.

"What kind of work do you do?" she asked.

"I'm in sales."

"How often are you in Cedar Key?"

"Just on Tuesday nights, usually, but I'll come over on a Saturday night every now and then if there's a good band playing."

"Where else do you go?"

"Oh, all over Levy and Marion counties, and I get over to Citrus, too. I like Dunellon, Ocala and Crystal River. I don't go much further than that."

"Where do you usually go on Saturday nights to have fun?"

"There's a nice little bar in Ocala that usually has a country band. I like to get up and dance every now and then, and they have some pool tables in the back. Think you might want to go there sometime?"

"Maybe. I can't go out in Cedar Key, or even Chiefland. Everybody knows me. I just can't do that, not with Jeremy bein' in jail and all."

"Well, anytime you want to go have some fun, and want some company, just let me know."

"I just might take you up on that," she said.

Chapter Fifteen

When she visited Jeremy the next day, she asked, "What's the latest? When are we going to know something? I can't go on like this, Jeremy. It's driving me crazy. I miss you so much!"

"Me, too, baby. I miss you two so much, too, but there's nothing I can do."

"What about that bond reduction? What happened with that?"

"My lawyer filed the motion but the Judge would only lower it to $50,000. We can't make that."

"Why is it still so high?"

"The State argued that Cowboy and the Mexican are still making arrests and that if I got out I could ruin things for them."

"But I saw them in court. I could identify them if I saw them," Sally said.

"They look different when they go into a bar. I almost didn't recognize Cowboy in court that day. He was all cleaned up. Gonzalez looked like any ordinary Mexican you see walkin' down the street. I'm not sure that I could recognize him if I saw him again. Anyway, the Judge wouldn't lower it any more than that."

"So what about that entrapment deal? What's up with that?"

"My attorney filed a motion to dismiss the case and there's a hearing set for next month."

"Next month!"

"That's the earliest time she could get."

"I don't know if I can make it through another month of this, baby. It's killing me."

"Killing you? I'm the one in jail, Sally, not you."

"It's hard out here without you, Jeremy. I don't know how to act without you around. We've been together so long, you're the only man I know."

"I'm sorry about all this, Sally. I really am. I wish it had never happened."

"How are you doing in here anyway, Jeremy? Are you over all that drug stuff? All the shakes and things?

"Yeah. It took a while, but I think it's out of my system. Now I just feel like shit because of being in here, but it's not the effects of the drugs that are causing the trouble any more, or at least I don't think so."

"That's good. I'm glad to hear that. So will you get out if you win that motion to have the case dismissed?"

"No, that will just get rid of that Sales and Delivery charge. I'll still have the other charge against me for having pills in my pocket when they arrested me, but my lawyer says I should get out on probation pretty easily on it, so if we win that motion to dismiss she says I could be out not long after that."

"God, I hope you win that motion, Jeremy."

"Me, too."

"If you don't you could be going away for a few years. This isn't fair to me and Samantha. We're gonna be punished, too."

"I know that. We gotta wait and see what happens. My lawyer says we've got a good chance of winning."

Sally started to cry.

"What's wrong, baby? Did something happen you're not telling me about?"

"No, I just miss you, that's all."

"Don't cry, baby. It makes it all that much harder for me bein' in here and not bein' able to do anything about it."

"I gotta go, Jeremy. I love you."

Sally stood and rushed out of the cubicle. Jeremy went back to his cell and stared at the same page of the book he was reading for the next fifteen minutes. He tried not to think about what was going on in Sally's life. He had to be patient and hope for the best. If he got too anxious about things, time went even more slowly and he worried too much. If he just kept his mind on whatever it was that he was doing, time went by faster.

He'd read all of the Louis L'Amour books that the library had. He had started to read Zane Grey books. He read Riders of the Purple Sage first and was hooked. He made a list of all the places he'd read about and his dream was to take a trip out West to see some of those places, even though he'd never been out of the state of Florida before. There were dozens of Zane Grey's books available to him.

After Sally left, he began to worry more about her and what was going on with her and Samantha. He had been worried about what was going to happen to him and hadn't really given too much thought to what it was like for Sally. The thought of Sally going out and finding another man never entered his mind, until now, and that began to eat at him like nothing else before, not even the threat of prison.

Jeremy immediately put in a note to have his attorney come see him. A few days later, Ms. Panther came to see him. When she did, he asked her,

"How much longer is it gonna be before that motion is going to be heard?"

"Why? What's going on?"

"I'm afraid my wife is getting tired of being alone. I'm thinking she may be ready to start looking around for somebody else."

"Jeremy, there isn't much I can do to hurry this thing along. I'll see if I can't get this thing heard any sooner, but that's only going to happen if a cancellation comes up on the Judge's calendar. I was supposed to have a week-long trial in front of this Judge, but the Defendant decided to change his plea and take the deal the State was offering him, so I know that some time has freed up on his calendar. I'll see what I can do."

A few days later, Jeremy received a notice in the mail informing him that a hearing on his case would be re-scheduled to the following Friday.

Sally didn't show up again until Sunday afternoon. He was afraid she wasn't going to come at all. They didn't have much to talk about and she left before the time was up. It was obvious that she was going through some changes, he just didn't know what they were.

He was sure she was still taking the pills, though she denied it. He could see changes in the way she looked and talked. He tried to warn her, but she wouldn't listen. He prayed that she hadn't become as dependent on the pills as he had been before he was arrested. He wondered to himself if his uncle and his mother noticed a change in his behavior back then, before he got arrested. If they had, nobody had said anything to him. He wouldn't have listened anyway. He knew that Sally wouldn't listen to him, either, and it made her mad when he tried to talk to her about it.

The hearing was scheduled for the following Friday afternoon, which displeased Jeremy since it meant that he'd miss basketball. He had established himself as one of the stars of the league and he enjoyed that notoriety amongst the other inmates, but this was clearly more important, much more important. Sally said she'd try to make it, but Jeremy wasn't too sure that she'd be there. After lunch, while the rest of his cell went out for recreation, he sat waiting to be transported to the courthouse.

When he was led into the courtroom, he was happy to see Sally sitting in the front row. The Assistant State Attorney was there, with two other people from the State Attorney's Office, plus two clerks and a court reporter, plus a bailiff and two deputy sheriffs, who were there to make sure Jeremy didn't try to escape. Jeremy had the leg irons on and the handcuffs, as before, and he wondered how in the world he could ever manage to escape with those things on.

Everyone sat waiting until another deputy sheriff opened the door to the back of the courtroom and said,

"All rise. The Circuit Court of the Eighth Judicial Circuit in and for Levy County, Florida is now in session, Judge Frederick Frick presiding."

Once Judge Frick sat down, the bailiff said,

"You may be seated."

The Judge then opened the file which lay on the table in front of him and said,

"Alright. We're here this afternoon on Defendant's motion to dismiss the charge of sale and delivery of a controlled substance, pursuant to Rule 3.190 (c)(4). So you are saying that there are no material facts in dispute and the undisputed material facts are such that your client is entitled to have the charge that he sold or delivered a controlled substance to an undercover Police Officer dismissed because the Officer 'entrapped' him, as a matter of law. Is that correct, Ms. Panther?"

"That's right, your Honor."

"What do have to say about that, Mr. Whistler?"

"Well, obviously the State disagrees with that position, your Honor, and…"

"Are the facts as Ms. Panther has presented them in her motion undisputed?"

"I think she has accurately quoted from the testimony this Court heard at the preliminary hearing conducted in this matter, your Honor. We disagree with the conclusions she draws from that testimony."

"I remember this case…this is the one where the delivery took place at a Laundromat in Cedar Key, right?"

"That's correct, Judge," Ms. Panther said.

"And the Defendant, who had purchased some form of RoxyContin, was paid some money by the first undercover Officer to deliver the drugs to the second undercover Officer, or had money taken off his bill. Is that this case?"

"That's right, your Honor," Mr. Whistler replied.

"Okay, we don't need to take any testimony here today, do we?"

"No, your Honor," both attorneys responded.

"So I've read your motion, why should I grant it, Ms. Panther?"

"On the basis of the case of the State of Florida versus Munoz, your Honor. It is a case out of Florida's Supreme Court, cited at 629 Southern 2d, page 90, and it says that the case should be dismissed if either one of two things happened, those being, number one, if this Court finds the conduct of the police was so outrageous this Court could bar the State from obtaining a conviction under the circumstances, and…"

"You're not suggesting that the conduct of the undercover Officer, called "Cowboy" as I recall, was outrageous in this case, are you, Ms. Panther? What did he do other than ask the Defendant to deliver illegal drugs to another Officer? You don't think I would be outraged because Cowboy reduced the bill which your client paid to buy drugs in order to catch your client in the act of committing a crime, do you?"

"Judge, I don't think it's too far off the holding in the State versus Glosson case, found at 462 Southern 2d, page 1082, another Supreme Court case. In the Glosson case law enforcement authorities were giving informants ten percent of all civil forfeiture proceedings resulting from any case the informant provided. The Court held that the conduct of the police was improper and dismissed all charges, and..."

"That's a completely different situation from what we have here, Ms. Panther. There the concern was that the paid informants might manufacture a crime in order to get paid, that's not what the Cowboy did. He didn't stand to gain any money from this deal."

"No, but the point is that the conduct of the Officer in paying Mr. Thibodeaux money..."

"Or reducing the bill for drugs..."

"Or reducing the bill, gave a cash incentive to induce a citizen to commit a crime."

"I don't buy it. What's your other argument?"

"My other argument is that the Officer, Cowboy, did more than just give my client the opportunity to commit a crime which my client was supposedly pre-disposed to commit, he created the crime and improperly induced my client to commit the crime."

"Isn't that called the subjective test, Ms. Panther?"

"Yes, Judge, the Supreme Court's decisions articulate an objective test and a subjective test and I acknowledge that the subjective test is, by definition, one that usually requires a determination by a fact-finder, but that's not where I'm going with this argument, Judge, but here's my argument... in the Munoz case the Court said the two questions to be asked are:

"Number one: Did the agent induce the Defendant to commit the crime? The answer to that question in this case is clearly yes. Cowboy set the whole thing up. It was Cowboy's idea entirely; and

Number two: was my client predisposed to commit the offense willingly, without any persuasion whatsoever? The answer to that is clearly no. Cowboy talked him into it.

Now, if the Court agrees that those are the answers to those two questions, then that is entrapment as a matter of law, based on the objective test standard, and it's not a factual issue for a jury to decide."

"It's not a factual issue, Ms. Panther? Whether or not your client was pre-disposed to commit the crime is an undisputed material fact?" The Judge asked. "I doubt that the State would agree with that."

"But when the facts are as clear, unequivocal and undisputed as they are in this case, your Honor, a jury doesn't need to hear them and you can rule as a matter of law. In this case it has been admitted and established that Mr. Thibodeaux has no prior record of arrest for anything and, of particular importance to this case, no record of arrests for drug use or the sale of drugs. Further, Mr. Thibodeaux didn't have a reputation as a drug dealer or as one who sold drugs. There is no evidence to suggest that he had ever done it before or since."

"The police knew that he was a drug user, Ms. Panther. They just decided it was time to arrest him, correct?"

"Actually, I think the Deputy said they weren't quite ready to spring the trap on this entire operation, Judge, and by the Officer's own admission, he had no reason whatsoever to think that Mr. Thibodeaux would be inclined to commit the crime. He just thought he'd give it a try because another individual hadn't shown up that night. He was not the "target" of an investigation as being one who was selling drugs. This is a classic case of a situation in which the criminal design originated with the police Officer and they implanted the idea to deliver an illegal substance, not sell it, in the mind of my client."

"And what says the State?"

"The facts are that once Deputy Fowler offered the Defendant $50 Mr. Thibodeaux jumped at the offer. This case isn't like the Hunter case, 586 Southern 2d, page 320, where the agent kept going back to Mr. Hunter continuously and, after many efforts, succeeded in convincing Mr. Hunter to help the agent find drugs from another individual. In this case, all the

Officer did was provide Mr. Thibodeaux an opportunity to commit a crime, and all the courts say that is a legal police tactic."

"What about Ms. Panther's argument that this man had no prior record, no reputation for being a drug dealer and the Officer had no reason to suspect that he was one who would sell or deliver drugs?"

"Well, your Honor, this isn't like the Sorrells case where the defendant had never been known to possess an illegal substance. In that case it was alcohol. In this case it is drugs, and it can't be argued that the Defendant wasn't inclined to commit a crime...the Officers KNEW that he was a drug user. He WAS a criminal. It's true that they didn't know if he would be someone who would sell or deliver drugs until they asked, but it's not entrapment just to ask."

"No, the argument the Defendant is making is that he wasn't pre-disposed to commit the crime of sale and delivery of OxyContin... OxyContin, correct? Or was it RoxyContin?"

"In this case it is RoxyContin, your Honor." The prosecutor responded.

"RoxyContin, thank you, and he would not have committed the crime except for the actions of the Officer. I remember the testimony of the chemist as well. What about the fact that this man was basically in a weakened condition as one who had, apparently, become addicted to the use of that particular drug, and the State took advantage of his weakness? Do you think that has any place in this discussion, sir?" the Judge asked.

"On behalf of the State, most definitely not. They are criminals because they use drugs. It is not a defense to say that there is some "diminished capacity" to know right from wrong as a result of becoming dependent on drugs as a result of using them. If that was permitted, the use of alcohol could become a defense to the crime and, as we all know, voluntary intoxication isn't a defense to a crime. It can reduce the "intent" required in some instances, but it isn't a defense to the underlying crime..."

"I disagree, your Honor..."

"Wait, Ms. Panther. Are you finished with your argument, Mr. Whistler?"

"Yes sir. I have nothing further to offer, other than to say that if the

Court thinks that there is an issue here as to whether or not entrapment occurred, then it should be an issue for a jury to decide."

"Alright, I'll hear from you now, Ms. Panther."

"First of all, the mental condition, or state of mind, of the Defendant is extremely important with regard to the question of the pre-disposition of the Defendant to commit the crime. It would be our argument that the Officer basically preyed on that weakness."

"Pffff," the prosecutor snorted.

"But more importantly, the facts of this case, which are undisputed, are such that this Court can rule as a matter of law as to whether or not Mr. Thibodeaux was entrapped. There is no need for a jury to hear and decide this case. You are permitted to make that decision, your Honor, where, as here, the facts aren't in dispute."

"What facts are you saying are not in dispute that would allow me to find entrapment as a matter of law, Ms. Panther? Be specific."

"This Defendant didn't arrange the sale, it wasn't his idea, he didn't participate in negotiating the price of the drugs, or the amount of drugs to be purchased, or where the exchange was to take place, he never saw the drugs, he never saw the money, he didn't want to do it at first, but the Officer talked him into it…all he did was simply deliver a package at the insistence of the Officer. There is absolutely no evidence to suggest that he was one who had any inclination whatsoever to commit the crime of selling or delivering drugs before the Officer set the whole thing up and convinced him to do it. That's entrapment."

"Alright. Thank you, counsel. I'm going to read the cases you cited and I'll have a ruling for you in a couple of weeks. When is trial set?"

"Six weeks from now, your Honor."

"You'll have my ruling in two weeks, more or less. That will be all."

The Judge stood and exited the courtroom.

The guard came up and stood by Jeremy, ready to take him back to jail. Ms. Panther turned to him and said,

"Can Mr. Thibodeaux talk to his wife for a minute, Officer?"

"No. She can do that at the jail."

"Can I have a word with my client?"

"Just a minute. I can't wait much more than that. I've got other prisoners waiting to be transported back to the Detention Center," the guard responded. He turned and walked away in order to give Ms. Panther a little privacy.

"So how do you think that went?" Jeremy asked.

"We've got a chance. The Judge could've ruled against us right then and there, but he didn't. That's a good sign."

"If he does grant that motion, you think the State will agree to let me out on probation on the possession charge?"

"I'll talk to the prosecutor and see what he says. First we've got to win that motion. Don't get your hopes up too high just yet. Motions like this aren't granted all that often."

"So what's next?"

"Trial."

"Trial?"

"Even if the Judge rules against us, we have a right to argue the case to a jury. Basically what the prosecutor said there at the end was that a jury should decide if you were 'pre-disposed' to commit the crime or if the undercover cop just 'gave you the opportunity to commit the crime.' The Judge could very easily say that those are factual issues for a jury to decide."

"But you're saying this Judge can decide himself and I won't have to go before a jury, right?"

"That's right."

"I never would have done it if he hadn't suggested it. He talked me into it. I was afraid he might punch me out if I didn't agree to do that for him. We, or I should say, I, only used that stuff in my own house or when no one was around, and that's the truth. I never sold or delivered anything to anybody, ever."

"I believe you. Like I said, we've got a chance. Take care, Mr. Thibodeaux. Keep your fingers crossed."

She then turned to the guard and said,

"Thanks."

Jeremy was led away and back to jail.

Chapter Sixteen

On a Saturday night a few weeks later, Sally put on her best blue jeans and her most colorful blouse and headed for Ocala to replenish her supply of RoxyContin. She left Samantha with her mother-in-law, telling her that she was going out with some girl friends to a movie and dinner in Gainesville.

"It's good to get out of the house for a little while, child. Enjoy yourself."

"Thanks, Mom."

"What movie are you going to see?"

"We haven't decided yet. Say, if we get home too late, would it be alright if I pick Samantha up in the morning?"

"Of course! I'll put her to bed at about 8:30 or 9:00, so if you're going to be any later than that, don't bother. I'll see you in the morning for church. Don't worry about a thing."

Sally had no trouble finding the Ghostriders Bar. It was just north of town on Highway 27, just like Slim had told her. It was a large, one story, wooden building, with a big porch on the front. There was plenty of parking in front and on both sides. It looked like a big log cabin.

It was still early, and the sun hadn't gone down yet, but the lot was filling up. She parked off to the side on the left and walked in. There were tables and chairs off to the right where people were eating dinner and a big dance floor with a stage in the room to the left. In front of her was a large bar which extended some sixty feet from the dining room to the dancing room with four bartenders standing together in the middle. They greeted her as she walked in.

"Good evenin', little lady! Would you like somethin' to drink?"

"Not just yet. I think I'll get me something to eat first."

She looked around, hoping to see Slim. She felt awkward walking into the bar by herself, but she didn't want any of her friends to know what she was doing, so she had no choice other than to go to a place where no one knew her. She didn't see him so she walked into the dining room on the right and took a seat in a booth so she could look out and watch as cars pulled in. It was 8:00.

A waitress came up and handed her a menu. When she did, Sally asked, "What time does the band start playing?"

"Not until 9:00 or so," the waitress responded. "Want something to drink?"

"I'll just have a glass of water for now. Give me a minute to look at the menu and I'll order some food."

The waitress turned and walked away. When she came back with the glass of water, Sally asked for the fried shrimp special, which came with fries and a salad.

Once it arrived, and as she was eating her food, she saw Slim enter the bar. He happened to look over at her at the same time. He immediately walked over to her booth and sat down.

"How're you tonight, Darlin? Good to see you here."

"I'm good. Thought I'd come down and do a little dancin' tonight. It's been a while and I needed to get out."

"Well I'm glad you did. I'm supposed to meet up with a couple of fellas here in a minute or two, but I'll be back. Enjoy your dinner."

She watched as Slim made his way through the bar, over toward the pool tables which were off to the side of the dance floor in a separate room. It was obvious that he'd been there before. It seemed as if he knew most everybody who worked there and a good number of the patrons, too. He picked up a bottle of Bud from the bar and disappeared out of sight into the pool room.

Just as she was finishing up with her dinner, she noticed Slim strolling through the bar and back to her booth. He sat down and said,

"Are you going to drink water all night or would you like something a little stronger?"

"I'll have a beer, thanks."

"What flavor would you like?"

"I'll take a Corona, with a lime."

He motioned to the waitress, and said,

"Let me have a Corona with a lime for the lady and I'll take the usual. Put it on my tab at the bar, would you, Donna?"

"No problem, Slim."

She was back with the beverages in no time.

"So this is your first time here, right?"

"Yeah."

"You're gonna like this band. This place really jumps when they start playin'. They should be starting up any time now. Here's to a good time! Cheers!"

She raised her bottle and clinked with his glass and said, "Cheers!"

They sat there talking for a while and then, when the band started up, he said,

"So you came here to dance. Let's dance, girl!"

The band played country rock. Sally hadn't been dancing in years, since high school, and she felt self-conscious at first, but then she realized that nobody was paying any attention to her, although a few guys looked her over, and she just started doing what came naturally, dancing the only way she knew how.

The band played mostly fast songs for the first three or four, and then the singer said,

"Let's slow it down a bit."

She knew what was about to happen, and she was ready for it, but it felt strange putting her arms around another man's body. Slim was a good six inches taller than she was and her head kind of fell on his chest. He put his hands on her low back, and moved them up and down. She felt some tingling throughout her body, knowing what else was in store for her.

They stayed out on the dance floor for the next hour until the singer said,

"We're gonna take a little break now. Don't go away. We'll be back in twenty minutes.

As they were walking off the dance floor, Slim asked,

"Would you like another beer?"

"Yeah, that sounds good. Thanks."

"I think I'll have one, too."

Slim ordered the beers and they stood next to the bar, without saying much, drinking them. When they had finished their drinks, Slim asked,

"Did you want to pick up a little somethin' while you're here?"

"Yeah, I was hopin' I might."

"Well, let's go on back to my place and take care of that right now. We'll be back before the band comes off its break."

"Okay."

"Want to take one car or two?"

"I'll drive my own."

"Suit yourself. You can follow me, but you know the way, right?"

"Yeah, but I'll follow you, just in case. I was only there once and that was in the day time."

It took ten minutes to get from the bar to Slim's house. Though she'd only had the two beers, she was feeling tipsy. Once inside, Slim held up a blue pill and said,

"Want to sample the product? "

Sally couldn't resist, even though she knew what was about to happen. The RoxyContin is a fast-acting pill and it worked as advertised. It wasn't but a matter of seconds after Slim gave her the pills she wanted, and taken her money, that she was on his bed taking his clothes off as he was doing the same to her, all the while plunging tongues into each other's mouths.

It happened so fast that Sally hadn't had any time to think about it. The pill and the alcohol certainly had an effect on her, but it wasn't as if she didn't know that what was happening might happen.

There was a part of her that resented Jeremy for what was happening to her. In some twisted way, this was payback to him. He was the one who introduced her to this drug and it was because of him that she'd become dependent upon it. She was feeling dizzy and light-headed, and not thinking too clearly, but the rage of passion was upon her and there was no turning back now.

There wasn't much foreplay, nor was there any care given to protection against an unwanted pregnancy or any sexually transmitted diseases. This was rough and tumble sex, and after a few minutes, he was rolling off of her, moaning,

"Oh baby! That was great!"

She had felt his thrusts, but he was finished way too soon for her to get her engine running. Since she hadn't taken any precautions, her first thought was that she hoped she didn't get pregnant. Her second thought was that she should have made him use a condom. Her next thought was that she'd better get to a pharmacy and use one of those things that can prevent a pregnancy within twenty four hours of sex that she'd heard some of her friends talk about.

Slim rolled off of her and onto his back. He leaned over, grabbed a cigarette, lit it, and said,

"Whew! That was nice. I've been wanting to do that with you ever since I first saw that sweet ass of yours at that bar in Cedar Key singin' karaoke."

"That was a few months ago, wasn't it?" Sally responded.

Sally wasn't sure what to say or how to act. This was all new to her.

"Yeah, but it was worth the wait, baby."

Sally lay there quietly, allowing all of her body parts to check in. She was trembling. The excitement of the moment was a thrill for her. She was also feeling the effects of the RoxyContin. Someone had told her that it was more powerful than heroin. She had no idea what heroin was like, but this stuff changed the channel like nothing she had ever had. She loved the high, with little concern for the consequences.

"You want to smoke a little weed?"

"Yeah, why not."

"Want anything a little stronger?"

"No, I've got to drive back to Cedar Key and it's a long drive, so I've got to be careful."

"You don't have to run off, you know. You can stay here if you'd like."

"Not tonight. Maybe next time. I didn't bring any change of clothes or anything."

"Suit yourself."

They lay quietly, not talking, as Slim took the last few drags on the joint they were sharing, let out a puff of smoke and said,

"I told a few people I'd meet them back at the bar later, so maybe I should be getting back, too. You sure you don't want to go back to the bar and do some more dancing?"

Sally sat up and started to put on her clothes.

"No, I've had enough fun for one night. Thanks."

"You sure you're able to drive?"

"I'll be fine."

"You're sure?"

"I'm sure."

"Okay then, whatever you say."

Slim sat up on the other side of the bed and started putting on his clothes, too. Moments later, they were standing at the doorway to the bedroom. He put his arms around her and said,

"We're gonna have to do that again sometime."

"Yeah," she whispered.

"Real soon," he added.

"Yeah." she gave him a hug as he squeezed her. They kissed, but the moment had passed. They were both on to the next event. It would be a long drive back to Cedar Key for her and she was in no condition to drive. This was the first time she'd ever taken a pill outside of the confines of her bedroom. She was woozy. For him, it was back to the bar to do some business, and maybe even to find somebody else to spend the night with.

They drove off in opposite directions, both deep in their own thoughts. She stopped at the Walgreen's on U.S. 27 on her way out of town to pick up some "after-sex" medicine, called "Plan B," and she was relieved to find out that she didn't need to have a prescription to get it, only girls under age eighteen needed a prescription. She took what she needed and hoped that it would work.

It was almost midnight by the time Sally got back to Cedar Key. She went straight to her home and to her bed, and she didn't need another of the little blue tablets to fall asleep.

Chapter Seventeen

On Thursday of the following week, three weeks prior to Jeremy's scheduled trial date, Sally paid Jeremy a visit.

"Hey, Sally! Good to see you! Where've you been? I haven't seen you since the hearing and you're never home when I call. What's going on?"

"About the same. I've got no money. It's hard raising Samantha by myself, and I'm tired all the time. How about you, Jeremy?"

"I'm so tired of being in here…thinking about getting out and being with you and Samantha is the only thing that keeps me going. What's wrong, Sally? You seem angry at me today. Why?"

Sally raised her voice and said,

"Part of me blames you for all that's going wrong in my life, Jeremy. It's because of you that I'm unhappy with myself and the mess that I'm in."

"I know, baby. I'm sorry. I'll make it up to you. I promise."

"How are you going to do that, Jeremy, when you're stuck in here? You can't help me and Samantha at all, can you? I've got to do it all by myself, don't I?"

Jeremy lowered his head, acknowledging that she was right, and said,

"I'm sorry, baby. I'm so sorry about all of this. I don't know what else I can say."

"Well that's not good enough, Jeremy. I'm real sorry about all of this, too."

"What else is wrong? Is something else going on that I don't know about?"

"I received a subpoena in the mail the other day."

"For what?"

"For your trial, that's what."

"Oh yeah? I didn't know she was doing that. She didn't tell me she was going to do that."

"You still haven't heard anything on that motion to dismiss, I guess."

"No, but the Judge said he'd make a ruling before the trial."

"The Judge said he'd make a decision in two weeks. That was almost a month ago. My lawyer says the Judge can take as long as he wants, so we wait. There's nothing we can do to hurry him up."

"So why'd she subpoena me? What am I going to say? I wasn't there."

"I don't know. Maybe to say that I'd never sold drugs before. I don't know."

"She'd better not ask if I'd ever taken any of those pills. I don't want to have to lie."

"You aren't taking them anymore, are you?"

"You worry about you, Jeremy. Let me worry about me."

"I know it's been bad for you, too, Sally, but I don't want to see you end up like me."

"Yeah? Well first you gotta get out of here, and then we'll see about me. Things have changed in the last five months, Jeremy. Things aren't what they used to be. I'm not the same person I was before you got locked up. You being locked up has changed me, too."

Sally started to cry. Jeremy didn't know what to say. When Sally straightened up a bit, and began drying the tears from her eyes with a Kleenex, Jeremy said,

"Yeah. Samantha's must have grown a few inches in the last five months. I can't wait to see her."

"That's not the only thing that's changed, Jeremy," Sally sniffled. "I just don't feel the same way towards you as I did. I'm angry with you, Jeremy!" Sally started to cry again.

"I know, I know. I'm sure this has been as hard on you as it has been on me."

"Maybe even harder, Jeremy. You don't know all that's been going on in my life now that you're not in it."

"I'm still in your life, baby. We just can't be together right now. That's all. I love you now even more than before, if that's possible. I see how much I've lost because of what I've done."

"Yeah, well I can't say the same thing, Jeremy. This hasn't made me closer to you. It's made me feel further and further away from you, and we owe my parents a lot of money, Jeremy. They've been supporting us for a while now."

"I'll pay 'em back. I promise."

"Yeah, right. We'll see. You may be going to prison for a few years first."

"Let's hope not."

"I'm tired of waiting, Jeremy. I can't go on like this."

"I'm the one who's gonna have to go, not you. You want to trade places?"

"Not hardly," Sally stiffened, stood up and said,

"You tell that lawyer of yours not to ask me any questions about drugs. You know I took some when I was in pain like I was. I don't want her to ask me about that."

"I'll tell her."

"I gotta go, Jeremy."

"Our half hour isn't up yet. Can't you stay a while longer?"

"No. I don't like it in here. It gives me the creeps."

"You hardly visit me but once a week anymore. You used to come every day."

"Like I said, it gives me the creeps."

"Don't go! Stay a while longer, baby, please!" Jeremy begged.

Sally turned and said, "Jeremy, I'm not happy with myself right now, and I blame you for all of this. I can't help it. That's how I feel…and you tell that lawyer of yours what I said."

"I will."

Jeremy knew things were bad, but he had no idea how bad. This was bad.

Three days later, he was sitting quietly in his cell, waiting for lunch to be served, when a guard called his name.

"But it's right before lunch! I'll miss lunch if I go now!"

"It's your lawyer. I think you want to see her, right?"

"Can they save me a plate?"

"You know the rules."

"Damn! This better be good."

Jeremy walked into the room and saw Ms. Panther sitting there, holding some pieces of paper in her hand, smiling.

"What are you so happy about?"

"We won!"

"We did! Really! You're kidding, right?"

"I'm not kidding. I wouldn't kid you about a thing like that."

"We won?"

"Yep."

"Can I give you a big hug?"

"No, but here, read it for yourself. I've got some other people to see in here. When I get back to the office I'll call the prosecutor and see if we can't work out a deal. I might be able to have you out of here by this afternoon."

"You're kidding!"

"I'm not kidding. It depends upon whether or not the State wants to appeal this thing or if they will let it go. I'll find out."

"Wow! That would be hard to believe. One minute I'm thinkin' I'm headed for prison and the next I might be goin' home!"

"Don't get your hopes up too high, but I'll see what I can do. Take this with you and read it over. You're a lucky man, Mr. Jeremy Thibodeaux."

She stood and walked out to have a guard bring in her next client. Jeremy stood and was trying to read what she had handed him, but his hands were shaking too much so he had to wait until he got back in his cell. Lunch hadn't been served yet. He sat on his bed and read,

In the Circuit Court of the Eighth Judicial Circuit,
in and for Levy County, Florida

State of Florida
versus
Jeremy Thibodeaux
Case No. 28-2011-CF-000147

ORDER GRANTING MOTION TO DISMISS

This cause came before the Court upon a Motion to Dismiss the charge that the Defendant unlawfully sold and delivered a controlled substance in violation of Florida Statute 893.03. This Motion is filed pursuant to Rule 3.190 (c) (4) of the Florida Rules of Criminal Procedure.

The facts are not in dispute. On the 14th day of March of this year the Defendant purchased a hundred RoxyContin tablets from an undercover law enforcement Officer at a bar in Chiefland, Florida, which is in Levy County. As the exchange of the pills for the money was being made, the law enforcement Officer, who was and is a Deputy Sheriff for Levy County, asked the Defendant to deliver a package to a person in Cedar Key who the Defendant did not know. The Defendant lived in Cedar Key, which is approximately thirty miles from Chiefland.

At first, the Defendant balked at the idea. The Officer then persuaded him to do it for him, saying that he would, in essence, be saving the Officer from making the trip, or doing the Officer a favor, if you will. The Defendant was still reluctant to make the delivery. The Officer then told the Defendant he would reduce the amount of the bill by fifty dollars if the Defendant would do as the Officer asked.

At that point the Defendant relented and agreed to deliver the package. The delivery was made to another undercover deputy sheriff at the Wash 'n Go on State Road 24 in Cedar Key. It took less than two minutes. It is not disputed that the Defendant was told that the package contained illegal drugs. It is also not disputed that the Defendant never saw the drugs and had nothing whatsoever to do with arranging the "buy" in terms of how many pills were to be bought, where the exchange was to take place, the price to be paid for those pills or any of the details of the sale. Defendant received no money from the second deputy sheriff to whom he delivered the package.

Defendant urges the Court to dismiss the charge that he unlawfully sold or delivered the controlled substance in question on the basis that he was "entrapped" by the actions of the law enforcement Officer and that 'but for' the actions of the Officer no crime would have been committed.

A few other salient facts, which the State of Florida does not contest, are that the Defendant had never been known to sell drugs in the past; that he did not have a reputation as a seller of drugs in the community; and that neither the Officer who sold the drugs to Defendant nor anyone else in law enforcement in Levy County had any information to suggest that the Defendant was involved in criminal activity other than as a user of a proscribed narcotic substance. In other words, he was not a "target" in an investigation of those who are in the business of selling illegal drugs. The testimony of the Officer was that he had information which indicated the Defendant had been a "user" of an OxyCodone derivative, nothing more. The Officer had sold OxyCodone pills to the Defendant on several prior occasions.

Of particular interest to the Court was the testimony of the chemist in this case, who explained the addictive nature of OxyCodone products. He referred to it as "hillbilly heroin." The witness explained that RoxyContin is an extremely effective pain relieving medication, but that it is also a dangerously addictive drug. It is often introduced to people by a physician who prescribes the medication to patients.

It is not uncommon that, after the medical treatment ends, patients find that they have become dependent upon the drug and they proceed to procure it illegally. The Court finds that testimony to be of significance as it bears upon the ultimate issue to be decided in this case, and that is the issue of whether or not the Defendant was "pre-disposed" to commit the crime. Defendant suggests that a drug user who is addicted to a particularly powerful drug has, by definition, a diminished capacity to make rational decisions and the Court should take into consideration that, in his weakened condition, the Defendant was easily manipulated.

The Court rejects that notion. Defendant is a legally competent adult and he is responsible for his criminal actions, and though this Court is of the opinion that a hospital or medical treatment facility might be a better place for criminal defendants such as Mr. Thibodeaux, that is an issue for the legislature, not the judiciary, to consider. It is not a defense to this crime.

The State argues that the Officer merely provided Mr. Thibodeaux with an opportunity to commit a crime and that the telling point came when the Officer agreed to lower Mr. Thibodeaux's bill by fifty dollars.

Though the facts are not in dispute, and this Court is loath to usurp the function of a jury by imposing its view of the facts, this Court has a duty to apply the law to situations such as this, when appropriate, where the material facts are not in dispute, thereby obviating the need for a jury, if and when justified. This Court heard argument on this issue over a month ago and after carefully reviewing the cases cited by both sides and giving the matter much consideration, it is the decision of this Court that the motion filed by the Defendant should be granted.

This Court has no doubt in its mind that this crime, that being the delivery of a controlled substance, originated in the mind of the Officer and that the Defendant would not have committed the crime but for the persuasive tactics and techniques of the Officer. The Officer did more than merely provide an opportunity, he created every aspect of the crime except one, that being the delivery of the drug. The Officer effectively induced the Defendant to step into the "trap" the Officer had created. The law calls that 'entrapment' and the further prosecution of this Defendant under these circumstances will not be permitted. The charge that Jeremy Thibodeaux unlawfully sold and delivered a controlled substance on March 14, 2011 is hereby dismissed.

Done and Entered in chambers, in Bronson, Levy County, Florida on this the 20th day of August, 2011.

Frederick Frick, Circuit Judge

"Hey! Thibodeaux! Are you going to eat or what! Last call!"

"Oh! Sorry, sorry, sorry. I was so busy reading I lost track of what was goin' on. Yes, yes, yes. Here I come."

Jeremy ran up and got a turkey and swiss sandwich, with potato chips and a drink. He sat back down and stared at the three page order in utter disbelief. He might be going home that day. He couldn't believe it. He felt like crying he was so happy, but he wasn't out of jail yet. He'd believe it when he walked out of the gate, out from behind the metal bars.

Chapter Eighteen

"Can you believe that shit? Judge Frick, of all people, granting that motion? What is the world coming to?" Mr. Whistler said.

"Hey, I think he made the right decision," Ms. Panther responded.

"Of course you do. He granted your motion!" Mr. Whistler replied.

"So what are you going to do, Whistler? Appeal? I don't think so."

"No, I already talked to the boss and, though he's not happy about it, he says we're just going to take this one on the chin."

"Judge Frick rules in your favor almost all of the time. You can't win 'em all, Whistler."

"He's real tough on search and seizure issues. We hardly ever lose motions to suppress. This is the first time I've ever had him find entrapment."

"And he's always going to take the word of a Police Officer over any of my clients any day of the week."

"That's true. He does."

"So maybe he just threw us a bone on this one."

"Hey, stop blowing smoke up my ass. You won. I'm not happy about it. Congratulations to you."

"So what are we going to do with this case?" Ms. Panther asked.

"What do you want?" Mr. Whistler responded.

"Two years of probation, with the requirement of drug counseling, court costs, jail fees and a withhold of adjudication."

"Withhold? Are you kidding?"

"This is a first offense for this guy. There's no need to be too hard on him, is there?"

"He caught a big break today, and you know it. I still think he's guilty of the Sales and Delivery charge. At the very least I want a conviction on the possession charge. He had the pills in his pants pocket at the jail for Christ's sake! I can convict him on that charge in my sleep!"

"Come on, Whistler! Maybe the Judge will find it was an illegal arrest and throw the whole case out."

"I doubt that. The best I'm going to do is two years of probation and the rest."

"If my guy will agree, can we do this today?"

"Why are you in such a hurry to get this done?"

"The guy's been in jail for five months. He's got a wife and young kid he hasn't seen in a long time."

"It's okay with me if the Judge will do it, but not too late. I'm going into town to ride my bike on the Gainesville-Hawthorne trail. I want to get in before the 5:00 block party, otherwise known as a traffic jam, starts up, so I want to be out of here by 4:00."

"I'll see what I can do."

Ms. Panther hurried out of the office and drove the mile and a half to the Levy County Detention Center. Her secretary called over to the jail and asked the guards to have Jeremy in the room waiting for her when she got there.

"The prosecutor will agree to two years of probation, with all the standard terms, if you'll plead no contest to the charge of unlawful possession."

"That's it? Two years of probation?"

"He wants a conviction, too."

"Which means?"

"You'll be a convicted felon. I wanted him to agree to a withhold of adjudication, so that you could honestly say that you'd never been convicted of a crime."

"I had the pills in my pocket, Ms. Panther. You told me that there was no way you could win that case."

"That was before the Judge ruled in our favor. He might throw the whole case out because the arrest was illegal. I doubt he'll do that, but it's possible."

"If I agree to plead no contest, when can I get out."

"Maybe this afternoon."

"If you can get me out this afternoon, I'll do it."

"Avoiding a felony conviction is a big deal, Mr. Thibodeaux. I think I might be able to get them to agree to a withhold of adjudication, but it might take a little while, maybe a week or so. Right now, he's still upset that the Judge ruled against him so we caught him at a bad time."

"Ms. Panther, I've been in here for five months. My wife is fixin' to leave me and I can't wait another day to see her and my baby. If you can get me out of here today, that's what I want you to do. I don't want to wait a week or two to find out if he'll change his mind."

"Okay, if that's what you want. I'll see what I can do about getting you out of here today."

Ms. Panther called her office and asked her secretary to see if the Judge was available to take Jeremy's plea. The Judge said he had an opening at 3:00, but nothing any later. Ms. Panther then called the prosecutor and said,

"The Judge can do this at 3:00. Can you arrange the transport?"

"I'll take care of it. See you then. I've got to run to get some things taken care of before 3:00."

A guard came and took Jeremy back to his cell as Ms. Panther left to get back to her office.

"I might be getting out of here today," he told his buddies, once he was back inside the room that had been his home for the last five months. Not long after that, another guard returned, and said,

"Thibodeaux! Let's go! You're going to court."

Jeremy's hands and knees were shaking as the van weaved its way along the road from the jail to the courthouse. When it arrived, he was immediately ushered into the courtroom where the attorneys, the clerk and the bailiff were in their seats. The Judge was sitting on the bench as well. As soon as Jeremy was seated, the Judge asked,

"Are we ready to proceed, or do you need a moment with your client, Ms. Panther?"

Ms. Panther stood and said,

"We're ready to proceed, your Honor."

"Alright then, Mr. Thibodeaux, if you and your attorney will please rise. Raise your right hand, Mr. Thibodeaux. Do you swear or affirm that the statements you are about to make will be the truth?"

Jeremy raised his right hand and said, "I do."

"I understand that you wish to change your plea from not guilty to no contest to the charge that you unlawfully possessed a category II controlled substance, namely OxyCodone, on March 14, 2011, is that correct?"

"Yes, your Honor."

"Mr. Whistler, would you please proffer what evidence the State is prepared to prove, if this case were to go to trial?"

"Yes, your Honor. The State is prepared to present evidence from Levy County Deputy Sheriff Gavin McCarthy that on the 14th day of March, 2011, the Defendant did unlawfully possess RoxyContin, which contained OxyCodone, a controlled substance, in violation of Florida Statute 893.03 (2)(a)(1)(o). Mr. McCarthy is a guard at the Levy County Detention Center and he will testify that when Mr. Thibodeaux was being booked into the Levy County Detention Center on another charge he, that being Deputy McCarthy, found two RoxyContin pills in the front pocket of Mr. Thibodeaux's pants. A chemist would testify that the substance which the Defendant possessed that night was RoxyContin, an OxyCodone derivative, your Honor."

"Alright, Mr. Thibodeaux, do you understand that by entering a plea of no contest you will be waiving your right to a trial by jury to contest, or challenge, the charge against you?"

"Yes sir."

"Do you understand that a plea of no contest means that you do not contest the charge, but the Court will find that you are guilty of the charge made against you and you will be convicted of that offense, which is a third degree felony.?"

"I do, your Honor."

"And do you understand that the maximum penalty for the offense is five years in the State penal system, as well as a fine of up to $5,000?"

"I do."

"And it is my understanding that an agreement has been reached between the State and your attorney by which you will be placed on probation for a period of two years with the requirement that you attend and satisfactorily complete a drug treatment program. Do you understand that?"

"I do."

"And does the State agree with that? Is that the plea agreement that has been reached?"

"Yes, your Honor. It is," the prosecutor responded, "plus the usual terms and conditions of probation, including a fine, community service and the fees for the Public Defender and the costs of incarceration.

"And Mr. Thibodeaux, do you understand that you will also be required to pay the costs of supervision as well as the cost of incarceration, as well as a fine, and that you will be required to perform 100 hours of community service?"

Jeremy looked over at his attorney with a puzzled look on his face. She nodded her head up and down and Jeremy responded,

"Yes, your Honor."

"And are you satisfied with the assistance provided to you by Ms. Panther, an assistant Public Defender who I appointed to represent you on this case?"

"I am, very much so, your Honor."

"And other than what I have told you, no other promises or assurances have been made to you?"

"No, your Honor."

"And you are not under the influence of any drug or narcotic such that you are unable to understand the nature and consequences of your actions here today?"

"No, your Honor.

"With that understanding, I will accept your plea and I will find that it is freely and voluntarily entered, that you understand the nature of the charges and you are competent to enter this plea, that you have been represented by competent counsel with whom you are well satisfied, and that there is a sufficient factual basis for this plea.

"Therefore, I do hereby find you guilty of the offense with which you are charged and I adjudicate you guilty of that charge. I sentence you to serve five years in the State Penitentiary for that charge, but I suspend that sentence and place you on probation for a period of two years, with the requirement that you attend and satisfactorily complete a drug rehabilitation program, plus pay the costs of supervision and the costs of incarceration."

The Judge, who had been reading much of what he said, then looked up and over at the two attorneys and said,

"Is there anything else, counsel?"

Both attorneys replied, "No, your Honor."

"Then this case is now concluded. However, I want to say this to you, Mr. Thibodeaux…"

And the Judge looked straight at Jeremy, measuring his words carefully,

"I don't want to see you back in my court ever again. Do you hear me?"

"Yes, your Honor, I do."

"You were very lucky to have avoided prison for your actions earlier this year and you were saved by some fine lawyering by Ms. Panther. If I see you again, I won't hesitate to send you to prison. Do you understand?"

"Yes, your Honor, I do. I want to get home and see my wife and my little girl. I don't ever want to be back behind bars again."

"And that includes doing anything to violate the terms of probation as well."

"I won't."

"Alright then…now, go and sin no more."

The Judge stood and started to walk out of the courtroom. As he did, the bailiff hollered, "All rise," and everyone stood. When he was out of the room, Jeremy asked,

"So when do I get out? Am I free to go now?"

"No, you have to be processed out of the jail and someone from the Probation Office will have to meet with you. It will be a couple of hours before you're a free man, but you'll be out today. Congratulations, Mr. Thibodeaux."

"Thank you, Ms. Panther. I'm so happy! Thank you for all you did for me."

"You're welcome. I'm as happy about it as you are, I think. Winning a motion like we did doesn't happen every day. In fact, that's the first one I've ever won on entrapment."

"Really? Wow! I guess I was lucky."

"Yes, you were."

"Say, before I go, what was that cost of incarceration all about? Do I have to pay for being in jail?"

"Yes, you do, but every prisoner does, so it wasn't something that applied to only you. There was nothing we could do about that. That's a state statute. The Probation Officer will explain all of that to you."

"I've got to get going, Ms. Panther. If you want to talk to your client any further you'll have to do it at the jail." The guard interjected.

"No, that's all. Good luck, Mr. Thibodeaux."

Chapter Nineteen

‹⋯⋯›

O n the ride back to the jail, Jeremy's mind was swirling. He wasn't prepared for all the things that were happening. He hadn't taken the time to get anything together, and he hadn't made arrangements for anyone to come get him. Everything he had in his possession was the property of the County, except for his underwear, socks and T-shirts, and they could keep them or throw them away. He didn't want them. He'd just leave everything behind and find himself a way home. He could do it.

Once he was back in his cell, he told the guys what was happening, and sat waiting to be called out of his cell for the last time. He became impatient the later it got, fearing that the people from the Probation Office would go home at 5:00.

"They won't let you out 'til you sign those probation papers," one of the other inmates told him. "You might not be getting out today."

"Shit! How bad would that be! Knowin' I'm supposed to be out of here and not bein' able to get out! I hope that doesn't happen."

At twenty minutes to 5, a guard called him out. An unhappy older woman sat at the desk and said, curtly,

"Good evening, Mr. Thibodeaux. We have a lot to do in the next twenty minutes. Have a seat."

She immediately put down a stack of papers in front of him and said,

"Sign each document on the line which I have highlighted for you.

If you have any questions, speak up. Otherwise, we can discuss this in more detail on Monday. My office is located directly across the street from the courthouse. I will want to see you first thing in the morning on Monday."

Jeremy flipped through the pages and signed where she told him to sign. Every now and then he'd ask,

"What does these mean?" or, "What am I signing?"

When he came to the piece of paper regarding the costs of incarceration, he looked up and said,

"You mean I have to pay $50 a day to live in this hell-hole, wake up at some un-godly hour every day and have guards scream at me all day long?"

"That's right, Mr. Thibodeaux, and you will be required to pay that debt off before your probation is terminated."

"And there is a charge for the Public Defender's Office? I thought they were free."

"The Court appointed a lawyer to represent you, and you didn't have to pay any money for that lawyer, since you didn't have any money at the time, but you owe a small amount of money for her services. And if you don't pay, a judgment will be entered against you and it will act as a lien against anything you might acquire in the future, like land."

"I didn't know that."

"Any other questions?"

"I can't go out of the County without your permission?"

"That's right."

"And I can't..."

"Mr. Thibodeaux, we're going to be here all night if you keep this up. All of these rules apply to every person who is placed on probation, not just to you. We can talk about anything you'd like on Monday. You have five other documents to sign and it's now 5:00. Do you want to get out of here today or not?"

"Yes, I sure do, Miss..."

"It's Mrs. Smythe. Thank you."

Jeremy signed the last of the documents and said,

"Can I leave now?"

"No, you can't. I'm finished with you, and I can leave now, but you'll have to wait until the jail finishes its paperwork."

She stood and said,

"I will expect to see you at 9:00 sharp on Monday, Mr. Thibodeaux."

"Yes, ma'am. I'll be there."

Once she had left the room, he expected to be taken back to his cell, but he wasn't. He sat there for another ten minutes until a guard yelled,

"Thibodeaux!"

"Yes sir."

"Come here."

Jeremy walked to the front desk and saw one of the deputies emptying a manila folder onto the desk."

The deputy handed him a sheet of paper with a list of the items taken from him on the day he was arrested.

"Make sure that you receive everything on the inventory, which should be every piece of personal property taken from you when you were booked in here five months ago. If it is, sign here."

Jeremy looked over everything, didn't see anything missing, and signed the sheet.

"Can I go now?"

"Yes you can."

Jeremy was stunned to hear him say those words. He turned and walked hesitatingly to the entrance door. He'd believe it when he was out of the building. He heard the buzzer, pushed on the door, walked into a small entrance way, and waited until the buzzer sounded and the door locked behind him. When he heard another buzzer, he then pushed on the next door. When it opened he was out in the enclosed area where the police vehicles parked when bringing in prisoners. He walked the thirty feet across the driveway to yet another door. When he heard the buzzer he pushed on the door. It opened. He walked through the door and out into the parking lot. He was a free man again.

"What am I going to do now?" He thought to himself. Since he hadn't had time to make any phone calls, and no one knew what had happened, he started walking. He wanted to get as far away from the jail as he could. A few hundred yards to the south was County Road 32. He turned west and walked half a mile to U.S. 27. Once there, he crossed over the highway and started walking south to the traffic light in Bronson. It was three miles away.

He stuck out his thumb and a pick-up truck gave him a ride to the light. He then started walking west on State Road 24 towards Cedar Key, thirty five miles away. He kept his thumb out as he walked. Five minutes down the road another pick-up truck stopped and picked him up. The guy was going to Coconuts to drink some beer. The thought of a beer sounded good, but the thought of getting home to Sally and Samantha was all he could think about.

The man dropped him off in front of the Dollar General store and Jeremy started to walk the last mile to his home, all the while thinking of what he would do when he saw his wife and daughter. It had been five months since he'd seen Samantha and he wanted to hold her, hug her and kiss her, but he wanted to make love to his wife more than anything else. He had dreamt of it and thought of her for so long he was in a frenzied state of mind. He fought back tears and began to run.

As he turned past the bushes which blocked the view of his home from the road, he slowed to a walk. He was disappointed to see that there were no cars in the driveway. He wondered where his truck was and thought to himself that Sally must be at her father's house, or maybe his mother's house.

It was a Friday night and it was starting to get dark, but there would be another hour or so before the sun went down. They should be home any minute. The door was locked and the spare key wasn't under the mat, where it usually was. He waited a few minutes, sitting on the front porch in one of the lounge chairs, but the bugs started to get to him, so he walked around to the back of the trailer, found a rock and broke one of the small panes in the rear door so that he could get his hand inside and unlock the door. The first thing he did was take off his clothes and jump in the shower. He wanted to be clean when he saw her. He was ready to "jump her bones."

He stayed in the shower for a long time, much longer than he'd spent in a shower in the last five months, and shampooed his hair twice and scrubbed himself extra hard, hoping to get the smell of the Levy County Detention Center out of his body, sticking his head out of the shower curtain every so often, listening to hear the sound of his arriving family.

After showering and drying himself off, he put deodorant under his arms and found his favorite shirt, the one Sally had given him for Christmas, and a clean pair of bluejeans, plus some blue socks, anything other than the whites he'd been wearing. He opened the refrigerator, looking for a beer, but found none. Sally never was one to drink much beer at home.

He took out a can of coke and lay down on the couch in front of the television. He wasn't interested in watching any television, even though he hadn't watched any in months. The only thing on his mind was seeing Sally and Samantha. He got up and walked into Samantha's room. He gazed at her toys, her clothes, her bed, felt them and smelled her presence. He smiled.

He walked all over the house, re-acquainting himself with all that was his. It was now almost 7:30, where could they be?

He thought about calling his father-in-law or his mother, but he didn't want to spoil the surprise. He kept thinking that they were going to arrive at any second. He thought about hiding, waiting until the door opened, but then he thought he might scare them. He decided he would rush out and greet them the moment the he heard the car pull in the driveway.

By 9:00, he had paced over every square inch of their 24 x 60 mobile home. He worried that something had happened to them. He kept telling himself to call her, but that would spoil the surprise. He lay down on his bed and thought about where he'd be if he was still in jail. It was hard for him to believe all that had happened in less than nine hours.

It had been shortly after noon when he'd found out that Judge Frick had ruled in his favor on the Sales and Delivery charge, and then not even five hours later, he was walking out of the jail. It was so good to be lying in his own bed, but he was so disappointed that his wife and child weren't home to greet him. He closed his eyes and told himself to relax, that they'd be home soon, that he was a lucky man. He was free again. He drifted off to sleep.

Jeremy awoke to the sound of a car door slamming. Then he heard another door slam. He bolted upright, sprang out of bed, and ran to the door. He turned on the outside light and opened the door. When he walked outside he saw two cars in the driveway and a stranger walking towards him, with Sally ten feet behind.

Jeremy's smile turned to a frown.

"Who are you?" he demanded.

Slim stopped in his tracks, realizing what was about to happen. As Sally was rushing to get in between the two men, Slim responded,

"My name's Slim," and then, though he knew full well who it was, he asked, "Who are you?"

"What are you doin' here, Jeremy?" Sally demanded. "When did you get out?"

Her tone of voice was not welcoming, warm or close to friendly.

"Who's he, Sally?"

"He's a friend." She turned to Slim and said, "You'd better go."

Before Slim had time to leave, Jeremy persisted,

"No, who the fuck is he, Sally? What's going on here!"

"That's none of your business, Jeremy! You haven't been around for five months and now all of a sudden you show up and think everything is going to be just like it was? It isn't!"

Sally got in between the two men and said to Slim, "Go! Now!"

Slim stood his ground at first, but then walked backwards, very slowly, toward his car, keeping his eyes on Jeremy as he did so. Jeremy walked towards him, keeping the same distance between the two men. Sally stayed in between them, facing Jeremy, keeping her arms up, pushing against Jeremy's chest, to stop his advance. He threw her hands to the side several times and kept walking.

"Who is he, Sally! You found yourself a boyfriend, did you?"

"He's just a friend, let him go. I'll explain later," she responded, in a softer tone of voice, trying to lower the tensions that were escalating.

"Oh yeah? I doubt that! Hey, you! Come back here!"

Slim reached his car, opened the passenger side door, reached underneath the seat and pulled out a Smith & Wesson 45. Then he sneered,

"I ain't goin' anywhere, Mister, and you'd better watch your mouth!"

Jeremy saw the gun and stopped.

"This is my house! Get your fucking ass off my property! Now!"

"What you gonna do, little man? Call the police?"

Jeremy's mind was racing. All he'd wanted to do was make love to his wife and see his baby. He wasn't ready for this.

"You put that gun down and I'll kick your fucking ass, that's what I'll do!"

"Oh yeah? You and who else you scrawny, little mother fucker!"

Sally stayed in between the two men, but Jeremy kept moving forward, pushing her out of the way, but she managed to stay in the middle. The men were less than six feet from each other. Jeremy stopped. The two men stared menacingly at each other.

"Okay! That's it! You get out of here, Slim! And you go back into the house, Jeremy! Now!" Sally shrieked. She put her hands on Jeremy again, pushing hard on his chest. He pushed her away, again, but this time she fell down. Jeremy stopped when he was a foot away from the gun which was pointed in his face and said,

"I ain't afraid of you! Go ahead, pull the fucking trigger! You fucking coward! Steal a man's wife while he's in jail!"

Slim pulled back the hammer until it clicked and said,

"Make one fucking move towards me and I'll blow your head off, mother fucker!"

The two men stood their ground, neither moving an inch, glaring at each other, less than a foot apart. As they did, they heard,

"Yes, this is Sally Thibodeaux. I need a deputy out here now! Somebody's about to get killed!"

Though both men heard what she had said, neither moved and neither looked away. Slim thought to himself that he'd better get out of there before the law arrived. He had some things in the car he'd rather they not find.

Jeremy thought to himself that he didn't want the law coming to his house for any reason. He didn't want to do anything that would put him back behind bars. Despite that, neither made the first move, until Slim slowly released the hammer, and said,

"Don't do anything stupid, little man. The law's gonna be here any minute."

He took a few steps sideways, angling to get around the car and into the driver's seat, while keeping the gun pointed at Jeremy's head, not saying another word.

Jeremy looked him straight in the eye and said,

"Get your fucking ass out of here and don't come back!"

Slim opened the door with his other hand, while keeping the gun pointed at Jeremy, got in, started the engine, and peeled out of the driveway, leaving Jeremy standing where he was and Sally still sitting on the ground with her cell phone in hand, giving directions.

"Tell them not to come, Sally. I don't want the law here." Jeremy said sternly.

"It's too late for that, Jeremy. They're on their way. Yes, I'll stay on the line. Yes, I'm safe now, I think. Yes, that's right, about a mile behind the Dollar Store."

Jeremy was angry, and hurt. His heart was pounding. He didn't know what to say or do, but he knew that he'd better get out of there before the police arrived.

"Where's my truck?" he demanded.

"I sold it." Sally replied, defiantly.

"You sold it?" he said, accusingly.

"That's right! I needed the money, Jeremy! We didn't have any!"

Jeremy didn't know what to do. He didn't want to be there when the police got there. He was afraid of what he might say or do.

"Give me the keys to your car!"

"No!"

"Give me the keys to your car, Sally! My name's on it, too!"

"No! Then what will I do for a car?"

"Sally, give me the damn keys! I'll go over to my mother's house and leave you alone. We can figure all of this out tomorrow!"

They heard the siren of the approaching police car.

"Too late now, Jeremy! You're going back to jail!"

"You'd like that, wouldn't you, Sally! So you could run around on me! What the hell happened to you!" he screamed.

"You weren't around to take care of me, so I had to find someone who could, Jeremy," she screamed back at him.

Jeremy let those words sink into his heart and then his head. Before he had time to do anything he might regret, a Levy County Deputy Sheriff's vehicle sped into the driveway, with its' lights swirling and the siren still sounding, kicking up gravel and sand as it did. An Officer leapt from the car, walked up to Sally and said,

"What's the problem here?"

Before Jeremy had a chance to say anything,

She told him, "He pushed me down and I'm afraid he's going to hurt me."

"Are you the person who called in the complaint?"

"Yes, I am. I'm still on the phone with 911."

"Let me have a word with her."

Sally handed him the phone.

"This is Deputy Sandlin. I'm on the scene and it seems as if everything is under control. There's no need to send back-up."

The deputy handed the phone back to Sally and said,

"Are you going to want to file a formal complaint about this?"

"Yes, I am."

"Are you hurt?"

Sally showed a bruise on her knee which was bleeding and said,

"I can't stay here with him. Unless you take him away, I've got to leave. He just got out of jail today. He hasn't been here in five months. I'm afraid he's going to beat me."

The Officer turned to Jeremy and said,

"Is that true?"

"It's true that I just got out of jail, but she just came home and she came home with some dude with a gun and I…"

The deputy turned back to Sally and said,

"Where's the man with the gun?"

"He's gone. Jeremy was going to kill him, so he pulled out a gun to protect himself."

"Alright, I've heard enough. Put your hands behind your back, sir. I'm taking you to the Detention Center."

"But Deputy, I…"

"Do what I say!" he commanded.

Jeremy did what he was told and after he was handcuffed, he was placed in the back seat of the vehicle and watched while the Officer took a statement from Sally. He couldn't hear what she was telling him, but he knew it wouldn't be good. Fifteen minutes later, the Officer was back in the car telling Jeremy that he was on his way back to jail.

"But Officer! I come home from bein' in jail for five months and I find my wife with some dude named Slim, who pulls a gun on me and I'm the one going to jail? Does that sound fair to you?"

"Stow it, Mr. Thibodeaux. Anything you say to me can and will be used against you in a court of law…"

"I know. I know. I know."

Chapter Twenty

———— ᐧᔑᐧ ————

The Officer at the booking desk couldn't believe it.

"You're back already, Thibodeaux? Did you miss us? You must like it here."

"You wouldn't believe it if I told you, but this guy wouldn't listen to a word I had to say. He just took my wife's side of the story and hauled my ass in here."

"Well, you know the drill. Let's do it."

When the booking process was completed, the guard said,

"In the morning, I'll put you back in the same cell. That should make you feel right at home. For now, you're going in a holding cell. Everybody should be asleep in your pod."

"Yeah, right. You really think those guys are sleeping?"

"They'd better be."

Jeremy spent a sleepless night, unable to believe his bad fortune. He couldn't imagine that he'd be sent to prison for violating his probation based on what had just happened, but he was worried about it, and feeling more depressed than he'd ever been. He hadn't even seen his daughter, and he'd lost his wife. He cried himself to sleep.

In the morning, Jeremy was taken in front of Judge Salter, the same County Court Judge as before, and told that he was charged with Domestic Battery. Bail was set at one thousand dollars on that charge, but there was a Violation of Probation hold placed on him as well, and there was no bond on that. He wasn't going anywhere for a while. The Public Defender's Office was appointed to represent him again.

A few days later, he received a notice in the mail informing him that Sally had filed papers seeking an injunction preventing Jeremy from having anything to do with her and giving her the exclusive use and possession of the marital home. It was called a Domestic Violence Petition. A Judge had signed it and it said that a Temporary Injunction had been issued. A final hearing was scheduled in two weeks.

"I guess the next thing will be divorce papers," Jeremy told the guard who served it on him. "How am I supposed to be a threat to her while I'm in here?" he asked.

"I can't answer that, Thibodeaux. Who knows, maybe you'll get out of here one of these days and stay out. Either that, or you'll be going up the road to the Department of Corrections…one of the two. You can't stay here too long."

Two days later, he received a copy of an Information. It charged that on the 20th day of August in the year 2011, he did unlawfully, and without provocation or excuse, strike one Sally Thibodeaux, against her will, and in so doing commit the crime of Battery, in violation of Florida Statute 784.03. On the Information it indicated that the offense of Battery was a misdemeanor, punishable by up to a year in jail."

"Shit! They are going to just bury me in here," he thought to himself.

Before he saw anyone from the PD's office, a detective called him out on the Tuesday following his arrest.

"Mr. Thibodeaux, I'm Detective Hanshaw of the Levy County Sheriff's Office, and I want to ask you some questions about this guy named Slim who supposedly pulled a gun on you. I know you have a lawyer, so you don't have to talk to me if you don't want to, and I'm not going to ask you anything about what happened or why. I just want to know about him. Would you be willing to talk to me about him?"

Jeremy thought about it for a second and immediately responded, "Yeah."

"Would you describe him for me, please?"

Jeremy proceeded to describe him.

"And I read the Domestic Violence report in which it says that he supposedly pulled a gun on you. Is that true?"

"Yes, it is."

"Where did he get that gun?"

"From his car."

"From what part of his car?"

Jeremy told him what he'd seen and asked why the officer wanted to know.

"That guy is named Stanley Foreman. He's a convicted felon. We suspect he's dealing pills in the tri-county area but we haven't been able to set up an arrest yet. If he has a gun, that's a felony. If we find one on him it will give us a basis to arrest him and get him off the street."

"Will it help me get out of here?"

"Maybe. Maybe not. I can't promise you anything, but I will agree to tell the prosecuting attorney and the Judge that you cooperated with us. Will you sign an affidavit regarding the gun?"

Jeremy thought about it for a few seconds and said,

"Yeah. I'd like to see that guy in here. I'll sign it."

"And it's the truth, right?"

"Damn straight it's the truth. That mother-fucker is why I'm back in here. He stole my wife from me!"

"I mean that part about the gun being in his vehicle."

"Yes, that's the truth. Otherwise I might have killed the son-of-a-bitch."

"And describe the vehicle for me."

"It was a black Jeep Wrangler, with a hard top."

"You don't know what kind of gun it was, do you?"

"One with a huge barrel on it."

"That's good enough. I can get the rest. Okay, Thibodeaux. Just sit here for a few minutes. I'll be right back."

The deputy left and when he returned he placed a piece of paper in front of Jeremy and said,

"Read it and sign on that line where your name is."

After Jeremy did as he was told the detective said,

"That's it, Thibodeaux. Have your attorney call me."

Armed with the affidavit, the detective went to the State's Attorney's Office and obtained a Warrant, signed by a Judge, to allow the search of Slim's black 2009 Jeep Wrangler, with license plate number 51KP64, owned by Stanley Foreman, for a hand gun. The warrant read, in part, that "Mr. Stanley Foreman, also known as "Slim," is a convicted felon, whose civil rights have not been restored, and he is not allowed to own or possess a firearm. Upon information and belief, there is a reasonable basis to believe that a firearm is located within said vehicle."

Ten days after he was put back in jail, Ms. Panther came to see him.

"Three hours after you got out of jail you were arrested and put back in here?"

"Yeah, how about that?" Jeremy acknowledged, with a half-smile and a rueful laugh.

"What were you thinking? How did that happen?"

When Jeremy explained the situation and how it all went down, she said,

"That was truly sad, and unfortunate, Jeremy. I'm really sorry to hear it, and now you've got a Battery charge and the Violation of Probation to deal with."

"And I never did see my baby girl."

"I'm sorry to hear that, too."

"So how much trouble am I in?"

"The Battery charge is a misdemeanor. I could probably get you out of here today on it for time-served. It's the Violation of Probation that I'm worried about. Has your Probation Officer been over to see you yet?"

"No."

"I'll give her a call. Those are pretty extenuating circumstances. As long as she's not wanting to put you in prison, you should be alright."

"It's up to her?"

"No, but she makes a recommendation, and that carries a lot of weight. If the prosecutor and the Probation Officer recommend that you be put back on probation, the Judge will usually go along with it."

"What about this Domestic Violence thing? Can you help me with that?"

"No. That's a civil matter and we don't get involved in those things but, I must warn you, when you go to that hearing, anything you say in there can be used against you in either the Battery case or the Violation of Probation case, so you need to be very careful about what you say."

"You mean like if I admit that I pushed her I'll be admitting I committed a battery and I'll be admitting that I violated my probation?"

"Exactly."

"So what should I do?"

"When is the hearing on the Domestic Violence charge?"

"In two weeks."

"Let me see what the State wants to do with you. I'll be back in touch in a few days."

"Say, Ms. Panther, I spoke to a detective the other day. He said he might be willing to help."

"You did?"

"Yeah."

"After I'd been appointed to represent you? He's not supposed to do that."

"It wasn't about the charges against me, it was about that dirt-bag Slim."

"Why? What was that all about?"

"They think the guy is selling pills and he's supposedly a convicted felon who is not allowed to have guns. I signed an affidavit saying that I saw him take a gun from his car and point it at me."

"Hmmm. He said he'd help you if you did that for him?"

"Yes, he did."

"That should be helpful. What was the detective's name?"

"Hanshaw. Hank Hanshaw."

"I know him. I'll give him a call. Okay, Mr. Thibodeaux, I'll be back in touch in a few days. Take care."

The next Saturday night, Sally and Slim were driving from his house back to the Ghostriders bar in his car, after having sex with each other for over an hour. They'd smoked some weed and were feeling relaxed. Sally had purchased some more pills and had them in her purse. She was planning on driving back to Cedar Key that night because Samantha was going to a birthday party early the next day. They were "stoned," but not high on the pills.

As he was pulling into the driveway of the bar, a Marion County Deputy Sheriff pulled in behind him. As he did, the overhead lights came on.

"Shit! I hope that cop isn't after me. I didn't do anything wrong."

Slim kept his eye on his rear-view mirror as the deputy followed Slim to a parking spot.

"Damn! The son-of-a-bitch is after me! Stay here. I'll see what this is about."

As Slim started to open the door, a voice was heard telling him.

"Stay in your vehicle and put your hands where I can see them."

Slim closed the door and said, "Shit!"

"You didn't do anything wrong. You weren't speeding or anything. Maybe it's just a tail light warning or something," Sally offered.

"Roll you window down!" the voice commanded.

Slim did as he was instructed to do. The Officer had yet to walk up to the vehicle. Sally turned around and saw him standing outside of his car, which was stopped directly behind their vehicle, within a foot or two, and she watched as he drew his pistol.

"Oh my God! He pulled out his gun!"

As she said that, a second Marion County Sheriff's vehicle pulled into the driveway and positioned itself to the right of the first one. Sally watched as the second deputy exited his car and drew his weapon, too. A third vehicle came in shortly after that and pulled next to the other two vehicles. The driver jumped out of his vehicle and drew his gun.

"Damn! What the hell is going on!" she exclaimed, becoming increasingly alarmed.

"Keep your mouth shut and let me do the talking!" Slim told her.

When the third Officer was in position, the first Officer, who was in the middle of the other two, said,

"Come out of your car, with your hands up!"

"Does that mean me, too?"

"Do what they say, Sally!"

Slim and Sally exited the Jeep, with their hands up, and stood next to their vehicle, as ordered.

"Close the car doors!" the deputy commanded.

Again, they did as they were ordered to do.

At that, the three deputies converged on Slim and Sally. Two deputies went after Slim and one approached Sally.

"With your hands above your head, move to the front of your vehicle and place your hands on the hood of your car!"

Once they had done what they were told to do, the first Officer approached them, and said,

"Are you Stanley Foreman?"

"I am."

"Mr. Foreman, a Warrant has been issued which allows for the search of your vehicle. A Levy County Deputy Sheriff is on his way with the Warrant. Do you want to wait until he arrives or will you allow us to search your vehicle at this time?"

"I'm not allowing you to search my vehicle, period, with or without a Warrant! You've got no right to do that!"

"You can take that up with a Judge, Mr. Foreman."

"I want to call my lawyer! You've got no right to do this!"

"You'll be given an opportunity to call your lawyer at a later time, Mr. Foreman. You are not under arrest at this time. We are going to search your vehicle, as allowed by the Search Warrant that has been issued, nothing more, at this time."

"What are you searching for anyway? I didn't do nothin' wrong."

"The Levy County Deputy will explain all of that to you. Stay where you are until he gets here."

"What about me? Do I have to stay here, too?" Sally asked. "It's not my car. I'm parked right over there. I'd like to go home now. I just have to get my purse and…"

"Stay where you are, ma'am. No one is going into that vehicle until it is searched."

Ten minutes later, another police cruiser pulled up. It was the deputy from Levy County. He walked up, spoke to the other Officers for a few seconds and then said,

"Mr. Foreman, my name is Deputy Parish. I have in my possession a Warrant, issued by a Circuit Court Judge, allowing me to search your vehicle. I am about to do so."

"I want to see that Warrant! You've got no right to do this!"

The deputy handed the Warrant to one of the other Officers and said, "Show this to Mr. Foreman, would you?" and he began to search the vehicle. He went first to the passenger side door, opened it, lifted up the seat and found the weapon. When he did so, he returned to where Slim and the others were standing and said,

"Mr. Foreman, you are under arrest."

"What for?" Slim demanded.

"You are a convicted felon and you are in possession of a firearm, in violation of law."

"That's not my gun! It's hers! It was under her seat, not mine."

"Mine!" Sally shrieked. "It's not my gun!"

"Put your hands behind your back, Mr. Foreman."

"This ain't right! You've got no right to do this!" Slim protested.

"Put your hands behind your back, Mr. Foreman!"

Slim reluctantly did as he was told. When he did, the deputy led him over to his cruiser and placed him in the back seat, after conducting a pat-down search.

"What about me? Can I go now?"

"Sorry, ma'am, but you'll have to wait until we have completed an inventory of this vehicle. We can't leave it where it is. Mr. Foreman might claim that somebody stole something from his vehicle and it was our fault for not properly securing his personal property."

Sally immediately realized that she had the pills in her purse.

"Can I at least get my purse? I need to use the restroom."

"No ma'am. You can't." One of the Officers responded. "Just stay where you are."

"But I need to use the bathroom!" she protested.

"I'm sorry, ma'am, but you'll just have to wait."

The Marion County deputies methodically removed each and every item from the vehicle, placing it in a box as they did so. When they came to Sally's purse, they discovered the pills. When they did, one of the Officers walked up to her and said,

"Mrs. Thibodeaux, you are under arrest for the offense of illegally possessing a controlled substance."

"I have a prescription for those!" she responded.

"You do? May I see it?"

"It's in my purse."

The Officer then said,

"I will allow you to reach in your purse and get the prescription you say you have. I will be watching every move you make, so don't do anything too suddenly. If I tell you to stop, I want you to stop. Understood?"

"I understand."

Sally reached into her purse and pulled out one of the old prescriptions Dr. Malpartido had given her. The Officer looked at it and said,

"This prescription is for 15 milligram RoxyContin pills. Those are the green pills. These are the Roxy Blues. You are under arrest, ma'am."

"But that's not fair! I really do have a prescription! I must have left the right one at home," she protested.

"You can tell that to a Judge. A female Officer is on her way here now. Stay where you are."

Minutes later, a female Officer arrived. She immediately patted Sally down for weapons and placed handcuffs on her. Sally was then led to the female deputy's vehicle and placed in the back seat.

"Where are you taking me?"

"To the Marion County Detention Center, ma'am."

"Can't I go to Levy County? That's where I live."

"No ma'am. The crime with which you are charged occurred here. You are going to our jail."

"But I have a little girl!"

"I will notify Protective Services, ma'am. Where is she now?"

"With her grandmother," Sally responded.

All the police vehicles still had their lights on. A crowd had gathered around, watching everything that was going on. Sally watched out of her window as the Levy County Deputy drove north towards Bronson, while she was being driven in the opposite direction towards Ocala.

The following morning, she was taken before a Judge and told what she was charged with. Her bond was set at $25,000 on the charge that she had unlawfully possessed a controlled substance, OxyCodone, and she could be sent to prison for five years and fined $5,000, if convicted. The Public Defender's Office was appointed to represent her.

Chapter Twenty One

On the following Monday morning, a woman from the State of Florida, Department of Children and Families, Division of Protective Services, arrived at the home of Jeremy's mother.

"Good morning. Are you Mrs. Thibodeaux?"

"I am."

"And are you the paternal grandmother of Samantha Thibodeaux?"

"I am."

"My name is Jean Easterly and I'm employed by the State of Florida with the Department of Children and Families. As I expect you know, your daughter-in-law, Samantha's mother, is presently in the Marion County Detention Center and…"

"Yes, she called me yesterday morning. I'm so upset I don't know what to do. I just sit around the house crying over all of this. The both of them are in jail now."

"Where is Samantha?"

"She's inside, playing."

"May I see her?"

"Of course."

The two women walked inside and found Samantha in her room, on the floor, playing with some toys. A television set was on and Samantha was watching a children's show.

"Samantha, this is Mrs. Easterly. Say good morning."

Samantha said "Good morning!" and smiled.

"Good morning, Samantha. And how are you?"

Samantha didn't respond. She kept doing whatever it was she was doing, somewhat oblivious of the two.

"Well, she seems to be a happy little girl."

"She is, and she's a delight to have around. She rarely acts up, but she'll throw a tantrum every now and again, just like any young 'un her age will."

"Let's go back outside. She doesn't need to hear any of this." When they were back on the porch, Mrs. Easterly said,

"Mrs. Thibodeaux, I have an order, signed by a Judge, directing me to pick up Samantha and take her into the custody of the Department of Children and Families. After meeting with you and meeting Samantha, I'm not going to do that, because I can see that this is a safe place for her to be and I am responsible for making sure that she is in a safe place. I'd rather see her here than in the home of a stranger, and I'm sure that would be much better for her, too. I assume that you are willing to keep Samantha with you while all that is going on with your son and daughter-in-law gets resolved. Is that right?"

"Of course I am. That child has been with me most of the time here lately as it is, ever since Jeremy got arrested a while back."

"Where is your husband, if I might ask?"

"He died a couple of years ago."

"No other men in your life? No other men living in the house or visiting on a regular basis is what I mean."

"No, no man in my life."

"Alright. Here's my card. I'll leave you with a copy of this Order which you can show to anyone who might ask. I am also giving you a sheet of paper which I have signed which says that you are the person who is being entrusted with the care of Samantha. Until the further Order of a court of law, or unless I change my mind, no one has the right to take this child from you."

"You have no idea when Sally might be getting out, do you? Or Jeremy?"

"I have no involvement in that whatsoever. My only interest is in the well-being of that child in there. I'm sure she's in good hands now."

"She is."

"I will be back every now and then to check up on her and see how you are doing. If you ever have a question or a problem, just call. We have a number of things that we can do to help you and Samantha, too, if you need help. Here's my card."

Mrs. Thibodeaux took the card, looked at it, and said, "Not now I don't. We're fine. I just wish the both of them would come back home real soon."

"Well, like I say, if you do, just call."

She turned to leave and said,

"I'm sorry about all of this, Mrs. Thibodeaux, as I'm sure you are, but that little girl is lucky to have you."

"And I'm lucky to have her. She's a blessing."

A week after Sally was arrested, Ms. Panther returned to see Jeremy.

"Your wife's been arrested. Did you know that?"

"No, I didn't. For what?"

"Drug charges. When the police arrested the man she was with, Sally was in the car and she had some pills in her purse."

"So is that guy in here?"

"I believe so. He's got a private lawyer, so I don't know if he bonded out or not."

"I thought I saw a guy in here the other day that looked like him. I mean…I only saw the guy once, and that was at night, and everybody looks different in an orange uniform than they do on the street, but I walked by a cell the other day and thought to myself it was him. I don't think he recognized me. They must be makin' sure to keep me away from him and him away from me."

"That's because you're the reason he's in here and you may well be an important witness against him."

"And he's the reason I'm in here."

"So I'd say they'd better keep the two of you apart."

Jeremy lowered his head, pondering what he would do to the man if given a chance, then asked,

"So how's Samantha? Where's she?"

"She's with her grandmother."

"That would be my mother. Sally's mother is in Crystal River and I doubt they took her there. They wouldn't have taken her there, would they?"

"No. She's in Cedar Key. She's here in Levy County. That much I know."

"So what's going to happen to me?"

"Well, first of all, that Domestic Violence thing will probably be dismissed since you're both in jail, but I could be wrong. You'll have to attend the hearing, I'm sure, but that's what I expect will happen."

"That will be good. I hope you're right."

"Also, regardless of what happens at that hearing, the State will allow you to plead no contest to the Battery charge and give you time served on it. You'll have another conviction, but it is only a misdemeanor, so that is up to you as to whether or not you want to fight it."

"As long as it doesn't violate my probation, I don't care. I just want out of here."

"I can't tell you just yet what's going to happen with the violation of probation charge."

"But what if I say I want to fight it? That means I have to sit in here until the trial, right?"

"Probably, but maybe not. Could you bond out if the bond was set at a low amount?"

"I don't have a dime to my name right now."

"Not even a hundred dollars?"

"I could borrow that much, I expect, from my mother, but I did push her down. I mean, I didn't intend to. I was trying to get at the guy. You know."

"Then you should probably just plead no contest to that charge and take time-served."

"I'll do that, so long as it doesn't violate my probation. Will it?"

"I'll talk to your Probation Officer and make sure she agrees to recommend that you be placed back on probation before we do anything."

"Does the State agree to that?"

"Yes, if the Probation Officer agrees."

"So if the Probation Officer agrees, let's do it."

"Okay. I can't get a hearing until next Friday, but if she does, I'll take care of it."

"Next Friday? I'll have to sit in here until then?"

"Afraid so, Mr. Thibodeaux. We only have one Circuit Judge here in Levy County handling criminal matters and he has a busy schedule."

"Damn!"

"The good news is you may be getting out. If you do get out, try to stay out a little longer this time, will you?"

"I know it sounds funny, Ms. Panther, and everybody in here laughs at me when they hear about it, but I don't know how I could have handled that any different. I think any man worth a damn would've done the same thing. There are some things that a man has to put up a fight about and that's one of them"

"Well, try to be smarter about it next time. If not, you know what's going to happen to you. And you're risking prison if you do what most men would do when faced with that situation. You're going to have to keep in mind that you're not like most men now. You're a man with a criminal record and you're going to be treated differently. You're going to have to turn the other cheek from now on…no bar fights, no drinking, no guns, no drugs…none of that."

"No guns…not even for hunting?"

"No guns! That's what got Slim arrested. It wasn't the drugs, it was the gun in his car, and that was because of you. You are a convicted felon, too. You know that. Have you read the terms of your probation?"

"No. I didn't have time to even get them."

"The Probation Officer hasn't been over to see you since you were re-arrested?"

"No."

"Well, that is one of the terms of your probation. As I said, it's a felony for you to have a gun, unless and until you get your civil rights restored and a Judge says you can."

Jeremy pondered that for a few seconds and then said,

"That detective helped me, didn't he?"

"Yes he did. The State Attorney didn't agree to all this until after talking to the deputy. You should be happy, Mr. Thibodeaux. It could've been worse, much worse."

"Yeah, you're right. I just have to be patient."

"I'm pretty sure the Probation Officer will go along with this. She has no reason not to. Unless you hear from me to the contrary, I'll make all the arrangements and plan to see you in court next week."

When the day came for the hearing on the Domestic Violence case, Jeremy was transported to court. When his case was called, he was led into the courtroom, but just before he was taken into the courtroom the deputy took the handcuffs and leg chains off.

To his surprise, Sally was in the courtroom, too. When he looked over at her as he was walking to his table, she averted his glance. There was a deputy sheriff sitting right behind her. It looked like she had a lawyer representing her. There were two women sitting at the table with her. Once he was seated, the Judge said,

"We're here today on a Petition filed by Sally Thibodeaux against Jeremy Thibodeaux. Both parties are present, although it appears that both parties are presently incarcerated. Is that correct?"

"Yes, it is, your Honor," one of the two women sitting with Sally said, standing as she did so.

"Thank you, Mrs. Winters, and let the record reflect that Mrs. Thibodeaux is being represented at this hearing by Three Rivers Legal Services. Have you filed a Notice of Appearance?"

"I did so moments before the hearing began."

"And I see Ms. Flowers from the Another Way program is here, too. Now, Ms. Flowers, she's not in shelter with you, is she? She's in jail, right?"

"That's right, your Honor. She came to see us before she got arrested."

"I see. Let the record reflect that Ms. Flowers is present as well. I have no problem with you sitting there at counsel table, Ms. Flowers, though I know you are not an attorney. You may stay where you are. Alright, well, let me ask…is it necessary for us to proceed with this hearing, given the circumstances of the two parties?"

"Yes, your Honor, it is," Mrs. Winters responded. "Mrs. Thibodeaux hopes to be out of jail before too long, with all charges against her either dropped or dismissed, though there is no guarantee of that at this moment"

"And what about you, Mr. Thibodeaux? What is your status?"

"I'm told that I might be able to get out next week."

"And how is that going to happen, if I might ask?"

"I am to plead no contest to the Battery charge and get time-served for it. The State's not going to violate me. I'm going to be put back on probation, I'm told. That's not for certain, but that's what my lawyer said she was going to try to do for me."

"Well, let's hope that happens for both of you. Alright then, let's proceed. Call your first witness, Mrs. Winters."

"I call Sally Thibodeaux to the witness stand."

Sally rose and walked up to the box next to where the Judge sat. A clerk asked her to raise her right hand and to swear or affirm that she would tell the truth. Sally responded that she would. When she sat down, Mrs. Winters said,

"Please state your full name."

"Sally Thibodeaux."

"And are you married to Jeremy Thibodeaux, the man seated over there?"

"Yes, I am."

"Tell the Judge what happened on August 20 of this year."

"I got home around 8:30 or 9:00 that night, and I had a friend of mine follow me home, and he was right behind me in his car. So when we pulled in the driveway, Jeremy comes running out of the house, and he…"

"Let me stop you there. Were you surprised to see Jeremy?"

"Yes I was."

"Tell the Judge why you were surprised."

"Because he had been in jail for five months on drug charges and I had no idea that he would be there."

"And then what happened?"

"Well, as soon as Jeremy saw this other man, he immediately started cussin' at me and at this other guy, so I stepped in front of him and…"

"You stepped in front of who?"

"I stepped in front of Jeremy and tried to keep him from goin' after this other guy."

"And what happened when you did."

"He pushed me to the ground, cussin' at me, and sayin' he was going to kill this other guy and things like that."

"What happened then?"

"This other guy pulled out a gun and that stopped Jeremy dead in his tracks."

"Were you injured as a result of being pushed to the ground?"

"I was. My knees were bruised and bleeding."

"What did you do?"

"I called 911 right away. I could see that somebody might get killed that night."

"And are you afraid for your safety if your husband is allowed back in the home, assuming that the both of you get out of jail?"

"Yes, I am. He's thinking all these terrible things about me and I don't want to be in the same house with him until he settles down and gets adjusted to being out of jail and me not being with him. He can't go around acting like that."

"And are you considering filing for divorce?"

"Yes, I am."

"I have no further questions, your Honor."

"Mr. Thibodeaux, do you wish to ask your wife any questions?"

"I do, your Honor."

"Go ahead."

"Sally, have I ever hit you in my entire life, except when we were small kids?"

Sally looked away and responded,

"Not before that night, and not before you went to prison. Things have changed. You've changed. I've changed. Things are different now."

"And isn't it true I wasn't trying to hurt you I was trying to get at that guy you were with?"

"I don't know what you were thinking. You were acting like a crazy man. All I know is you pushed me down and made threats to kill us both."

"That's not true and you know it!"

"Just ask your next question, Mr. Thibodeaux. You'll have a chance to tell your side of the story later," the Judge interjected.

"I never made one threat against you that night, did I? Tell the truth!"

"You were acting so crazy. I can't recall exactly what you said or whether you were speaking to me or Slim."

"And that guy Slim and you got arrested together, didn't you? That's why you're in jail, isn't it?"

"Do I have to answer that question, your Honor? That has nothing to do with him pushing me down."

"Maybe not, but I'd like to know the answer to the question. What is your answer?"

"Yes. I was a passenger in his car and I was arrested at the same time he was."

"And you are in jail on what charges, Mrs. Thibodeaux?"

Sally looked down, not wanting to answer the question. Her attorney stood and said,

"Objection, your Honor. That has nothing to do with the Domestic Violence case."

"It might. Over-ruled."

Sally had to answer and she said,

"Possession of a controlled substance,"

"And what was that substance?" the Judge continued.

"Your Honor, with all due respect," Mrs. Winters said, "I would ask that my client not be required to answer any questions along these lines. She does have her Fifth Amendment rights and she could say something to incriminate herself."

"I understand, Mrs. Winters, and your point is well-taken. Let me clarify the question…without telling us anything whatsoever with regard to the facts and circumstances surrounding your arrest, what is the controlled substance that you are charged with allegedly unlawfully possessing?"

"Your Honor. With all due respect, I would renew my objection and ask if this is relevant to the issues to be decided here today?"

"Well, Mrs. Winters. I believe your client is going to ask that she be allowed to have me award her custody of the child of these two parties, if I read the petition correctly, so I think drug usage, or the potential for drug usage, is a relevant issue for me to be aware of and concerned about. Do you want to answer the question for her, Mrs. Winters? That will be fine with me."

"RoxyContin, your Honor."

"I don't have anything else to ask her, Judge."

"Any other witnesses, Mrs. Winters?"

"No, your Honor."

"Would you like to make a statement to the court, Mr. Thibodeaux, regarding the request that I issue an injunction that will prevent you from having any contact with your wife, among other things?"

"No, your Honor, except to say that I was so happy when I got out of jail that night, and I was so much looking forward to being with my wife that night, and seeing my little girl…"

Jeremy started crying.

"I still haven't seen her…neither she nor Sally were home, and then when Sally gets there she's with this other guy…"

He started crying again.

"I didn't want to go back to jail. I knew that if I violated probation I could be sent to prison. I hadn't been out three hours! I just wanted to be with my wife and my daughter. I didn't want any of this to happen."

"I wasn't trying to hurt her…I love her….,"

"Do you want to take a minute to gather yourself, Mr. Thibodeaux?"

"No, your Honor. That's all I have to say."

Jeremy slumped down in his chair, rubbing his eyes to wipe away the tears.

"Do you want to call any witnesses, Mr. Thibodeaux?"

"No sir," Jeremy blubbered.

"Any closing argument you wish to make, Mrs. Winters?"

"Just to say that it is clear that an act of violence occurred that night. In fact, the State has charged Mr. Thibodeaux with Battery and if I understood Mr. Thibodeaux correctly, he's going to plead guilty or no contest to that charge. It's clear that he pushed her to the ground. It is also clear that unless you issue an Injunction it is very likely that a further act of violence could occur, given what we've heard here today, your Honor, assuming both parties are released from jail, and then there is the issue of the marital home to consider, as well as custody of the child."

"The child is in the custody of DCF, correct?" the Judge asked.

"I believe that is correct, your Honor," Mrs. Winters responded. "I'm not handling that aspect of the case."

"I'm not going to do anything with that issue. I can tell you that much. Not at this point I'm not,"

The Judge turned to Jeremy and asked,

"Would you like to say anything, Mr. Thibodeaux?"

"Only that I didn't mean to hurt her. I never hurt her in my life. I wouldn't hurt her even now, after what she's done."

"Alright then, unless there's something else, I'm prepared to rule."

When nobody said anything, he continued,

"Domestic Violence is a serious matter and an Injunction, if issued, can remain in effect for up to one year, or longer in some cases. The purpose of an Injunction is to prevent any acts of violence within a family unit or, in some cases, the extended family. This Court does not take these matters lightly. There is no doubt that an act of violence occurred, but the Court finds the circumstances under which that act occurred to be extremely extenuating ones. I have no doubt in my mind that Mr. Thibodeaux did not intend to hurt his wife that night, given the fact that he was just released from jail that very day after five months of being incarcerated. I have no doubt that he wanted to be with his wife that night and re-unite with his daughter. I cannot, in good conscience, issue an Injunction under those circumstances. Therefore, the Temporary Injunction that was issued is hereby dissolved and the Petition for a Domestic Violence Injunction is denied. Case dismissed."

The Judge raised his gavel, smacked it on the bench in front of him as he stood, and began to leave the bench. Mrs. Winters asked,

"But your Honor, what about the marital residence, custody of the child and those matters?"

"That can be dealt with in the divorce case, Mrs. Winters, if one is filed, or they can figure that out between themselves, if and when they get out of jail. This case is dismissed."

At that, he exited the courtroom as the bailiff said,

"All rise!"

Jeremy looked over at Sally, who turned her head away, again. He was led out of the courtroom. Once in the van, on the way back to jail, he asked the driver,

"So does that mean I can go home?"

"Ask your lawyer. I can't answer that, but it's your house, isn't it? I heard him say you should take it up in the divorce. Have you filed for divorce?"

"No."

"Has she?"

"Not that I know of."

"Then it's your house as much as it is her house. That's what I'd say."

"Makes sense to me."

"But I'd get a court order, Mr. Thibodeaux. You don't want to get into a fight with her over it and find yourself back in jail. I know that. Are you going to file for divorce once you get out?"

"I don't know what I'm going to do. Right now, I just want to get out, and stay out."

"That's a good idea, Thibodeaux. We don't want to see you back here again. Nobody likes you, man!" he said, jokingly.

"Very funny, Mueller."

Chapter Twenty Two

On Monday of the following week, as he was sitting in his cell after dinner, staring at the pages of another Zane Grey book, not reading a word, just counting the minutes until he'd be out of jail again, one of the guards came up to the cell door and called his name. He walked to the door and said,

"Yes, Officer?"

"You've got some mail that you have to sign for. Here's a pen. Sign on the line where you see your name."

"What is it?"

"Just sign the damn paper, Thibodeaux, and you can read it all night. It's about your kid."

"My kid?"

"Yeah."

Jeremy signed the piece of paper and took the legal-size envelope back to his bed, opened it, and began to read.

In the Circuit Court of the Eighth Judicial Circuit in and for Levy County
In the interest of:
SAMANTHA SUSAN THIBODEAUX, DOB 07/08/08
PETITION FOR ADJUDICATION OF DEPENDENCY
Comes now the Department of Children and Families (DCF), by and through counsel, and petitions this Court to adjudicate the above-named

minor child to be a dependent child within the meaning and intent of Chapter 39, Florida Statutes. As grounds, it states as follows:

1. This Court has jurisdiction over the minor child, SAMANTHA SUSAN THIBODEAUX, a female. At the time the dependency arose the child was in the custody of her mother in Levy County, Florida.
2. The mother of the minor child, namely SALLY ANN THIBODEAUX, is a resident of Levy County, Florida.
3. The father of the minor child, namely JEREMY ROY THIBODEAUX, is a resident of Levy County, Florida.
4. Both the mother and the father are presently incarcerated for criminal offenses. Both parents are believed to be involved with the use of controlled substances, without a prescription from a medical doctor allowing them to do so. It is presently unknown when either or both parents will be released from incarceration.
5. The child is a dependent child within the meaning of Chapter 39, Florida Statutes, in that the parents are presently unable to care for the child due to their incarceration. Furthermore, due to the apparent level of drug usage known to exist, there is a substantial question as to whether or not the child would be safe with either parent until such time as the drug usage ceases entirely.
6. This Court conducted an emergency shelter hearing on October 2, 2011 at which time the child was placed in the custody of the Department until such time as a formal Petition for Adjudication of Dependency could be filed.
7. Since that time, the Department has placed the child with the Paternal Grandmother, ROSEMARY LOUISE THIBODEAUX, who resides in Levy County, Florida.

Wherefore, the Department asks that this Court formally determine and declare that the said minor child, SAMANTHA SUSAN THIBODEAUX, be adjudicated a dependent child within the meaning of the law. The Department further requests that this Court enter a judgment and order granting the following relief:

1. Adjudicate the child a dependent child by a finding of clear and convincing evidence that the parents are presently unable to properly care for their child;
2. Place the child into the temporary legal custody of the Department; and
3. Such other and further relief as this Court deems just and proper as further evidence develops.

THIS PETITION IS FILED IN GOOD FAITH

_____

EMMY ROSALIE HOLLY, ESQ.
Attorney for DCF

Jeremy felt his chest, stomach and all his internal organs drop a foot. Although he didn't think it possible, he had reached a new low. Now he was going to lose his child, too.

At least she was with his mother, he thought. He tried not to think about it, but he was unable to keep those bad thoughts out of his head. He hoped that this was the bottom. He didn't want to go any lower. The only good news was that his attorney told him that his Probation Officer would not be recommending that his probation be violated. A hearing on his change of plea on the Battery charge was scheduled for Friday afternoon. She told him that he'd be getting out of jail then, if all went as planned.

Since he knew he was getting out, he called his uncle to come get him on Friday afternoon, after work. When Friday finally arrived, after he entered a plea to the Battery charge and was sentenced to time-served, he was allowed to walk out of the jail, again, but not until Judge Frick again threatened him with prison if he ever saw him in court on criminal charges another time, Jeremy saw that Ray, one of the other guys who worked for his uncle, was there to meet him when he walked out of the jail a second time. This time, he knew he was going home to an empty house.

"Ricky told me to come get you. He wants to see you first thing Monday morning. He wants to talk to you before he'll let you come back to work."

"Yeah. He's not happy with me. I got myself all messed up with those drugs and now people think I'm a druggie and a wife-beater and all kinds of bad things."

"Yeah, that's probably what he's thinking, but you ain't alone on this. There's a lot of guys doin' those pills and getting messed up on them all over this county, especially in Cedar Key."

"That's no consolation to me, Ray. I've been in jail for almost six months now. I don't ever want to go back. I just want to go to work and raise my daughter."

"What's gonna happen with Sally?"

"I don't know. She's in jail now herself, in Marion County."

"That's what we heard."

"Say Ray, no offense, but I don't want to talk about any of this shit right now."

"That's cool. I don't blame you for that, man. You been through some serious shit, haven't you?"

"You can say that again."

"Is it as bad in there as they say?"

"I didn't get sent to prison, so I don't know how that is, but the Levy County jail is no place you want to be. It's as boring as hell, they treat you like shit, plus the food ain't worth a damn. That much I can say for sure."

"But I'm talkin' about guys doin' shit to other guys and all that."

"It happens, but it didn't happen to me. It's no place you want to be, Ray. Trust me on that. I am never going back."

When Jeremy got home, the first thing he did was call his mother and ask if he could see Samantha.

"Well I don't know, Jeremy, if I can let you do that. She was put in my custody by the Department of Children and Families. I think I'll have to ask them about that."

"But it's Friday afternoon, Mom! They won't be there until Monday morning. I can't wait that long."

"Well, alright. You can come see her, but you can't take her from my house. How's that?"

"That'll be fine. You're in charge. I just want to see her. I haven't seen her in six months."

"I just can't let you take her away from me, Jeremy. What would they do with her then? They might take her away from me and take her to Crystal River to Sally's mother's house, or put her in some stranger's house. I doubt that they'd put her with Sally's father, but I don't want to take a chance. You know I want you to see your daughter, son, but I have to be careful, too. You understand, don't you?"

"I know, Mom."

"And she misses you so much, too. She asks 'where's my Daddy' all the time. I told her you went away to make some money and you're coming back to see her any day. She'll be so excited."

"I've got to shower and get cleaned up, and that's going to take me a little while, but could you come get me? Sally sold my truck and her car is in Ocala someplace. I'll have to see about going to get it. Would you do that for me?"

"Of course I will, but you have to promise me that you won't say a word about this to that DCF worker, and you won't cause me any trouble when it's time for you to go."

"I won't. I promise."

His mother paused, hesitated, and then said,

"I'll tell you what, Jeremy…I'll bring her over to your house in an hour. How's that?"

"That'll be great, Mom. Thanks."

"I'm just so sorry about all that has happened to the two of you. I hope you get this mess straightened out."

"I don't know what's going to happen. I'm just glad to be home. See you whenever you get here."

Jeremy made some calls and found out where Sally's car had been towed. Since his name was on the title, he had as much right to it as she did. There was a large fee to be paid for towing and storage. Jeremy was going to have to borrow some money to pay for it, plus get a ride over to Ocala. With his father dead, and his mother financially strapped, his uncle Ricky was his only hope. He'd have to talk to him and hope for the best.

Later that afternoon, after Jeremy had cleaned himself and the house up as best he could, he ran outside when he heard his mother's car pull in the driveway. She opened the door, took Samantha out of her car seat, and helped her as she scrambled out of the car. She immediately went running towards her father, yelling,

"Daddy!"

Jeremy got down on both knees, holding back tears of happiness, and greeted her with open arms.

"I had to go away for a while but now I'm back and I'm not going away ever again. I promise."

He looked at her and saw that she had grown in the six months since he'd seen her. Her hair was longer. He felt a strange sensation as he looked at her, having nothing but love for his little girl and, at the same time realizing how much she looked like Sally did when she her age.

"I think you've grown a foot, Sweetheart! But you're still Daddy's little girl, aren't you?"

He squeezed her tight until Samantha exclaimed, "Daddy! You're hurting me!"

"I'm sorry, Samantha! I'm just so happy to see you, that's all."

He picked her up and carried her inside. His mother followed them in, but not before Jeremy looked over at his mother and said, "Thanks, Mom. I'm sorry about all this."

As Jeremy and Samantha were rolling around on the floor in her room, playing with whatever toys and whatever game Samantha wanted to play with, Mrs. Thibodeaux looked in the pantry and in the refrigerator, and said,

"Jeremy, I'm going to run down to the Dollar Store and get a few things. Don't go anywhere."

"I won't," he hollered back. "I can't! I don't have a car!"

She bought some food, milk, juice, cereal and some bread and sandwich meat, and returned half an hour later. Jeremy and Samantha were still lying on the floor in her room, getting re-acquainted.

"I'll tell you what…you just call me when you get tired, or she gets sleepy, and I'll come get her. It's 6:00 now. I'll be back by 8:00 if I haven't heard from you. She goes to bed by 8:30 most every night, at least when she's with me she does."

"Great! Thanks, Mom. What are you going to do?"

"I'm going to rest for a while. That daughter of yours tires me out."

At 8:00, she came back for Samantha, who asked why she couldn't stay at her home. Mrs. Thibodeaux told her she could come back in the morning if she wanted to, and that made her happy. It made Jeremy happy, too.

That Monday, Jeremy went in to work to meet with his uncle.

"Jeremy, I want you to know that if it weren't for the fact your father was my brother I wouldn't be talking to you, do you understand?"

"Yes, Uncle Ricky, I do."

"And if he were here to take care of you I'd leave it up to him, and I know what he'd do…he'd whip your ass, and good. As for me, I don't want anything to do with you until you get yourself cleaned up."

"I've been in jail for almost six months, Uncle Ricky. I haven't had so much as a drop of alcohol since I first got arrested that day."

"I've heard it before, Jeremy. Over the years I've had a whole lot of people workin' for me who were drinking too much, doin' drugs and takin' pills and they'd steal from me, wouldn't show up for work, and when they did they weren't worth a shit. I don't want that Jeremy. I've got no use for anybody who wants to do that shit, you hear?"

"I hear, Uncle Ricky."

"If I see you do anything that makes me think you've been takin' that shit again I'll fire you so fast it will make your head swim. You understand?"

"And if you so much as show up ten minutes late for work without asking permission, I'll fire you! You understand?"

"I understand."

"And if I even hear a rumor that you're goin' out to the bars and runnin' around acting crazy, I'll fire you. You understand?"

"I understand, Uncle Ricky."

"And if I hear that you aren't takin' care of that baby of yours, I'll fire you. Understand?"

"I understand."

"I'm not happy about this, Jeremy!"

"I know."

Ricky walked around in circles for a few seconds, calmed down a bit, and said,

"Alright, I'll give you your old job back, but you're starting out at a beginning salary, you hear? You're being punished for what you did!"

"I know. I understand. I'm sorry for what I did, Uncle Ricky."

"Alright. I got that out of my system. Now come here and give me a hug. You're my nephew and I love you."

The two men embraced.

"Now get out there and go to work."

"Uncle Ricky, before I do, there's one more thing."

"What's that?"

"I need to borrow $500."

"$500! You're kidding, right?" Ricky laughed out loud, certain that Jeremy was trying to be funny. "That's not funny, Jeremy. I'm serious about this shit. I hope you don't think I was kidding about anything I said to you, because I'm not."

"No, I'm not trying to be funny. Sally sold my truck and her car was impounded by the police when she got arrested. I've got to get over to Ocala and get her car. My name's on it, too."

"She sold your truck while you were in jail?"

"Yeah. I didn't know anything about it. I guess she needed the money to buy those pills she got caught with."

"Jeremy, if you weren't my nephew...."

Ricky scratched his head, walked around in a circle once or twice more, and then said, "Yeah, I'll advance you the money. Come see me at the end of the day. How'd you get here this morning?"

"I walked."

"You walked?"

"Somebody picked me up, but I walked a mile or so. I was here by 6:30. I didn't want to be late."

"How are you going to get home?"

"I haven't figured that out yet."

"How are you going to get to Ocala?"

"I have no idea."

"Damn, Jeremy!"

He hesitated for a few seconds and then said,

"What time does that place close in Ocala?"

"6:00."

"I'll give you a ride over after work. We'll leave at 4:00. You're going to owe me big time for this, Jeremy. I'm going to take a hundred dollars out of each paycheck until I'm repaid, agreed?"

"I agree. Thanks, Uncle Ricky."

That afternoon, the two men drove over to Ocala and retrieved the silver, 2005 Toyota Corolla that Sally had been driving before her arrest.

"That's going to make her day when she finds out about that, won't it?" Jeremy remarked.

"She shouldn't have sold your truck without asking you first, Jeremy."

"Those drugs are bad news, Uncle Ricky. It makes you do stupid things."

"Well, I hope you learned your lesson."

"I did. If I mess up again, the next time I'm going to prison, and I don't want there to be a next time."

"And you'd better get that car put in your name right now, Jeremy, or else when she gets out she's gonna come get it, just like you just did."

"Can I do that?"

"If it's says Jeremy or Sally, you can. If it says Jeremy and Sally, you can't. What does it say?"

"It says 'or'."

"Then you can. Do it!"

Chapter Twenty Three

The Public Defender's Office had been appointed to represent Sally, since she had no money and no ability to retain a lawyer. Ten days after she was arrested, an investigator came to interview her. Sally was having a hard time adjusting to the "cold turkey" treatment jail offered for drug users. Many of the worst side effects were plaguing her, including nausea, headaches, constipation, anxiety, irritability and insomnia. She was a nervous wreck and behaving like never before.

"So why'd it take you so long to come see me?"

"We're very busy, Mrs. Thibodeaux. We do the best we can."

"Ten days? I could have died in here and you all wouldn't have known a thing about it? What kind of lawyers are you?"

"Actually, I'm not a lawyer, I'm an investigator."

"Great! When do I get to see a lawyer? Sometime before the trial I hope."

"As soon as I can get a report prepared, and a lawyer has an opportunity to review it, someone will be over. Now, if you would, please tell me what happened."

Sally explained, in rambling fashion, all that occurred that night.

"So the pills were found in your purse, not in your clothes or on your person, right?"

"That's right."

"And you didn't consent to them searching your purse, right?"

"No. Of course I didn't. I knew the pills were in there."

"And you weren't under arrest for doing anything wrong, correct?"

"No. I didn't do anything wrong. I was a passenger in Slim's car. Don't you get it? I was framed! I'm being held here illegally. You need to get me out of here…now!"

The investigator lowered his head, let out a sigh, and continued,

"And he wasn't arrested for drugs, correct?"

"No, just for illegally possessing a gun. That's what they said. I heard something about him being a felon. They had a search warrant."

"To search his car, not your purse, right?"

"That's right. They had no right to search my purse. Are you listening to me?"

"I heard you, but I'm not the lawyer, remember? I'll discuss it with a lawyer and let him or her tell you what the law is."

"You're not a lawyer….that's right," Sally said, shaking her head. "So when will I get to see a real lawyer?"

"Once I get my report written up and hand it to the administrative assistant, an attorney will be assigned and that's when someone will come see you. We represent so many people we have to do things in an orderly fashion of some kind or people could get lost in the system."

"And I'm not getting out of here until I see a lawyer, am I?"

"Not unless you post a $50,000 bond."

"That's not going to happen. Say, can you do one thing for me?" she asked with dripping sarcasm, "Can you find out if Stanley Foreman is still in the Levy County jail or if he bonded out? He might post my bond if he's out."

"I'll see what I can do and let you know. I should be able to find out if he's still in the Detention Center or not. That shouldn't be a problem."

"That will be great. So even though you aren't a lawyer, don't you think I have a good case? Shouldn't I be getting out of here soon?"

"It sounds like a good case to me, but I didn't go to law school. I'm not the lawyer."

"I know. I said that. I just asked what you think."

The investigator sat silently, hoping the interview was over and either he could leave or Sally would go away.

"Would you please tell the lawyer assigned to my case to come see me immediately? I need to get out of here, and soon!"

Sally stood and huffed out of the room, unhappy that she didn't achieve her purpose, which was to get out of jail that day. The young investigator, a Criminal Justice major at a local college on a summer internship with the Public Defender's Office, breathed a sigh of relief when Sally finally left the room where the interview was conducted.

Sally's mother, who lived in Crystal River, over an hour away from Ocala, accepted Sally's collect phone calls but she wasn't willing to make the drive to Ocala to see her right away. She promised to visit at the first opportunity, as soon as she could find someone to go with her. It was too long a drive for her to go by herself, and she wasn't particularly sympathetic to her daughter's demands.

Sally began crying uncontrollably when she received the Petition for Adjudication of Dependency from the Department of Children and Families. She was even more upset when, a week later, her mother told her that Jeremy was out of jail and visiting with Samantha every day.

"How did you find that out?"

"The DCF worker came by my house to interview me. She told me. She said she was going to visit you, too. She hasn't been there yet?"

"Not yet."

A few days later, the DCF worker arrived at the Marion County Detention Center, unaware of what awaited her.

"I don't want him having anything to do with Samantha. He's liable to take her and run off to Alaska! Don't let him have her!" She shrieked.

Mrs. Easterly told her that Jeremy wasn't allowed to have her, either. The court Order took Samantha away from both of them and put her in the custody of the closest relative, other than the parents, and that was Mrs. Thibodeaux.

"I don't want his mother to leave my daughter alone with him! I don't trust him! What if he were to run off and get arrested again. That could happen. And what would become of Samantha? That's his mother! What's she going to do? Why can't my mother have Samantha?"

"I understand your concerns," Mrs. Easterly responded.

"Well, I don't think you appreciate how strongly I feel about this, Mrs…..."

"Easterly, and yes, I do, and I'll do what I think is best for Samantha. She's the one who has done nothing wrong and she's the one I'm most concerned about now. Until you get out of this place you're in, you'll have to just trust me to do what's best for her, Sally."

"I'm sure you will, Mrs. Easterly, but you've got to listen to me! Please! Please! Please! Believe me when I tell you not to trust Samantha's father. It's his fault that I'm in here. I'd never taken so much as an aspirin before he brought that junk into my house! This is all his fault! When I get out of here I'm going to want to get her back right away. You can do that for me, right?"

"That's up to the Judge, Mrs. Thibodeaux. We'll have to see about that. I'll make sure she's well taken care of until then."

When Sally called Jeremy's mother, she was pleasantly surprised when her collect call was accepted.

"I think jail changed Jeremy for the better, Sally. I hope it helps you, too. All he wants to do is be with Samantha."

"Don't trust him! I know he's your son, but he's my husband. I know him better than you do. He'll be back doing those drugs again. I'm sure of it. Is he back working?"

"Yes. He's back working with his uncle, every day except for Sunday."

"When I get out, Mrs.Thibodeaux. I want my daughter back!"

"That's not up to me, Sally, but you're welcome at my house anytime. You know that. You just can't take her from me. I can't let either you or Jeremy do that. She's been put in my care for now."

Sally wasn't happy when her conversation with Mrs. Thibodeaux ended. She was sure Jeremy was getting Samantha whenever he wanted and doing whatever he wanted. She was going to have to talk to Mrs. Easterly and have him watched.

Jeremy began a pattern of living that involved working in the water with the clams, and doing all the things he was able to do before the injury, and going home, seeing Samantha, then going to sleep. He spent all of his spare time with Samantha. Every Monday, he would have to report to his Probation Officer, take a urine test, fill out a form, and pay some money towards his cost of supervision and towards the cost of his incarceration.

Since one of the terms of his probation was that he not consume alcohol, he didn't even think about going into one of the bars in town after work. He was squeaky clean, and didn't miss a day of work or show up late even once. Seeing Samantha was the highlight of every day.

It was early September and temperatures were still in the high eighties, and even though he spent time in the waters of the Gulf, working with clam bags, he liked to take Samantha to Blue Springs or Henry Beck park, both of which were a good half hour from his house, but the cool waters refreshed him and his daughter, and both parks had swings and sand for her to play in. His mother went with him every time. She never let him take Samantha by himself, ever.

"That worker from DCF said it was up to me. I'm in charge, but I can't entrust her to you, Jeremy, and I won't entrust her to Sally, either. She'd get mad if she found out and make a great big stink over it. I know she would. I'm not going to risk that."

Sally was learning all about the criminal justice system, just as Jeremy had. Many of the inmates were "jailhouse lawyers," and they told her that she'd been wrongly arrested. Very early on she had become convinced that she shouldn't even be in jail, that she should be released right away. She grew angrier and angrier as each day went by.

She was especially miffed by the fact that she couldn't get her Public Defender to come see her as often as she wanted him to. Even after a month of "cold turkey" she was still feeling many of the adverse effects of a forced withdrawal. For most of her life, she had been a person with a sunny disposition and an even temperament. She never cursed, at least not when people might hear her, and she always had kind words for people. Jail did not become her. Every day was a "bad hair day," and she didn't look good in orange.

"God damned son-of-a-bitch! That's what he gets paid for, to represent my ass! I haven't seen the bastard since I've been here. It's been five weeks now!"

She started writing letters and lodging complaints, and telling everyone who got within earshot of her situation. A week later, attorney Rupert Dowling went to see her. He was a short, painfully thin man, with thick black glasses, straight black hair and a sheet white complexion. He wasn't prepared for Sally.

"So where have you been? You didn't get my messages?"

"Yes, I did, Mrs. Thibodeaux, but I have a caseload of over a hundred clients. You're not the only one."

"I hope you don't treat all your clients the way you treat me. If you do, you should lose your job!"

"Yes, well, I tried to find another assistant Public Defender to take your case but nobody volunteered. Nobody likes a client who complains about everything, especially one who sends a letter a day to our boss."

"Hey! I'm real sorry about that, but I want out of here. I was illegally arrested! You agree with that much, don't you?"

"Actually, we do think you have a very good case and that you have a good chance of having the charges against you dismissed."

"So why haven't you done something about it?"

"Because the State Attorney's Office doesn't agree with us."

"Why not?"

"Because they say that the drugs were found in your purse as a result of a routine inventory search, not as part of the Search Warrant."

"What difference does that make? It's illegal, right?"

"We think so. Our position is that once they found the gun there was no need to conduct any further search of the car and that they should have let you gather your belongings and leave."

"What do they say?"

"They say that they had an obligation to inventory what was inside the vehicle before having it towed away."

"Why couldn't they have just left it where it was? The bar wouldn't have minded, I'm sure. Slim was a regular customer and everybody there liked him."

"I have no doubt that is true, but the State says once it arrested your companion they had a duty to make sure that all of his personal belongings were protected."

"That's bullshit! Why couldn't they just let me drive Slim's car off?"

"That's a good point. You weren't under arrest for anything. Slim would have agreed to that, and we think the police should have offered him that option."

"So how do we make them agree with us and get me out of here?"

"The only way is for a Judge to enter an order making them let you go."

"So how long do I have to wait until that happens?"

"I have to take some depositions of the arresting Officers and establish the facts so that the court can have a basis on which to make a ruling."

"How long does that take?"

"It could take a couple of months."

"A couple of months?" To take a few depositions, whatever those are? What kind of lawyer are you? Can't we sue them?"

"No, our office only defends people. We don't sue people."

"Great! I'm glad I'm not paying you any money for this. You don't deserve any. So what's the deal with depositions? How come they aren't set yet if we have to have them?"

"Well, the depositions are set for next month, but then they have to be typed up after the deposition is over, and then we file a motion to suppress the evidence, and then we go before the court and make our argument. It all takes time."

Sally stood up, raised her voice, started waving her hands above her head, and said,

"Oh, shit! This is not right! I shouldn't be in here! Who do I have to talk to about this? Who is your supervisor?"

"Mrs. Thibodeaux, you know who my boss is. You write to him every day. I have been assigned by him to represent you and I am your lawyer, but I'm not going to put up with this. Either you lower your voice, and sit down, immediately, or I am leaving. Do you hear me?"

Sally huffed, sat down, and glared at him, not saying a word. He continued,

"So please keep in mind that I am on your side and I am the ONLY person on your side at this time. I wish someone else would take over this case, but no one else will, and you are facing a serious charge, a second degree felony, which carries fifteen years in jail. Those were some seriously illegal pills you had on you and you will be very lucky if we can get these charges against you dismissed on a technicality. You are guilty of possessing an illegal substance and the only reason you're going to get off, if you do get off, is because the police made a mistake when they searched your purse. Do you understand that? And please understand that is our argument. The Judge has to agree with it. He or she might not. You are, in fact, guilty of possessing an illegal substance!"

Sally started screaming again,

"They violated my Fourth Amendment rights! I'm a citizen and I have a right to be free from an illegal search and seizure! That's not a technicality! Where did you go to law school anyway? You didn't learn that in law school? I should be suing them, but you can't help me with that! What good are you anyway."

"Okay, Mrs. Thibodeaux. That's it. Stop screaming at me. I am leaving right now."

Mr. Dowling stood and began to leave.

"As I told you before, I can't help you with any case you wish to file against the state. The Public Defender's Office only defends people. We don't handle civil cases. We only do criminal law. We cannot sue the State on your behalf. You can call some private lawyers and see if any of them are willing to help you."

Sally looked down at her feet, shaking her head back and forth and said,

"This ain't right!"

"Mrs. Thibodeaux, if you want a different lawyer you can always hire yourself a private lawyer."

Mr. Dowling was standing in the doorway to the visitation room, with one foot inside the room and one foot outside the room. Sally responded,

"I don't have the money for that and you know it! Don't be a smart ass!"

"Then you're stuck with me and I'm stuck with you. And you'd better start acting a whole lot nicer to me than you do. I'm leaving now. Is there anything else I can do for you today?"

Sally looked at the pale, thin, weakling who stood in front of her and thought to herself that she might be able to kick his ass all by herself, but she knew she'd get in trouble if she did, so she bit her tongue and said, in the sweetest voice she could muster,

"No. That's enough for today, but I want you to do your best to get that Motion heard as soon as is humanly possible. Can you do that for me, pretty please?" Sally asked, in a tone of voice that wreaked of insincerity.

"Yes ma'am. I'll do the best I can."

Sally stood and walked out of the room, right past Mr. Dowling, muttering to herself something about him being a sorry son-of-a-bitch.

After Jeremy had been out of jail for a few weeks, he made a phone call to Mrs. Easterly, the DCF worker. He asked if it might be possible for him to get to see his daughter without his mother being there all the time.

"Mr. Thibodeaux, right now the only thing that is important is the well-being of that child of yours. The Court has to be certain that if she's put back in your care that she will be well taken care of."

"I can promise you she will be."

"She needs to stay where she is, I think. Don't you?"

"She's my daughter. I think she needs to be with me. I'm okay now."

"And what will you do with her while you're working?"

"I guess my mother can watch her."

"The Department can provide a variety of services to assist you, if and when the child is returned to you, including some child supervision services, homemaker services, training, counseling and things like that, but first we have to complete our investigation, write some reports and decide whether or not we believe it's safe to return her to you, and we're not at that point yet."

"How long will that take?"

"It could take a few weeks or a few months, depending upon what our investigation reveals."

"Your investigation?"

"Yes. We're going to talk to your employer, your friends, people who know you, get your school records…find out everything we can about you. That takes a while."

Jeremy heaved a deep sigh and asked,

"Would it help if Sally and I were divorced?"

"It might, but it might not. We'll have to do an investigation into her background as well. If the two of you are together, then that is one situation. If the two of you are divorced, that's a different situation. I can't tell you which one is better. I don't know either of you well enough yet, but I will tell you that your wife is not particularly pleased with the fact that you get to see so much of Samantha. She would much prefer that her mother have some custodial rights."

"I'm sure she does," Jeremy responded, "but she's still in jail, so we don't have to worry about that just yet, do we?"

"No, but once she gets out, if she gets out, then, based on what she's said to me, I think we both will be hearing from her quite a bit."

"Yeah. You're right about that. Maybe I should file for divorce now, while she's still in jail, while there's no question of her having any right to see Samantha."

"That's up to you. I'm not going to say one word about that to you, either way."

"That divorce Judge might get me Samantha back sooner maybe?"

"Maybe. I can't say. The judges work together and they all rely upon us. It takes time."

"I'm thinking it might be better off to be divorced."

"That's up to you, Mr. Thibodeaux. I don't know what else I can tell you about that."

Jeremy paused, thinking about the likely costs of hiring a lawyer and filing for divorce, and then asked,

"So do you need anything from me?"

"I'll need for you to complete some forms and I'll call you if I have any questions. I'll put them in the mail to you today."

After Jeremy had saved up enough money, he found a lawyer in Cedar Key who was willing to take his case and allow him to pay over time. The Clerk's Office took a partial payment towards the $408 filing fee, with the requirement that he pay it all off within four months. Jeremy signed the necessary papers and had filed for divorce a week later. He had to pay $40 to have a Marion County Sheriff serve Sally in jail. She was not happy when she received a copy of the summons and the complaint.

"Well if that don't beat all! He's suing me for divorce!"

One of the other women asked,

"What did you expect? You run around on him while he's in jail and he catches you…"

"You shut up, bitch!" Sally grabbed her hair and the two began to fight. The guards came in, restrained both of them and put them in separate cells. When she was alone, she started to cry. Her life was a mess and there was no way she could straighten it out, not while she was in jail. She couldn't recognize the person she had become. She didn't like what she saw.

Jeremy was required by the DCF case worker to take various tests and to complete the Drug Treatment Program offered by Meridian, the local mental health clinic. Since he'd been ordered to do that as part of his probation, he was well along on the thirteen week program. Since he had taken the Parenting Class in jail, and received a certificate a few months earlier, he wasn't required to take it again.

After two months of steady work and regular reporting, the case worker was willing to recommend that he be allowed to have overnight visitation with Samantha, and since Sally was still in jail, there was no one to oppose him. Her recommendation was approved. His mother still cared for Samantha on a daily basis, since Jeremy was at work all day, and she was still the legal custodian, but Samantha was allowed to spend more and more time with Jeremy, in her own home. She missed her mother, but she was glad to have her father back in her life.

"Now what's going to happen when Sally gets out of jail?" his mother asked.

"I don't know. My lawyer is working on getting the divorce over with before she gets out of jail. That's what we're hoping for."

"Well when she gets out of jail, if she gets out of jail, you know she's going to want to get Samantha from the both of us, don't you?"

"Yeah. That is for sure. My lawyer says if I can get a divorce now, the order will probably say that she can't have any rights to see the child until she gets permission from the court to do so. That will slow her down some."

"I hope you two find a way to be civil to one another, and keep the lawyers and the rest out of it all."

"Right now, that isn't possible, Mom. I am stuck in a world of lawyers, lawsuits, Probation Officers, Police Officers, DCF workers and who knows what else. Life was a lot simpler before I got hurt that day, wasn't it?"

"That it was, son. I hope you can get back to that someday."

"Me, too, Mom."

When Sally didn't respond to the divorce complaint twenty days after being served, a default was entered against her by the clerk. Less than two weeks after that, Jeremy obtained an uncontested divorce which included language in the order which prohibited Sally from having any visitation with Samantha, which was not supervised by a DCF worker, until the further order of the court, which meant that Sally would have to petition the court and get a Judge to sign an order allowing her any unsupervised visitation. That would take a while for Sally to accomplish.

The Court Order also gave Jeremy the exclusive use and possession of the marital home until Samantha turned eighteen or graduated from high school, or the further order of the Court, if and when Sally got out of jail. There were no marital assets other than the house to consider, except for the car, and the order said that Jeremy would have to sell the house and split the proceeds once Samantha turned eighteen, graduated from high school, or became emancipated, whichever came first, but he could keep the house, provided he made all the payments, until then.

"Good riddance to him!" She told her cell mates, when she received her copy of the final divorce decree. She wasn't happy when she read the part where she couldn't have unsupervised visitation with Samantha until she petitioned the court and obtained an order allowing her to do so. When no one was watching, she cried.

Chapter Twenty Four

⊹⊹⊹

After four and a half months in jail, the day finally arrived when the motion Sally's attorney had filed to suppress the evidence seized by the Marion County deputies who searched her purse on the night she was arrested finally was to be heard. Sally was transported to the courtroom and she was able to hear the argument. The Judge began,

"So let me understand, Mr. Alvarez, the gun was found exactly where it was said to be, exactly where the Search Warrant indicated it would be, correct?"

"Yes, your Honor."

"And it is your contention that after the purpose of the Search Warrant had been fulfilled, the police still had a right to continue to search the vehicle, is that correct?"

"Yes, your Honor. The State is not contending that the pills were found as part of the search authorized by the Warrant, although it is the State's position that a further search of the vehicle would have been permissible since there could have been other guns inside the vehicle, including inside the purse. It is not at all inconceivable that Mr. Foreman could have put a gun in Mrs. Thibodeaux's purse once the Officers stopped him, but…"

"But surely you're not suggesting that the Officers had a right to search a woman's purse, pursuant to that Warrant, are you?"

"No, your Honor. We won't make that argument, but we think a search of the vehicle at that time, under those circumstances, for additional weapons, was reasonable and proper."

"But the search warrant authorized a search of the vehicle and was very specific about what part of the vehicle was to be searched, wasn't it, sir?"

"Yes, sir. That's true, but…"

"So, as I understand it, the primary basis for legitimizing the search of Mrs. Thibodeaux's purse is that the purse was found while the Officers were conducting an inventory of the vehicle, because the vehicle had to be impounded once the owner of the vehicle was arrested, is that correct?"

"Yes, your Honor. That is correct. That is our main argument, but we have the others."

"So basically you are saying that it wasn't a search at all. Your position is that the Officers were doing nothing more than protecting the personal property of the man arrested. Have I got that right?"

"That and the Officers had to inventory the vehicle so that no one could later come back and say that the Officers had improperly removed items from the vehicle or that someone else had come along and taken items from the vehicle, and they were also making sure there were no more guns in the vehicle."

"So law enforcement was performing an administrative function at the time, not an investigation, once Mr. Foreman was arrested, handcuffed and placed in the back of a police vehicle, is that correct?"

"Yes, your Honor. I think that's a fair statement."

"But the Officers never specifically asked Mr. Foreman about the vehicle and what should be done with it, is that correct?"

The Assistant State Attorney, squirmed a bit and replied, "That is correct, your Honor."

"And your argument, Mr. Dowling, is that they had no right to search the purse since they knew the purse didn't belong to the owner of the vehicle, Mr. Foreman, and that it belonged to your client, who was a passenger in the vehicle, and the Officers had no reason whatsoever to think that she had committed a crime, at least not at that time. Is that correct?"

"Yes, your Honor. We have a couple of other arguments, too, but that is certainly the strongest."

"And the other arguments are that there was no need to impound the vehicle because your client could have driven it off or the vehicle could have been left at the scene, since it was in a private place and not in a place which might have constituted an obstacle for other citizens. Is that right?"

"Yes, your Honor, it is, but we also would suggest that it was a pretext. The Officers wanted to search that vehicle and they were looking for an excuse to do so. They suspected that Mr. Foreman was dealing drugs and this gun charge was a ruse to allow them to arrest him."

"A ruse?"

"That may be a little strong, your Honor, but…"

"The man was a convicted felon in possession of a firearm. There is absolutely nothing improper about the search or the arrest, or at least nothing that I have seen or heard which would indicate it was improper."

"I'm not suggesting that it was. What I'm saying is that they went too far. They made a valid stop; they conducted a valid search; they found exactly what they were looking for, and then they went too far. For them to argue that it wasn't a search is disingenuous. Those Officers were going to search that vehicle that night no matter what. The argument that they were simply inventorying the man's vehicle for the protection of his property is laughable. That was a search."

"Your Honor, I take offense at…"

"That's enough. I've read the motion and the memoranda you have filed, and I've read the cases you both rely upon and I think the decision of the Florida Supreme Court in the case of State vs. Miller, 403 Southern Second at page 1307, is the most persuasive. As the Court said, and I quote,

"…We hold: (1) the purpose of an inventory search is a caretaking function exclusively for (a) protection of the owner's property; (b) protection of the police from claims and disputes over lost or stolen property which has not been impounded, and (c) protection of the police from danger; (2) an inventory search is not conducted in order to discover evidence of a crime, and any suggestion that standard police procedure for an inventory search is actually a pretext for an investigative search will require the search to meet traditional probable cause standards or be invalidated; (3) there must be a threshold inquiry by the trial court to determine that the impoundment was for the above purposes and was reasonable and necessary under the circumstances; and …"

The Judge stopped reading, looked up, and said,
"I want you two to pay particular attention to this statement…"

"…and (4) when the owner or possessor of the vehicle is present, the arresting Officers must advise him or her that the motor vehicle will be impounded unless the owner or possessor can provide a reasonable alternative to impoundment…"

"So, unless the State has some further basis upon which to suggest that the search, or non-search, was justified, I am required to follow the law, given the facts of this case. And it is my considered opinion that the Officers did not have a right to inventory the vehicle under any of those criteria. Most significantly, by your own admission, Mr. Alvarez, the Officers failed to follow the procedure established by the Supreme Court in that they failed to advise Mr. Foreman that his car would be impounded and they failed to ask him if there was a reasonable alternative to impoundment.

"Clearly, in this case, the Defendant was present and, presumably, able to drive the vehicle away if Mr. Foreman wished for her to do so. That option was not, apparently, even considered."

The Judge then cleared his throat, put down the papers he was reading from, turned to the two attorneys and said,

"And having made those findings of fact, it is my conclusion that the Officers were, in fact, conducting what was, at that point, a warrantless search of the vehicle, and that it was a search which they didn't have the right to conduct. And they certainly had no right to search this woman's purse pursuant to that warrant, or for any legally justifiable reason that I am aware of.

"Hence, the search of Defendant's purse was unlawful. Therefore,

I grant the Motion to Suppress the drugs found in Defendant's purse pursuant to that unlawful, and warrantless, search. I assume the State won't be able to proceed without the evidence, correct Mr. Alvarez?"

"Yes, your Honor, but we may wish to appeal the decision of the Court and we would ask that you not release the Defendant from jail until the time for filing a Motion for Rehearing has expired."

"No, I'm not going to do that under these circumstances. If I had any doubt about the merits of your position I might be more inclined to grant your request. In this case, I am going to order that she be released on her own recognizance at this time. I'll leave the case on the docket and you can decide how you wish to proceed. That will be all for today."

The Judge stood and left the courtroom. Sally turned and said, "So that means I get out of jail?"

"That's right. You should be out of jail by the end of the day. Congratulations, Mrs. Thibodeaux. You dodged a huge bullet."

Sally started to cry. Then she said to her attorney,

"Yeah, I know what you're thinking...I'm sorry for being such a pain in the ass but everybody told me that unless you were the squeaky wheel you didn't get any grease."

"Well you certainly were the squeaky wheel, Mrs. Thibodeaux, weren't you?"

"Yeah. I guess I was. Thank you for all you did for me."

Sally leaned forward as if to give the man a hug. He quickly backed up.

"You're welcome," he said. "I hope I never see you again inside this courtroom or in the Marion County jail."

"I'm sure you do."

"And maybe a nice letter of commendation to my employer would be a good thing, too."

"I'll do that for you. I will."

"Good luck, Mrs. Thibodeaux." He turned and walked away, without even so much as a handshake.

Sally was released from jail several hours later. She was extremely angry to learn that her car was no longer at the lot where it had been towed, but she didn't have enough money to get it out anyway. Fortunately for her, she had enough money to get a bus ticket to Crystal River to get to her mother's house. She called first, told her mother she was coming and asked her to pick her up at the bus terminal.

By the time they arrived back home at Mrs. Richards' place it was way past the time Mrs. Richards normally ate her dinner, and she didn't want to go home and cook. So they picked up an order of fried chicken, potatoes and beans from Kentucky Fried Chicken on the way home. As they were sitting down for their meal, after listening to an earful of Sally's complaints about how miserable her life and her circumstances were, her mother said,

"Sally, you're my only daughter and I love you very much, and you're welcome here, but I don't want any trouble and I don't want to hear you complain all the time. I have a very quiet and peaceful life here. I don't bother anyone and no one bothers me. I don't want you to change that."

"I'm not going to cause you any trouble, Mom. I just want to get my life back together, that's all. I have nowhere else to go."

"Well, let's eat our food, and take things one day at a time. How's that?"

The next day, the first thing Sally wanted her mother to do was to drive her up to Cedar Key so she could get her car back and to see Samantha. Somewhat begrudgingly, Mrs. Richards agreed to do so. She really didn't have a choice. It was either do it or hear about it all day long.

Jeremy was at work when they arrived at his mother's house. Mrs. Thibodeaux, who knew that something bad was about to happen, immediately called Jeremy, who immediately called the Sheriff's office. A deputy was dispatched to the scene and arrived to find Jeremy and Sally having a heated discussion. Jeremy showed him the divorce decree and a copy of the title to the vehicle. The deputy turned to Sally and said,

"Mrs. Thibodeaux, this car belongs to Mr. Thibodeaux and this decree says that you can't take your daughter with you. In fact, unless Mrs. Thibodeaux here says you can be here at all, you can't, and apparently she says you can't."

He then turned to Jeremy and said,

"What do you want me to do, sir? Do you want me to make her leave?"

"This is my mother's house, so you'll have to ask her. I just want to make sure that she doesn't take my car or my child and run off some place."

"If she does, I will arrest her."

The Officer turned to Jeremy's mother and asked,

"Do you want me to make her leave the premises, Mrs. Thibodeaux?"

"That won't be necessary, as long as she doesn't cause any trouble, and doesn't try to take Samantha, or Jeremy's car, or anything else, she's welcome here."

The Officer than turned to Sally and said,

"Do you understand that you are not to take this car and not to take this child from these premises, ma'am?"

"But that's not fair! That's my car! And that's my daughter!"

"You'll have to take that up with the Judge, ma'am. This Order says you can't do either. Do you understand?"

Sally lowered her head and said, "I understand."

The Officer then turned to Jeremy's mother once more and asked,

"Last chance. Are you sure you don't want me to ask her to leave?"

Mrs. Thibodeaux looked first over at Jeremy and then back over to Sally and said,

"Yes, I'm sure. I've known her all her life. I hate to see her like this, but I still love her, almost as much as I love my son."

"Alright then. Unless there is anything else, I will be on my way. If you have any trouble, I'll come back, but if I do, somebody's going to jail. Do you all understand that?"

He looked at Jeremy and Sally and waited for them to agree. When they did, he drove off. Jeremy didn't want to go back to work until Sally left and Sally stayed for a few hours, visiting with Samantha. The two grandmothers left the mother and daughter alone. Jeremy stayed in his car, outside the home, leaving Sally to be with Samantha by herself inside the house. The two grandmothers went in to town for some lunch at Kona Joe's Island Café, sitting on the back porch overlooking the back bayou.

When her mother came back to get her, Sally asked her to drive her back through the streets of Cedar Key. She'd been away for several months. She'd never been away from her two homes in Cedar Key, the only homes she'd ever known, for more than a week in her entire life, and she felt the pangs of remorse and regret at what had taken her away from her island paradise. When they drove off Jeremy went home. It was too late to go back to work.

As the two women were driving down Dock Street, Sally asked her mother to stop at Coconuts.

"You're not wanting to have something to drink, are you, Sally?"

"No. I just want to walk in and see the place. That's all."

"I'll stay in the car."

"No. You come in, too. We'll have an iced tea out on the pier, looking over the water."

"I'd rather not."

"Oh, come on, Mom! I need this. I'm at the lowest point in my life right now."

"At least you're not in jail anymore."

"That's true, but I lost my husband, my daughter, my job, my house, my car…everything I ever had… I've got nothing."

She started to cry.

"You've still got me, Dear, and I still love you."

They sat in the car, hugging each other, until Sally sat up and said,

"I needed that, Mom. Let's go inside."

Sally and her mother walked into Coconuts. As they did, Sally noticed Brianne seated at the bar. She was going to walk past without saying a word, but Brianne saw her and said,

"Hi Sally! How are you?"

Sally was taken aback by her friendliness, given their long history of dislike for one another. She stopped momentarily to respond.

"I'm fine, Brianne. How are you?"

"I'm doing great, thanks. How's Samantha?"

"She's growing up."

"What is she about three now?"

"She turned three in August."

"I heard about that trouble you got in. Is everything okay with that?"

Sally looked around and saw some familiar faces. Some people were over-hearing their conversation. She said,

"You remember my mother, don't you?"

"Yes. We met many times at school functions over the years. Nice to see you again, Mrs. Richards."

"Nice to see you again, Brianne."

"We were just going outside to have some tea. If you wanted to join us…"

"I'd be delighted, just for a minute or two. I was about to leave when you walked in."

The three women walked out on the dock to a table with an umbrella, where they had some privacy, and Sally said,

"Yeah. The charges were dismissed. It was illegal what they did to me. I never should have been arrested."

"Really?"

"Yeah. It was an illegal search. They searched my purse when they had no right to."

"And you had drugs in your purse, right?"

"Yes, I did."

"RoxyContins, right?"

Sally looked at her through squinted eyes, wondering how she knew about all of that, glancing at her mother, who was learning things she hadn't known.

"Yeah, that's true. How did you know?"

"I got arrested for the Roxy Blues, too, a while back. It just about ruined my life. They took my daughter away for four months or so. Scared me to death."

"Really? I had no idea."

"Jeremy never told you about me?"

The question startled Sally.

"No. What is it he didn't tell me?"

"I was his source of pills there for a while until I got arrested."

"Really? He never mentioned it."

"Well you and I were never too close, you know. Maybe that's why he didn't tell you."

There was a lull in the conversation while Sally pondered Brianne's last remark. She bristled a bit, recalling the years of discord between the two, then asked,

"Maybe that's why. So why are you being so nice now, Brianne."

"Sally, I'm like a born-again Christian. Once I got out of jail, I changed my life. I don't mess with drugs or alcohol or anything that might take me away from my child. In fact, that's where I'm going, to pick her up from school. I stopped here to meet a friend and have a glass of tea. My daughter is the most important thing in my life. I'm sure you feel the same way about your daughter."

Sally thought about Samantha and what had happened earlier in the day with the deputy sheriff.

"Yeah. That's right. Samantha's the most important thing in the world to me right now."

"Say, Sally…I've got to run now, but if there's anything I can do to help, please call."

Sally looked at her suspiciously. The two women really hadn't liked each other at all for most of their lives.

"Why would you want to help me, Brianne?"

"It's part of my recovery. It's the twelfth step in my program. It's my obligation and my responsibility to help others who face the same problems I faced. In return, that gives me strength. Here…here's my telephone number." Brianne handed Sally a napkin after she scribbled her number on it. "Call me…and please call me before you take another pill. I know what you're going through."

Brianne stood, smiled and said,

"So good to see the two of you. Take care. I hope to hear from you, Sally. Bye."

Sally and her mother watched as Brianne left the restaurant. There was an awkward silence until her mother said,

"Do you think you might call her, Sally?"

"I don't know, Mom. I'm going to have to give it some thought. I never liked that woman. I really didn't."

"I think you should call her."

"There's a lot of things I should do, Mom. I'll think about it."

The two women were quiet on the ride home. Sally was deep in thought. Not being able to see her daughter hurt the most. That night, she called Brianne.

"So what do you suggest I do, Brianne?"

"I want you to attend a meeting with me."

"What kind of meeting?"

"It's a meeting of a group of people just like you and me…people with the same kind of problems you have and I had."

"You had…you don't have those problems anymore, Brianne. Isn't that what you told me? Why would you go to one of those meetings?"

"I was an addict and I'm still an addict."

The sound of the word, "addict," sent a chill through Sally.

"Why would you do that for me?"

"Because that's part of my cure, Sally."

Sally thought about what she was hearing and said,

"So where are these meetings?"

"They're all over the place. Where are you living now?"

"I'm in Crystal River with my Mom."

"Crystal River, huh? That's a long way from where I am. Are you planning to move back any time soon?"

"Yeah, just as soon as I can. I can't be that far away from Samantha. I'll only get to see her for an hour or two at a time unless I move back."

"I'll tell you what…I'll find out where there is a meeting in Crystal River and call you back. Maybe I'll come down there for the first meeting and then when you get back here you can attend meetings up here with me."

"Alright. I'll think about it."

"But Sally, I've got to ask you one question…"

"What's that?"

"Before we do this I need to make sure that you really want help. If you don't, it's a waste of time. Do you want help?"

There was a pause. Brianne continued,

"Well, think about it, but when I call back I want you to answer that question for me, okay?"

"Okay," Sally responded.

Sally wasn't too sure about doing what Brianne was suggesting. She had disliked the woman for so long, she was having a hard time getting past that, but she was also at the end of her rope. She had no place to go and nothing to do. Who was going to hire her? She was too ashamed to call her father after what she'd done.

All she could think about was finding someone with some pills so she could forget about things for a while, but she didn't want to end up back in jail again. That much she knew. That and she wanted to be able to see Samantha again. She wrestled with the idea of going to a meeting with Brianne, and hadn't made up her mind when Brianne called back.

"There's a meeting every Tuesday night at a local church. I'll come down next Tuesday and go with you to your first meeting. How's that?"

"I don't know, Brianne. I've been thinking about it and I just don't think I can go meet with a bunch of strangers and that's gonna help me. I just don't see it happening."

"You're feeling hopeless, aren't you, Sally, like you don't know where to turn, but you know you can't go back to doing what you were doing, right?"

"Yeah, that's true."

"And your brain keeps telling you to take one of those pills and that's going to make you feel better, even if it's only for a little while."

"Yeah. I have those thoughts all the time now it seems, but I'm not an addict. I just used those pills after I got hurt, that's all. A doctor prescribed them for me."

"But you couldn't stop using them, could you?"

"They made me feel good and helped me go to sleep."

"But you couldn't stop, could you? I know I couldn't. I admit I was addicted to them. It took me a long time to admit that I was an addict."

"I don't want to sit there and listen to addicts talk about what they've been through. How's that going to help me?"

"It's helped me, Sally, and I've been clean for almost a year now."

"And you keep going back?"

"Yes, I do."

"Why?"

"Because I was an addict and I still am. I need help to keep me from going back to it, just like an alcoholic or someone with a gambling problem. The first step is to admit you have a problem. The next step is to do something about it."

"I'll admit that I have a problem, but I think I can deal with it on my own."

"But you want help, right?"

Sally hesitated and then answered,

"Yes. I want some help. I'm just not sure that what you're talking about is going to help me."

"Just come to one meeting. See what it's like. If you don't like it, you don't have to come back. Give it a try. What do you have to lose?"

Sally thought about it for a few seconds. She had nothing else going on and couldn't think of a good reason not to.

"Alright. I'll go to a meeting with you."

"I'll pick you up. Tell me where you're living."

Sally gave her directions to her house. When she told her mother of her decision, her mother supported her and offered to go with her, but Sally declined the offer.

Chapter Twenty Five

······························· ·ılı· ·······························

The next morning, Sally went out looking for a job in Crystal River. The only thing she knew was the clam business, but she figured she could wait tables if nothing else. She made some phone calls and went on some job interviews. When she filled out applications every one asked about criminal convictions. Since the charges against her had been dismissed, she could honestly say that she'd never been convicted of a crime and wasn't on probation.

A few days later, she got a job at a McDonald's within walking distance of her mother's house. Most of her co-workers were either in high school or just out of high school. She felt out of place and much older than they were, though she wasn't that much older, but she needed the money so she kept her mouth shut and did her best to fit in. She could tell that some of them were using drugs, because of things they said and did around her, but she avoided the conversations and suggestions that she join in.

When the day for the meeting arrived, she was nervous and apprehensive. She kept telling her mother she wasn't going to go, and her mother told her to call Brianne and tell her so. It wasn't fair to her not to do that. Sally never made the call and Brianne arrived at the house half an hour before the meeting was to start. Sally was nervous as she walked into the building where the meeting was to take place.

"Do you know anybody who will be here? Sally asked.

"No." Brianne responded.

"And you're not nervous about this?"

"Not anymore. I'm sure this group will be supportive of both of us."

A dozen chairs were placed in a circle in the middle of the room. A woman was sitting in one of the chairs, shuffling some papers.

"Welcome! You're the first to arrive. Have a seat anyplace. My name is Donna. I've got a few things to do before we get started."

The two sat quietly as others came in and sat down around them. Most of the early arrivals were older than she was. Most were men, but there were several other women, too. It was a diverse group, with some African-Americans and Hispanics, but mostly Caucasians. Sally's stomach was so tight it felt like she was having a contraction.

"We have more chairs in the back if we need them," Donna offered.

One of the men went and brought back a few more chairs and everyone moved back a few feet to widen the circle. More people arrived as the top of the hour approached. At exactly 7:00, Donna said,

"Okay. It's time to begin our meeting. If you would, please stand."

Everyone stood. Brianne grabbed hold of Sally's hand and the person to Sally's left extended her right hand to Sally and Sally took hold of it. Donna began,

"Let's begin with the Serenity Prayer."

All of the people bowed their heads and said, "God, grant us the serenity to accept the things we cannot change, the courage to change the things we can, and the wisdom to know the difference."

Everyone then sat down.

"Let's begin by having everyone introduce themselves. I'll start and we'll go around the circle to my left. I'm Donna. I'm a recovering addict. I have been clean for three years now."

The man to her left said,

"My name is Peter. I am a recovering addict. I have not taken a drug or a pill in six months. I'm glad to be here."

They went around the room. Brianne went before her. When it was her turn, she said,

"My name is Sally. This is my first meeting."

Everyone stopped, smiled at her and said,

"Congratulations! Welcome!" and "Glad you're here!" which made her feel better.

After everyone had introduced themselves, Donna said,

"Let's have someone read the twelve steps. Peter, would you mind doing that for us?"

Peter read,

Step One: We admitted that we were powerless over our addiction, that our lives had become unmanageable."

"Step two: We came to believe that a Power greater than ourselves could restore us to sanity."

"Step three: We made a decision to turn our will and our lives over to the care of God as we understood Him."

"Step four: We made a searching and fearless moral inventory of ourselves."

"Step five: We admitted to God, to ourselves, and to another human being the exact nature of our wrongs."

"Step six: We were entirely ready to have God remove all these defects of character."

"Step seven: We humbly asked Him to remove our shortcomings."

"Step eight: We made a list of all persons we had harmed, and became willing to make amends to them all."

"Step nine: We made direct amends to such people whenever possible, except when to do so would injure them or others."

"Step ten: We continued to take personal inventory and when we were wrong promptly admitted it."

"Step eleven: We sought through prayer and meditation to improve our conscious contact with God as we understood Him, praying only for knowledge of His will for us and the power to carry that out."

"Step twelve: Having had a spiritual awakening as a result of these steps, we tried to carry the message to addicts, and to practice these principles in all our affairs."[1]

Sally pondered those words. She hadn't been to church in a long, long time and hadn't even thought about Him, or Her, at all. She hadn't admitted to herself or to anyone else the nature and extent of her problems.

"Alright. Thank you all," Donna said. "Next, let's have someone else read the twelve traditions of Narcotics Anonymous. Stephanie, would you do that for us?"

Sally hadn't asked what the group was called. It surprised her when she heard it. This was like Alcoholics Anonymous. Stephanie began reading,

"Number one: Our common welfare should come first; personal recovery depends on NA unity."

"Number two: For our group purpose there is but one ultimate authority—a loving God as He may express Himself in our group conscience. Our leaders are but trusted servants, they do not govern."

"Number three: The only requirement for membership is a desire to stop using."

---

1 The Twelve Steps of NA reprinted by permission of NA World Services, Inc. All rights reserved.

"Number four: Each group should be autonomous except in matters affecting other groups or NA as a whole."

"Number five: Each group has but one primary purpose—to carry the message to the addict who still suffers."

"Number six: An NA group ought never to endorse, finance, or lend the NA name to any related facility or outside enterprise, lest problems of money, property, or prestige divert us from our primary purpose."

"Number seven: Every NA group ought to be fully self-supporting, declining outside contributions."

"Number eight: Narcotics Anonymous should remain forever nonprofessional, but our service centers may employ special workers."

"Number nine: NA, as such, ought never be organized, but we may create service boards or committees directly responsible to those they serve."

"Number ten: Narcotics Anonymous has no opinion or outside issues; hence the NA name ought never be drawn into public controversy."

"Number eleven: Our public relations policy is based on attraction rather than promotion; we need always maintain personal anonymity at the level of press, radio, and films." and

"Number twelve: Anonymity is the spiritual foundation of all our traditions, ever reminding us to place principles before personalities."[2]

---

2 The Twelve Traditions of NA reprinted for adaptation by permission of AA World Services, Inc. All rights reserved

Sally thought about that for a second. That was why Brianne was helping her, because of that twelfth step. The meeting coordinator, Donna, then said,

"Thank you all. I'd like to read one passage from one of our pamphlets and ask all of you to share your thoughts on it. I've chosen the topic of 'Why we are here.' The passage reads as follows:

Before coming here to the fellowship of NA, we could not manage our own lives. We could not live and enjoy life as other people do. We had to have something different and we thought we had found it in drugs. We placed their use ahead of the welfare of our families, our wives, husbands, and our children. We had to have drugs at all costs. We did many people great harm, but most of all we harmed ourselves. Through our inability to accept personal responsibilities we were actually creating our own problems. We seemed incapable of facing life on its own terms. Many of us ended up in jail, or sought help through medicine, religion or psychiatry. In desperation, we sought help from each other in Narcotics Anonymous." [3]

Sally thought that some of those words were directed to her. Donna then said,

"Nancy. Let's start with you. How do those words resonate with you? Share your thoughts with us, please."

"I've been in NA for three years now. I remember being so lost and so confused that I didn't know what to do with myself. I don't want to talk about the things I did to get drugs, other than to say it put me in prison for a while. I'm just so thankful that I found NA. It saved my life. I know I'm still addicted and that I need to be here or I might go back to the streets, and I don't want that."

Sally looked at her and thought she might have been a school teacher. She no more looked like an addict than her mother did. It shocked her to hear the woman talk.

The next man, who was in a wheelchair, said,

"My name is Mark. I've been in the program for five years. When I hear those words, I remember what got me here. I used to work for a

---

[3] Reprinted by permission of NA World Services, Inc. All rights reserved.

landscape company. I was a climber. I fell out of a tree one day and broke my back, basically. I was in so much pain. They gave me Oxycodone in the hospital. There I was, my life ruined, but when I was on Oxycodone nothing else mattered. Everything was fine as long as I got that medicine. Once I finally got out of the hospital, I was so hooked on Oxycodone I had to have it, and I was able to get it, legally, but it was ruining my life. I had no life. One day a friend of mine convinced me to come to one of these meetings. I thank him for that and I thank God that I did."

The next man said,

"My name is Joel. I've been in the program for two months. I still crave the pills. I was shooting up the 80 milligram oxycodone pills two and three times a day. I remember thinking one time, after I'd just shot myself up, that if someone poured gasoline on my foot and lit a match, I wouldn't have cared. I was completely under the spell of that drug. One of my best friends, a guy I grew up with, got arrested and is now in jail. He's probably going to prison for a long time. When he got arrested, something inside me snapped and somehow I found my way to one of these meetings. I attend as many meetings as I can every week. I drive to Tampa, Bradenton, and even over to Orlando every now and then to attend a meeting. I'm afraid if I don't, I'll get back on that damn drug again. This program has saved me."

When it was Sally's turn, she said,

"My name is Sally and this is not only my first time at this meeting, it's my first time at a meeting like this. I had no idea what to expect." She turned to Brianne and said, "She talked me into coming here tonight. I really didn't want to, but I'm glad I did. I don't know what to say, but I just got out of jail after being in for almost four months. I haven't admitted to anyone, not even myself, that I have a problem with drugs. I guess I'm a little like you, Nancy,…"

"Sorry to interrupt," Donna said, "But we don't allow cross-talking. Talk to all of us, not any one of us. I know this is your first time so you don't know our rules. Go on."

"Sorry about that. As I was saying, when I was in jail it was like it was everybody else's fault that I was there…my husband's, the police who unlawfully arrested me, my lawyer who refused to come see me and get me out…everybody else's fault but mine. I'm going to think about everything I heard you all say here tonight, and I think I'm going to come back. I've lost everything I ever had. I have a problem. I think this program can help me. Thanks."

After everyone else spoke, Donna said,

"That concludes our meeting. I will now pass around a basket in keeping with our traditions. If this is your first time, we ask that you not put anything in the basket this time."

After the basket was passed around, Donna said, "Please stand and join me in the Serenity Prayer."

Everyone stood, held hands and said,

"God grant us the serenity to accept the things we cannot change, the courage to change the things we can, and the wisdom to know the difference."

Several people then exclaimed,

"Keep coming back! It works if you work it!"

Once the meeting was over, five or six people gathered around Sally, introduced themselves again, and encouraged her to come back. Donna handed her a few pamphlets and a list of other women in the program who she could call, if she wanted to, and said, "Here, take these with you and read them, if you'd like. Good luck!"

When they were in the car headed home, Brianne asked,

"So what did you think?"

"It wasn't like what I expected it to be."

"Do you think you'll go back?"

"Yeah. I think I will."

"You're going to need a sponsor. I'll be happy to sponsor you."

"What does a sponsor do?"

"It's just another person who has been through what you're going through. You're supposed to call your sponsor whenever you feel an urge to take a drug or do something you're not sure of. You're going to doubt yourself and your decisions for a while, I expect. You'll want to have someone to talk to about things, I'm sure, and your sponsor will help you work the 12 steps."

"You'll do that for me?"

"I will. That's part of my recovery, too, as you heard."

Sally was quiet for a few moments, thinking about all that had happened that night. Brianne handed her a pamphlet and said,

"Here, take this. It's a pamphlet that I used when I was first starting out. I still use it. I suggest you read it to yourself every night before you go to bed, if it helps. It helped me."

Sally looked at the pamphlet. It read, "Living the Program."

It was almost nine o'clock by the time she got home. Her mother was in bed already. Before she went to sleep, she read the first few lines of the pamphlet Brianne had given her. After doing so, so said to herself, "Today, I was clean today. Today, I didn't let my disease ruin my day. Today was a good day."

She stopped there, turned off the light and said to herself that she was starting down a new path.

Chapter Twenty Six

Sally called Brianne the next night. They didn't talk long, but Brianne asked Sally if she'd stayed clean since she last saw her, if she had read any of the NA literature, if she had prayed, and other such things. Brianne told her,

"Remember, I'm here to talk to you any time you'd like, but the rules are that you should call me, not the other way around."

"Why's that?" Sally asked.

"Because it shows that you are reaching out for help, not that I, or anyone else in the program, is trying to get you to do something you don't really want to do."

Sally called every night for the next several days. When Tuesday rolled around again, Brianne decided that the trip to Crystal River, which took her an extra half hour longer than the drive to Williston from Gainesville, was worth it. She wanted to be with Sally at the next meeting. She felt that it was giving her a real opportunity to fulfill the twelfth step of her journey to sobriety by helping someone who was in dire need of help, and that was definitely Sally's situation.

Sally felt much more comfortable going to the meeting when she knew Brianne was going to be there with her. Though she was still self-conscious, and sure that she was the lowest form of a human being in the room, she went.

The meeting was conducted in the same manner as before, beginning and ending with the Serenity prayer and reciting the twelve steps. The part that she liked the best was hearing others tell their tales of woe. It made her feel better, as if she wasn't the person with the most problems in the room. She recognized most of the people from the week before, but there were a few new people, too.

One man, about her age, told of how he "railed Oxys." Another man talked about how he crushed up pills on one of his credit cards with the use of another card and then snorted it with a straw. Yet another talked about shooting it into a vein with needles. One of the new people, a woman in her thirties, talked about having a relapse and how glad she was to be back with the group.

When Sally spoke, she opened up a little bit and told of how she wasn't able to have her daughter with her because of what drugs had done to her. She cried as she did. Though there were a few people she hadn't seen before, but she was still the newest of the newcomers to the group.

When the meeting was over, on their way home, Brianne asked,

"Why don't you go back to work with your Dad?"

"Oh, I know him. He won't even talk to me after what I did."

"When was the last time you talked to him?"

"The day before I got arrested."

"He never came to see you?"

"No."

"Did you call him?"

"I tried. I called a few times. He wouldn't accept the call. I could only make a collect call from the jail."

"You don't think he'd let you go back to work there?"

"I'm sure of it."

"Hmmm. Have you talked to your mother about it?"

"She wouldn't know. She doesn't talk to him. They haven't talked in years, ever since the divorce."

"But does she think you should talk to him?"

"I haven't asked. I know how he thinks."

Brianne thought about that for a few seconds and then added,

"If you could work in Cedar Key, you could see your daughter every day."

"That's true."

"Think about it, Sally. It can't hurt."

"Thanks, Brianne. Thanks for being here. You're helping me."

"That's why I'm here, but it's also good for me, too. I'm not doing this just for you. Please believe me when I tell you that I'm doing this in order to help me continue to fight this addiction we both have. It's a daily struggle. Tonight, before you go to bed, read something to lift your spirits. I do….every night."

As the days went by, as she continued to live her life without using any pills, Sally began to feel better about herself, but she still had the urges to use drugs again, and sometimes those urges were very powerful. To counter them, she would go with her mother to the beach after work. Being by the waters of the Gulf of Mexico made her feel better. She began to get some color on her skin. Because of her being in jail for over four months, she had an unhealthy ghost-like look about her.

Every weekend, on either Saturday or Sunday, whatever day she didn't have to work, she and her mother would drive to Cedar Key so that Sally could visit with Samantha. Jeremy made sure that he wasn't around when she came. Samantha was always glad to see her and cried when she left. So did Sally.

One night, a month after she'd begun the NA program, Brianne asked Sally to do her a favor.

"I'd like for you to read steps eight, nine and ten before you go to sleep tonight. Will you do that for me?"

"Okay. No problem," Sally replied.

"I'd like to talk about it with you tomorrow night."

Before going to sleep that night, Sally read the three steps. They involved talking to the people who were affected by her actions and trying to make things right with them. The first person she thought of was Jeremy, but she wasn't ready for that. The next person was her father. She told herself she wasn't ready for that either.

She had been thinking about herself and her problems and not giving too much thought to the people who were hurt by her actions. The next night, she talked about it with Brianne.

"So you think I should apologize to Jeremy?"

"I didn't say that."

"But that's what you're thinking, isn't it?"

"No, not really. I could think of some other people who might come before him."

"Like who? Samantha? She wouldn't understand. My mother? Who?"

"Like maybe your father."

"My father...that's who I thought you meant. I don't think I'm ready to talk to him."

"Don't you think he's hurt by what you've done?"

"He's angry is what he is. I made him mad. He doesn't want to talk to me. I'm as sure of that as I can be."

"Read those three steps again, and pray on it."

The next week, the two went to the meeting again. As with the other two times she'd been there, Sally met some new people. This time, a man about her age was there. He looked familiar, but she couldn't place him. When the group was going around the room making introductions, it hit her. She remembered seeing him at the bar in Ocala. He acted like he recognized her, too.

When it was his turn to talk, he said how he had been in a very dangerous situation involving the law, and he knew that he had to get clean or he'd be going to prison. He said that he'd been trying for years, and attending programs in other cities, but had fallen off the path a few times. He said he was determined to make it work this time.

After the meeting, he approached her and said,

"Sally, remember me? My name's Jeff."

"Yes, I do. You're a friend of Slim's, right?"

"I was. I'm trying to get away from all of them people right now."

"Whatever happened to him anyhow?"

"Say, no offense, but I'd rather not talk about any of that here. I'd be glad to meet you someplace and tell you all about it, but not here."

Sally wanted to know what had happened to Slim. Jeff was a good-looking man, and he seemed nice, so she said,

"I can do that. I'm living here in Crystal River now. How about you? Are you still in Ocala?"

"I live in Dunellon. I could come meet you here anytime."

Sally gave him her number and said,

"Give me a call. I'll look forward to hearing from you. I'm real curious about what happened to Slim. I spent almost four months in jail because of him."

On the ride home, Brianne asked if she thought that was a good idea.

"I don't know the man, but I will say this…in this program they tell newcomers not to get involved with anyone, and especially no one in the group, for at least a year, so I'd have to say it's not recommended.

"I'm not talking about getting romantically involved with the guy, I just want to know what happened to Slim. I really do."

"Did you care for the guy, or was he just the person you got your drugs from?"

"I cared for him some, I guess. He's the only other man I'd ever been with, other than Jeremy, but it wasn't like I was in love with him or anything."

"Be careful, Sally. They tell you to try not to put yourself in situations that could tempt you."

"I'll be careful," Sally assured her.

The next day, Jeff called. They arranged to meet at the Fish House on U.S. 19 for dinner that night. Sally was surprised at how nervous she was while getting ready to go. Her mother encouraged her.

"Go on! Have a good time. You haven't been out for a long time, but be careful. No drugs."

"I won't, Mom. There are a few things I need to find out from him. He's in the group. He's in the recovery program, too."

They sat in a corner booth, looking out over the water. He ordered a beer. At first, she was alarmed, because she hadn't had any alcohol since the night she was arrested. She didn't think people in NA were supposed to drink alcohol, but she wasn't sure. She thought about it, and she told herself that she had a problem with drugs, not alcohol. And since he was having a beer, she figured it must be okay. So she ordered a beer, too.

"So what happened to Slim?"

"After the two of you got arrested that night, the police searched his house. They found a whole lot of drugs. He got charged with trafficking in that RoxyCodone shit and that man is looking at some serious time in prison."

"Did they do that the same night I got arrested?"

"No, it was the next day or two."

"Was that legal? How'd they do that?"

"Some people apparently told the police that he was selling drugs and that was enough for them to get the warrant to search the house. Some people thought it was you at first, but then when they heard you were still in jail, they got to thinking that it must've been someone else."

"It wasn't me. I sat in that jail until my case got dismissed because of that being an illegal search. They had no right to go through my purse like they did."

He looked at her curiously, as if he wasn't sure she was telling the truth and said,

"So they didn't offer you a deal or anything?"

"Nope. They never offered me anything. I sat there until a Judge told them that they didn't have a right to search the car at all, at least not after they found the gun. They were supposed to ask Slim what he wanted to have done with the car before they impounded it."

"I wonder why they didn't offer you some kind of deal."

"I didn't know what I could have told them. I didn't know anybody else who was buying from him or anything. I wasn't buying very much and he was the only person I had ever bought stuff from."

"That's probably why they didn't offer you any deal."

"I guess."

"I heard he got sentenced to twenty five years in prison."

"Twenty five years!"

"And that was the minimum he could get, from what I was told. He supposedly gave them some names and cooperated with them or it could have been worse."

"Wow! Twenty five years in prison! I can't believe it. My husband…I mean we're divorced now, so he's my ex-husband, was charged with sales and possession of Oxycodone and it was a maximum of fifteen years in prison, as I recall."

"Slim had a lot of stuff. The penalties get heavier the more you've got in your possession when they catch you."

"Was he a friend of yours?"

"He'd been selling drugs to me for years, ever since high school. He had some prior felony convictions, too, so he was what is called a repeat offender, or something like that."

"You went to school in Ocala?"

"Yeah. Class of 2005. How about you?"

"Cedar Key, class of 2007."

"So how did you meet him?"

Before Sally could answer, the waitress brought them their beers.

"Would you like to order now?"

"We haven't even looked at the menu," Sally replied. Give us a few minutes."

"To our recovery!" Sally said.

They clinked their bottles.

"I met him in Cedar Key."

"You two had a little something else going on, didn't you?" he asked with a knowing smile.

Sally giggled and replied, "Nothing too serious."

"Yeah. Slim was a real ladies man. He knew what made some of you women happy…sex, drugs and alcohol! Or I should say, alcohol, then drugs and then sex."

Sally looked down and ruefully said, "That's the way it was for me. I'm glad I'm away from all that. I was really messed up back then."

He looked at her and asked,

"Do you still get an urge to do those pills every now and then?"

"Most every day," Sally replied, "But I know better. It's hard though."

"Yeah. I know what you mean. I've been trying to quit for years."

"So what about you? What's going on with you? You said you were in some serious danger or something like that. What was that all about?"

"When Slim got arrested, everybody who had ever done any business with him headed for cover. Some people rolled over on other people. I'm sure a whole bunch of people rolled over on Slim and agreed to testify against him in exchange for having charges dropped or lighter sentences, whatever."

"I don't know what I would have done if they'd offered me a deal like that. I guess I'd have probably taken it. I'm glad they didn't, but I was so messed up. After taking that stuff for over a year, when I was in jail and couldn't get any, it messed me up big time. While I was locked up, I heard stories of the police doing more than just taking names. I heard they used people to set up other people, including their friends, and make them do all kinds of bad things, like go on the street and make the buys…things like that. It can be dangerous."

"That stuff happens. I don't want it happening to me, that's why I moved away, and I'm glad it didn't happen to you," Jeff said.

"Me too," Sally replied.

"The police came looking for me several times. I was never home when they came. My neighbors told me about it. They asked a lot of questions. I had to move out of my place and out of town. I found a new job and everything in Dunellon. I'm serious. They were after me. I'm sure of it."

"How come they never caught up to you? If the police are looking for someone, they usually find them, don't they?"

"They found me, but they didn't have anything on me. They just wanted to ask me some questions and kind of let me know that they knew I'd been using, and they just wanted to give me a warning. I didn't let on about anything, but it scared me."

"So you had to get out of town, huh?"

The waitress interrupted,

"So have you two decided?"

"Give us another minute or two. We've been talking, but I'll take another Bud, thanks."

Sally hadn't taken but a few sips of her beer. Jeff had downed his. She took another sip as they looked at the menu.

When the waitress returned, she ordered the boiled shrimp. Jeff ordered the fish of the day, which was grouper. He had another beer once the dinner was served. Sally ordered a second beer at the same time.

At Sally's request, they talked about things other than Slim and drugs. They were telling each other about the types of things they liked to do. He liked to fish and was surprised to hear about how much Sally liked to fish, too. He had a small boat and they talked about going out on it some time. He liked going to movies. Sally was used to watching movies at home through Netflix. She'd never been to the theatre in Crystal River. They talked about going to see the latest action movie. He was happy to know that she liked movies like that.

Sally hadn't been with a man in six months. She also hadn't had anything to drink in six months. The alcohol was having an effect on her, and she was enjoying herself. Jeff laughed easily and Sally found herself laughing at silly things.

After dinner, he had another beer and they shared a piece of Key Lime pie. When dinner was over, Jeff asked if she wanted to go listen to some music at a bar down the road.

Sally thought about it but declined. She was feeling a more than a little light-headed and was unsure of herself. She was attracted to him, though, and gave it some thought before turning down the invitation.

When she arrived home, her mother was asleep, but there was a note on the door to Sally's bedroom that said Brianne had called and to call no matter what time she got in. Sally didn't want to talk to her after having the two beers. She had her doubts about abstinence from alcohol not being a part of the program. That night, as she prepared herself for bed, she read out of the "Big Book," which applied to Alcoholics Anonymous primarily but NA used it as well. Her thoughts drifted to Jeff as well.

She called Brianne the next night and gave her all the news. Brianne was concerned. "Guys like that are called 'thirteenth steppers."

"What's that mean?" Sally asked.

"It means that they've got something else on their agenda other than the twelve steps. There are guys who are looking to meet women at these meetings because the women, like you, are so vulnerable. It's not a good thing, and Sally…you're not supposed to drink alcohol. The NA means 'sobriety' from all kinds of mind-altering substances, not just narcotics. He knows that. He's not being faithful to what NA is all about."

Sally listened to what she had to say, and told herself to be careful. After four months in jail, she was happy just to get out of the house and he was the only man who was showing any interest in her.

When Jeff called her about going to a movie that weekend, Sally accepted for Friday night, saying she had to go to Cedar Key with her mother to see her daughter on Saturday and they made a full day of it when they went. The two went to see an action movie called 'Thor,' and neither was disappointed.

It was an action-packed thriller about an extra-terrestrial being possessed with super-natural powers who comes to planet earth, falls in love, kills bad guys and lives happily ever after. It was a great "escape" movie for the both of them. After it was over, they decided to go listen to some music at the bar inside the Holiday Inn on U.S. 19 just north of town.

The group was a dance band that played mostly sixties and seventies music. Jeff had a few drinks, but Sally declined any alcoholic beverages. She told him what Brianne had told her. He said, "That's probably why I can't see to make it past Step One in this program." Sally laughed, but an alarm inside her head went off. Despite that, they danced, and laughed and had a good time together.

At eleven o'clock, Sally was ready to go home. She had made plans to leave early the next morning and she didn't want to do anything to disturb those plans. Jeff was disappointed, but said he understood. Since they drove separate cars, she left and he stayed, listening to the band.

Again, there was a note on her door telling her that Brianne had called. Again, she decided not to return the call. It was too late, she told herself.

Sally and her mother arose early the next morning and drove to Cedar Key. They drove straight to Jeremy's mother's house. Jeremy had gone fishing with a friend from high school. Samantha was dressed and ready to go when they arrived. The three women and Samantha then drove together to Fanning Springs, which was half an hour or so north of Cedar Key on U.S. 19. Jeremy's mother had packed a picnic lunch and they planned to swim and enjoy the cool spring waters. There were also swings and a small playground for Samantha to play on.

On the way there, they stopped for breakfast at the Burger King not far from the Kringle in Chiefland. Sally couldn't bring herself to eat at the McDonald's. She ate so much of it at work every day that she was sick of it.

By mid-afternoon, Samantha tired of all the activity and was in need of a nap, so they left. She fell asleep on the ride home. When they arrived home, Jeremy was outside, washing his fishing poles and cleaning some of the fish he had caught. When he saw them turn in the driveway, he gathered his equipment and tried to get away, but wasn't able to. Sally's mother walked over to him and gave him a big hug.

"How are you doing, Jeremy? I haven't seen you in ages."

Sally carried Samantha into the house, taking as wide a berth from Jeremy as she could and avoiding his glance as she did so.

"I'm hangin' in there, Mrs. Richards. How about you?"

"I'm still kickin', just not as high as I used to."

"Would you like some fish? I caught a bunch of trout and redfish today."

"I'd love some. I don't eat much fresh fish anymore, not like I used to when I lived around here."

Jeremy retrieved a few pieces of fish from the cooler in the back of his car and handed them to her.

"Thank you so much, Jeremy! We'll eat these tonight."

"I hope you enjoy them."

"I'm sure we will. I enjoy coming up here every week and seeing Samantha so much. I didn't realize how much I missed this place. It brings back a lot of memories, but seeing Samantha is the best part. The two of you have a beautiful daughter to share."

"How's Sally doing?" Jeremy asked, in a low voice, so Sally couldn't hear.

"She's doing better, I think. It's going to take some time."

"Those drugs are hard to get out of your system."

"How are you doing with that, Jeremy?"

"I haven't taken a pill or a drop of alcohol since I got out of jail. I think my uncle would kill me if I did."

She laughed and said, "He wouldn't do that, I'm sure."

"No. He would. I'm serious."

"Well, let's hope he won't have to."

"Well, it's been nice seeing you, Mrs. Richards. I've got to get going. I'm going out to dinner with some friends later and I'm running a little late."

He didn't really have any plans, but he felt uncomfortable being there while Sally was there.

After he'd gone, Sally came out of the house and she and her mother returned to Crystal River.

That night, Sally talked to Brianne. When she told her about her meetings with Jeff, Brianne was relieved when Sally told her that she refused the invitation to have a beer, but she was very concerned when she heard about what Jeff had said and about how many beers he had consumed that night.

"Sally, I am more than a little worried about you. I know you think you can control the situation, but you've got to be very, very careful. The reason NA has these rules is because people like you are so vulnerable. You think you aren't, but you are. People have to stay completely sober, meaning no alcohol either, to be successful in this program. Jeff isn't going to be successful this time if he acts that way, and from what he told the group, he has tried and failed at this several times."

"But this is a Narcotics Anonymous program, not an Alcoholics Anonymous program. I didn't think it would matter that much."

"The important thing is that you stay off of drugs, that's true, but it could lead to something else if you're not careful. It's up to you, but I'm your sponsor and I'm telling you that it would be best if you stayed sober, and it would be best if you stayed away from him. That's the NA way, girl. No one said it would be easy."

Sally took offense.

"I haven't taken any drugs, Brianne, and I'm doing the best I can. I haven't had any fun in six months, or more, more like almost two years, ever since Jeremy first got hurt. I don't know how to act, Brianne. I got married to the only boyfriend I ever had my whole life. You know that! This is all new to me!" Sally weeped.

"I understand. I understand. Just do the best you can, okay? I'm your sponsor and I've given you my advice. What you do with it is up to you. Sometimes people have to learn from their mistakes. Just be careful."

"I will."

At the meeting the following week, Jeff was there again. Brianne could tell that there was a definite connection between the two, but she wasn't getting good vibes from the man and purposefully avoided engaging him in conversation.

"Be careful, Sally," she cautioned. "You're in a fragile state. Take good care of yourself."

That Friday night, Jeff and Sally went to a movie again. After the movie, they went to listen to music again at the Holiday Inn. When it was time for Sally to go, Jeff followed her outside. As she was about to get in the car, he kissed her, and she kissed back. Her car was parked in a far corner of the lot which was not well lit. One kiss led to another. He pressed his body up against hers, pushing her back against the car. The first kiss unleashed a flood of emotions. He groped her body and she groped back. Fifteen minutes later, they came up for air.

"Want to get a room?" he asked.

"No, not tonight. I've got to go to Cedar Key in the morning. Next time maybe."

She got in the car and drove off. Unhappily, he watched her go without any further contact, but the games had begun and they both knew it. Sally reminded herself of what Brianne had told her and told herself that she probably needed to stop seeing him altogether. If she didn't, she knew where the relationship was going.

She didn't love Jeff. She didn't know him well enough to love him. It was all about the physical attraction and the desire to be loved. She told herself it was a lot like she felt when she thought about having one of the blue pills. It was a craving she'd have to resist, and she told herself she was going to have to do it.

Chapter Twenty Seven

---·⑃·---

The next morning, since it was a Saturday, Sally was awakened by her mother. Usually she let her sleep as long as she wanted to.

"Get up, girl! We have a big day ahead of us."

"Okay, Mom. What's so big about it, other than we get to see Samantha."

"That's big enough, but I have a surprise for the two of you."

"What is it?"

"I'm not telling. If I did, it wouldn't be a surprise. You'll see."

Sally showered and dressed in a hurry, all the while probing her mother about the surprise, with no luck. Once they arrived at Jeremy's mother's house, and the four were in the car, she drove into town.

"Where are we going, Gramma?" Samantha asked.

"You'll see."

When they drove past the Blue Desert Restaurant and the Mermaid's Landing cabins, she turned into the parking lot of the Marina.

"We're going fishing?" Samantha exclaimed.

"We're going out on a boat!" Mrs. Richards responded.

"Out to Atsena Otie and beyond!" Mrs. Thibodeaux chimed in.

"Oh, so you're in on this, too, are you?"

Sally asked.

"You bet! We've been planning this all week." Jeremy's mother said.

"It was hard for me to keep the surprise a secret," her mother added.

Mrs. Thibodeaux pulled a large picnic basket and a cooler out of her trunk.

"Here, give me a hand."

Sally grabbed the other end of the cooler and the two of them walked down to the dock, where a pontoon boat was waiting for them. Mrs. Richards walked inside the large blue building to make payment as the other three loaded their gear onto the boat.

"How much did this cost you?" Sally asked.

"Never you mind, girl." Mrs. Thibodeaux replied. "This is our treat for the both of you."

"You know how to drive this thing?"

"I've been running boats up and down, over and through these islands since long before you were born, thank you very much." she responded.

"Me, too." Mrs. Richards said as she jumped on board. "Let's go."

It was three hours past the low tide, so there was plenty of water for them to maneuver in, but they went slowly. Once the four were out of the channel and into the Gulf, Mrs. Thibodeaux throttled up the engine and they felt the wind in their faces. Samantha sat in her mother's lap, giggling with excitement the whole time.

"You've even got fishing poles! Did you remember to get bait?" Sally asked.

"Of course I did! Who taught you how to fish, child?" her mother responded. "Or at least I told them to put some in the boat. Better check that compartment, Sally. Would you do that?"

Sally opened the lid to the bait well and said, "Yep. There are a few dozen shrimp swimming around in there."

"We're going to catch our dinner. That fish Jeremy gave me last week made me think about us catching some fish for ourselves. I called Mrs. Thibodeaux and she agreed. Let's go out past Sea Horse Key and see what we can get into. We ought to find a few trout swimming around in these grassy flats."

Samantha had been on boats many times before, but going out with her two grandmothers and her mother was a completely new and different experience for her. She was happy sitting on whichever lap would have her and she had her choice of all three.

They anchored a few hundred yards off of the island called Sea Horse Key, outside of the channel and baited their hooks. Samantha was given her own pole and a place to sit and watch if her bobber went down. Sally sat next to her.

The other two positioned themselves at opposite ends of the twenty foot long and eight foot wide vessel. Before too long, they started to get hits and everyone, even Samantha, caught a fish or two, although Sally helped her reel it in.

When they had caught enough fish, which was about the time when Samantha became a little impatient when the fish didn't bite as quickly as she wanted them to, they pulled up the anchor and motored around Snake Key, Grassy Key, North Key and Atsena Otie islands for a while.

They stopped for lunch on the back side of Atsena Otie, in a well-protected area. When the winds began to pick up after noon, the four headed back in, though they had rented the boat for the full day. They'd had enough and they'd had a great day. For Samantha, it was an adventure and she enjoyed it thoroughly.

On the ride back, as her mother was handling the wheel, and it was difficult to have any conversation, Sally sidled over to Mrs. Thibodeaux and asked,

"Does my Dad ever come to see Samantha?"

"All the time."

"Really?"

"At least once a day, though he usually doesn't stay too long. He'll bring Samantha a little something most every time he comes."

"You never told me that."

"You never asked."

"Hmm." Sally mused.

"I think he'd like to hear from you, Sally."

"No way. He won't even speak to me, I'm sure."

"You might be surprised."

Sally thought about it, but said nothing more.

Once they were in the car and on their way back to Mrs. Thibodeaux's house, Samantha fell asleep in her mother's arms. After they'd said their good-byes, but before heading back to Crystal River, Sally asked,

"Say, Mom. Would you mind if we went by Dad's house, just to see if he's home?"

"I'll drive by, and see if he's there, and if he is and you want to talk to him, you can drop me off at the coffee shop and go back and see him. I have no desire to see the man."

"Okay, let's do that."

They drove by the house where Sally had been born and raised, and where her mother had spent most of her adult life. They saw the tattered and dented blue pick-up truck her father had driven for years.

"The old coot must be there," her mother remarked. "I'll get myself a cup of tea at Kona Joe's and sit outside under one of those fans. Stay as long as you'd like, I'll take a walk around the town if I get bored. When you're ready, give me a call and I'll be there waiting for you. I haven't spent much time here in years."

Sally drove back to the house after dropping her mother off in town. She stopped at the end of the block, not sure if she really wanted to talk to him. After sitting there for several minutes she said,

"What the hell! He can't shoot me and I'm too big for him to spank. What can he do to me?"

She walked hesitatingly to the front door and knocked. Her father must have been taking a nap as it took him a few seconds to respond.

"Just a minute. I'll be right there," he hollered.

When he opened the door, he seemed surprised to see her.

"I didn't recognize the car. Is that yours?"

"No, it's Mom's."

"How is the old battle-axe?"

"She's fine. I'm living with her now."

"That's what Mrs. Thibodeaux was telling me. Come in, girl, and give me a hug."

Sally was taken aback. She wasn't expecting any warmth from her father, who had been unfailingly gruff and stern with her from the time she was born, as best she could remember. She put her arms around him and he embraced her with both arms.

"It's good to see you again. I've missed you," he said.

"Really? I didn't think you'd want to ever talk to me again," Sally responded.

"You're my only daughter. I don't have another one to talk to."

"But you refused all my calls while I was in jail."

"I didn't want to talk to you while you were in that place. Besides, you weren't thinking too clearly at the time. Care for something to drink?"

"A glass of water would be fine."

"Well get one for me while you're up. You know your way around the place. It hasn't changed any."

Sally walked back to the kitchen as he sat down in his favorite easy chair. She walked by what had been her bedroom.

"Looks like you've kept my room up better than I used to."

"Mrs. Lambert comes and cleans the house for me every week or so. She does a good job. I can't take any credit for that."

Sally returned to the living room moments later with two glasses of water, sat down on the sofa, and said,

"I'm sorry, Dad, for all the heart-ache I've caused you."

He looked over at her and said,

"Thank you for saying so. You have caused me an awful lot of heart-ache over the last year or so. How are you doing? Have you got that stuff out of your body?"

"I'm working on it. I've been clean ever since I got out of jail, and I was in there for almost four months. I'm not having any of the withdrawal side effects anymore, so I'm pretty sure I've got it out of my system. I just have to keep it out."

"Well I don't want you back until you've rid yourself of that disease, and it is a disease. It's just like a sickness, as bad as cancer or any of the others. I want to see you well again, Sally. I miss you."

There were tears in his eyes as he spoke. Sally lowered her head, wiped the moisture from her eyes and said,

"I'm going to meetings on a regular basis."

"What kind of meetings?"

"It's called Narcotics Anonymous."

"Never heard of it. Like Alcoholics Anonymous, I suppose."

"Yeah. That's right."

"Whatever works, Sally. I'll help you the best I can, but not when you're under the spell of that devilish stuff you've been on. There was nothing I or anyone else could say or do to change your way of thinking back then. It was probably a good thing you got arrested, though it about broke my heart when you did."

"I lost Samantha because of it."

"You haven't lost her. You just went away for a while. She's still here and she's doing fine. She's still your daughter, so you haven't lost anything… yet. Mrs. Thibodeaux is taking real good care of her."

"She tells me that you go to see Samantha just about every day."

"That's true. Wouldn't think of missing a day. I enjoy it. She's a beautiful little girl and she's my only grandchild."

"Thanks, Daddy. I miss being here."

"This is still your home, Sally, and it always will be. I'm glad to have you back."

"Does that mean I can have my old job back?"

"It's waiting for you. All you've got to do is promise me you won't use those pills anymore or take any kind of drugs."

"And can I have my old room back?"

He looked over at her and said,

"Of course you can. It's yours. I haven't changed it a bit. It's just the way you left it."

Sally started to cry. She stood up, walked over to him, gave him a hug and said,

"Thanks, Daddy. I'll be back by Monday."

"Work starts at 6:00, like always. Don't be late!"

She laughed and said,

"I won't."

Her mother had mixed emotions when Sally told her of her plans. "I'm going to miss you, Sally, and I'm going to miss our trips up here to see Samantha, but it's for the best, I'm sure. You don't belong in Crystal River. This is your home."

"You can still come visit, or Samantha and I can visit you."

"I hope you do."

Sally packed her bags and what little she had and moved back in with her father that Sunday night. When she told Brianne what she had done, Brianne was happy for her.

"You made amends to someone you had harmed."

"And he took me back."

"You never know what will happen until you try. Have you ever read the book called The Four Agreements?"

"No."

"Well, anyway, it's about agreements, or understandings, that you make with yourself. One of them is that you never assume anything. You assumed that your father could never forgive you."

"I was wrong."

"Now, he may never forget what happened, and it may take a while for him to forgive you for what you did, but he still loves you."

"What are the other ones?"

"The second one is 'Be your word.' That means always speak the truth. What comes out of your mouth should be who you are and what you are. Don't lie to yourself, especially. The other two are 'Don't take anything personally,' and 'Always do your best'."

"Sounds like good advice."

"So will you continue going to meetings?"

"Not in Crystal River. That's too far. Is there anything closer? Like in Bronson, Chiefland or Williston?" That's where you used to go, isn't it? Williston?"

"Yes. There's one in Williston and that's where I started going almost a year ago. They meet on Thursdays at 8:00 at the Women's Center."

"The Women's Center?"

"Yep."

"Pretty hard to be anonymous, isn't it?"

"People know who does what in a small town. That's true."

"But nobody will know me."

"That's what you want, isn't it?"

"Yes, it is."

"Well, it doesn't matter where you go as long as you keep going, that's the important thing. I'll look and see if there is a group that meets in Bronson. I'll let you know what I find out, but wherever you go, I'll be there with you. Good luck, Sally. I hope this works out for you."

"Thanks, Brianne, for everything you've done for me. I doubt I'd be where I am if it weren't for what you did for me."

"You're welcome. That's part of my job as your sponsor, and my commitment to myself."

Before she left, Sally called Jeff. He wasn't at home so she left a message on his recorder. She told him she was moving back home. She also told him he'd better stop drinking if he wanted to be successful in the program. She didn't want to see him again unless and until he did.

Chapter Twenty Eight

Sally was welcomed back at work as if she'd never been away. Of course, her father being the boss didn't hurt. When Jeremy found out about it, he wasn't too thrilled. She stopped by his mother's house the second night back and said that she'd like to see Samantha on a daily basis. When Jeremy heard about it, he called Sally and said,

"Don't think that just because you moved back home that you're gonna get whatever you want. Until a Judge says diffcrent, it's up to my Mom. I gotta see that you've changed until I tell her that it's okay with me to let you see her as often as you want."

"I know I hurt you, Jeremy, and I apologize for that. It was those drugs and you're the one who turned me on to all of that in the first place. I did you wrong but you did me wrong, too."

Jeremy didn't respond at first. He knew that what she said was true, but he wasn't ready to admit that to her.

"I didn't make you take them like you did while I was in jail," he said, haltingly.

"No, you didn't, but you know what they made you become. The same thing happened to me," Sally responded.

"And I didn't make you hook up with that dude like you did," Jeremy said.

"It was the drugs, Jeremy. Don't take it personal. It wasn't about you.

I've loved you since I was a little girl. You know that. I was sick and now I'm trying to get well."

Jeremy felt himself tearing up. He wasn't expecting this conversation.

"You were my wife, Sally. How can I not take that personally?"

"I wasn't thinking straight. That wasn't me. That's not how I am. You know that. The drugs had control over my brain. They had control over you just the same, maybe even worse. You know that, too."

Jeremy thought about what she said. He knew it was true.

"It's gonna take some time, Sally."

"I know."

"I don't know that I can ever get over the hurt you caused me."

"I know that, too, but are you going to object to me seeing Samantha? She's my daughter, too, and I love her just as much as you do."

Jeremy took the receiver from next to his ear and looked at it, seeing her face on the other side. She was still the same girl he'd known all his life. She'd made wrong turns. So had he. He heaved a deep sigh, put the phone back up to his mouth, and said,

"Yeah. I'm willing to share her with you. I know we will both want to see her after work every day. You can have her from 4:00 to 5:30, but you've got to have her home by 5:30 most every day, because that's when she eats her dinner. I'll have her from dinner until it's time for her to go to bed. She doesn't stay up much past dinner anyway. We can start with that."

"Can I come get her now?"

"You can tell my Mom I said it was okay."

Sally took Samantha down to the park in Cedar Key and played with her in water up to her knees and on the swings. She had her home before 5:30. Jeremy was there when she brought her back.

"Thanks, Jeremy."

"You're welcome, Sally."

"Maybe we can be friends again."

"Maybe."

"And let's just do the best we can…for Samantha, and for us. We don't have to be enemies, do we?"

"It's gonna take some time, Sally."

"I know, but we can try. Let's take things one day at a time."

THE END

Epilogue

············ ⫶⫶⫶ ············

This book is a story about two people whose marriage unravels as a result of the innocent use of OxyContin, a prescribed pain medication which is known to have a high potential for drug dependency. Both are arrested and put in jail for the illegal use of the extremely powerful drug, after the legal usage ends. They lose custody of their child, they divorce, and they must deal with the aftermath of the chaos which is created.

I decided to write this book after hearing so many truly incredible stories about how the use of OxyContin had destroyed lives. One might wonder why I, one who lived through the sixties, might be so surprised to hear of drug usage destroying a life, since that is certainly one of the legacies of the "peace and love" generation. I hasten to add, in defense of my fellow baby boomers, that there were many extremely positive things to come from those incredibly turbulent days as well but, whether we like it or not, illegal drug usage was rampant during those days and some would say that was when the drug problem began in this country.

To be honest, I had never heard the term Roxy Blues before this year. However, when a person in the community who was placed on probation for a drug offense, was arrested for possession of RoxyContin on the very same night after being warned by the Judge that if he saw him again he was going to prison, I was surprised and took note. And when another individual I know of, who was recently released from prison, was arrested for possessing RoxyContin, not long after being released, knowing that another arrest would cause him to be sent back to prison, I was surprised. And when yet another person I heard about, who was involved in a nasty divorce in which custody was being hotly contested, was arrested for using RoxyContin and, as a result, lost the child who she had just successfully obtained custody of, I realized that this particular drug is not only truly incredibly powerful, it also has the effect of completely dominating a person's thought processes. It is not called "hillbilly heroin" for nothing. Those are just a few of the many stories I have heard about this drug.

In fact, when I mention the term, Roxy Blues, or RoxyContin, to people it seems as if half the people have never heard of it before. The other half, however, not only have heard of it, those people usually have a horror story or two to tell about it. Florida is said to be one of the leading "pill mills" in the country, which is to say that people come to Florida to have prescriptions filled for pain medications such as RoxyContin, because it is much easier to do in Florida than it is in other states, for a variety of reasons.

There is no question whatsoever that it is an extremely effective pain reliever. I have a former client who is taking OxyContin, pursuant to a prescription, for pain resulting from a personal injury incident. He tells me that OxyContin is the only thing that relieves the severe pain he continues to experience. The doctor is afraid, quite understandably, that the client is becoming dependent. From everything I have heard, or read, although the drug is an extremely effective pain reliever, it is also known to be a drug which has an extremely high risk for chemical dependency.

Having never taken an OxyCodone product, I have no idea how compelling the urges must be which drive people to do things that they know, deep in their conscious minds, they should not do. For the benefits they apparently experience to be worth the risks they take, the use of that particular drug is, in and of itself, a story that needed to be told.

I wrote this book in mid-2011. As I was writing it, I listened with amazement as two candidates for the GOP presidential nomination presented impassioned arguments as to why drugs, and they were talking specifically about marijuana, should be legalized. It was even more amazing to me when, last year, the State of California had a ballot initiative which would have legalized marijuana. That was not hard to understand, but what was surprising to me was that a substantial number of law enforcement officers and agencies, though not all of them, favored legalization.

The "War on Drugs" initiated by former President Reagan in 1986 resulted in a staggeringly high increase in those placed behind bars due to the illegal use of drugs. The amount of money spent on trying to prevent drugs from entering our country is astronomical. It seems as if the problem will be dealt with based on the financial considerations involved more so than any moral or other reason, which is what the two GOP presidential hopefuls were suggesting.

As part of that overall change in the policy towards drugs which seems likely to occur, a different approach to the treatment of those addicted to drugs will likely be necessary. Tens of millions of Americans currently use prescribed medications to relieve pain. Millions of Americans use barbituates, or pain medication, illegally, at the present time. The problem is epidemic. The solutions are not simple. Many otherwise law-abiding citizens are violating the law by illegally using drugs intended for medicinal purposes. Without question, a large component of the problem is the "recreational" use of illegal drugs, but there is the component of excessive use of prescription drugs, too.

One solution is to legalize the private use of marijuana. Fourteen states have done so provided medical doctors have found that usage is for medicinal purposes. That, however, is not likely to become our national policy for quite some time, if ever. Another solution, which seems more reasonable and more humane, given the psychological dependency issues discussed in this book, is to treat those people with drug addiction problems as medically ill persons, not criminals.

Our policies and procedures regarding the drug problem are in crisis. The issues of legal drug usage, illegal drug usage, drug trafficking, over-crowded jails and prisons, not to mention the immigration and interdiction problems we have at our borders with Mexico, are matters of great concern and much public debate at this time.

The United States of America incarcerates more people than any other country in the world. In 2008, there were 2.3 million criminals behind bars, more than any other nation, according to Wikipedia, citing data maintained by the International Center for Prison Studies at King's College London. China, though it has more than a billion citizens, over three times more than the United States, is second, with 1.6 million people in prison.

The United States is also ranked first in incarceration rates. It has 751 people in prison or jail for every 100,000 in population. Russia imprisons 627 prisoners for every 100,000 people. England's rate is 151; Germany's rate is 88 and Japan's rate is 63.

Most of those 2.3 million prisoners are imprisoned for drug related crimes. Most of those are imprisoned for simple possession and use of drugs, not trafficking. The drug world is a dangerous and violent market dominated by hard-core criminals. There is an incredible amount of money being made by criminals, as well as drug manufacturers. That is the lure for the traffickers, and the lure for the consumers is, apparently, the incredibly powerful addictive drugs themselves.

At the present time drug lords in Mexico are battling police along the southern border of the United States and innocent civilians are being caught in the cross-hairs. The fight is about money. The demand for drugs, even though they are illegal, is so high in the United States and so pervasive in our society that the benefits far outweigh the risks since there is so much money involved in the drug trade. Those issues, of course, have nothing to do with the story I've told in this book.

Jeremy and Sally can be viewed as victims of the drug culture which pervades our society, or they can be viewed as criminals, who knowingly engaged in criminal acts. Did they belong in a jail or in a prison, or did they belong in some sort of drug rehabilitation facility?

Who is to bless and who is to blame for the problem? Is it the drug traffickers? The drug manufacturers? Are doctors and the medical profession to share any of the blame? Is our country to blame for its permissive policy towards the prescription drug industry, or for the failing penal system from which people come out worse, not better? Or is it the user?

It seems to me that, as in most cases, the least powerful share the biggest burden. The poor, the ignorant, the weak, the injured and yes, the criminal users, are the ones who will be found in prisons and on the streets, usually without homes, money, or possessions…all lost as a result of what is not only a deadly addiction, it is an extremely expensive proposition. Hundred dollar a day habits are normal. Thousand dollar a day habits are not uncommon.

The point which I sincerely hope that I was adequately able to convey is the compulsive nature of the drug, which apparently deprives users of any ability to combat the dependency which users of Roxy Blues are left with. I leave that issue to you, the reader, to decide for yourself if I did so. Unless you are a user, or have been a user in the past, it can be hard to understand, or sympathize with, one who uses drugs illegally, despite the risks and the harmful side-effects. We can read about it, and think about it, but to know it is something else again.

However, another issue presented in this book is that of forgiveness. It is a difficult one for all of us. There is the Lord's Prayer in which Christians recite: "Forgive us our trespasses as we forgive those who trespass against us."

I thought about the many, many situations throughout the history of the world in which atrocities of such magnitude were perpetrated by one nation, or a race, upon another, and how the enmity could ever be resolved. Being of Irish descent, the centuries of wrongs and oppression by the English immediately came to my mind. The "troubles" continue to this day and will never be forgotten, nor can they be rectified, but can they be forgiven? Time will tell but it doesn't appear that will occur in this generation.

The same can be said of Jews and what happened to them in Germany, or of the current Israel-Palestine situation where atrocities are being committed by both sides. The racial struggles of African Americans in the United States sadly remains a problem. And then there is the issue of the Native Americans. One can only wonder what they think of the concept of forgiveness.

As an economics major many years ago, I was taught in macro-economics that the rules which apply to countries, races, or large groups of people, are also applicable in micro-economic theory, or to individuals.

The suggestion is that before countries, or races, can forgive atrocities, or wrongs, individuals must do so. Infidelity is just one of many causes of severe marital discord. Some marriages can overcome such a problem, but most cannot.

Can Sally forgive Jeremy for bringing the drug into their home? Can Jeremy forgive Sally for her marital infidelity while he was in jail? Can they put their marriage back together? I leave that for your imagination.

As with all of my books, I included legal issues. I hope that you found the issues of entrapment and an inventory search of interest. Even though you might disagree with the results in this case, and there are many who have a problem with issues of police misconduct and how it should be handled, the law as found in this book is the law in the state of Florida, to the best of my knowledge. In sum, I hope you enjoyed the read and I thank you for taking the time to do so.

Pierce Kelley

About the Author

·⫴·

Pierce Kelley is a lawyer and educator turned author who received his undergraduate degree from Tulane University, New Orleans, Louisiana in 1969. He received his Doctorate of Jurisprudence (JD) from the George Washington University, Washington, D.C. in 1973. Following his admission to the Florida Bar, Pierce began his legal career as an Assistant Public Defender in Clearwater, Florida. In 1979 he moved to West Virginia and became the managing attorney of a Legal Services office in a rural five county area in the northeast corner of the state called the Potomac Highlands. In 1985, Pierce returned to Miami, where he was raised, and served as an Assistant Federal Public Defender for the Southern District of Florida.

Since 1986 Pierce has worked exclusively in the area of civil law, concentrating on personal injury, consumer and family law matters. He has served as lead counsel in over 100 jury trials and has successfully argued before the Supreme Court of Florida and the Supreme Court of Appeals for the State of West Virginia. He is currently an active member of the Florida Bar and an inactive member of the West Virginia Bar Association. He is admitted to practice in the United States District Courts for the Southern, Middle and Northern Districts of Florida, the 11th Circuit Court of Appeals and the United States Supreme Court, though he has yet to do so. He is now a sole practitioner in Cedar Key, Florida.

Pierce began writing in 1989 when a freak accident in a softball game resulted in a broken ankle. While convalescing, he wrote <u>A Parent's Guide to Coaching Tennis</u>, which was recognized by the United States Tennis Association as being <u>the</u> perfect introduction and primer for parents of beginning players. Over a span of 50 years, Mr. Kelley was a nationally-ranked player as a junior, in the open Men's Division, and as a senior. He was also the president of the Youth Tennis Foundation of Florida from 1987 until 2007.

In 2000, Pierce authored his second book, <u>Civil Litigation: A Case Study</u>, while teaching paralegal students as an Adjunct Professor at St. Petersburg College in St. Petersburg, Florida. He taught at various colleges and universities as an Adjunct for over 25 years.

Pierce completed his first novel, <u>A Very Fine Line</u>, in 2006. Since then seven more have followed, which are <u>Fistfight at the L and M Saloon</u>, <u>A Plenary Indulgence</u>, <u>Bocas del Toro</u>, <u>Asleep at the Wheel</u>, <u>A Tinker's Damn!</u>, <u>A Foreseeable Risk</u> and <u>Thousand Yard Stare</u>. He has also written <u>Pieces to the Puzzle</u>, which is a collection of personal essays, and <u>Kennedy Homes: An American Tragedy</u>, which is an account of a major Fair Housing case Mr. Kelley was involved in during the years 2004 and 2007. <u>Father, I Must Go</u>, published in 2011, is a work of non-fiction about a man from the Yucatan who lived illegally in the United States for almost twenty years.

<u>Roxy Blues</u> is his ninth published novel.